A LONG WAY TO DIE

Other books by the author include:

A Wing and a Prayer (1st Book Of Gabriel)

Belladonna (2nd Book Of Gabriel)

Dealing with the Devil (3rd Book Of Gabriel)

Past and Future Sins (5th Book of Gabriel)

A LONG WAY TO DIE

THE FOURTH BOOK OF GABRIEL

ERNEST OGLESBY

iUniverse, Inc.
Bloomington

A Long Way to Die
The Fourth Book of Gabriel

iUniverse books may be ordered through booksellers or by contacting:

iUniverse
1663 Liberty Drive
Bloomington, IN 47403
www.iuniverse.com
1-800-Authors (1-800-288-4677)

ISBN: 978-1-4759-3594-3 (sc)
ISBN: 978-1-4759-3595-0 (hc)
ISBN: 978-1-4759-3596-7 (ebk)

Library of Congress Control Number: 2011901153

Printed in the United States of America

iUniverse rev. date: 03/05/2013

This book is dedicated to Olga, whose mysterious dark eyes I first dreamt about when I was sixteen, not knowing it would be another thirty five years until I actually met her. She helped me understand a lot about the differences between Eastern and Western cultures.

Chapter One

March 18th

Spring was slow coming to this part of northern Pakistan, and the cold March winds coming down off the mountains still stung with the biting cold of winter, bitter and harsh to anyone unprepared for the vagaries of weather in this part of the world.

The two Mossad agents struggled head-on onto the wind, wrapped up in their thick sheepskins. Their eyes stung as they trudged wearily onwards. The village could be seen in the distance, and a young boy tended a herd of goats in one of the nearby fields, but he paid the men little heed. A village like many others in this region, but one in which they finally hoped to find their prey. If it had a name, it wasn't on any map they knew of, situated on the northern bank of the Indus River valley. To the south, the peaks of Nanga Parbat could be seen, still covered in snow. It was a bleak and inhospitable place.

Mullah Ali Bin Wazir was one of the last surviving Taliban who had sought sanctuary in northern Pakistan, where many of the people openly supported his former regime, still declaring their allegiance for Bin Laden. This was a volatile part of the world, as Bin Laden's followers frequently crossed into Kashmir, engaging Indian forces and generally fomenting unrest in a region inhabited by two religions, where both nuclear powers claimed sovereignty. It was now a very dangerous part of the world.

Bin Wazir had fled here from Afghanistan, seeking to consolidate a new power-base, whilst avoiding the long arms of the American President in his self-declared 'War on Terror'. Like most Americans he

1

talked big, but delivered very little, and the Mullah thought himself safe here, for he knew that President Musharraf would not dare allow any American operation within Pakistan's own borders, for fear of an uprising against his regime by the more extreme religious elements, all followers or supporters of Al Qaeda.

Israel did not respect international borders when it came to anti-terrorist operations, and a quiet word from the American CIA was all they needed to mount an operation of their own within Pakistan. President Musharraf was indeed aware of it, but would never publicly admit it. He was playing a delicate political game, only too aware of the extremists within his own country who were trying to undermine his rule. Should the mission become public knowledge, he would publicly condemn the Israelis, who knew they walked a thin line across international opinion. They had been walking such a thin line ever since the foundation of the modern nation of Israel, and they weren't afraid to cross it if the need arose.

Ali Bin Wazir was one of Osama Bin Laden's Military Commanders, responsible for planning a number of atrocities. Lots of different nationalities had died when those two mighty towers fell. A lot of them had been Jews.

* * *

For all the unrest and claims of persecution from the Muslim world, 95% of the world's terrorists were Muslim. That was a fact that couldn't be argued. Religion was ever an excuse for acts which its own faith forbade, yet one man's martyr was another's terrorist.

Al Qaeda was worldwide these days, as the world emasculated itself by allowing the terrorist organisation to proliferate, hiding behind supposedly 'legal' front-organisations. Much of the funding came from the rich Saudi families that Bin Laden was connected to, who looked upon Israel's very existence as an affront.

Too many countries opened their borders too freely, and both legal and illegal, immigrants or refugees were allowed free access. Not many even pretended allegiance to their new homelands, but continued to live their lives the way they had always done, knowing they were free from persecution under many countries' laws. Muslims now spread over the earth much further and more freely than they had ever done under the Ottoman Empire.

Many Western countries gave too much weight to ethnic and minority groups, and politicians were too afraid of losing votes to be seen to do anything against any of these groups, yet in places like America and even England, whites were now considered ethnic minorities in some towns and cities.

Islam was slowly being allowed to spread across the face of the globe almost unhindered, and it's followers were intent on spreading it's doctrine by any means necessary, for it was a very unforgiving religion and would suffer no others.

For sheer fanaticism, Islam couldn't be beaten, because children were made to learn the Koran before being given any other education. Indeed, some never got any further education, as the Koran was supposed to contain all the knowledge its followers needed. Islam looked on the rest of the world's religions with scorn, particularly the Christian faith, often ridiculing the New Testament as a prophet's versions of the Word of God, whilst their own Koran itself was looked upon as the Actual Word of God, though Muslims conveniently forgot to mention that it is "as told by the Prophet Mohammed" so no more reliable, really.

All Muslims were devout, at least in public, and most sincerely believed in its doctrines, sure that their reward for carrying out Allah's Will would be a place in Paradise. Allah's Will, unfortunately, was not usually dictated by Allah himself, but by a variety of Mullahs, who were more practical than devout. Allah's Will was more hearsay, if truth be told, but none dare disagree openly with a Mullah's interpretation, for fear of reprisals by the rest of the Faithful. Blind faith was never blinder.

Anyone critical of Islam could be condemned by a Fatwah, for the Koran told that it was a Muslim's duty to slay any and all followers of any other religion, if they couldn't be converted to Islam, and thus save their souls. Conversely, anyone converting from or denouncing Islam, automatically sentenced himself to death in the eyes of the Mullahs.

*   *   *

The two Mossad agents knew what their fate would be if they were caught on such a clandestine operation deep in a Muslim country.

Yet, knowing that, they had volunteered for the mission, and had been dropped into Northern Pakistan at night by one of the American Black Hawk helicopters flying covertly. Three other teams were operating across the area, but their whereabouts were unknown, and the single-burst one time radio they carried was to be used only for extraction.

They had followed the trail diligently for the last four days, listening and observing, fluent in the northern dialects. Bin Wazir and one of his three wives had been staying in this village, stationary finally, to attend a meeting of some kind. They would observe this meeting, and then make a decision on whether to take out their target or not.

*   *   *

Inside the house, Bin Wazir and his followers enjoyed the warmth of a fire, whilst listening to the wind outside. The old man felt the cold more in his bones these days, and he sat close to the flames. He still had plenty of fat on those bones, though a couple of old wounds ached unless he kept well wrapped up against the elements, and he needed a stick to walk, these days. Of average height, he was still dwarfed by his guest, who looked taller, even sitting down.

The house had windows of glass, keeping out the elements, unlike most of the dwellings in the town, which put up shutters in the colder months. Bin Wazir had a good view out across the valley and surrounding hills. So did his bodyguards.

The Mullah took the first small cup of coffee from his wife and sipped, nodding to the only other man in the room, who sat on the broad sofa across from him. Masoud Al Asmi took up his own cup, and drank also, though he now had a taste for western coffee in preference to this strong bitter brew. Al Asmi dressed in western clothes, and he could pass for a Westerner with ease, which was one of the reasons he had been put forward for this assignment. Trim the beard, tidy the hair, and he could pass for any number of different nationalities.

The woman offered him fruits, dates and nuts, which Masoud respectfully sampled. She left them on the low table when Bin Wazir dismissed her from the room to talk in private with his guest.

"The West thinks itself strong, secure even, now that it has broken our power base in Afghanistan," Bin Wazir began. "If they know of our reach across the world, they will certainly not publicise it," he chuckled to himself. Al Asmi nodded. "But the world weakens itself from within. It is corrupt, and has not our strength. Islam is the word of the one true God, and this 'War on Terror' will not silence us. Islam is the one true religion, and as the rest of the world wages war on us, we in turn will wage war on them!" Bin Wazir's eyes blazed, reflecting the inner fury he felt. "Islam is about to wage war on the very religions of the world," he told Al Asmi. "Centuries ago, the Christian Pope authorised a Holy Crusade to control trade across the Mediterranean, and the Moors and Turks were expelled from their conquests in Northern Europe. Our religion suffered serious setbacks at the hands of these heathens," he went on, fervently. "It is time we embarked on a Jihad of our own, and showed the nations of the world that our time is coming." His voice, well used to oratory, was having the right effect on Al Asmi, reaching deep inside him. "I want you to spearhead that Jihad, Masoud Al Asmi. I want you to take the fight to the Infidel!"

*   *   *

The two Mossad agents befriended the boy with the goats, talking to him fluently, with not a trace of any accent. It wasn't long before he had revealed to them the location of the house used by the Mullah. In their backpacks and within their clothing, as well as the radio, they carried some explosive charges, two machine-pistols, and one broken-down sniper's rifle. The lie of the land would determine how they planned their assault.

*   *   *

"Imagine if you will, the religions of the world brought down by the power of Islam." Bin Wazir went on. "Not just the religions of the West but those of the East too, all of them falling in turn, as we strike against them, one by one." He had vision, and no mistake, thought Al Asmi, a part of him reacting to the Mullah's fervour, and yet his western upbringing dredged up doubts from his subconscious.

His parents, Arab father, Pakistani mother, had raised him in the English town of Keighley, in North Yorkshire, where there had been much racial tension, as his own race soon grew to outnumber the native white community. Answering the call of the Taliban, he had made his way to Afghanistan to fight for Bin Laden against the Americans. After the rout, Bin Wazir, on hearing of his bravery and his background, had arranged this meeting, deeming him highly suitable for the mission he was about to bestow upon him.

"I want you to wage war, Al Asmi," Bin Wazir exclaimed. "Your first target will be the Holy Catholic Church, as revenge for the Crusades which drove us out of Europe those many years ago. You will take a small squad of hand-picked men and women, and infiltrate the Italian sub-continent. Once there, you will bring that country to its knees by a series of well-coordinated strikes against the very heart of its religion," he revealed. "Your code-name will be Torquemada, and I want you to test the faith of the Infidel like never before. Let him feel the fires of our Inquisition."

*   *   *

The town-house was on the very outskirts of the sprawling village, halfway down the slope of a low range of hills. It had a commanding look across the valley beneath it. Three cars were parked up outside the house. Vegetation was scarce, and there was no way the two Mossad agents could approach the house in daylight without being seen. They could only observe from a distance until nightfall, and even that was dangerous, lest their attentions be noted by the villagers.

There was an abandoned car, long since burnt out, by the side of the road, but it would not give either of them sufficient cover in the light of day, for there wasn't much of the bodywork left, and it was far too obvious.

They went back into the town, and managed to find a small bar-cum-coffee shop on the road that led back out to the Mullah's house. It was the best they could do till dark. At least in here their presence would be disguised, and they could watch the traffic to see if any of those cars came back along the road. It also helped shelter them from the bitter wind, and so was a welcome relief.

*   *   *

Back inside the house, Bin Wazir and Al Asmi were deep in conversation whilst the bodyguards did their rounds, alternating their positions every hour, lest they became too complacent watching the same piece of terrain for too long.

"I'll need a list of operatives," Al Asmi insisted. "People who can pass themselves as Italians, or foreign exchange students. They all must be able to speak Italian. Fluent would be best, but not essential. Italy is a cosmopolitan country which sees a lot of tourists. It should be easy enough to move around. Two cells of four. I'll need cars buying. No rentals. They're too easy to trace. Forged documents. Good ones. Cell-phones to communicate. Pay as you go. They can't be traced or located unless they know who's got them. We keep it as simple as we can," he advised Bin Wazir, who was pleased to see the reports about the man's tactical strategies lived up to expectations. "Co-ordinated attacks in different parts of the country, which we publicise to force them to accept their own helplessness." He indicated towns and road-systems on the map, making notations here and there as Bin Wazir looked on, nodding in agreement.

Bin Wazir smiled. "I will look forward to hearing of your exploits on CNN," he chuckled.

"What about weapons and munitions? How will they be arranged?"

"Many of the Arab nations are sympathetic to our cause, and one in particular hates Italy with a vengeance. They will assist your efforts," he grinned. "I have already spoken to contacts in the Balkans to arrange delivery of the more important items," Bin Wazir assured him.

"I am ready to give my life for Allah," Al Asmi assured the Mullah, who smiled knowingly.

"The home of Catholicism will be destroyed, and if it is necessary, your martyrdom will assure you of a place in Paradise," he promised the devout younger man.

*   *   *

Dusk was coming, and the three cars all passed the coffee shop within seconds of each other, as the two Israelis shook their heads in frustration. So near and so close, but Fate was cruel. There was only a slim chance that anyone was left in the house, but they had to check it out.

Back out into the cold wind and dying light, they retraced their steps along the pitted road, seeing no lights in the house in the distance. Cautious, they approached carefully, taking their time and using what cover there was. Finally, satisfied that if they hadn't drawn any fire by now, they never would, they ran the last hundred yards to the house, alert as ever for anyone inside.

Controlling their breathing, they waited for nearly sixty seconds outside the door, but could near nothing inside. One of them put his shoulder to the door, and it fell in over, splintering the frame, and breaking the poorly made lock.

One covered the other as they conducted a quick search of the place, but their suspicions had proved correct. There was no one left in the house, no clothing. Only foodstuffs had been left behind. They searched for information now, and any documents that the Mullah had left behind to reveal his plans of movements.

The upstairs rooms proved that the house was normally occupied, though the occupants had moved out to allow the place to be used by Bin Wazir. Clothes still hung in the wardrobes, though westernized, and nothing like the traditional robes worn by the Mullah, so they wasted little time searching through these.

The kitchen was fully stocked, and the dishes had been left piled up in the sink for someone else to wash, as Bin Wazir and his bodyguards had vacated the place.

The main living area was sparsely furnished. Thick carpets were richly woven, in bright colours with some sort of hunting scene. Matching large scatter cushions were sprinkled about the room, for those who preferred more traditional seating methods than the westernized sofa, of cheap plastic imitation leather, and the coffee table looked like a flat-pack from the likes of IKEA. Functional furniture, but not that expensive. Even the bulb that hung from the ceiling bore no shade, just a bare bulb.

In the large fireplace, in front of the embers of a dying fire, lay a burnt remnant of a map, which must have fallen out of the fire. The outline of the southern coast of Italy was unmistakeable. Still visible in the bottom corner of the map were four still-legible lines of Arabic script, obviously names, written in ink.

One of the men carefully picked up the map, and slipped it into a small plastic bag which he then sealed and put inside his clothing. A further search revealed nothing else of value in the house. The place was otherwise sterile.

Leaving the house, the two men climbed the slopes of the hill, seeking clear high ground, and one of them pulled the single burst radio. He thumbed the ON switch, and spoke softly into the mouthpiece. "Taxi. Repeat. Taxi." and he gave the co-ordinates legible on the GPS device built into the side of the radio, for the Americans to pinpoint their transmission point. Then he switched the device off, and hunkered over against the cold wind to wait for the helicopter extraction.

Chapter Two

Lesya stirred, still half-asleep, wrapped snugly in her blanket, and stretching out on the thick carpet, her feet reassuringly pressed against the fleece-covered hot-water bottle, an unusual but welcome Christmas present from her Englishman friend. She often slept on the floor like this, a legacy from her yoga training days, as she did not like beds that were too soft.

She dreamed strange dreams sometimes, a gift of her heritage through her mother's line, witches every one, and the powers manifested themselves in her sometimes as strange, possibly visionary, dreams. At other times she was receptive to the 'voices' of kindred spirits, holding 'conversations' in her sleep, on the spiritual plane, with people in far away places. Other people scoffed when she told them, and just wrote them off as dreams, but it didn't affect her own beliefs.

Tonight's dream was full of shadows, half-glimpsed figures, a warning of some kind. Some future event in her life, or meant for others? She didn't know. Her dreams weren't always clear to interpretation. The future had its own way of unraveling.

The alarm on her cellphone rang at four am, and Lesya was waiting for it, grumbling to herself as she threw back the blanket, and killed the alarm. She got up, and did a brief series of stretching exercises, to get the kinks out of her system, before putting on a robe, and going into the bathroom, which was usually hers all to herself at that time of the day. She looked at her face in the mirror, elfin short dark-hair, and a cute little nose which held up the round-rimmed glasses. She screwed up her face and stuck her tongue out at her own reflection, chuckling to herself as she did so. Did it really give him a 'hard-on' when she did that in front of him? She did it again, and smiled to herself, before continuing with her ablutions.

Finally, dressed and refreshed, she grabbed an apple to eat on the bus for her breakfast, and put on her thick quilted winter coat, filled with swans' down. She left her apartment and took the stairs down, descending the flights carefully. Putting up her fur-lined hood against the biting wind, she walked across to where the regular bus awaited her. The temperature today seemed about minus 20 with the wind-chill, snow crunching underfoot and she was glad to get on the bus which had its heaters running. Nodding to a few acquaintances, she settled herself down into her seat, and took out her apple, biting into it.

Fresh fruit was hard to come by out in the remote areas of Kazakhstan, and Tegriz was pretty remote. Full-circle, or so it seemed, for Lesya had taken a government sponsored educational programme that had ended up with her going to University in the United States, after her divorce from her first husband. Signing on for the programme meant that she got work experience for Chevron once she got her Degree, and she worked in the labs for a while before being interviewed and considered for a posting for one of the Oil companies back in her home country of Kazakhstan. One of the conditions of her own educational programme was that she had to return to work in Kazakhstan within a certain time period, and remain there for a minimum of two years. She got regular leave, but could not re-enter America, until those two years were up.

Being a pretty girl in a male environment was hard enough here, with everyone, even her own fellow engineers hitting on her, and Tegriz itself was a close community of men and women, some of them married, some of them not. Relationships formed between sexes irrespective of their marital status. Some people looked upon it as living half their lives out here, so the idea of a Tegriz Wife or Tegriz Husband was how they justified their behaviour. A lot of the girls out here, both Russian and Kazakh were looking for a way out of the place, and she didn't blame them for trying to latch on to one of the many ex-pats, but they weren't fussy about whether the men were single or already married. Everyone seemed to assume the worst of everyone else in this place. You were assumed to be doing it, even if you weren't.

Lesya was friendly with most people, but she enjoyed the attentions her Englishman friend bestowed upon her. He was nice to talk to, flattered her a lot, and she enjoyed his company, even if she didn't always feel 100% safe in it. He wasn't married, but his girlfriend was in America, though he hadn't seen her for around 9 months. She had family problems, and he found them frustrating and hard to deal with. The relationship had gone sour, or so he had told her. Everyone needed a bit of company now and then, and he was seeking hers, but for reasons she wasn't quite sure of. She called him her 'Magician', for he had a way of making things happen, and was always full of pleasant and unexpected surprises. He had organized a delivery of flowers for her birthday. Flowers, in the middle of a desert. Tears had welled up in her eyes when she received them.

Older than her, and possibly worldlier, he was certainly charming and well-mannered, good to talk to, and on an intellectual level they seemed well-matched. The thought of entering into another relationship was doubtful, unwise even, but not outright impossible. Where would this friendship lead? Where should she let it lead? Was that the sort of relationship this man wanted of her? He was at least open in his feelings, or was he?

He was quite good with words, and his e-mails, which were frequent, as were hers to him, were full of all manner of nuances. One said that she *could* seduce him. But did she want to? True, they enjoyed each other's company. It was limited mainly to the office as they lived on different camps, and she didn't deem it wise to be seen out and about in male company, however discreet. Women at the plant were already talking about her, assuming she already had a lover, assuming her behaviour mirrored their own. Who did they think it was? Her Magician?

Their friendship was good, and it certainly helped her get through each rotation, with all the stress and worry of both the job and her personal issues. It would grow with time, but how far should she let it grow? It was as though both were testing the water, teasing and flirting, which was good for the ego, and gave her the emotional support she so badly needed at the moment. He made her smile, and feel good about herself, which was a good thing. More than friends, more than good friends, even. She was getting out of her depth, if she wasn't careful.

It was something she needed to think about in the days ahead. Right now, she was going to snuggle up in her coat and try and doze as the bus drove from the RV to the Plant where she worked. It was a 40 minute journey, past the OCTV camp, and too dark to see anything at this ungodly hour, even if she was of a mind to sightsee. This part of Kazakhstan was flat, barren and desolate, so not much to see unless you wanted to see it, and could appreciate such a wilderness. She would be glad when this rotation ended, and she could go and relax for a few weeks, and get her head together.

*   *   *

The day started in predictable form, after she checked through the main-gate just before 6am, nodding to one of the bored security guards and showing her pass, her mini-filter that they'd all just been issued with and was now mandatory, as if it would do that much good in the event of a real H2S emergency. The usual people trooped in with her off the bus. Most days were quite predictable in this regard at least, though the rest of her day could often be filled with unexpected problems. She said Hi and Good Morning, Dobroe Utro, to friends and colleagues, even being polite to that prick of a Kazakh Engineer who had the audacity to think she was easy-meat. Indeed that was often how he looked at her.

Once in the office, she was pleased to find another offering on her desk, waiting for her. Some of that delicious English cheese she liked, from her Magician, and she smiled as she took off her coat and hung it up, before booting up her PC and waiting to draft him a nice e-mail as a Thank You.

Once done, she started going through her list of outstanding jobs. There were numerous projects assigned to her, in various stages of completion. The Englishman was one of the Senior Designers in the Cad Group, and he was of great help to her in moving her work along, though he claimed no preference was given to her own work ;-)) Still, he didn't argue with her like he did with some of the other engineers. A good thing, as she had a temper, and sometimes wasn't afraid to use it. She grinned at the thought. She may have been a lady, but she not only dressed like a tom-boy, she could fight like one too.

The Lead Engineer came over to check with her on the status of a few of her jobs later that morning, and he assigned her another couple of jobs to work with some of the more junior Engineers on, to Mentor them in effect. Everyone was used to helping each other down here, and so she got on with it, and the day went by in its usual manner, breaking in with the odd e-mail from her friend to lighten her mood and ease her frustrations. Adam only worked across the corridor, but both were here to work, and it wouldn't do to be seen to be paying her too much attention with the gossips down here. A strange way to conduct a relationship, and she knew he wasn't entirely happy with it.

This place was like Heaven and Hell all mixed up into one. Easier to conduct a homosexual relationship than a heterosexual one, with all the eyes and wagging tongues around the place. She smiled at that thought, too, as she had often contemplated exploring 'her feminine-side' when her relationships with men had broken up, though so far she had only toyed with the idea. She sighed, and brought her mind back down to Earth.

A lot of the work she was getting lately was tedious and not that interesting, a bit beneath her capabilities, but they all needed doing. She didn't fool herself that she could do this sort of thing all her life. She had plans, and they included a climb up the management ladder, going on to more complex projects once she had proved her worth down here at the Plant. Then in a few years time, she wanted out of OCT altogether. She had her heart set on a home in the sun.

*　　*　　*

"Lesya, what's happening with the material on my job? I just got copied on an MR which says the 24" control valve is on its way back to Europe." Csaba, one of the Hungarian Engineers, looked down at her over her desk, interrupting her train of thought.

"What are you talking about? Can you explain? I don't know what happened to your material. I ordered it. It arrived. For sure. I checked. That's all I know." She shrugged her shoulders. Lesya was just as puzzled by the revelation as Csaba.

"I checked myself with the warehouse, and they told me you had arranged for the valve to be returned to the manufacturer for some internal adjustments."

"I ordered no such thing." She protested, raising her head and her eyes warningly. "My involvement stopped after the materials arrived. It's your job, and up to you to do with it as you like."

"The authorization for the return came from you, according to the Transport representative and it was shipped out by train the day before yesterday." Csaba went on, obviously annoyed.

"Look," Lesya's eyes glared. "That valve was there in the Warehouse a couple of days ago. I saw it myself, and I wrote no authorization to send it anywhere, let alone back to the manufacturer." Csaba was getting frustrated, and started becoming more accusatory.

"You must have got confused, and sent the wrong part back to the wrong place."

Her eyes hardened. "No, I didn't!" her voice raised now, along with her eyebrows, and the other two Engineers in the room tried to look elsewhere. "You must have lost it yourself. I didn't do anything with your stupid valve, except order it for you." At the sound of raised voices, the Lead Engineer popped his head around the corner.

"Hey, guys . . . . cool it down here, okay? What seems to be the problem?" asked Bruce, the American Lead Engineer.

"This 'woman' has sent one of my control valves back to the manufacturer, and I need it installing next week." Csaba accused, using the description of her gender as an insult. Lesya felt like using the ice-pick on her desk.

"I didn't do anything with his valve!" she retorted. Csaba sneered as he opened up the Job-Pack he was carrying.

"Well what is this? Is this not your name?" he showed both her and Bruce a copy of an e-mail, authorizing the return. Her name was on the end of it, and Lesya's mouth dropped. She could not remember writing any such e-mail. Bruce shook his head, and Csaba started to swagger as he had seemingly proved his case against her. She was used to such attitudes from Hungarians, who did not think women were their equals.

"Lesya, see what you can do to get this valve back here. Get in touch with Transport and see if you can stop the return. Failing that, get onto the manufacturer and ask him to get another one out here as quickly as you can. Air-freight, if need be. Csaba, you start checking out the other project stocks and see if there's something we can borrow or utilize to do a quick workaround on this problem."

He was not pleased, and Lesya felt diminished in his eyes. Her temper was simmering under the surface, in the face of this new evidence, and she determined to get to the bottom of it.

As the two men went off, Lesya went back behind her desk. The other two male Engineers were seemingly determined to mind their own business, and were pointedly concentrating on their own computer screens, as Lesya now did with hers, tracking back through all her electronic e-mail, which she kept neatly filed in her Personal Folders in Outlook. They had witnessed her moods before, and she was in quite a black one at the moment.

It didn't take her long to track through that particular job folder, but there was nothing there that matched the paper copy Csaba had shown her. She picked up the phone and called ICS, the computer support people. "Saule? Hello. It's Lesya. I need your help. I'm trying to find an e-mail which I don't seem to have on my P drive. Maybe I deleted it by mistake. I don't know. It went to Transport in the last few days. Will you look for it for me, and if you find it, restore it to my In-Box? Oh thank you so much." It always proved beneficial to maintain a good working relationship with people in other departments.

As it was, it didn't take Aisaule long to get back on the phone to her. "Lesya? I'm sorry, but I could not trace any such e-mail from your computer over the last few days. Do you want me to check back further?"

"Nyet. But could you check whether such an e-mail was received by Transport? The supervisor's name was Kairat Abilkhasov."

"Okay. I'll run another check, and I'll get back to you." Lesya put the phone down and called Transport.

"Could I speak to Kairat Abilkhasov please?" she asked, trying to keep hold of her temper.

"I'm sorry, but he is not available at the moment. Can I be of help?" answered a male voice.

"Perhaps. My name is Lesya. I'm one of the Reliability Engineers, on extension 7911. There seems to be some sort of mistake. A control valve was sent back to the manufacturer a couple of days ago. Can we recall it?" she asked. Lesya heard the rustling of papers at the other end of the phone.

"Ahhh, yes. There was a valve shipped out the other day. Sent by train. It may well have left Kazakhstan by now."

"Could you please check, and see if there is any way to recall the valve?"

"Very well. I'll see what can be done. I'll inform Kairat upon his return, and get him to speak to you."

"Thank you." Lesya put the phone down, and started writing an e-mail, a genuine one this time, to the valve manufacturer, trying to explain what had happened, and asking them to arrange for another valve to be air-freighted out here in time for the shutdown. Her fingers rattled on the keyboard, and the two Engineers who shared the office with her could feel her mood all the way across the room. It wasn't a pleasant atmosphere, and they avoided eye-contact with her.

Half an hour later, Saule rang back. "Lesya? I'm sorry, but I've checked Kairat's e-mail account and I can't find that particular e-mail either."

"Okay. Thanks, Saule. I'll discuss it with him personally." She put the phone down, puzzled. How did that e-mail exist? She opened one of her previously sent e-mails, and others that other people had sent to her. A bit of creative cutting n pasting, and she had managed to create a similar facsimile. She sent it off to the printer, and went to collect it. *Look at my butt if you want, creep*, she sent a mental message to Khanat, the Kazakh Engineer, whom she knew was now ogling her as she walked to the printer. *That's as close as you'll get to it.* Kazakh men were so backward in their attitude towards women, and there was ill-feeling towards Russians by Kazakhs, and even in-fighting between the different Oblasts in Kazakhstan. Lesya considered herself more Russian, of Russian parents, even though born a Kazakh,

She went around the corner to Csaba's desk. "Csaba, could you let me have a copy of that e-mail, please?" she asked sweetly, through grating teeth. "I'm trying to get in touch with the manufacturer, and I've been onto Transport to try and recall the valve." Csaba grunted as he took the copy from his file and went over to photocopy it for her.

"We need to resolve this, Lesya. We don't have much time before the shutdown." He handed the copy to her. Lesya took it, and returned to her desk. That man exasperated her at times. So damn macho, and with as low an opinion of her as her own was of him.

She studied the photocopy in her hand. So if it wasn't electronically sent, then how did Transport get it? It looked every bit as genuine as any other printout. Okay, easy enough to forge. But who had done it, and why? Was it an attempt to cause trouble for her in her job? Kazakhs called that sort of behaviour 'attrition' and it was generally accepted as common practice out here. It hadn't been done accidentally, but she was puzzled as to the reason behind it.

* * *

The Kazakh Rail network was a tried and trusted method of transportation, slow but methodical, as were most systems in the former soviet block country. North to Makat, then west to Atyrau and beyond the Kazakh borders to Astrakhan, and further afield to Grozny.

The control valve itself was currently stuck on a reinforced steel-plated support base for its long journey, the steel plating hiding a hidden consignment which the weighty valve helped to conceal. The train waited to acquire customs clearance, as a methodical customs guards pocketed the sizeable wad of notes that accompanied the consignment notes, and rubber-stamped the clearance papers. There were problems and problems. Most could be solved with the same solution. Customs positions were very sought after in ex-communist countries. For such a poor salary, the customs officials always seemed to drive the nicest cars.

* * *

It was after lunch that she got a return call from Transport. "Lesya? Kairat Abilkhasov from Transport here. I was given your message when I got back into the office. Unfortunately, the train has now passed beyond our borders, and we have little option but to let it continue its journey," he explained.

"Kairat, this e-mail you received. I got ICS to check, and it doesn't officially exist. How did you receive it?" she asked. There was a pause on the other end of the phone, before Kairat spoke again.

"My e-mail normally gets printed out by the clerk and left on my desk for me to deal with. I must have just picked it up from the pile and dealt with it as I normally do. I suppose anyone *could* have added something to the pile, but why would they do that?" he asked, before she could ask him the selfsame question. There was something in the man's voice that raised Lesya's suspicions. His answer sounded contrived. No one was supposed to allow another individual access to their Personal Computers. Passwords were *supposed* to be closely guarded, and the man was hinting at a breach of security that ICS would not take kindly to.

"Okay. Thank you for the information," she replied, and put the phone down, puzzled over his strange manner. Out of curiosity she pulled up "White Page" on the screen and went down the range of employees' photographs until she found the man. Vaguely familiar. Tall, thin, with pockmarked skin and most of his top teeth capped with gold, as were a lot of Kazakh men. Then she placed him. She had seen him in the Tropicana nightclub on a couple of occasions her girlfriends had persuaded her to get out of her apartment. She did love to dance, and enjoyed the loud music they played there.

She pulled up her own employee photo, realizing the changes in her appearance since it had been taken. The photo made her face look a lot rounder than it was, and her hair was a different length these days. Unless someone pointed her out to him, then he would probably not know who she was. A chance encounter at the Tropicana might yield some information out of him. It was a rare man who stayed sober there, away from Group 4 Security, and a loose tongue might throw some light on what was happening. Saturday was tomorrow, so she would bide her time till then.

The phone rang once more, and she answered it, holding it to her ear. "Allo?"

"Hey, what's up with you? Having fun over there?" It was her Englishman. Lesya smiled, picturing him on the other end of the phone.

"Oh, hello, Adam. No, I'm not having fun at all today," she complained. "Lots of hassles. Csaba is driving me mad, screaming on me and blaming me for something I didn't do."

"Perhaps you should have done it, then?" he suggested, amusedly, and Lesya stuck her tongue out at him down the phone, although he couldn't see her do it. "I'm cooking again tonight," he explained. "Why don't you join me and take the late bus back?" he suggested. Lesya pulled a face, wanting to say Yes, but realizing she'd have to say No.

"I can't. You know what people are like."

"I'll have other people there besides you. No wagging tongues."

"The last time your friends were there, they were looking at me like a fresh piece of meat," she complained.

"What can I say?" he apologized. "You know what this place is like. Always people looking for attachments or trying to spot attachments between others. You're new here, so people don't know you that well yet," he explained.

"I'll think about it," she promised. "I've got a busy day ahead. I'll call you later, I promise." Lesya put the phone down reluctantly. Should she attend? He was quite a good cook, but she didn't quite trust herself with him, or did she? Did she feel just safe or *too* safe in his company?

*   *   *

The rest of the day was busy enough, and she had to go upto the Hungarian Camp for a meeting with some of the other Project Engineers. There was talk of transferring her up here, away from the Plant, once this year's shutdown was completed, and she had mixed feelings about it. Possibly good for her career, but she was worried about the money aspects, already having had some tempting offers from other companies since her return to Kazakhstan.

It was a boring meeting, lasting most of the afternoon, in a different building to where most of the ex-pat designers and Engineers worked, and then by the time it was all over, she was too tired to go to the gym, so she caught the early bus back upto her accommodation block, for a hot bath and early to bed. She used her mobile to phone Adam's extension whilst on the bus, and unluckily didn't catch him, so just left a message apologizing, without feeling too bad about letting him down.

*   *   *

Saturday night finally came, and Lesya went with her friend Nataly late in the evening, knowing most of the men would have been drinking for an hour or two. Eyes turned as the pair of them left the cloakroom, for the two women were quite striking, both in appearance and in their choice of dress. Nataly was always getting attention because of her resemblance to that Latin-American singer Gloria Estefan, and tonight she was wearing all white—a tight suede t-shirt with a scoop neckline, skin-tight suede jeans which contrasted nicely with the olive complexion of her skin. Lesya was her own woman, with her own style, which tonight consisted of a long red dress with breath-taking pompadour cleavage, slit high up her left thigh to reveal a black silk stocking top. A giggle-band, as her English friend had laughingly revealed to her. Black jet necklace, and high-heeled black and red shoes were the final addition to her battlefield outfit.

The two women got drinks from the bar first of all, and then found a small table where they sat and discussed the plan for the evening they had worked out, before eventually taking to the dance-floor.

They danced with each other to start with, which often brought curious stares in this part of the world, but they allowed various men to cut in, and danced with different partners. Men, more often than not, didn't dance as well, which was a shame, as Lesya could really throw herself into the music, and more and more men found their eyes drawn like a magnet to her body, 'snake-moving' and revealing her shapely legs. She was getting the attention she intended to get tonight.

Easy as always, she thought, used to going out in extreme outfits designed to shock, when her former husband or her friends decided to have some fun. Tonight she wanted to attract one man in particular, and after nearly an hour, she saw him. His eyes, like those of many men around the dance-floor, were on her, and she danced her way over to the edge of the onlookers, smiling invitingly as she held out her arms to beckon him forward to join her.

Kairat's face lit up, and he put down his drink on a nearby table, to join her gladly, and Lesya danced in close, laughing, as he did his best to keep up with her. Sober, he might have been better than average, but she could tell from his co-ordination, that he wasn't sober. "My name is Kairat," he shouted in her ear over the loud music.

"Liya," Lesya replied, just as loudly as she leaned close, not wanting to reveal her real name and letting him look down her cleavage. Conversation was difficult on the dance-floor, jostled as they were by the heaving crowd of people.

Kairat began to sweat more noticeably as he danced, and Lesya decided she had better continue her questioning somewhere quieter, before he ended up too drunk entirely. When she took his arm and made to leave the dancefloor, Kairat was only too pleased to follow, retrieving his drink from the table, as she allowed him to escort her over towards the secluded booths on one side of the room. Kairat didn't notice how Lesya nodded to her friend Nataly discreetly as she passed her.

She sat down in the booth, and Kairat slid in alongside her, closer than she would have liked. This close, she could smell the sweat through his clothes, and by the table-light, she noticed the sallowness of his skin. He didn't look well, obviously having had a lot to drink, but he called the waiter over regardless and ordered himself another shot of vodka and Lesya asked for a Bailey's. She would have preferred not to have anything alcoholic, but it would have looked odd for what she was about to do, and she didn't want to make him suspicious just yet.

"So, pretty Liya, I have seen you in here once, or twice. You are a good mover out there," he complimented her on her dancing.

"Yes, I love to dance, but it's so hard to find a good partner," she smiled back, slightly leaning toward the table so her cleavage was exposed more. "You dance well," she lied, but made it sound convincing. "Did you learn while working here?"

Kairat proudly raised his head. "Dance-floor with a woman like you is the best teacher," and looked deep down into her cleavage, as Lesya gave him a charming smile

"Then I am really jealous of your female colleagues. No matter how many you have, they are so lucky." She looked into his eyes with an innocent admiration.

"Oh, I do have many. I work in the Transport Office," he revealed, "and I have to arrange shipments of materials in and out of the country, communicating with lots of women, but none of them as good-looking as you," he said with a sly wink. "What is your work about?"

"Oh, I just help out in the Mail Room," she said, vaguely. "Boring job, but the money is okay. Your job sounds much more interesting," she turned the conversation back to him again. The waiter returned with their drinks and took the empty glass as Kairat drained his glass in a single quaff. Lesya thanked him for her Bailey's and took a light sip.

"Yes, I have much responsibility there," Kairat agreed, eager to boast of his own self importance to such an obviously impressionable young woman. "I arrange flights, shipments, rail-movements of goods and materials for the various projects we do here in Tegriz."

"Do you do any other form of shipments?" she asked, mischieviously, over the rim of her glass, pretending to be more drunk than she really was.

"What do you mean, little Liya?" he leered, and put his hand on her thigh under the table, massaging it lightly, as he leaned closed. Lesya could smell the alcohol on the man's breath.

"Slow down, boy," she chuckled, and took his hand and gently put it on the table, holding it gently in case he decided to repeat his action. "I have heard you can arrange 'other' shipments. For friends," she smiled, taking her glass in the other hand, and slowly licked the rim, mischievously, so Kairat appeared amused watching her, and stayed calm for a minute before speaking again.

"It is true, my position allows me certain privileges," he smiled, and moved closer while she put her glass back on the table, and continued to play with his hand. "I have influence with certain officials, and I know ways and means of by-passing official channels to get things done. What are we really talking about here?" he asked. Lesya shrugged nonchalantly.

"A friend of mine has asked me to arrange to ship a large quantity of caviar out of the country, but with all the Customs Regulations, I don't know how I can do such a thing." She feigned ignorance. Kairat smiled broadly as he replied.

"Such things are of little consequence to a man in my position. My influence extends way beyond the boundaries of OCT and Tegriz. I know people with the real power in Kazakhstan. What I cannot arrange, they can, for they owe me many favours," he boasted.

*   *   *

In the next booth, Usen, Kairat's co-worker in the Transport Office was sat, listening discreetly to the conversation between his boss and the pretty little thing he had picked up off the dancefloor. Kairat always did have a loose tongue on him when he was drinking. They both took the same risks in the illegal activities that took place, under the auspices of OCT, but the money they both got for breaking the law was not in equal proportion. This conversation would be reported to their 'real' bosses, he thought, and then we will see whether Kairat's loose tongue is allowed to remain in his mouth or not.

As Kairat continued his boasting, one of the names he mentioned was known to her, though she managed to hide her surprise. The man, Feliks Kovacs, was rumoured to be connected to the Russian Mafiya, and reportedly operated out of a secure complex about 30km north of her home town of Almaty, the former capital of the country, now replaced by Astana, due to it's location on a fault-line, which meant it was occasionally susceptible to earthquakes.

*   *   *

Kairat's eyes were getting more and more glazed. Lesya puzzled over the significance of the discovery. If the Russian Mafiya were getting involved with some sort of scam to steal industrial equipment, what did it mean for the future of the country's economy?

She smiled sweetly towards Kairat, who was understandably flattered by her attentions, and eager to please her by talking and boasting about his accomplishments. How far should she take this, Lesya wondered, as she listened to him? She already had enough information to report the matter to her supervisor, but without proof, it would be his word against hers, and she was new to Tegriz. This illegal operation had obviously been going on for years.

"So, Kairat, do you think you could arrange such a shipment for me? I would be ever so grateful." She leaned closer, and put her hand on *his* thigh now, which made the man smile wider. She had made her mind up. "It all sounds so thrilling. You'll need to tell me where and how my friend can pick up the consignment?" she half-queried.

"Not a problem, my pretty one. I know the network inside out. I am on first-name terms with all the important people." His breath stank as he leaned in closer, and Lesya permitted him to kiss her, turning her cheek at the last moment. The last thing she wanted was those lips on hers.

After gently 'milking' him for information, Lesya decided enough was enough, and gave a nod to her watching friend, who came over to remind her that it was time they left. "Thank you for the evening, Kairat. Perhaps I will see you here next Saturday, and we can talk some more?" She got up from the booth as Kairat reluctantly got to his feet to let her past.

His ideas for the rest of the evening were suddenly in disarray, as both Lesya and Nataly smiled readily enough at him. He knew how the women worked things out here. Always moving around in pairs. He smiled, and nodded, but under his breath he muttered "Cock-teasing little bitch." Perhaps he would see her next weekend. Perhaps not. He hoped he would, for little Liya was extremely nice.

*   *   *

Next morning, Lesya awoke late, for Sunday was a half-day officially, allowing people a bit of leeway to enjoy themselves on a weekend after working 12 hour days the rest of the week. Truth be told, she had found it hard to sleep, thinking over last night's revelations. Illegal shipments were being made at the company's expense, and possibly with Russian Mafiya involvement. How far did all the corruption spread? Was it wise to enquire?

She had had experience of the Russian Mafiya before, as one of her male acquaintances had been involved, and persuaded by her to let her tag along for the ride one day on a meeting between rival factions.

Gunfire had broken out, and at least one person shot and killed, though her friend had quickly driven her away from the danger, but at least two bullets had hit their car. A wild and exciting experience at the time, but one she ought not to repeat, even though a little danger often appealed to her. She liked walking the edge occasionally, sometimes more than was good for her.

*   *   *

She discussed her findings with her Englishman friend that afternoon in the Mosquito Bar, aptly named in the summer months, though they were restricted in what they could say to each other as they were quickly joined by other friends.

It irritated him, she knew, meeting in public like this, but Lesya didn't want wagging tongues, and she wasn't quite sure yet just how much she could trust herself to meet privately with him. Things could easily go too far, and part of her wanted them to.

It sometimes felt like dipping her toes in the water, going in a little further each time, and then it felt like the sand beneath her feet was turning into quicksand, and she was forced to withdraw from him, fearful of her own feelings, as well as his own. They were from different worlds, and she had already learnt that relationships were not always what they seemed to be.

"It seems a rather elaborate charade this guy's playing for just a small scam, unless he's into it big-time," Adam mused. He reached across the table and took her hand. "I'd be careful pushing this too far if I were you, Lesya. The Russian Mafiya have been known to be rather ruthless, if that's who he's really working for. He'd need contacts to get away with this sort of thing, and they've always been into everything."

"Okay, I won't do anything with what I've learned so far, at least until after my leave. I'll give it some thought and maybe talk it over with my Father. He's a manager with a company in Balkash, and he knows a thing or two about the way business is run in this country." What she didn't tell him was that she also knew a bit about the Russian Mafiya from personal experience. She didn't want to worry him, but a Russian knew more about what was going on in Russia than did an outsider. Only Russians really understood Russians.

Finishing their drinks, they walked outside, buttoning up their coats against the cold and the chill wind. He walked her to the entrance to her accommodation, and she turned to hug him and give him a brief goodnight kiss under the watching eye of the security guard. No tongues yet, as he was quite tender, and not pushing this further or faster than she wanted for the moment. She bade him good night, and he walked off down the darkened uneven streets to find a taxi back to the Hungarian Village.

*   *   *

While this little friendly chat was going on, her conversation with Kairat in the nightclub the night before was being passed on to higher-ups in the Russian Mafiya by Usen, causing slight concern, with both her own involvement and Kairat's loose tongue. "Lesya Romanova. She works for Reliability as an Engineer, though that's not what she told that idiot Kairat." There was a pause down the other end of the phone.

"Just how much does she know, and what does she intend to do with that knowledge? We need to be sure before deciding what action to take. Arranging some sort of accident would be difficult in a secure facility like where you work. Anything more deliberate would attract the attentions of the Militia, and we don't want that. Watch her for now, and I will discuss the matter with my superiors. If we decide to take decisive action, I will contact you again with the arrangements, and will leave it to you to carry them out. We may also need to make arrangements to include Kairat in any such 'accident' as his bumbling may bring unwanted attention down on our illegal shipments."

The phone disconnected at the other end, and Usen smiled as he put the receiver down, already imagining how his life would change when he replaced Kairat in the hierarchy. Decisions needed to be made, to ensure nothing came of this Engineer's investigations.

The name Lesya Romanova was passed along, and enquiries were begun into her background. The tentacles of this fledgling Mafiya were farspread, advancing further and faster than the Italian Cosa Nostra had ever dared. Already they were making inroads into America and Europe.

*　　*　　*

Over the next couple of weeks, Lesya lived life as normal, working, exercising, aerobics and such, and enjoying hot baths every night to get the kinks out of her system, and occasionally having her sleep interrupted by her neighbour and her Scottish boyfriend. Valentina was a squealer.

She didn't go to the Tropicana again, purposely staying away from Kairat, yet she visited the Mosquito Bar a couple more times with her Englishman friend.

The eventual burglary in her room came as a bit of a surprise to her. There were no locks on any of the apartment flats, just the main entrance downstairs, and she had complained about that before. Fortunately, she hadn't brought much in the way of jewelry with her, and usually wore most of it, or kept it with her in her handbag. She still felt violated by the intrusion, finding her things roughly strewn about the place, and she was still quite upset when she discussed it with her English friend that night over a couple of drinks.

Not wanting to worry her, he said nothing about the shifty looking character he had noticed a few times watching the two of them say goodnight just outside the compound gates, but he was determined to find out more, possibly speaking to security himself on the matter. It was all he could do to remain calm as he saw the man again as they left, standing away just out of reach of the one streetlight that still worked. He couldn't see the face, but the shape and size and attitude were unmistakeable. It was the same man.

As Lesya walked through the gate, and he turned, the figure turned away also, slowly moving back further into the darkness. Adam followed him along the road, walking slowly, but at a slightly faster pace than the furtive character, determined to catch up with him. He closed the gap slowly, till by the time they'd passed the 69 Bar, he had closed to within a few yards of the man.

Adam called out suddenly, "Ei, shto ty delaesh? Pochemu ty nabludaesh za nami?", and made a grab for the shifty character as he tried to pull away, and then he gasped as the man lashed out, and the sharp blade of a knife ripped through his jacket. The thick material ripped, but slowed the blade enough not to slice through skin as well, and he cried out as the man came at him again, cutting and ripping low, aiming for his abdomen. He parried hastily with his arms and thick winter mitts, backing off and stumbling over the uneven ground.

As the man rushed him, he fell backwards, trying to kick out with his legs, but the man avoided them and threw himself down on top of him, trying to stab him and force the knife through the thick material of his coat.

He tried to force the blade back, the shiny length glinting evilly in the cold moonlight as the two men strained and rolled about the road. The smaller wirey man was wriggling about, and hard to hold onto.

A knee slammed into his balls and he gasped, losing his grip. The knife raised up, about to plunge down once more, when a shadowy figure came into peripheral vision, launching a kick into the attacker's side, and he cried out as he fell away, rolling, and taking the knife with him. The smaller man quickly scrambled to his feet, and ran off into the darkness.

"Boney, thank fuck!" Adam gasped, getting his breath back. "Don't let the bastard get away," he gasped, getting to his feet. The welcome assist had come from a friend of his who was just leaving the 69 Bar. Mike then turned to help dust his friend off.

"Best let him go, Adam. There'll be hell on if the other nationals see us give him a good kicking," he suggested discretion rather than valour. "What the fuck was all that about, anyway?" Mike asked. "You must have been flashing your money around too much," he supposed. "Not the best place to walk on your own. You're asking to get mugged.

It's like fucking Beirut down here, some nights. Let's grab a cab back to camp, quick," he suggested, and helped Adam along the road as more people, both ex-pats and nationals began leaving the 69 Bar as it was throwing-out time. Best stay with the crowds till they got clear, in case the little bastard came back, with friends.

Adam stayed silent over the cause of the attack, though he was sure it was nothing to do with any chance mugging. Lesya was getting in over her head with something. Stubborn little bitch had better be careful. He didn't get much of a look at the man's face in the dark. A discreet call to Security was the best he could hope for out here, but he doubted if they could really do anything under the circumstances.

Chapter Three

May 2nd

Security chiefs throughout Europe were made privy to the information retrieved by Mossad. Al Qaeda was planning a strike somewhere on the Italian mainland. The scrap of map did not show where, and all they had to go on were four hastily scribbled names;

Ali Kalfan Achmed

Mustafa Rachid

Achmed Al Wali

Fatima Khalid

Handwritten, and not in the best of script, the names were uncertain, possibly aliases, but they were all they had, and people behind the scenes were running them through a variety of computers trying to put faces to the names.

CIA liaisons were cross-checking possible American targets in Italy as it was an Al Qaeda operation. It was thought that American interests were the most likely subject of any such terrorist operation.

Special Forces Anti-Terrorist units were working in close proximity with their respective government agencies. Now all supposedly working under the auspices of the EEC, they were co-ordinated under the umbrella of Europol, from a building in The Hague, where Jim Maddox had his office.

"Any luck running those names through, Tom?" he asked his subordinate, as he studied a tactical map of the Italian mainland. All major ports, airports and railway networks were shown on the map, colour-coded after the last risk-assessment exercise had verified their vulnerability. Another map showed likely points of access into the country. Effectively a peninsula, Italy was a woman with her legs spread-just asking for it. If the terrorists wanted in, there was little chance of stopping them entering the country. Simply too many points of entry.

"Nothing yet, boss. Early days though. We're cross-linked with the CIA and FBI computers across the pond, as well as Europe-wide. Mossad's being more tight-lipped than usual. No access, but they've promised full co-operation on anything they come up with." Tom Brady smiled hopefully.

"I wouldn't trust those bastards any further than I could throw them," Maddox exclaimed. "They're good, but they've been fighting Arabs for so long they can't think straight any more. They get side-tracked too easily. Got to stay detached for these sort of ops," he explained.

"Easier said than done, Jim. At least we never had suicide bombers to contend with on the Donegal Road," Brady pointed out.

Maddox sneered. "Fucking Yanks!" he complained. "All this shit with the Arabs wouldn't be half as bad if they'd stop supporting Israel every time they make inroads into the Palestinian lands. 9/11 was long overdue, but the Americans hadn't a clue how to fight a terrorist war. All they wanted was a nice stationary target for them to use their 'overwhelming military might' against, and Iraq and Hussein had been begging for it for years. Didn't take much of an excuse, thanks to the chickenshit UN, and Blair was so keen to get caught up in Bush's little vendetta his head almost ended up stuck up Bush's ass!"

"Yeah, Boss. Now we've got Al Qaeda and other Muslim terror threats spreading all over the world. We've let them in, a lot of them illegally, and now have no way of tracking them. Even the ones we do know about like that twat Abu Hamza, we end up paying him legal aid to fight extradition. I can't believe it!"

"All goes with letting too many people wander around uncontrolled, in the first place," he insisted. "You or me go abroad into a foreign country, particularly a Soviet or an Arab one, and there's all sorts of paperwork to fill out before they even let you in. Once you do manage to get in, your movements are strictly controlled, and you need passes to go anywhere. What do we do in Britain? We let anybody in." He gestured in exasperation. "Fucking Politicians! Bastards, all of them. Won't say boo to a goose if they think it'll cost them a single vote. Just wait till we get a black Prime Minister, it's only a matter of time," he forced a laugh.

"You sound like Enoch Powell . . ." Brady joked.

"Cheeky bastard!" Maddox scrunched up a sheet of paper from his desk and threw it at him, and Tom grinned as he headed the missile away. "I was a bit young to hear the old 'Rivers of Blood' speech, but I read about it as I was growing up. He talked a lot of sense. Trouble was, the rot had already set in by then. Political correctness meant you couldn't speak the truth without being shouted down." Brady could only nod his head in agreement.

"Yeah, boss. Old Maggie, for all her faults, sorted the Argies out over the Falklands. I remember all the shouting about the Belgrano." He took a sip out of his mug of tea. "Fancy people complaining 'cos we sunk an enemy warship in a time of war. Who cares which way she was fucking sailing? She could have turned around again a few minutes later, couldn't she?" Maddox nodded, pushing the maps to one side. His eyes were hurting after studying them in this harsh light for the last couple of hours. He looked out of the office window across the cityscape. April always brought rain, and the windows were streaked with it, smearing the view somewhat.

"Yeah, Maggie was alright. Sorted out the Argies. Sorted that twat Scargill out, too," he laughed. "Fancy calling a strike in direct contradiction to his own Union rules? Served the silly sods right for listening to him. He bears the bulk of the blame for ruining the mining industry as far as I'm concerned," Maddox opinionated. "The Tories were just waiting to get their own back after he brought down the Heath government. Too busy playing politics, the communist bastard! He played right into their hands. She never built up those stockpiles for fun, you know. Just a shame Maggie couldn't sort her own party out. They sold her down the river, and that's why we now have an office here in The Hague, my old son," he gesticulated. "The arsehole of Europe (next to Brussels)," he laughed, and Brady laughed with him. "Come on, I've had enough for one night. These threat assessments go on and on, and usually nothing comes of them. Let's go find a bar. I need a drink," Maddox announced. Brady grinned, and pushed his mug of tea to one side.

"Now yer talking, boss!" Tom got up and pulled his coat off the back of his chair. The bright lights were calling. The paperwork would keep for another day. He knew the strain Maddox was under with his personal problems. These long tours of duty in The Hague took their toll of him. A little livener would help take his mind off things for a while.

*   *   *

Mossad had its own anti-terrorism units, and they dealt primarily with Arab threats to the safety of Israel. They were well familiar with the Arab mindset and the various networks of terrorist cells which operated against them. Al Qaeda was simply the latest in a long line of organisations used by the Arabs to attacks Jews.

The four names on the remnant of the map were indeed aliases, which certain Arab terrorists had used before, and some were still in use. The trick was in putting a face to the name, and then a location to the face. Whatever name they used, they were still a threat to Israel.

Alexi Davidovich was a Russian Jew, who had sought out what he saw as his natural homeland in 1974, and had since risen to take control of Israel's Mista'arvim, an elite unit, controlling the undercover operatives who risked their lives on a daily basis to infiltrate terrorist cells on the West Bank, Gaza and Jerusalem.

He had come across one of those four names previously in intercepted communications reports from one of his units. All his efforts were now being concentrated on tracking down the person who used that name.

His people were out and about, using what contacts they had within the underbelly of the Palestinian society, to try and locate the terrorist concerned. Israel controlled much of the movements of the Palestinians, and the airports were on alert, but there were so many places where an individual could cross the border into Egypt, Syria, Jordan or the Lebanon, none of them particularly friendly towards Israel. Once there, they were out of Israel's control, and free to move as they pleased. Which meant that capturing the terrorist on Israeli soil was all the more imperative.

The search was underway within hours of the remnant map being found, though Davidovich withheld that particular piece of information from the Americans and their other European allies. If this terrorist was on Israel's soil, she was an Israeli problem, and would be dealt with accordingly.

*   *   *

The town of Dimona lay to the south-east of Beersheba and the airport. Austensibly a quiet enough place, on the face of it, away from the trouble spots in the east and north of the country, and government patrols kept people away from the military facilities on the outskirts of the place, but within the town itself, life was lived as normal. Two jeeps followed the road south from Beersheba, towards Mamshit, taking the right-hand fork towards Dimona, and then switching off their headlights. They approached the town slowly and quietly from the north, headlights off now, and driving only by the light of the pale moon above.

The apartment block was one of many such on the eastern side of the town, and their target lived on the third floor. It was not going to be an easy extraction, and the men of Israel's Mista'arvim checked their weapons as they slowed to a halt as close to the building as they dared.

Like black shadows, they drifted across the road and into the building. Speed was of the essence now. Once they were spotted, all hell was likely to break loose.

Single file on the stairs, one man covering the one in front as they rounded the landings, trying to keep it as quiet as they could. The first cry came as they made the second floor landing, as an old man in a string vest and pajama bottoms opened his apartment door to let out his cat, and he cried out in alarm at seeing armed men in the stairwell.

More cries soon followed, as the unit rushed up the stairs. One by one the residents of the building were starting to waken. Fatima Khalid was in bed when she heard the ruckus. Coming awake quickly, she slid the small automatic out from under her pillow, and chambered a round. Somehow they'd found her. Her passport and papers were good forgeries, but they obviously hadn't worked. Hiding out in the Jewish towns in plain sight, was often easier than trying to hide away on the West Bank.

Hastily, she threw on some clothes, hearing the noise in the stairwell growing louder and nearer. She slipped her feet into soft rubber-soled shoes as she heard the first sounds just outside her apartment door, and fired two quick shots straight through the panelling, hearing the cries from men outside as the bullets struck home.

Grabbing a small satchel, which was already packed for her intended trip the next day, she backed off quickly towards the fire escape, sending one more round through the door to delay her pursuers. Fatima climbed though the window, and off down the fire escape, the flimsy iron structure shaking under her weight as she descended rapidly. She had a car parked two streets away, fully fuelled and sufficient to get her across the border into Egypt. The men were breaking down her apartment door in the room above as she dropped the last few feet to the alley floor, not waiting for the ladder to fully descend. If she stuck to the shadows, she had every chance of escape. The Jews could not have planned a large raid on her building, else the clamour from the residents would be much louder than it was. She had no doubt that it was herself they were after. Things were hotting up in Israel. The climate in Italy was much cooler, but only for the moment. She had no doubt it would heat up once she arrived there.

*   *   *

The story didn't warrant great headlines, and it was buried away on Page two of The Times, and other newspapers worldwide. Two men shot and wounded in a raid on an apartment building in Dimona. Suspect escapes. It went on to give brief details of the attempted arrest of a female suspected terrorist by security forces, and explained how the raid went wrong. Security alerts were in place, seeking to apprehend said terrorist, and a photo was published, obviously old, and sufficiently distorted to pass for any old passport photo.

Chapter Four

May 14th

May in Italy usually signals the start of the tourist season, as the unpredictable spring weather gives way to the more familiar summer sunshine and oppressive humidity of the Mediterranean climate.

With the influx of thousands of these tourists flooding into the country, Masoud Al Asmi and his newly recruited band of terrorists disguised their arrival onto the mainland, each of them entering through a different port of entry, some by the airports of Milan and Naples, whilst others arrived by boat at a variety of ports and fishing villages. Two of them drove overland from France, through the Massif du Pelvouz, and entering via Turin.

Their instructions had been clearly understood. They were to gather in two teams of four. One team would rendezvous in Salerno in the south, the other in Genoa in the north of the country. Communication would be by cell-phone only to co-ordinate their terrorist strikes up and down the country. The strategy was brilliant in its simplicity. As one struck in the south, within a day or so, an attack would be carried out in the north, leading the authorities to keep switching their resources up and down, assuming only one terror group was responsible for the atrocities, and moving back and forth to carry them out. In truth, their movements would be slower, taking place while the authorities were looking in a different place for them. It would take them some time to catch onto the fact that more than one group was responsible and that all the actions were well co-ordinated.

*   *   *

In a small hotel in Salerno, three men and one woman met in Room 316 on the third floor at the appointed time of 3pm. They introduced themselves to each other. "My name is Fatima Khalid." Her reputation was well known, from Palestine, a known member of Hamas. She stood about five feet eight inches if you discounted the heeled shoes she was wearing. Mid to late forties, a few streaks of grey in her otherwise black hair, but still attractive despite the hard mouth. Her body was still impressive, as the western clothes fitted it snugly, and the three men noticed it, as they listened to her.

"Ali Kalfan Achmed" another introduced himself. He was from Saudi Arabia, and belonged to Islamic Jihad. He was using a toothpick to clean otherwise gleaming white teeth, behind a tightly cropped beard. He was younger than the woman, in his late twenties, fit and around 6 feet tall. He stared openly at her, enjoying the freedom to let his eyes wander.

"Mustafa Rachid," announced the third terrorist, a Pakistani who had fought against the Americans with the Taliban. He was in his early twenties, and impressionable. He was also shorter by far than the rest of them in the room, about five feet three inches tall.

"Achmed Al Wali," the fourth terrorist introduced himself. Ex-Libyan military, but changed allegiances when dissatisfied by Qaddafi's softening stance against the West. He was by far the toughest looking amongst them, standing five feet ten inches tall and as wide as a barn. He looked to be in his early thirties. A thin moustache drew a line across his upper lip.

Some were known to the others by reputation, though none had ever met before. These four made up the first of Torquemada's terrorist cells, and they settled down to study maps of the Italian mainland, which had been left in the room for them, awaiting their first instructions which were expected by a telephone call which would be made at 5pm.

*   *   *

Similarly, about an hour later, four men gathered in another hotel room in northern Genoa. They introduced themselves as "Anwar Rachman." He spoke with a good English accent, despite having fought for the Taliban in Afghanistan. He stood about six feet two inches tall, slim, late twenties, though his eyes looked somehow older. He wore a small goatee beard.

"Abdul Aziz." He was a Yemeni, large and rotund, about five feet nine inches tall, and slightly balding.

"Mohammed Al Shair," from Saudi Arabia. He looked like a hot-head, and such could get them killed. He was about thirty years old, of average build, and about five feet seven inches tall. His eyes were those of a true fanatic.

"Omar Akhtar," the fourth man introduced himself. He was a Palestinian, with Fatah. He looked too young to be on such a mission, hardly out of short pants, and standing a mere five feet six inches tall. "I have come here to kill the Infidel," he said with the conviction of a true Believer of the Faith.

They too sat down to study the paperwork that had been left in the hotel room for them, and await telephone instructions. Italy didn't know it, but the Jihad had already begun.

*   *   *

In Genoa, the phone call rang exactly on time, and Ali answered it. "Did everyone make it through okay?" asked a cultured voice.

"All four of us arrived safely," was his response. "A few minor delays, but we all made it here to the hotel on time," he verified.

"Good. My name is Yusef Abdullah. I work as a Language Professor at the University here in Rome. I will be your contact for the duration of your mission. I have arranged for cars to be left in your hotel car-park. Keys and documentation you should have found in the hotel room."

"Yes, we have them," Ali confirmed.

"In the boot of the cars are a selection of munitions and weapons in the recess normally used for the spare wheel. The spares are loose on top of the carpet, deflated as though you had just changed a flat tyre if for some reason the police stop you and ask to look in the boot. It will pass a cursory inspection," he assured Ali. "Leave any vehicles you arrived in. I will arrange to have them collected and moved or returned to any rental agencies you may have used. Leave keys and documentation in the hotel room when you leave. You have my telephone number. Memorise it and use it sparingly. I do not wish to know your itinerary.

The newspapers will tell me where you've been, after the event. Let me know in advance of your needs, and I will arrange what I can. We can discuss pick-up points as and where required, but try and keep your requests realistic. I can only do so much, lest my superiors here realise I am exceeding the duties of my office. We do not all sympathise with your cause," he explained.

*   *   *

Naples was chosen as the first target of Torquemada's Inquisition. St Magdelene's was a Catholic school which catered for young children in the inner city. Set amid a dull lifeless industrial backdrop, on the southwest of the port, it represented a breath of fresh air for the children who took their morning exercise in the walled playground every morning and every afternoon. It was just one of many such schools in the city, and it had been picked purely because of its ease of access to the main thoroughfares to ensure a quick and easy getaway.

A small pale blue Fiat cruised down the main street towards the school. The two men inside the car were carefully watching the surrounding streets and buildings. They drove all the way down the street, turning right at the junction, before making a complete circuit, and approaching the school for a second time. A large white dollop suddenly splattered the windscreen, which caused a curse from the driver, who instantly switched on his windscreen wipers to clear the mess away. "I hate those seagulls. All they ever do is shit on everything!" he cursed.

This time they slowed as they approached, seeing the children cavorting and playing over the brickwork and meshed fence. The car finally pulled over and stopped, though the engine was kept running. The two men sat within the car, watching and waiting, till, at a nod from one, both the men got out of the car and slowly and deliberately approached the fenced playground.

The children ignored the two men, who stood there, looking in through the mesh. Both of them had strange set expressions on their faces, and Sister Anna Catherine thought they looked odd, suspicious even, worldly enough to realise that not all of the people who stared into children's playgrounds could be trusted with her young charges.

One man was slightly taller than the other. Swarthy skinned, the smaller one had a thin moustache, the other a tightly cropped beard. Both wore long raincoats, which she thought was unusual considering the fine sunny weather, though neither of them looked like they might be 'flashers', though she had never heard of such perverts operating in tandem.

One of them caught her curious stare and grinned brazenly back at her, flashing gleaming white teeth which showed one gold tooth glinting in the bright sunlight. He picked at his teeth with a small wooden toothpick and blew the nun a kiss as he returned her stare, before laughing coarsely to his friend. Sister Anna Catherine determined to go and have a word with the two men, and started off across the playground towards them, working her way through the playing groups of children, when one of the men reached inside his raincoat and pulled out what looked like a ball of some kind.

As she looked, he threw the ball into the air and over the fence. Her eyes followed the trajectory, realising far too late what it was she was seeing. "Oh, my God!" she cried, as the first grenade went off, scarcely ten feet from the ground, and showering everyone within a thirty foot radius with deadly shrapnel.

The neighbourhood rocked with the sound of the first explosion, which was quickly followed by three more. The two men hastily got to their feet and ran back to their car, which had been safely sheltered by the low wall from receiving any damage from the shrapnel. Controlling themselves well, despite the huge adrenaline rush, they drove away slowly, controlled, heading south back out of the city.

Behind them they left carnage in their wake, for the four grenades had ripped most of the children in the playground to shreds. A few survivors wailed and cried helplessly, as in the distance, sirens could be heard and alarm calls alerted the Emergency services, flooding the switchboards. Sister Anna Catherine's body lay unmoving in the playground, though beneath it, the little girl she had attempted to save, cried pitifully, soaked in the nun's blood.

*   *   *

The Mayor of Naples had scarcely been given the news of the atrocity, when one of her aides patched a call through to his office. "I think you'd better listen to this, Madame Mayor. It's a tape that's just been delivered to the local TV networks. The editor there had the good sense to keep it off the air and contact ourselves."

The Mayor listened as they played back the recording down the phoneline. A well-cultured voice, fluent in Italian, thought with just a hint of accent, introduced himself. "Friends, Romans, Countrymen, lend me your ears," the voice laughed and taunted. "You may call me Torquemada, and today's events are my doing. Consider this the hour of your Inquisition!" he laughed. "It is only the first strike in what will be a long campaign of terror, I assure you. In Allah's name, many more will die. You will hear from me again," the voice promised, then was promptly cut off.

*　　*　　*

By the time the emergency services got their act together, the two terrorists were well on their way back to Salerno. Tomorrow, as the manhunt began, another attack would be carried out in the north of Italy, and it would serve to make the authorities switch their attention many hundreds of miles away, and leave them free to continue their journey northwards.

The second team, in turn, would be heading generally south, where they would in all eventuality rendezvous in Rome itself, the grandest of stages, where the final act of this drama would be played out.

*　　*　　*

"It's started, Tom," Maddox had just received word from his counterpart in Italy. He reiterated the news about the attack on the Catholic school.

"Jesus! That's horrible, but how do you know it's the Arabs? Why would Al Qaeda attack a target like that? It has no military value," Brady pondered.

"All but admitted it on a tape he sent into the tv network, which they've kept off the air. Tape and the envelope it came in are both in forensics being examined as we speak. They're not very hopeful. Sounds like this bastard wanted something spectacular, and this is bound to be on tonight's news and tomorrow's front pages," Maddox pointed out. "We've got a madman out there!"

*   *   *

Belle smiled as she opened her apartment door, pleasantly surprised to see that Achille Ratti had been as good as his word, and that her flat had been well maintained in her absence. Her little jungle of plants had been well watered and cared for, and she delighted in stroking the delicate blooms and vines.

Now that this 'truce' between themselves and the Church was holding up, she was free to return to Rome and take up her former modelling career once more. Argentina was nice, beautiful even in its own way, but she had grown to love Rome over the years.

Months had passed while she adjusted to the parents she had never known, coming back into her life. It had at times been awkward, but gradually she had felt more and more at ease with her mother and father, pleased now that she could call them by those names so readily.

She went back to the door to bring in her luggage, carrying the heavy cases in both hands. Only a few months ago, she had been an amputee, but now looking at the wrist of her right hand she could no longer see any trace of a scar. The operation had been a complete success. She could use the hand as she had always done.

The offer to resume her modelling career had come from some of the forwarded mail from her server, which she had access to via the computers in Gabriel's villa. Out of the blue it might have been, but a welcome excuse to get her own life back. Her parents, her 'real' parents she added mentally to herself, were nice and as loving as she could ever have hoped for, but she felt strangely claustrophobic living in such close proximity, for she was hardly a child, despite her looks.

A return to Rome and its nightlife was too tempting to pass up, and she had promised to meet with Donatello Grimaldi, and personally thank him for all the help towards herself and her mother after the incident at Borgia's nightclub.

It would be fun to strut her stuff up on the catwalk again, and see all the wondrous new creations, which she would automatically get a good discount on. She had plenty of money if truth be told, but like any woman she always had an eye for a bargain.

Belle finished unpacking her stuff and putting her things away, then went to open the window and stepped out onto her balcony for a moment, enjoying the sights and the sounds of night-time Rome. She breathed it all in, slowly. It was good to be back.

Satisfied, she stepped back inside the apartment and went into the bathroom to run herself a bath, adding some nice scented cologne and bubble-bath to the hot water. As it ran, she went into the lounge to pour herself a drink. She checked the fridge and found some orange juice within, which suited her mood, and poured herself a long tall Screwdriver, and took it into the bedroom with her while she got undressed.

She sipped at it slowly, as she walked naked into the bathroom, and put it down gently by the side of the bath as she tested the water. Finally satisfied, she turned off the taps and dipped a toe into the clouds of bubbles. She lowered herself into the water slowly, moaning sensuously as the hot water and suds caressed every inch of her body. She lay back in the water, submerging herself almost fully, and letting the heat soak into her pores. She rested her head back on the lip of the tub and just lay there, luxuriating in the feel of the warm water.

*   *   *

The manhunt for the terrorists was getting into full swing as Belle retired for the night. The authorities wanted a lid clamping down on this outrage, yet they knew time wasn't on their side. Unless they got very lucky, very quickly, the shit was going to hit the fan.

Chapter Five

May 17th

Two days later, shit was flying everywhere. Hardly had the security forces and police mobilised to restrict movement in and around Naples, and were trying to track down new arrivals in the area, than Torquemada's second cell struck near Modena, in northern Italy.

$$*\qquad*\qquad*$$

The busload of clergy had come down through the Brenner Pass, intending to travel down to Rome on the autostrada, with a brief stopover in Florence, before proceeding on to the Vatican City. Mostly elderly, the good Fathers and Sisters were enjoying the trip, sitting back in the comfortable bus and watching the odd video as the bus-driver coasted along, bringing them ever nearer their destination.

Father Klaus Wohlert was trying hard to work on the crossword in his newspaper, but the talkative nuns kept distracting him. He had been to Italy before, so the landscape and the sights were nothing new to him. It had been a long drive, even in such a comfortable coach as this one. He would much rather have gone through the Brenner Pass by daylight. The view was much more spectacular.

The grey Fiat followed them out of the city and out onto the autostrada, staying a set distance behind them. Traffic was light, this early in the morning, and the driver hoped to make Florence by mid-afternoon. In his mirror, he saw the grey Fiat pull out, and slowly begin to overtake him. He thought nothing of it till it pulled up level with him and then just stayed there, as the passenger window of the car slid down.

He gawped at the sight of the machine pistol that suddenly projected out of that window, and screamed briefly as his own side window shattered. The gun moved up and down, stitching bullets this way and that, killing the driver outright, and his shuddering body fell forward onto the steering-wheel. Inside the bus, the screaming started almost immediately, as they were at a loss to understand just what had happened, and the bus slewed wildly across the road surface as the grey Fiat sped up and accelerated away into the distance.

The bus hit the central reservation at an angle, bouncing off, almost at once, in a shower of sparks, and headed back across the lanes. Father Klaus fought his way to the front amid the panic, seeing the dead man, and trying to pull his limp body off the wheel, but it was too heavy and he had no time. The bus smashed through the barricade and off the road, as he tried to grab the wheel. It's momentum took it through the first line of trees, smashing them down in it's path, but then the uneven ground made it lurch, twist and finally overturn, throwing passengers everywhere, as it's chassis and bodywork twisted, before finally coming to rest on it's side, the bodies inside the bus piling up on top of each other, some alive some now dead.

Inside the overturned vehicle, in the silence immediately following the crash, still conscious survivors fought to claw their way out of the wreckage, over each other, but they were injured and mostly infirm. Some moaned and groaned, gasping as they found themselves still alive, and others began to scream in pain as the shock subsided and their injuries became suddenly, and painfully, apparent.

Father Klaus struggled to free himself of the nun's body which was pinning him down. His vision was gone without his glasses, and the steady flow of blood from his head-wound was running down his face, into his eyes. He finally forced his way free amid the carnage, holding a handkerchief to his brow to staunch the flow of blood. Around him, people were crying out in pain.

On the motorway, cars were braking to a halt, and drivers leaving their vehicles to try and help, climbing over the barriers to gain access to the broken bus.

The windows of the bus were shattered where it had landed on its side, leaving the broken yet still intact windows above their heads.

There was the smell of burning which drew his attention toward the front of the bus, and he saw flames there as the broken petrol line and oil ignited on the sparks from the shattered engine with a sudden awful WUFFFF . . . . The flames spread rapidly as the screams grew louder, as they realised what was happening, and Father Klaus just had time to cross himself as he realised what was about to happen. The resulting explosion as the petrol tank blew, silenced all the screams, and a huge pall of black smoke rose mournfully into the sky, as would be rescuers flung themselves to the ground. The long broken body of the bus turned into a funeral pyre.

*   *   *

As planned, the location of the second attack in as many days made the authorities switch their attention and their resources to the north of the country, and emergency and security services closed in around Modena. The first cell of terrorists was now free to begin their travels north, and they travelled in two separate cars, taking different routes, towards their next target. Each smiled as they mentally reviewed their own roles in the overall strategy. No ill-conceived rash act of terror was this, but a planned strategy. Let the authorities rant and postulate as they will. There was no way they could hope to stop what was to come. Torquemada's strategy was brilliant. There was no way to combat it!

*   *   *

Back in The Hague, news of the second outrage was being dissected by Maddox and his team. First Naples and now Modena. Opposite ends of the country. They must have made their escape from Naples before the roadblocks were fully in place. It was a bad time of the year for anything like this to happen. Once it got out, the tourism industry would be badly affected.

First a Catholic school, and now a busload of Catholic clergy. Deliberate connection, or just coincidence. Maddox didn't know as yet. Too many unknowns, and way too early. "I've got a real bad feeling about this one, Tom," he admitted to his sub-ordinate. "I've been listening to that recording, and the voice-analysts agree with my latest gut-feelings. My first impressions were wrong. This Torquemada is no psycho, even though he's acting like one. He's a cold one. Makes him all the more dangerous and all the more unpredictable."

"Suppose it is a pattern, boss? Makes a change from the usual American targets," Brady conjectured.

"If that's the case, you can bet the septics won't bust a gut to help us, if it's not their nationals being targetted. If it is a pattern, how the hell are we going to do anything about it? There must be millions of priests and nuns in Italy. They're all going around with a big red bullseye painted on themselves, and they don't know it. Think what'll happen when the Press figure that one out. Panic on a scale that's unthinkable," Maddox rubbed his brow wearily. "I'm getting too old for this shit," he complained.

"You're still the best, boss. Not many have your analytical mind. You'll work it out, and we'll catch the sonofabitch in the end. Just wait and see."

"Wish I had your confidence, Tom. Got too many other things on my mind."

"Julie?" Maddox nodded. "I know it must be hard. Christ, I can't know," Brady admitted. "If it ever happened to me, one of my kids, I don't know what I'd do."

"I pray it doesn't, Tom. I'm just glad she's still alive. Original prognosis wasn't that promising. Still, there's been no deterioration in her condition these last couple of months. No improvement either, though," he admitted. "I'm going back home for the weekend, unless something drastic comes up. I'll pop into the hospital to see her, spend some time with her, even if she's got no idea I'm in the room. Something I've just got to keep doing, keep my hopes up."

*   *   *

The second tape was delivered to the television networks that night, and again, it never made airtime as the authorities demanded the networks' co-operation. It was just two isolated incidents as far as the public were concerned, and that's how they wanted the situation to remain. Catholicism was the root of all modern Italian culture. If it was realised that the very fundamentals of their society were being targetted, then who knows how the members of the public would react, let alone the clergy themselves.

"Greetings, my friends. This is Torquemada. How goes the Inquisition?" the voice laughed, taunting. "First your children, and now your priests. More Italian blood has been spilled, and there will be more, much more," he promised. "Each atrocity will be worse than the one before it. Sooner or later the media will have no choice but to reveal who is behind these crimes. You yourselves are to blame for these acts, for they are only revenge for past wrongs your religion has done to mine. Yours will be but the first such religion to fall before Islam, for this is the Holy War that has been talked about and threatened for centuries. All will fall before the tide of Islam!" The tape ended there, and Achille Ratti switched off the tape recorder.

*   *   *

All eyes around the council table looked to one another, as they took in the words of the terrorist. Now leader of this Council, Ratti spoke finally. "What shall we do in the face of this threat?" he asked, and glowered around the darkened chamber. "It was bad enough when we just had those Red Brigade fanatics to deal with, but this man strikes at the very core of our beliefs, our civilisation. The Sword of Solomon was not formed to deal with such threats."

"What word from the authorities? How are they intending to deal with this matter?" asked Romanus, leaning forward, agitated.

"They can only react after the event. Terror is always the initiator, and thus has the advantage," explained De Grimoard.

"Unless the terrorists make a mistake, the authorities don't stand much chance of catching them. Such things are always difficult to dissect after the event. The longer this campaign of terror goes on, the more information they will have to work from, but such investigations take time, and by then the country will be at a standstill once word gets out of the truth of these terrorist attacks," Ratti revealed. "I think this situation warrants a rather unique approach."

"How so, Achille?" asked De Grimoard.

"We are presently helpless against this terrorist threat, therefore we need to seek assistance from an outside source," he explained. "I will go now to seek such assistance." Ratti stood up from the table. "I will keep you informed of results." Ratti then turned and slowly left the Council Chamber, followed by Marco Falcone.

"You mean to ask his help, then?" Falcone asked when they were out of earshot of the chamber. Ratti smiled wearily,

"What else can I do, Marco? His background proves he has the experience we need here. I can think of no one else who has the knowledge and the skill we need."

"And if he refuses to aid us, as I think likely, for he has no love for the Church?"

"Then I suggest you had better find some way of persuading him, Marco," Ratti grinned mirthlessly.

*　　*　　*

On the other side of the world, Gabriel's computer flagged an incoming e-mail alert. Manuel looked at it in disgust. The firewall was secure enough, but it rankled that his 'young' charge allowed any sort of contact with 'them'. Dutifully, he printed out the message, and took it down to where Gabriel was working out in the basement gymnasium.

Gabriel paused from his exercises, towelling himself down as Manuel handed him the hardcopy e-mail. He studied it carefully.

My dear Gabriel,

if you have been paying attention to the world news, you may be aware that terrorist attacks are being carried out in Italy. These attacks seem to be specifically targeting the Catholic Church.

Two days ago in Naples, a nun and thirty seven children were slaughtered in a school playground. Nine children survived the attack, all hospitalised with severe injuries and traumatised by their experience. Today, twenty one priests and fifteen nuns were burned alive in a bus which had been machine-gunned and forced off the motorway. One civilian was also killed in this attack.

The terrorists are Arab, possibly linked with Al Qaeda, according to preliminary reports. My own organisation was not designed to deal with this sort of outrage, and we currently find ourselves as helpless as the authorities. People are dying here, needlessly, and we find ourselves needing help. Your help.

Your previous links with ETA, and your known reputation puts you in a rather unique position to assist us. In light of the recent truce between us, and appealing to your good nature, I would ask your help in this matter. Perhaps with your insight, and my own organisation, we may be able to assist the authorities in apprehending this terrorist cell before many more people die.

Regards

Achille

Gabriel studied the e-mail long and hard, as Manuel studied him in turn. He raised his matted brow and handed the e-mail back to Manuel. "Send him a reply, Manuel. One word. No."

"As you wish, sir," replied Manuel smugly.

Chapter Six

Lesya was on leave, and back in her home-town of Almaty. She had moved away for a time, when she wanted her freedom, to Karagandar, but eventually decided the comfort of familiar surroundings was needed after a turbulent private life. Almaty was always described as a bit of an upside-down city, with the mountains to the south, north was always *down*, and the many streets were on a noticeable slope, aligned in an ordered fashion as they were.

She lived on the fourth floor of apartment building 64, close to one of the rivers which flowed down from the overlooking mountains. The lift rarely worked, as the tenants themselves were supposed to pay for its upkeep, but everyone was forever arguing over the cost, and many people using it without contributing themselves. Still, four flights of stairs helped keep her in trim. Exercise was a regime with her. Now that she had gotten her body into this perfect shape, she intended keeping it that way.

Lesya loved to just relax on her time off, enjoying doing nothing, as opposed to the hectic work schedule forced upon her in Tegriz. She didn't like to cook and so most evenings she used to frequent a little restaurant owned by a friend of her parents, called the Tropicana, strangely named like the nightclub back on the complex in Tegriz. She always looked upon the Manager as her Uncle Vanya. She had known him since she was a little girl, and he always gave her good food and discounted prices.

She tried to distance herself from her work while she was on leave, and the mystery surrounding the illegal movement of goods that she had discovered remained stored away in the back of her mind as she pondered what to do with the knowledge she had gained. Getting involved with the Russian Mafiya was never wise, and it was only hearsay evidence she had gained so far.

She noticed the well-dressed man eyeing her on the fourth night of her return. Middle-aged, and quite distinctive looking, he dined alone as did she. She was used to men staring at her, but this one was not giving her the same lustful stares. There was something different behind his eyes. He was there every night that she turned up, and always offered a smile when their eyes met, though he remained at his table and she remained at her own. Two single people each enjoying the same food, or so she thought.

Then, after nearly ten days at home, Lesya turned up to enjoy her evening meal to find the restaurant full, and no spare tables remained as she spoke to the maitre-de. The businessman was there, at his usual table, and noticed the conversation. He got up from his table, and came over.

"Excuse me, but I could not help but overhear the conversation. We both dine here alone, and under the circumstances, I would be honoured if you would allow me to share my table with you for the evening. My name is Pyotr Dmitriyevich Grechko, and I work for the Biology section of Kovacs Pharmaceuticals." He held out his hand, and Lesya took it, in greeting. Kovacs Pharmaceuticals was owned by Feliks Kovacs, the alleged head of the local branch of the Russian Mafiya here in Almaty. One of life's strange coincidences? But then Kovacs had fingers in any number of pies in the local industries.

"Oh, thank you. Under the circumstances, it would be a pleasure," she smiled. "I am Lesya Alexandrovna Romanova."

"A pleasure," Grechko smiled, and turned to escort her to his table. He held out a chair for her, as she sat. "The restaurant is busy tonight. I usually eat here on my way home from work."

"You must work late every night," Lesya commented as she studied the menu. The waiter hovered to take her order. Sturgeon in a white wine sauce, with some rice and vegetables. Some fruit juice, chilled.

"I must work hard to maintain my position. I am one of the directors of the firm, and there is much to do in this new world order.

We do business all over Europe," he revealed. "Business booms since we improved trade with the West," he smiled, and took another sip of his vodka. "So what do you do for a living, Lesya Alexandrovna? I have only seen you in here recently."

"I work in Tegriz, in the oilfields, for one of the big oil companies. I normally work a 4&4 cycle, but I have just had to do a 6 week stint, so I am a little tired after the pressures of work." Pyotr's eyebrows raised in amusement.

"Yes, industry is picking up all over Kazakhstan. It is a profitable time as all the big oil and gas companies seek to asset-strip our country," he mused.

"Without their help, our government could never capitalize on its resources by itself," she pointed out. Pyotr shook his head lightly from side to side. The grey streaks in his hair were distinguished, but there.

"All companies look to their own profits first, my dear Lesya. Business could not exist without profit. Capitalism has finally won out over Communism in this regard at least," he joked.

Lesya found the man charming, and attentive, a good conversationalist, and he revealed further details about his life, his loves, his hobbies, his divorced wife. Yes, Lesya knew *that* was coming. A good looking (*was he?* she suddenly asked herself) man, out on his own, always had some sort of similar tale to tell (either that or he was gay), but then her own experiences proved that marriages were difficult to maintain.

Lesya was a little reticent to be so open with a stranger, and so continued to listen rather than reveal details of her own troubled personal life. It was pleasant enough just listening to him talk, as he was cultured and well-spoken.

Her sturgeon arrived eventually, and she was persuaded to order some mulled wine to go with it. Grechko enjoyed watching her eat, for he liked fine food, fine wines, and fine women. This Lesya Alexandrovna was a very fine woman indeed, and his appreciation of her was obvious.

Partway through the meal, Grechko appeared in slight discomfort, and fished in his pocket for a bottle of pills. He popped two into his mouth. "I have a slight heart murmur," he explained, "and I need to keep taking medication till it clears up."

The evening meal ended early enough, and when he suggested giving her a lift back to her apartment, she was of a mind to refuse, until he said his chauffeur would drop her off. Curious, she decided to accept, and when they left the restaurant together, a large BMW pulled up with tinted windows. The front window rolled down smoothly to reveal a moustached man in a chauffeur's cap and uniform. "Nikolai, we are taking the young lady home," Grechko announced as he held open the rear door for her. The chauffeur smiled, and nodded to Lesya, who nodded back.

Lesya gave him the address of her apartment building, and she got into the back of the car with Pyotr Grechko. The engine noise could hardly be heard, as the BMW pulled away, and the drive was as smooth as silk. Grechko must be important indeed to warrant such luxury.

Nikolai opened the rear door to let her and Grechko out, and Grechko insisted on accompanying her to her door, though he was careful to take the four flights of stairs slowly. She let herself in, using her two keys on the different locks. "May I call you?"

"You don't have my phone number," Lesya smiled, sweetly enough.

"No, I don't, do I?" Grechko smiled back. But he had ways of finding it out.

"Thank you for the meal, and the company. I enjoyed the evening."

"My pleasure also," Grechko bowed slightly, and Lesya closed the door, listening for a moment till she heard his footsteps going back down the stairs. Her evening had been pleasant enough, so far, yet she had found the events strangely disturbing.

After a good long soak in her bath-tub, and a play with her rubber-duck in the water, a strange present from her Englishman friend, Lesya put on her pajamas, and decided to do a little surfing on the internet, and she switched on her laptop. Kovacs Pharmaceuticals was a big organization in Almaty, and after checking, she found the name of Grechko among that of three other directors of the company. They had subsidiary offices throughout Europe.

Kovacs himself lived on a private estate, to the north of Almaty. It was the hub of his empire, so to speak, housing a research facility where drug-research was carried out, under the strictest security, and it also housed his personal villa, further along the grounds, where he enjoyed the same security in his private life.

He was rumoured to live an opulent lifestyle, though when in residence here in Almaty, rarely ventured outside the grounds of his estate. He had too many enemies, an occupational hazard of the real business he dealt in. Avoiding this Grechko was unlikely if he ate at the same restaurant as herself, but should she cultivate the friendship? She might learn more of Kovacs' organization. She decided to sleep on it, and retired to bed, pulling the blankets around herself comfortingly.

*   *   *

Back in Tegriz, Adam was still on rotation, and he was concerned about recent events, so much so that he went in to see his Supervisor about it. Ian was a dour Jock, back to back with a useless Yank cunt, running the Cad Design Group. "Hi, Adam. What's up?" asked Ian, as he was collared in the corridor coming back from a smoke-break downstairs. Adam walked with him back to his office.

"I don't know if you heard, but last time I was up the RV, I was almost knifed," he explained, by way of introduction.

"No, I hadn't heard. It's like the fucking Wild West up there, man. Best stay away from the place," he advised.

"If it's that bad, why does the company still house some of its employees there? It has no security like the main camp," he pointed out.

"Not for me or you to say. Company policy," was Ian's only comment.

"Yes, and we all know Company Policy is not for the plebs to comment on. Just fucking put up with, right?" Adam continued.

"What are you trying to say, Adam. For fuck's sake, man, I've got enough on my plate at the moment, without listening to grief from you."

"Like I said, I almost got knifed. You know I'm friendly with Lesya, the Project Engineer?" Ian nodded. "Well, she's being stalked by one of the Nationals. I collared him one night, after I'd seen her to the gate at her accomodation, and the little cunt tries to knife me. Would have succeeded too, if a friend of mine hadn't of intervened." He deliberately didn't pass on his suspicions that the incident had something to do with her investigations into what seemed to be some sort of smuggling operation.

"If it happened off camp, there's not much I can do about it," Ian complained. "Group Four only work within the confines of the main camp. The local militia have jurisdiction up at the RV, and involving them would cause problems for the company in a situation like this," he explained.

"So you prefer to put one of the company employees at risk, rather than involve the militia, is that it?" Adam remonstrated. Ian was losing his temper.

"I don't make Company Policy. I just enforce it," Ian pointed out.

"I remember when people used to think of you as one of the boys, Ian. Of course that was before Fred came in and you realised you had no real authority any more. But your 'Company Policy' is putting the life of one of my friends at risk, and I'm not prepared to keep quiet about this. Either you do something about it, or I will," Adam warned.

"Look, you little cunt, don't you start on me with your own petty little problems." Ian stood up from his desk. "There are rules for working here, and you shouldn't have gotten involved with one of the Nationals anyway," he accused.

"As if you haven't, eh, Ian?" Adam countered back. "Either way, I want some action taken, officially or unnofficially. I want this little bastard found and dealt with. I don't care what kind of repercussions there are. I know it's difficult to get rid of a National employee, but he's a threat. If you don't want to make it public knowledge, then speak to the head of Group Four, and get something done *un*officially. If she comes to any harm, Company Policy is going to suffer when I go to the Press. I know enough about all the little scams going on around here, particularly yours, to cause a lot of problems."

"Don't you fucking threaten me! I'll have you out of here on the next plane!" Ian warned.

"And you'll be on the one after, once management knows about the way you manipulated tenders to give all that as-built work over that fucked up Plant Revamp project to a pseudo company run by a couple of the lads in your own E&I squad. 10% was it, or more? I don't fucking care anymore, Ian. You've got me working for that two-bit Maintenance department, and undermining me instead of supporting me while I'm trying to work to your procedures, which they prefer to ignore. I've had enough of being between a rock and a hard place. You want to sack me, then fucking sack me, but this time, just this once, we do things *my* way!" Adam insisted.

Ian's face went red, and he came around from his desk, going toe to toe with Adam. A typical fiery Jock, he found it difficult controlling his temper. "There are limits to what I can do unofficially, just as there are limits within Company Policy," he reiterated. "I'll speak to the head of Group Four, but it will be upto him as to what can be done. You're right, I do know my limitations. Know yours!"

*   *   *

The next evening, back in the restaurant, Lesya again accepted Grechko's invitation to join him at his table, and they dined on guinea-fowl with a nice thick gravy, and steamed vegetables. Topped off with a suitable wine, she found the conversation pleasant and relaxing. Pyotr was a charming man, well educated, and sure of himself. "Although I don't spend much time at the Research Facility, I get invited to the old man's parties every week. He invites dozens of people. Work and business associates. The one night of the week he gets a bit of relaxation. Oversees too much of the work himself, and all that stress isn't good for anyone, let alone someone of his age," he explained. "There is a party scheduled for tomorrow night. Would you care to accompany me?" he smiled, in invitation.

Lesya found herself taken aback slightly, by the sudden invitation. He was asking her on a date. Yet a look around Kovacs' private dwelling might give her the opportunity for a bit of snooping around. Should she chance it? Before she could stop herself, she found herself nodding. "Yes, that might be fun. I haven't been out to any parties in ages," she admitted. Grechko smiled at her acceptance.

"Good, I'll have Nikolai pick you up outside your apartment, at say eight o'clock?" Lesya nodded.

"Yes. That will be fine. Is it going to be a formal party?" Grechko laughed, as he shook his head.

"No, nothing too grand. Just dinner and drinks. Maybe watch a movie. He gets all the latest releases before they get into the shops. Clothes are whatever you feel comfortable with," he assured her. Lesya felt more at ease after his words. Still, if there were other women there, then she would not want to appear out of place, and certainly not look the frumpiest of them there.

*   *   *

In the end, Lesya decided upon a tight pair of black pants, and a beige blouse. The underwear, of course, matched, though she had made no conscious decision when choosing them. After all, she was not intending to seduce or be seduced. A simple black onyx cameo around her neck, onyx bracelet, and matching black handbag made up her ensemble, and she was ready and waiting as eight o'clock came around. She had a short black leather jacket with a black foxfur collar to help keep out the chill as she waited for the BMW to pull up.

Grechko got out of the car himself to greet her, beaming as he complimented her on her attire. "You look marvelous. I'll be the envy of every man there. You'd better stay close to me, or someone will try and steal you away," he joked. Lesya laughed, and got into the car as he held the rear door open for her.

They drove for nearly an hour, with the heater turned up against the cold evening, along roads which were at times less than perfect as they headed north from the city. They talked for a while, and then as Nikolai played some soothing Italian opera on the car stereo, Lesya just lay back and closed her eyes for the remainder of the drive. Grechko smiled as he noticed her enjoying the music, but let her enjoy it, and kept his conversation to a minimum.

*   *   *

The facility was floodlit when they pulled up at the security gate, and heavy steel gates slowly parted, as one of the security guards came to check on the identity of the visitors. Nikolai merely nodded to the guard, and he was allowed to drive through. Concrete fencing surrounded the outer perimeter, with an inner layer of mesh fencing, and guard dogs let loose and roaming in between as she could see. Kovacs took his security seriously.

A two storey building flashed past on the left, and warehouses were noticed on the opposite side of the car, before they were driving through blackness again, away from the research labs and towards

Kovacs' private villa. This too was well lit up as they arrived, and Lesya noticed dozens of cars parked in a crowded car-park, as Nikolai pulled up outside the main entrance to let them out. He got out of the car, and opened the door for them both to alight.

"I'll be round the back, in the ante-room down from the kitchen, with the other guys, when you need me, boss. Just page me when you want me." Grechko nodded, and let Nikolai enjoy a bit of leisure time.

"Thanks, Nikolai. Shall we go, my dear?" he offered Lesya his arm, and she took it, and allowed him to lead her inside the villa, as an aged manservant admitted them.

"May I take your coat, Madame?" he enquired, and Grechko helped her out of it, before handing it to the man to take away into the downstairs cloakroom. Lesya was staring around the place, admiring the décor, as the music and laughter could be heard coming from further inside.

Kovacs himself came out of the main lounge, through the polished oak doors, and he grinned as he saw them. He and Grechko hugged in familiar fashion. "Glad you could make it, Pyotr." He was a big bear of a man, still hearty despite his aged years. He looked to be in his sixties, hair and bushy moustache all white. Breaking the embrace, he turned to greet Lesya, though thankfully just took her hand instead of crushing her in his arms as he had done with Grechko.

"May I present Lesya Alexandrovna Romanova? This is Feliks Mikhailovich Kovacs, the head of the company."

"Enchanted, my dear," he smiled, and kissed the back of her hand lightly. Lesya smiled reservedly, a bit in awe of the man. He had quite a presence. "You look lovely. I hope Pyotr has been treating you well. Come on in and meet everybody. I can't remember all their names, but they're all having fun," he laughed, and began to usher them forward.

Lesya followed Grechko's lead, and entered the room just behind him. The large open doors gave way to a modern lounge, decorated a bit too lavishly for her own taste, with a big open fire in the middle, in a sunken hearth, with a huge copper canopy overhead to draw out the smoke. Large logs crackled and burned on the fire, giving out a noticeable heat.

Scattered around the room were a number of guests, mainly middle-aged men and much younger women, which put her on her guard straight away. They couldn't all be the men's wives, secretaries, mistresses perhaps. Some of them stood talking in little groups, while other sat around on the numerous sofas. Alcohol looked to be in plentiful supply, as Kovacs had another two servants going around the room with trays of drinks, keeping everyone supplied. Some heads turned to see the new arrivals, and Grechko waved at a few acquaintances he knew.

Kovacs left them then, and Grechko ushered her forward, making introductions to most of the men, and some of the women he knew. Lesya accepted a drink, and began to listen to the conversation started between Pyotr and a man he obviously knew. Another man came over to them with a broad smile holding a tiny woman by hand. Most of the men, if not the women, knew each other to greater or lesser degrees. Some of the women were indeed introduced as secretaries, or otherwise company employees. No wives present, which told her a lot. All of the women were well-dressed, some overtly so, and she was glad she hadn't dressed down too much.

Low pop music played in the background. The speakers were well-hidden, but obviously good quality. The group singing she recognized as TATY, a Russian female duo that were now making inroads into Europe and America. She preferred Latin acts like Ricky Martin and Enrique Eglesias herself. Latin music was so wild, and easy to dance to.

She found it hard to remember the names, as Grechko slowly worked her around the room, and she made small-talk with so many easily-forgettable men and women. The men were obviously a lot more interested in her than the women, but then that was to be expected. She was used to the way men looked at her, some with respect, but more often than not open lust. She could deal with it. Women of course looked upon her as a potential rival, so she wasn't fooled by the overtly friendly greetings she was getting.

"So nice to meet you, my dear."

Lesya accepted the interest with good grace and patience, sipping at her glass occasionally, though not wanting to get drunk, she changed to mineral water the next time one of the waiters came around with the drinks trays.

Eventually, after being introduced to virtually everybody there, Grechko guided her away from the main group. "Let me take you on the Grand Tour," he smiled. "Feliks lives here in grand style," he explained as he took her arm. Lesya went with him as they wandered from room to room, occasionally bumping into more guests who were doing their own touring around the place. The place was certainly sumptuous, and he had not scrimped with the décor. Only the finest of furnishings. Some of the paintings she recognized. Kovacs had taste alright, and the money to go with it.

The kitchen was bigger than her flat, and Grechko nodded to Nikolai who was smoking a cigarette with some of the other relaxing chauffeurs just outside the rear doors, leading into the grounds. Three chefs were busily preparing canapés and snacks. Once through the kitchen, he lead her through the grounds, past the swimming pool and Jacuzzi, and adjacent sauna, and back in through the front doors once more, before guiding her up the grand staircase to the upper floor.

The bathroom was huge, with a marble sunken bathtub. Lesya imagined herself soaking luxuriously in such a bathtub. It was a pleasant thought for a moment. Eight guest bedrooms followed, and one of them was obviously occupied, by the feminine laughter that was coming from within it, as Grechko discreetly avoided opening that particular door, and continued with her down the corridor. "Along here is the old man's business area, where he keeps in contact with his other companies worldwide. He has a modern computer and telephone system installed, so it's quite easy to keep on top of things from here. Modern technology is invaluable in a place like this. One can enjoy the quiet of the countryside and still get your work done." He showed Lesya the place briefly, and then turned her around to guide her back downstairs once more. "So how long are you home in Almaty for, Lesya? When do you need to return to Tegriz?" he asked as they walked back into the main lounge and he grabbed some more drinks off a passing tray. Lesya accepted graciously, though wasn't too keen to drink out of the glass.

"Fortunately, I am changing rotation slightly, so I still have a week left of my leave. Me and my backtoback are adjusting schedules to allow for holidays," she explained.

"It must be a harsh schedule to work in such a remote location?"

"Yes, it is," she agreed, "but there are compensations, not least of which are the long vacations."

As the evening wore on, Kovacs appeared at intervals, with just a towel wrapped around his waist, or in a bathrobe, spending some time in the sauna with guests. Lesya socialized as best she could among strangers, though Grechko was in close attendance to offer support, and she was starting to feel more comfortable when she noticed some of the guests disappearing, in pairs. It was gradual at first, hardly noticeable. If it hadn't been for the screams and laughter from outside, she might not have realized at all. But when she looked out through one set of French windows, she saw the naked partygoers frolicking in the swimming pool.

No prude, Lesya suddenly felt very uncomfortable, realizing the way people were pairing off. Not wanting to cause offence, she decided to feign a bad stomach, and disappeared upstairs to the bathroom. She had to wait to gain access, and when she did, made herself partially sick by sticking her fingers down her throat. Looking convincingly ill by the time she returned to her host, she pleaded sickness.

"I don't feel too well, Pyotr. It must have been some of the canapés upsetting my stomach. I have to watch what I eat. Could you please take me home?" she asked, apologetically.

Grechko showed immediate concern for her welfare, and no annoyance at all, as he paged Nikolai to return to the car-park. Collecting her jacket from the cloakroom attendant, he insisted on escorting her home himself, and they sat in the back of the BMW, whilst Lesya held onto her stomach and Nikolai tried to avoid the potholes in the road.

"I may have eaten something I shouldn't, too." Grechko tried to make light of the situation, as he held his own stomach momentarily. He reached into his inside pocket for his bottle of pills, which rattled almost emptily. He shook out the one capsule that was left, raised it to his mouth, and swallowed it dry. He grimaced a little as he waited for it to take effect.

Lesya looked concerned now. "Are you sure you're okay? That's one of your heart-tablets." Grechko nodded.

"I'll be okay. No need to worry." But as the drive wore on into the night and the city lights approached, she noticed the beads of sweat on his forehead. He looked ashen, and she rapped on the partition to alert the chauffeur.

"Nikolai, Nikolai, he's sick. Pull over." The driver pulled up and got out, opening the back door to let in some crisp night air. Grechko groaned, and held out the empty pill bottle.

"Stupid of me. Need all-night pharmacy." He was very conservative with his words, and in pain. Wasting no time, Nikolai got back into the driving seat, pushing the pedal to the metal as he tore into the outskirts of Almaty. Lesya gave him directions through the partition, to a small pharmacy she knew which stayed open late.

Fifteen minutes later, they pulled up hurriedly, and Lesya took the bottle from Grechko's weak hand. She rushed to get out of the car and into the pharmacy, stumbling and cursing as she caught her heel in the uneven pavement and went down hard. Nikolai rushed to assist, as Lesya grimaced, holding onto her twisted ankle. "Help me up," she gasped. "Worry about me later. Let's get this prescription filled," she suggested.

Her arm around the taller man, Lesya let him support her as they entered the pharmacy and hurriedly explained their requirements. The druggist hurriedly give them the similar bottle with the required pills, and Nikolai left her there in the pharmacy while he rushed to get the pills to his employer. "Do you have anything for a sprained ankle?" Lesya managed a feint smile, as she fished in her purse for some tenghe to pay the man.

After she had strapped up her ankle, Lesya managed to walk gingerly out of the pharmacy, holding her shoes in her hand, for she couldn't walk in them with her sprained ankle. Her pain was secondary. Of more importance was Grechko's heart-condition, and she hoped the pills had alleviated his pain by now.

Nikolai was sitting back behind the wheel as she approached the rear of the BMW, and the rear window was open to let in some fresh air as Grechko lay back on the seat, recovering from his murmur. He was also talking on his cell-phone, and she continued to approach the BMW when Lesya heard her own name mentioned. She froze momentarily.

"No Feliks, I don't think we have anything to worry about with this Lesya. She's done nothing to cause concern while she's been back in Almaty. When I haven't been with her, I've had her watched. Yes, I know what your contact in Tegriz told you. It was probably all just a coincidence that she made those enquiries, despite her giving a false name. So would you if you were trying to do something illegal,"

Grechko laughed momentarily. "Lots of girls look to make money on the Black Market. Some go to great lengths, as you know. She may have been telling the truth. Give me a few more days and I'll worm it out of her, to verify her story. If she's telling the truth, then no harm done. Just take care of that loose-lipped fool in Tegriz. If it turns out otherwise, then I'll take care of the situation." Lesya's blood froze. For a moment she stood there, like a rabbit caught in the headlights.

Her contact in Tegriz must have been reported, despite her giving a false name to Kairat. As yet, she had done nothing with that information, so they were undecided what to do about her. God, what should she do? She backed away from the car slowly, uncertain and frightened.

Then a car came around the corner, framing her in its headlights, and she saw Nikolai's head turn at her reflection in the mirror, and she found she suddenly had no choice but to walk painfully towards the BMW once more. Her heart was in her mouth as Nikolai got out of the car to open the rear door for her. He nodded courteously, and she managed a weak smile back as she stooped to enter the rear.

Grechko managed to smile as she sat down alongside him. "Thank you, my dear. That was a bad one. I don't know what I'd have done without you. I'm sorry about your ankle. Nikolai told me what had happened, but I needed to catch my breath after that attack," he apologized.

"It's okay. I'll live. I was more concerned for your health than my own," she explained, truthfully.

"Drive the lady home, Nikolai," he instructed the driver, as Lesya sat there silently beside him, not knowing what to say to a man who was no longer her friend, despite his charm and his manners. She didn't dare reveal she had overheard part of his conversation, yet how should she handle this?

As Nikolai pulled up in front of her apartment complex, Grechko put a hand on her arm. "Forgive me, but I can't escort you to your door, and I realize it may be hard for you to get about for a day or so till your ankle heals. I will call you tomorrow to see if you need something, ok? I've enjoyed this evening, my heart problem notwithstanding of course," he managed to joke.

Lesya smiled once more, and then allowed Nikolai to help her out of the BMW. He helped support her as they crossed to her apartment building, and swept her off her feet easily, to carry her up the four floors, once he realized the lift was not working. "Really, this is too much," Lesya started to protest.

"Nonsense. It's the least I can do. Thank you for *your* help, Miss. I don't know what Mr Grechko would have done without your assistance tonight." He was sincere, and half-supported Lesya from the stairwell to her apartment door on the fourth floor. He insisted on opening the door with her key, and bade her goodnight. Lesya found herself blushing momentarily, touched by his concern, as the older man turned and walked back towards the lift.

She undressed with difficulty, wanting a good soak in a hot bath, but settled instead with filling the bath with cold water to soak her ankle whilst sitting on the side, and thinking things through. She was under suspicion by the Mafiya. What could she do? If she made a move against them without evidence, they would bury her, probably literally. If she did nothing, could she live with the fear? Weighty thoughts indeed, and somehow Lesya knew she would get little sleep that night.

As she soaked her ankle, she mused over her problem. It didn't do to cross the Mafyia in Russia, more brutal and quicker to anger than their Italian counterparts.

So, if the Mafiya, read that as Kovacs, was suspicious of her, what could she do about it? Feign ignorance? What then would they find out about her actions? What would they do? She couldn't live in fear all her life. What could she do? There must be something at the villa that would implicate Kovacs, and if she could find it, then she had something to bargain with for her life. But finding such as that would mean getting back inside. She couldn't trust Grechko. He was sweet on her, but he followed Kovacs' orders, and spied on her for him.

*   *   *

Her ankle still needed a light strapping next morning, and it was still painful when Grechko phoned her to enquire about it. She wondered just how many people in this world were in the pay of the Mafia? They seemed more powerful than KGB these days but she knew it was not true. Appearances could be deceptive. "Forgive me, but it was relatively easy for a man in my position to find your phone number, and I really was concerned for you."

"Thank you for calling to enquire about my ankle. It was sweet and thoughtful of you. I think I need to rest it for a few days. Give myself time to catch up on my sleep," she suggested.

"I want to see you again, Lesya. Feliks is hosting another party at the end of the week. Will your ankle be up for it, by then?" he asked, hopefully. Lesya paused, considering her answer. To beard the old lion in his den would take all her courage. If she was caught in what she intended, she would be miles from anywhere and in his power.

"Let us see how I'll feel by the end of the week. My ankle should be okay as long as I don't dance," she frowned to herself. Can't exercise with the damn thing, either, she said to her herself, feeling like an invalid.

"Okay. You rest up, and I'll call you in a day or so to finalise arrangements, Feliks is hosting some bigwigs from Chechnya, and he wants to create a good impression. Should be a lavish party. You'll enjoy it, I'm sure."

"Time will tell. Goodbye then."

"Get better, my dear. I'll talk to you in a few days." She replaced the receiver.

*   *   *

By the time Grechko called for her on the Saturday evening, Lesya had had time to think things through. She would only have the one chance to do some snooping and she had to make the most of it. The only way to get the Mafiya off her back was to get Kovacs put away. Once the evening festivities were underway, she could slip away and try and get into Kovacs' private offices. He looked the meticulous type, and if she could get access, she was sure she could soon find what she wanted.

She dressed for the occasion in similar style to the previous evening, feeling somehow more secure wearing light sand coloured pants than a skirt or dress. Multicoloured brown, beige and opal shirt, with a matching bracelet, from Swarovski. (A present from her Magician). A matching brown leather handbag was big enough to hold her camera. She went downstairs to where Nikolai held the door open to the BMW. Grechko awaited within, offering her a huge red rose bouquet as she slipped into the back of the BMW beside him. "You look lovely, my dear."

"Thank you," she smiled, holding it on her lap. Grechko covered one of her hands with his own, as Nikolai got behind the wheel, and the vehicle slowly moved off into the night.

"I've been looking forward to tonight," he admitted. "I hope you don't have any more trouble with the food this evening. I told Felik's chef off after the other night."

"I do suffer from poor health, I'm afraid. I have to watch my blood-pressure and be careful of my diet all the time," she revealed, though already thinking of excuses to terminate the evening early. It would be more difficult than last time.

The BMW's suspension handled the rough roads well as they left the citylights behind, and the headlights illuminated the dark of the countryside as they headed north. The music from the front of the car was relaxing, and Lesya found herself settling back, and pretending to sleep, as the journey continued.

The kilometers soon sped by, and the glow from the compound lights could be seen in the sky above the steppes. "Nearly there," Grechko gave her a little nudge to ensure she woke up, and Lesya pretended to yawn.

"Already? I must be more tired than I thought," she explained. "The week before I go back to work is always hectic, running around and organizing things . . ." The gate approached, and two guards came over to check the occupants as before. Satisfied, the gates were opened to allow them in, and Nikolai parked up in the same car-park as before, alongside numerous other vehicles. He held the door, offering her his hand gallantly as she alighted. Lesya liked Nikolai. Old-world Russian charm. He must have been very attractive in his youth, though he was still an attractive man now, even though she put his age at close to sixty. He smiled as she accepted his hand, and she smiled in return. He closed the door behind her softly, as she walked with Grechko towards the large open doors to the main house.

As she left her jacket with the old retainer once more, Kovacs again came to meet them, shaking Grechko's hand heartily and giving Lesya a hug. "Lesya, isn't it? Welcome back. If you have problems with the food again, we'll roast the chef in his own oven," he joked, or did he? Grechko laughed anyway along with him, though Lesya managed a weak smile, unsure of how she was expected to react. "Make yourselves at home. I have some of the latest movie releases which are going to be premiered next month," he boasted, and ushered them inside, where Lesya recognized a few faces from her previous visit, some of whom acknowledged her return, whilst others, some of the women, pointedly didn't.

"Let's get some drinks." Grechko gestured to one of the waiters, who promptly came their way with a loaded tray of drinks, and Grechko took one for himself, another for Lesya. Martinis. He offered a glass to Lesya, with a toast. "To the beautiful women in the room," he smiled. Lesya nodded graciously.

"But of course," she grinned, and he laughed, as she took a sip from the glass. She was indeed beautiful, which was part of Grechko's problem. He was finding her company intoxicating, even without the alcohol. Tasked with keeping her under surveillance, and possibly arranging her death, he was finding it hard to be objective. He had hardly known her for more than a couple of weeks. A different type of woman from what he was used to, no empty-headed secretary or hanger-on eye-candy like he saw accompanied some of the other men he knew here. Envious eyes were on him as he escorted her around the room, and with good reason. He hoped she was as innocent as she made out. He would hate to be ordered to have her killed. He was capable of it, but he would regret doing so. Feliks would make the decision, and he would do what Feliks wanted. He had little choice in the matter. You did not disobey Feliks Kovacs and live to boast about it.

He kept close to Lesya as they wandered about, staking his claim pointedly to the rest of the men there, and careful not to let any of them talk to her too long, as they attempted to ingratiate themselves with her. He was actually starting to feel jealous, he realized, and laughed inwardly. Lesya flirted openly, naturally, though he could tell she didn't really mean any of it. It was just something that came naturally to her, enjoying being the centre of attention. He spotted some of the looks some of the other women were giving her. If looks could kill.

She seemed to be enjoying herself tonight, and used her camera to take a few photos of him, and he took some of her. Plenty of people offered to take photos of them together. "Nice camera," he commented, as she showed him the digital display on the back.

"A present from a friend," Lesya smiled.

"Must be a good friend," Grechko commented.

"He is. The best," was all Lesya would add. She snapped a few more, of the other partygoers, who were quick to pose on the promise that Grechko would see they were copied on the photos. Lesya was planning ahead, sure Kovacs' guest-list would be of interest to other interested parties.

The doors to the terrace and pool were open, but it was a bit chillier tonight, and no one was actually in the pool, in swimsuits or out of them, though plenty of people were milling around the poolside itself, and some hopped in and out of the sauna. The latest bootleg film Kovacs was going to screen was a popular choice, and most people seemed to be keen on seeing it. That might be her opportunity to try and access Kovacs' private offices. If not, she would have to hope for another opportunity later, and then find an excuse to get the hell out. She was outwardly calm, though drinking a bit more than usual to quiet her nerves and stop her knees from knocking. She was no coward, but bearding the Russian Mafiya in their own den was not for the squeamish. As long as she did not overtly act in a suspicious manner, nothing would happen to her tonight, she convinced herself of that. Think positive!

A light buffet meal was served after about an hour, with Grechko keen to try the food Lesya was eating himself, wanting to ensure she had no more stomach problems. That was one excuse she couldn't use tonight. She would have to think of another. Then Kovacs himself reappeared to inform everyone that the film was about to start in his home-cinema.

Lesya and Grechko followed everyone else to the upper floor, where they passed Kovacs' offices, and at the far end of the corridor, a large door opened up onto a mini-theatre, with rows of seats descending towards a large thirty-foot screen. There were seats for around sixty people, plush and upholstered with soft red velour padding. The architect had done Kovacs proud, squeezing all this into one modestly large room, utilizing the space well. Looking round, she guessed the projectionist's booth was up on the 3rd floor, above them. Lesya took her seat with the rest of them, and after a little while the lights dimmed for the start of the film.

The seats were broad enough with space for a small table on each arm-rest, to hold drinks and canapés while they watched the movie.

The copy was almost perfect, apart from the slightly tinny sound. Modern pirates were using digital technology these days, and even hand-held cameras in the back row of the cinema captured recordings good enough to mass-produce, even allowing for the odd silhouette of someone getting up out of the audience to go to the toilet.

Lesya was quite engrossed in the film, along with the rest of Kovacs' guests, and watched happily, allowing Pyotr Grechko to hold her hand as he sat beside her. The film was a long one, and no one thought it odd that Lesya got up to go to the toilet partway through, as some of the women had done already, the only difference being that she went on her own, but that was natural in itself as she was a stranger here.

Once the door to the cinema closed behind her, Lesya sprinted down the carpeted corridor, past the toilet to the door to Kovacs' offices. She tried the handle, and found it unlocked as it was on the previous evening. Quickly she stole inside, closing the door behind her. Going over to the filing cabinet, she tried the top drawer, and found this time it was locked. Trying the desk, she found those drawers locked too. Undeterred, she took her keyring from her bag, and one of the trinkets hanging from it was actually a small piece of spring-steel, made by a friend of hers, small enough and intricate enough to open most simple locks,. The filing cabinet took less than ten seconds, and Lesya began pouring through the contents.

Kovacs was neat and organized, or his secretary took good care of him. She pulled the file for last month, and started going through it. It didn't take her long to find the consignment papers, recognizing Kairat's name and matching it with the date. She had to be quick. Laying out the paper on the desk, she turned on the desk-lamp and quickly took out her camera.

*   *   *

Inside the home-cinema, Grechko was becoming concerned. Lesya had been gone longer than expected. Was she suffering a recurrence of her stomach problem? He was concerned for her welfare, and he excused himself and got up out of his seat, moving back towards the exit, to go look for her himself.

The noise and vibration from the big action scene on screen disguised the first brief rumble from deep below the ground, and he thought his legs were unsteady from being sat in one position too long, but then as he tried to move forward again, the second tremor struck more fiercely, and the floor and walls began to shake around him. Earthquake!

People were screaming as Grechko picked himself up, trying to avoid being trampled on in the crush to escape. The lights had gone out, and it was pitch-dark. Some people were resourceful enough to use cigarette lighters for illumination, casting scattered shadows of frightened people. His legs were shaking as much as the building around him, and everyone was panicking. "Outside . . . Everyone outside in the grounds . . . ." someone was yelling, and people were fighting to get out of what could be a death-trap. The capital status had been transferred from Almaty to Astana because of the frequent earthquakes in the south of Kazakhstan, in the shadow of the peak Khan Tengri.

Pyotr let himself be carried along in the tide, as the partygoers fought their way along the darkened corridors, trying to get out before the building fell in on them. Time seemed to stand still as the deep rumbling went on and on. Plaster was falling from the ceiling and a few light-fittings, though so far that was the limit of the structural damage. People weren't hanging about waiting for more, and he had little choice but to rush with them, fortunately seeing the toilet door open and assuming Lesya had already got out ahead of him.

*   *   *

Inside Kovacs' office, Lesya picked herself up off the floor, frightened by the powerful tremor, and the chance of discovery in the ensuing panic. She had been about to replace the file when the sudden loud rumbling and shaking had knocked her off her feet, and the filing cabinet had fallen to one side, lodging against the wall. There was enough light from the window to enable her to make her way over to it, and put it back into the still-open drawer, though she wasn't sure it was returned to the right place with the way the files were strewn. She swore when she couldn't close the drawer. It had jammed as it had fallen against the wall. Try as she might, she couldn't budge it, and decided there was nothing to do but leave it, and hope someone would think the tremor caused it to open. Grabbing her bag, she cautiously opened the office door into the darker corridor, hearing the screams from below as people were still exiting the building onto the grounds. She had to get down there and join them quickly, before her absence was noticed.

*   *   *

"Lesya! Lesya!" Grechko was calling as he wandered through the shocked guests, some of the women were still sobbing with shock and fright. Security guards were approaching with powerful lamps to throw some light on the scene. The tremor had stopped now, and the building still seemed more or less intact. "Lesya, thank God you're alright!" he cried out, hugging her as she threw herself into his arms, face wide with fright, as he thought, though more relief that she had managed to get back out without being seen.

"Pyotr, I was so frightened. One minute I am powdering my nose, and the next everything starts shaking. I thought the whole building was going to fall down," she blurted out, flushed and breathless from her ordeal.

"We're safe now. I think the tremor is over. If that's the worst of it, then I don't think we need to worry about aftershocks. Security is coming and they'll soon have the power back on again," he assured her, enjoying the feel of her in his arms.

The crowd of partygoers huddled together for warmth in the chill evening breeze, as Kovacs organized his Security Detail to go through the building and check for structural damage and make sure everything was safe to allow people back inside. Feint tired cheers of relief went up when the lights came back on, and shortly after that, one of the Security Detail announced it was safe to return inside. Catering staff hurriedly began to tidy up the scenes of panic, uprighting furniture and clearing away scattered bottles and glasses, bringing more as people wanted a livener to help their stresses nerves.

Lesya took a cognac, and Grechko a shot of vodka, as they looked around. So much panic in so short a space of time. Earthquakes were not uncommon, but still took some getting used to. Far better to experience them outdoors rather than inside, where a supposed refuge might fall down on top of you. "I think I'd like to go home now, Pyotr. I've had enough excitement for one night." Lesya managed a weak smile, and Grechko reluctantly nodded, realizing she was right.

"Wait here while I find Nikolai," he suggested, and then turned and headed off toward the rear of the property. Lesya could hardly contain herself. She'd gotten the evidence, now she needed to get the hell away from Feliks Kovacs while she decided what to do with it. She found her jacket herself, and was waiting in the foyer as Grechko returned to tell her Nikolai was bringing the car around.

They went outside, pausing briefly to speak to Kovacs, who nodded understandingly. It seemed a few other guests had similar ideas, as other engines were heard firing up in the car-park. The BMW pulled up in front of the broad stone steps, and Nikolai got out to open the rear doors for them. The plush seat felt so reassuringly comfortable as Lesya settled into it and Grechko got in beside her. Nikolai closed the door and then went around to get back into the driver's seat. "Take it steady on the roads, Nikolai," Grechko cautioned his chauffeur. "Those tremors may have caused some damage."

The BMW coasted towards the security gate, and stopped as one of the guards came forward. In the security booth a phone was ringing. The guards checked the occupants, and gave the signal to open the gates, which started to move slowly. Nikolai put the car into gear, and started to move forward, when there was a shout from the security booth, and the gates started to close once more. Lesya's heart froze in her chest as the guard approached the car again and Nikolai rolled down the window as he spoke. "There is a problem."

*   *   *

Back in the main building, some of the guests were rather indignant as Grechko ushered Lesya back inside. She hung onto her handbag nervously, trying to stop her knees from knocking with fright. One of the women suddenly stormed out from a side room, face black with fury, and she unleashed a volley of invectives at her male escort as he attempted to console her. One of the others explained to Grechko, as he stood looking puzzled at events. "The old man wants all the guests searched. He thinks something is missing. I don't know what." He shrugged his shoulders.

Lesya's blood was turning to ice, and she started to hyperventilate. Kovacs must have spotted the filing cabinet. He can't be sure as she had replaced the paperwork, but he must suspect or was being overcautious by ordering this search. Grechko tried to placate her, seeing the worried look on her face. "It's alright. Probably nothing. You're new here, so it's just a formality. We'll soon be out of here, don't worry." Lesya nodded agreeably, though not feeling quite so confident. Her handbag felt heavier and heavier.

When it was her turn, Lesya was asked inside the ante-room by a female security guard. Big and stocky, shorter but much heavier and well-muscled than Lesya herself. In close quarters, even as fit as Lesya was, it would be no contest. She was miles from anywhere, in the heart of Kovacs' empire. She had no one to turn to, not even Grechko. She would just have to hope her bluff would work.

"Undress," the female guard said simply, and Lesya's face flushed with mock indignation, though she had suspected this would happen. She put her handbag down on the adjacent sofa, and started to undress, removing her jacket and handing it to the woman to examine, which she did, running her hands over the material and going through the pockets. Satisfied, she handed it back, and Lesya put it down on the sofa, covering her handbag. Her blouse was next, then the pants, and then the underwear, all minutely examined by the female guard. Lesya shivered as the women's eyes ran up and down her naked body, half expecting some sort of full-cavity search, but pleased when the woman told her to simply get dressed, which she did, hurriedly.

Once she had put her clothing back on, Lesya lifted her jacket off the sofa, grabbing the handbag through the cloth and hoping her action would go unnoticed. She turned to leave, simply carrying the jacket and the concealed handbag.

"Not so fast, lady," smirked the female guard. "Show me your handbag," she ordered. Lesya cursed mentally, and put the bag on the table, opening it and emptying the contents onto the small table. The guard took the bag, examining it, and feeling in and around the lining. Then she examined the contents. Cosmetics, cellphone, addressbook which she leafed through. She examined the cellphone, and then reached for the digital camera, when Lesya reached for it herself.

"Careful, it's expensive," she protested, grabbing the camera case herself, and opening it up for the other woman. She took the camera out herself, and the guard held out her hand. Lesya reluctantly put the camera in it.

"I am used to such technology," she said, weighing the camera in her hand, and then switching it on. The back display began to illuminate, and she pressed the control buttons to display and slideshow all the photos that Lesya had taken with the camera, studying each one in turn carefully as Lesya watched her. The photos started with the ones Lesya had taken of some of the guests, then a few of Pyotr Grechko, then some of her which he had taken, and then some of the two of them together, and then . . . The female guard switched off the camera and handed it back to Lesya. "You may go," she announced, perfunctorily, and Lesya hid a sigh of relief as she replaced the camera inside the camera-case, on top of the spare media card she had actually used to take the photographs in Kovacs' office.

As she left the ante-room, another of the female guests was ushered inside to undergo a similar search, and Lesya felt elated as Grechko came upto her and gave her a hug. "See, I told you it was nothing to worry about. Come along now and we'll get you home. I can't go with you, I'm afraid. Feliks wants me to stay back and help him with something, but Nikolai will ensure you get home safely," he reassured her.

*   *   *

Nikolai waited with the engine running, and Lesya kissed Grechko's cheek as she bade him Goodnight. In the BMW once more, Lesya felt the heat as Nikolai turned up the AC against the evening chill, and she settled back to relax as the gates closed, only this time behind the vehicle as they sped off back into the dark of the night.

The older man watched Lesya from time to time in the driver's mirror as she gradually dozed off. He liked the girl, for she reminded him a little of his wife when she was younger and still alive. He liked his boss too, and he thought they made a good couple. Ahead of the car, powerful headlights illuminated the road, and he was careful to keep his concentration there, trying to make the ride as smooth as possible so as not to wake her.

*   *   *

Back in the complex, Feliks Kovacs was going through his office, concerned at the open filing cabinet. It could have opened during the tremor as things were shaken about, but his instinct told him otherwise. He took out the contents of the jammed drawer and started going through the files with Grechko, dividing them up between the two of them. It was Kovacs himself who spotted it, the one file that had been disturbed. Inside it the papers were no longer in date order, as his secretary always filed them, and more importantly, these papers were concerned with the shipment to Chechnya that the girl had been enquiring about in the Oil Company. "She's been in here," he announced to Grechko.

"But she was searched. She had nothing on her," Grechko protested, defending her.

"Whether she had something on her or not, she's been through this file. This is no coincidence, Pyotr. Details can be given to the authorities. I can't afford that to happen. This has gone on long enough. Terminate her," he ordered coldly. Grechko frowned, saddened by events. He was enamoured of her, true enough, but wise enough to know you didn't cross Kovacs. He picked up his pager, and started punching in a message to his chauffeur.

*   *   *

The beeper went off in Nikolai's pocket as the lights of Almaty appeared in the distance ahead, though they were still a few miles north of the city. He pulled the pager out of his pocket with one hand, and pressed the button to illuminate the message. His mood changed in the few seconds it took to read the message. In the back of the BMW, Lesya dozed, unknowing, and it was only the slowing of the vehicle that roused her, as Nikolai pulled over to the side of the road and stopped the car. They had just entered the outskirts of Almaty.

The big chauffeur got out of the driver's seat, and slowly came around to open the back door. "Miss, you are in big trouble," he announced, standing there, blocking any chance of escape. "I have been ordered to return you to Mr Kovacs' estate." Lesya gasped. Her charade had failed. They knew. She looked up at the big man, desperately trying to think of options. "Mr Grechko has instructed me to return you to the estate at my earliest convenience. That's a code word he uses to me sometimes. It gives me discretion to do what I think he wants, and not what he says he wants. My boss likes you, little lady, and I like you too, but you seem to be in big trouble with Mr Kovacs. Get out of the car," he ordered. He stepped back, and Lesya considered making a break for it. She didn't know what else to do. They were still on the outskirts of the city. Only the headlights gave any sort of illumination now, as the night sky was dark with clouds obscuring the moon. Tentatively, she started to get out of the car. Nikolai pointed across the road towards towards the waiting taxis outside the small nightclub. "I don't want to know where you go, but don't go home. I'll tell my boss, and more importantly Mr Kovacs, that you asked me to drop you off near a friends' place, before I got the message through on my pager. I'll just make up a streetname. They'll be looking for you, so don't stay around. That's all I can do for you," he apologized, and beckoned to her to start walking.

Lesya took a few steps, and then turned and stood on tiptoe to plant a kiss on the old man's cheek. "Tell Pyotr Thank You from me, if you get the chance?" she asked, and then turned to start walking once more. Behind her she heard the engine start up again, and the beam of the headlights turned and vanished into the night.

*   *   *

It was a long walk into the city, and once there, what would she do, where would she go? She debated whether to get into one of the taxis or not.

As she deliberated, she huddled her jacket tight about her against the cold, trying to assess her options. She needed advice, and checked her watch. It would still be early evening back on the Caspian and her friend Nataly would still be awake. She took her cellphone and called her friend. "Nataly, I'm in big trouble," she began the conversation.

"No shit, sweetheart," Nataly interrupted. "That guy you were quizzing got admitted into the clinic with a high dose of Radiation Poisoning. The company are treating it as an overdose from one of the isotopes they use to examine welds, but this is way too serious for that sort of exposure," she explained. "He had prolonged exposure to something much bigger," she speculated.

"Oh no, this is getting out of hand," Lesya suddenly decided. Her options were reducing all the time. She had heard rumours of illegal radiation dumps that the old Soviet Regime had left behind in various places in Kazakhstan, some not too far away from where she worked. If that was what they were smuggling, what the hell were they doing with it and where were they sending it? She was at a loss what to do, and then she remembered an old flame, Mikhailovanch. "Nataly, I have to go. I'll keep in touch. Bye," and with that, she severed the connection and called another number. It rang several times before being answered.

"Yes? Hello?" came a weary voice.

"Mikhailovanch? It's Lesya, Lesya Alexandrovna. Are you alone? Can we talk?" she asked.

"Lesya? Little Lesya? Bozhe moi, it's been years. How are you?"

"In trouble, and I need help. Will you help me, Mikhailovanch?" The voice at the other end stopped talking, as if considering. Then he spoke once more.

"Lesya, if you're contacting me now, after all this time, then you do need help, and if I can, I'll be glad to give it. Come over. Do you know my address?" he asked.

"Yes. Your reputation still goes before you, old friend. I'll take a taxi." She severed the connection and went across to grab one of the waiting taxis outside the club, giving him the address of one of the remote villas high up in the mountains.

*   *   *

Lesya knocked tentatively on the door of Mikhailovanch's house, pleased to see a light on inside. She and Mikhailovanch had been lovers years before, whilst he was still a junior lieutenant in the local Mafiya heirarchy. Now, he was at the head of one of many factions in this many-headed Hydra. He was older, more mature now, no longer the hothead she had known, and for a brief time, loved. "Hi," she forced a smile. Mikhailovanch smiled back. "Am I interrupting anything?" she asked. "I heard you had a live-in girlfriend. I don't want to cause a scene," she insisted. Mikhailovanch shrugged.

"Aigul is away visiting her parents. She won't be back for a few days, and what she doesn't know won't hurt her. Come in," he stepped back and held the door open for her. Lesya entered, nervously. He closed and locked the door behind her, and then took her coat before showing her into the living room, all swedish pine, and obviously very expensive, though typical of the housing here high up in the mountains, where only the really rich could afford to live, above the pollution clouded city of Almaty. "Take a seat, while I make some tea. Do you still like it weak?" he joked, forcing a small nervous laugh from her.

"Yes, I still like my White Rose tea," she confirmed, and watched him walk off out of the room in the direction of what she took to be his kitchen. He had lit a fire, prior to her arrival, and Lesya huddled over it, needing to get some warmth back into her bones after the evening she had just had.

After a few minutes, Mikhailovanch reappeared with two cups, one containing dark sweet tea as he preferred, and the other just plain boiled water to suit Lesya's tastes. He passed her her cup, and she took a sip gratefully. "So, where do we begin?" he asked. "Just what sort of trouble brings you back into my life at this time?"

Lesya started to explain slowly, letting the events of the last few weeks pour out of her, and finishing with everything that had happened to her earlier tonight.

"I know Kovacs. Not one to cross. I know Grechko too. I tried to get him to work for me, but Kovacs was paying him too much," he admitted. "It was good of him to try and help you. But there is a limit to how much he can protect you now Kovacs suspects you have information which can hurt him. Most people he dislikes usually disappear or turn up dead. You did right to come to me. The KND are infiltrated, by my people as well as Kovacs'. But this news is very worrying, and proves links between the Russian Mafiya and the Chechins. The authorities will not take kindly to this disclosure, but will be grateful for it. Right now we must move quickly, before Kovacs can get away," he insisted. "Your life will be in danger until we have him behind bars, or dead. You did a very brave thing by getting this information. Kazakhstan needs strong honest people like you," he complimented her as she sipped her cup. "This news about the radiation is serious. If they are indeed smuggling this type of material and the Chechins get their hands on it, anything could happen. The security forces all across the continent need to be alerted to get co-operation to track down this illegal consignment. It's too big for my own people to handle, but I'll protect you as much as I can." Lesya was aware that Kazakhstan had recently applied to join the EEC, and in a case of this magnitude, the government would go out of their way to be open and co-operative over this issue.

"Will you use the KND?" she asked.

"Only my own people within it. Enough to organise a raid on his complex. If we're lucky, we'll catch him unawares. I have a few phone calls to make. You'd better take one of the guest bedrooms, and I'll wake you in the morning. Not too early. I remember," he smiled, and Lesya reached out a hand to take his.

"Mikhailovanch, you are a true friend," she complimented him, and then let him show her to one of the guestrooms, where he left her to retire for the night.

*　　*　　*

The next day, the news came across Maddox's desk in The Hague, and it brought a worried frown to Jim's brow. The thought of the Chechins getting hold of fissionable material with their current attitudes to modern Russia was not a pleasant one. He reviewed the scanned photos of the documentation, and then reviewed the large wall-map of Eastern Europe, studying the rail networks against the timetable he had in his hand. "Looks like we need a favour off the septics. Let's see how good their spy satellites really are. Who do we have in Chechnya who can do some leg-work for us?" he asked his subordinate.

*　　*　　*

Midday in Almaty, saw Lesya awoken from her slumber, with a brief hurried knock on her door. She had slept with her clothes on for once, so it didn't take her long to answer the door. Mikhailovanch was stood there, a worried look on his face. "Kovacs and some of his key men got away in the firefight. I lost half my men in the shooting. You are the only witness against him, and your life is now in greater danger than before. The Mafiya has links everywhere. Kazakhstan is not currently safe for you. We need to arrange a holiday for you somewhere abroad until Kovacs has been captured."

Chapter Seven

Jim Maddox flew into Heathrow feeling tired. The drinks on the plane hadn't helped as much as he'd liked, and he still felt strung out. A hire car got him up to Hereford in a couple of hours, and he stopped off at his home to shower and change. The shower did him more good than the drinks had done, and he felt refreshed once more.

He drove to the hospital, parking up and feeding the meter for a couple of hours. Julie was kept in a private room, and he was glad the young blonde nurse was on duty and not that old dragon of a Welshwoman who was stricter about visiting hours. They both knew him by sight, and she gave him a welcoming smile. Strange that smile, all nurses seemed to practise it.

She showed him into the room and Jim pulled up a chair beside his daughter's bed. She lay there as if asleep, peaceful and angelic. But it didn't look like she'd ever wake up. Sensors were attached to various monitoring devices, and he knew she was getting the best of care. It didn't make it any easier. She was the light of his life now his wife had died a couple of years earlier. She didn't deserve this.

Tenderly, he reached out and took her hand in his, holding it, cradling it. He could feel her pulse, still strong, and the doctors 'had every hope', but she had been like this for months now. "I'm here, darlin'," he spoke softly, then, idly noticing the fresh flowers by her bed, he wondered who had left them there. He made a mental note to ask the sister on the way out. "Pleasant dreams," he said, as he gently stroked the back of her unresponsive hand.

He stayed at the hospital for four hours, till he felt he needed to go back home and get some sleep. He kissed his daughter's forehead before leaving her room, and then went back out to the car-park where he found he had overstayed his welcome on the meter. Luckily, his car hadn't been clamped, and he got in it and drove off.

Getting back to his home, he opened the door to the sound of his telephone ringing. Annoyed, he closed the door behind him and then answered the phone. "Guvnor, we need to talk," spoke a gruff yet friendly voice.

"No one is supposed to know I'm back, Nick," he said wearily, recognising the voice of one of his best lads in 22SAS. "How did you know I was here?" he asked.

"The sexy blonde nurse at the hospital tipped me off earlier tonight," he revealed.

"What were you doing at the hospital, Nick?" Maddox asked.

"Oh, just visiting a friend," he answered vaguely.

"Right. Now what's this about? I've had a bad week."

"Not over the phone. Take a walk down by the park. I'll pick up with you there," he explained.

"This better be good, Nick," Maddox warned.

"It's not good, guvnor, but believe me, you'll be interested in what I have to tell you," Turnbull promised.

*   *   *

The early morning news was awful, Belle thought as she treated herself to some pasta. The terrorist incident in Naples was bad enough the other day, and now this coach crash. As ordered, the media were playing down this second outrage, and had not revealed details of how the crash had occurred. Still, the visuals were quite graphic and not for the squeamish. So far, no one was connecting the two incidents, as horrific as they were.

Belle finished off her meal with a fresh fruit cocktail, rushing it slightly as she had a two o'clock appointment at the salon for a fitting. Preparations were progressing well for the show scheduled for tomorrow.

She did her makeup, keeping it to a minimum as she knew it would probably be changed once she surrendered herself to the dressers at the salon. Finally, she threw on a silk jacket, grabbed her purse and a hastily prepared overnight-bag, and left the apartment.

Taking the lift down to the basement garage where she stored her car, she fished around in her bag for her keys. The Aston Martin DB5 looked as good as new, once she pulled the dust-cover off it. Disabling the alarm, she stuffed the cover and her bag in the boot, and got into the car to start it up. The engine caught almost instantly after giving the pedal a few good pumps to get the petrol into the engine. It roared to life, coming alive as she played the throttle with her foot.

Grinning, she pulled away slowly, coasting up the ramp towards the street. The metallic gold paintwork caught the eye in the bright sunlight, and Belle enjoyed the turning heads, having fallen in love with the car when she had first seen the Bond film Goldfinger. She just had to have one, and although it took a year or two to finally get one, off the assembly line, she had looked after it lovingly ever since. Just a shame it didn't come with the same extras as the one had in the film, she chuckled to herself, momentarily fantasising about the fun she could have in traffic with the next jerk who tried to cut her up.

Momentarily, she mentally cursed as she realised the tax disk was probably out of date, and promised herself she would rectify that oversight as soon as possible. Until then she would have to rely on her smile to get her out of any trouble with any over-observant policemen. She had a very pleasing smile, and a very persuasive nature. Once in the car-park in Leonardo Da Vinci airport, it was safe enough until her return from the Fashion Show in Milan.

*   *   *

"He turned you down, then?" Falcone asked Ratti.

"Not unexpected. I appealed to his good nature. Apparently he doesn't have one," Ratti said resignedly. "Time now for Plan B. I hope you have one?" he asked, hopefully.

"I'm working on it," Falcone assured him.

*   *   *

Belle enjoyed being back on the modelling circuit again, though she hardly recognised any of the models these days. All her intimate friends had long since retired from the catwalk. No one knew her personally, which was advantageous, and made explanations unnecessary. She was known by reputation only, coming and going every couple of years, till her face faded from the public view, and then she would reappear, sometimes even changing her name, as well as her appearance.

She revelled in the designer dresses, so flambouyant, so daring. She would have to shave to wear that one, she thought as she held it upto the light. So translucent, and she couldn't possibly wear anything under it. The only problem with shaving was when the hair grew back, and she was all bristly for a few days, and itching like mad. Still she'd rather put up with that than staying bald, and having to shave her delicate areas so often.

Her long black hair was adored by the stylists backstage, as they combed and shaped it into various different designs to go with the creations she was being asked to wear. They pampered her incessantly. God, it was good to be back!

The show was scheduled for tomorrow, and all the important people in Italy were going to be there. Politicians and their wives, movie stars, all the paparazzi. It was going to be a blast!

* * *

Masoud Al Asmi scowled as he studied the media coverage of the bus massacre. Not unexpectedly, the authorities were doing their best to play down any terrorist link to the Naples incident, less they start a panic. That must not happen again. The next incident must be evident to the world. It was time to step things up a gear.

He smirked as he watched the police cordons tightening around Modena, for all the good it would do them. They didn't know it, but Act Three was already in motion and soon his men would spill more blood in his Holy Crusade.

* * *

The autostrada which ran between Naples and Bari on the two opposite coasts was currently undergoing a series of repairs to bring the road back upto standard. There were many sections of the motorway where traffic was at a virtual standstill due to the many roadworks, and a sea of red and white traffic cones stretched for miles. Traffic slowed down to a crawl as it passed them.

Stuck in the queue of traffic were two cars, quite innocuous in appearance and colour. As they drove slowly along, a hand came out from the rear window of the first car, and deftly picked up one of the cones, bringing it inside the vehicle. Some distance behind the first car, a similar theft occurred with the second vehicle.

Some time later, returning in the opposite direction, two more traffic cones were stolen, before the terrorists returned to their hotel rooms, to continue working long into the night. The promised munitions had been waiting for them when they had checked into the hotel, and they were keen to make use of them.

*   *   *

That evening, by prior arrangement, a BMW called to collect Belle from her hotel. Inside, waiting for her, was Donatello Grimaldi, head of the Grimaldi family, and one of the lesser powers in the modern Mafia. Still, he was happy with his lot in life, not as greedy or as unscrupulous as some of the other Dons, for if truth be told, he was following his dead uncle's advice to legitimise his business interests. Crime as it had been known in Italy was not as profitable as it once was, and there was more money to be made in Corporate Business.

A powerful man in his mid fifties, his black hair was starting to turn grey, but the moustache was still as black as ever, aided by an occasional bit of Marianne's mascara. His waistline was growing lately. Thank God for stretch pants, he chuckled, as he readjusted them.

Donatello thought of Gabriel as one of the 'family' so to speak, and Gabriel's family was 'his' family, as Gabriel had been one of his dear uncle's closest friends and confidantes. Belle was looked upon as a favoured niece, though in latter years, she had been considered one of 'them', an operative of the Church's secret Sword of Solomon organisation. But that was in the past, and Donatello was now prepared to accept her as a friend.

When Gabriel had phoned to tell of her intended return to Rome, he had been only too pleased to offer his hospitality and protection should she require it, and he had been delighted to accept her invitation to catch her return to the catwalk in Milan.

She looked gorgeous as she waltzed down the entrance steps, black sable fur wrapped around her bare shoulders as she stooped to climb into the car as his chauffeur held open the door for her. "My dear, you look like an Angel," and he took her hand to kiss it, and momentarily paused, as he couldn't help but marvel at the skill with which it had been reattached. Not a scar or even a blemish. If he had not seen it with his own eyes, he wouldn't have believed it possible.

Recovering his composure, Donatello charmed her from the second she entered his car, and Belle settled back in comfort, as the chauffeur drove through the city, heading for the restaurant in which Donatello had made reservations.

"So, how are preparations for the show? I will attend of course," Donatello insisted as he and Belle sipped at their champagne, waiting for the first course to arrive. Belle's fur was loosely draped over the back of her chair, and her shoulders were now bare. The low-cut bodice revealed the ample swell of her bosom, and Donatello knew every man in the place envied him his place at her table.

Donatello wasn't married, but he did have a favoured mistress, one who had carped like a harrion when she had found he was taking someone else out to dinner this evening, but such is life. A designer dress from Belle's fashion show would serve to placate her.

"It's on schedule for tomorrow. I'll have some tickets reserved for you. How many do you want?" she smiled.

"Should I bring my Marianne, or just surprise her when I bring home one of those dresses for her?" he mused. "She is currently visiting friends, while I have the onerous task of taking you out to dinner. Poor me," he joked, making her smile.

"Oh, you've got to bring her, Donatello. Don't be so cruel. She'll love the whole day. You'll have to introduce us and I'll show her everything behind the scenes." Donatello held up his hand.

"Okay, okay. I know when I am beaten. Two tickets then," he laughed. "So how do you find life with your parents?" he asked, changing the subject.

"Strange, if I told the truth," she answered truthfully, musing. "I'm a bit old to suddenly discover a new set of parents I never knew existed," she revealed, knowing that Donatello was privy to most of Gabriel's secrets, including his longevity. "It gets to be a little bit claustrophobic at times, so I decided to do a bit of travelling once more," she explained.

"My father has been spending a lot of time up in Cordoba recently, at that medical research lab he funds, and my mother is getting involved with the local Red Cross and helping the underprivileged children from the barrioes. Argentina would be more fun if I had someone to share it with," she admitted wistfully.

"There is no man in your life? But how can that be? Such a pretty one as yourself?" Donatello held up his hands. Belle smiled back.

"No, no one. Maybe I'll meet someone here in Milan or back in Rome who will sweep me off my feet?" she forced a weak laugh.

"Ah, but if I was only twenty years younger," Donatello mused.

"You're far too young for me as it is, Donatello." Belle made light of the conversation, though enjoying the flattery, and then the waiter brought over the first course, and they settled down to their meal.

It was shortly after midnight, when Grimaldi's BMW pulled up outside Belle's hotel complex, and Donatello walked her to the door herself, kissing the back of her hand gallantly once more. "It has been a wonderful evening, my dear. Just as well because my Marianne is apt to kill me when I get back. Those friends of hers are boring," he joked, and Belle laughed lightly.

"Thank you, Donatello. It's been lovely meeting you again. I'll be sure to leave those tickets for the both of you at the front desk. I look forward to meeting Marianne." Reluctantly, he let go of her hand, and she turned and entered the building. He walked back down the steps and back into his BMW. He settled back and tried to doze as his chauffeur drove through the brightly lit city-streets.

*   *   *

La Scala opera house in Milan was the venue for the fashion show, and tickets were selling out fast, despite their prices. Crowds had begun gathering since lunch-time though the show itself didn't start until three, and would likely go on into the early evening.

Lesya mingled with the throng, so pleased that her tourist agency had been able to fix up this holiday at such short notice, and even more so that they had been able to arrange tickets to this prestige fashion show. The Schengen Visa gave her easy access to most of Europe, and Italy had been her first choice. She loved high-fashion and her Italian was coming along well enough to handle most simple conversations, as long as people didn't speak too quickly, a greater problem than she realized with Italians in their own country, she had to smile to herself.

*   *   *

Grimaldi and his mistress turned up shortly after two, and his BMW dropped them off at the main entrance, where he collected the reserved tickets, and escorted his mistress inside. One of the concierges told Belle of their arrival, and she came out from the dressing rooms in a silk robe to greet them, before whisking a delighted Marianne off behind the scenes to show her around. Donatello found he wasn't allowed backstage where the models were changing and making last-minute adjustments to their gowns, and so he contented himself with strolling around the auditorium, watching the place slowly filling up.

He bumped into Lesya by accident. "Scusi, Signorina. My fault, I was preoccupied," he apologized like the gentleman he was, and bowed slightly. Lesya was momentarily taken aback, not used to such courtesy back in her own country. She started to speak, and then stopped herself. Her tongue wouldn't work and she ended up giggling as she tried to remember the words. Donatello, smiled as he realized the problem, switching to English. "Would this be better? I am quite fluent in the language," he announced proudly.

"Yes, for me, certainly," Lesya replied in her still less than perfect English. "I am Kazakh by birth, but not a native English-speaker. I have been studying English at University and am now studying Italian." Grimaldi's eyes widened.

"Ah, so you are over here on holiday, practicing your language skills? Allow me," he took two glasses of champagne from a passing waiter, and offered one to her. "I am Donatello Grimaldi," he introduced himself.

"Grazi," Lesya smiled, accepting the glass. "Lesya Alexandrovna Romanova. A pleasure to meet such a gentleman," she complimented him. "Yes, a sudden urge to take a holiday came over me, and Italy is somewhere I have dreamed of traveling. The climate, the people, the beautiful language, it's all so . . . . so . . ." she was lost for words to describe her feelings.

She had traveled extensively in her young years, to America, Holland, Cyprus, but there were still plenty of places she wanted to visit, and Italy had been top of her list for some time now. With Kovacs on the run from the Kazakh authorities, she thought that now was as good a time as any to visit foreign climes. Until they caught him, anyway.

She sipped at the champagne, the sparkling bubbles going up her nose momentarily, and she fought a desire to sneeze, which her charming companion found amusing.

*   *   *

At the back of the room, a tall man in dark sunglasses leafed through one of the expensive programmes. He looked vaguely familiar to Grimaldi, but he couldn't quite place him. He took one of the programmes himself, and went to his own seat, closer to the catwalk, where he waited for his mistress to join him, idly wondering just how much the afternoon would end up costing him, as he leafed through the glossy pages, noting the prices of each of the exclusive creations.

*   *   *

About twenty minutes before the show was due to start, Marianne came out from behind the stage, and her hackles rose instantly upon seeing her lover engaged in conversation with the beautiful slim dark-haired woman at the bank of the auditorium. Donatello's face paled momentarily as he caught sight of her, and hastily made introductions to ease the situation. "My dear, this is Lesya Romanova, who is over here to take in the haute couture of Italian fashion. I hope you don't mind, but I've invited her to sit with us? She'll get a better view up front, than at the back with the rest of the mob." Seeing Donatello's openness, and accepting the woman's hand, and reassuring smile, Marianne felt better about the situation, and introduced herself familiarly.

"Marianne Lazaridis. Very pleased to meet you." She shook Lesya's hand briefly, and then took Donatello's arm, possessively, as if staking her claim, and Grimaldi smiled. He turned to usher Lesya towards the front row seats at the side of the catwalk. Marianne was still enervated by her little adventure behind the scenes with Belle and the rest of the models, and happily recounted to Donatello and Lesya all that she had seen behind the curtains. He was pleased, and knew he had been forgiven for excluding her from last night's meal. Perhaps he might get away lightly this afternoon after all. He could but hope, anyway.

With a loud fanfare of music, the grand show began, and the leggy models sashayed out along the catwalk, to a multitude of flashes from the cameras of the paparazzi, eager to record the latest creations for the morning's papers tomorrow.

It was a mixed audience of wealthy socialites, for who else could afford some of these creations? The men like himself had more eyes for the models than the gowns and dresses they were modelling, only admiring how well they looked in them, not the actual clothes themselves. The women were more critical, examining the lines and the colours, and mentally cross-checking the contents of their wardrobes at home for suitable accessories, should they manage to persuade their spouses and lovers to actually buy some of the creations for themselves.

Belle came out from behind the curtain in a sheer black creation, which came down to mid thigh level. Semi-transparent, it clung in all the right places, and she paused as the cameras flashed, to smile down at Donatello and Marianne.

Lesya was lost in amazement. This was a world far removed from her own, and one she wanted to be so much a part of. The raven-haired beauty on the catwalk, looked down at her, brazenly, hands on hips, and winked at her, deliberately. Lesya blushed momentarily, till Belle broke the glance with a saucy smile, and headed off back down the catwalk. She turned sharply, letting those long sleek black tresses cascade around her, before finally relinquishing centre-stage to one of the other models.

* * *

As the afternoon wore on, the man in the dark glasses paid close attention to the catwalk, the programme now held folded across his lap. He wasn't so much concerned with the lines and colours of the gowns, but more with the movements and choreography of the models themselves, how they moved, the distances they kept between themselves, and the speed with which they walked. One hand was in his jacket pocket, and it stayed there the whole time he watched the catwalk.

* * *

Five o'clock saw the motorway traffic slow to a crawl in both directions as the lanes narrowed to accommodate the roadworks. Angelo Modana berated his two children as they fought in the back of the car. "Sit down and be quiet. I can't concentrate in this traffic," he complained. One boy took one last sly dig at his brother, before the two of them moved apart, and Angelo shook his head. "Don't think I didn't see that, Mario," he warned. The boy scowled and pulled a face.

"He started it," he accused.

"Did not!" the brother counter-claimed.

"Look, I buy you an ice-cream on the way home, eh? Just be good till we get there." He used a handkerchief to mop his brow, and then wound his window down slightly. It was a hot day out there. At this slow speed there was no fresh draught coming in through the open window, just petrol and diesel fumes from the long lines of congested traffic.

He looked at the temperature gauge of his car. It was slowly rising, and would doubtless overheat if things didn't start moving soon. Reluctantly he switched off his engine to be on the safe side, and watched the temperature gauge slowly sink back down.

In the adjacent cars, he noticed similar frustration. The heat haze from the bodywork of the cars caused a slight atmospheric distortion as he looked along the long line of cars, the thin red and white traffic cones guiding them as they moved ever so slowly forwards. The last few weeks had been murder along this stretch of road since the roadworks had started. The journey took twice as long as normal.

In the back of the car, the two children startled jostling again, as bored and as impatient as he himself was, and so he turned again to castigate them.

The explosion behind him was loud, and reflected in the eyes of Angelo's two children as he stared over the seats at them. Mouth open in shock, he whirled around, seeing the black smoke rising further down the line of cars, and seeing and hearing the steadily increasing rain of debris which was falling back to earth. "Mother of God!" he exclaimed, crossing himself, and suddenly rediscovering religion for the first time in many years.

He started to open the car door, to get out and get a better look at the carnage, as did a number of other motorists, trapped in this jam, when the second claymore mine exploded, considerably closer to his own car, its charge aimed at the adjacent vehicles, and ripping through them in less than a second. Angelo slammed the door shut again as he watched vehicles and their drivers being ripped apart. "My God! My God!"

The shockwave shattered the windscreen of Angelo's car and his two children screamed in the back of the car as Angelo himself ducked down, trying to escape the broken glass. He forced himself up again to turn and wave his children to the opposite side of the car, away from the traffic cones which had been altered to contain the explosive devices. "Get out of the car! Get out of the car!" he screamed at them, and tried to slide across to the passenger side as well.

The rear door opened, and the two boys fought to scramble clear as their father tried to follow them. One of them reached for the front passenger door to open it for him as he struggled over the gear-stick, and he reached for the open doorway. He almost made it before the third device went off right next to his car, and the full force of the claymore mine ripped through it, killing both Angelo and his children outright, blasting them apart as though they were no more than dolls, and scattering their remains about like bits of bloodied rags.

People milled about in panic, throwing themselves from their cars, and getting as far away from the stationary lines of cars as they could. Black smoke hung over the motorway as they waited for the next explosion, but mercifully it never came. Everyone sought cover, and hid and waited, hoping and preying that the carnage was over, but not daring to show themselves, just in case.

*   *   *

The fashion show was well underway, and received much applause from an appreciative audience. Belle was having the time of her life. It felt so good to be up here again. She walked boldly, swinging her hips, enjoying the eyes on her, defying the cameras to catch her looking less than perfect. She flashed another smile down at Donatello, flanked by two beauties. The shorter-haired one had caught her eye. Maybe it was the glasses. Something about her certainly appealed. Trust Donatello to surround himself with beautiful women.

*   *   *

The man in the dark glasses was sweating slightly now. Timing was everything, and he couldn't afford a mistake. His hand was still in his pocket, and he could feel the perspiration making the small plastic device slick in his palm. As Belle rounded the bottom of the catwalk, she paused once more to display herself as well as the exotic design she was wearing, ever the peacock, and then she started on her way back up towards the curtains. The button on the small transmitter was finally pressed, and the front of the catwalk exploded in a huge fireball.

*   *   *

It was early morning in Buenos Aires when the phonecall came through, and it was Laura who took it. Manuel brought her the remote handset as she worked in the garden, tending the little spice garden she had recently planted. She took off her gardening gloves and took the handset from him.

"Yes, Donatello? It's so nice to hear from you again," she began the conversation.

"Madame Laura," Grimaldi spoke in a trembling voice. "I have some bad news."

Chapter Eight

June 7th

As news of the latest terrorist outrages hit the media, Maddox watched it all unfold on Sky News. He picked up a phone and made a reservation on the next plane to The Hague. He would have to cut his intended weekend break short. Two cells. There had to be two cells operating in Italy. He was right, but for the wrong reasons. The strike on the fashion house had come less than an hour after the slaughter on the motorway, and those tv helicopters kept on zooming up and down the long line of ripped apart cars. The images were haunting. Sitting-Ducks in a row. So unbelievably fucking easy, as long as you had no qualms about mass murder, and this Torquemada obviously didn't.

Nick Turnbull handed him another beer. He cracked open another can for himself, and then continued eating his takeaway curry. Maddox had suddenly lost all appetite.

"It'll keep, guvnor," Nick said reassuringly, for this latest outrage demanded Maddox's full attention now.

"It'll have to," agreed Maddox, though it would be hard to readjust his priorities following the news Nick had just given him. Raising the can to take a good swig of the cold sharp lager, he checked his watch as he swallowed. "You can run me to the airport if you've nothing better to do. There are a few things I'd like you to do for me while I'm gone," he suggested.

"Sure thing," Nick agreed.

* * *

The flight from Ezeiza was long and understandably strained under the circumstances. "Thank God she's still alive," Laura clung to her small gold crucifix that she rarely took from around her neck. Gabriel pulled her close against him, for she needed his warmth, his presence.

"She was lucky, by all accounts," agreed Gabriel. "So were the rest of the people there," he added. "Less than a dozen hospitalised, and no fatalities. Apart from Belle's broken leg and minor burns, the subsequent fire caused more damage than the explosion itself. Some sort of incendiary device, or so they reckon. Grimaldi is still making enquiries. He was lucky to be sitting on the far side of the catwalk when the device went off."

Laura cuddled closer. "Bastards!" she exclaimed as she pressed into her chest and accepted Gabriel's arms around her. "What sort of scum would do something like that? Innocent people out enjoying themselves, and they get caught up in something like that."

"That's what terrorists do, Laura," he explained, his thoughts dark now, remembering his own past. He hadn't wanted to get involved in this thing, but it seemed like events were drawing him in, back to times best forgotten. ETA had seemed to offer him a way of attacking the Church, payback after Madrid and the death of Matthias, but their outrages went beyond Gabriel's anger, forcing him to sever all ties with them.

Laura fell asleep in his arms, and Gabriel drew the blanket across her, keeping her warm. He found sleep more difficult, and preferred instead to brood, mulling things over in his mind. Belle would be up and out of the hospital in a couple of weeks if her recovery rate was as great as his own, and it should be, for she was his daughter, and the same miraculous blood ran in her veins as it did in his own, the famed Blood of Christ as it was named by the Church. They'd laugh if they realised that his blood was extra-terrestrial in origin, Gabriel thought. Perhaps not. Might affect their moral sensibilities.

Malevar's revelations of his origins had at first shocked him, but then they answered so many of his own questions as to his nature, and his history. His creation was simply an experiment in DNA splicing, one of many, to create a perfect host body in which Malevar could live on and breathe this planet's atmosphere without harm. No real mother, no father, to speak of, just a cold glass test-tube. His cells must have had origin in some nameless human on this planet, but he was destined never to find out. It was something he was still coming to terms with, his history, his legacy. Someday soon, he would have to consider everything in detail, and assess his options on what to do with that awareness.

If it hadn't have been for the intervention of Laura and Belle, he realized, Malevar might have well succeeded in his scheme of psychic transferrence and taking over his human body. Then it would be someone else sitting here, thinking these thoughts, and making their own different plans.

He had spent the last few weeks in Cordoba, going over the findings of the blue liquid the alien had used to inhibit Belle's regenerative powers. He had taken it from Malevar's laboratory on a whim, as the place burned around them. He had half an idea of growing his wings back once upon a time, yet now he realised the futility of this. Still, who knew what the future held? Belle's recent amputation had proved there was a use for this fluid, and he had been pleased to learn that the research scientists could recreate it. Alien formulae, but humans could recreate it. Should either he or Belle require similar surgery in the future, it would prove highly beneficial, but only to those of a similar cell-structure.

*   *   *

Maddox had hardly took his coat off as he swept back into his office when Tom Brady came in, holding a fax in his hand and grinning like a Cheshire Cat. "We got a break at last! You're not gonna believe this, Jim," he announced. "There was a fourth device on the motorway. It didn't go off. As the bomb squad dismantled it, they found a note." Maddox's jaw dropped. "It was addressed to you!" His jaw dropped even further.

"What? Are you joking?" he asked, in disbelief. "Give me that!" He snatched the fax out of Tom's hand, and read the scanned copy of the note.

The words were hastily scrawled, and they were in Hebrew. Maddox could read the words without a need for translation. PISA, TUESDAY-TELL MADDOX-REBEL

His heart stopped for a brief moment as he caught his breath. Could it be? How in Hell could he be reading such a note, in such circumstances? The two names together brought back instant memories, of years gone by, and the pain that had gone before. It couldn't be!

"What does it mean, boss?" Brady asked.

"Apart from the obvious, we've got a ringer," he announced. "One of those terrorists is on the side of the angels. Mossad's got someone on the inside." Maddox shook his head slowly from side to side. "Okay, we've got two days. Get me all the maps and intelligence data we've got on Pisa. I want checkpoints on all major routes south of the city. They'll be heading north from today's little incidents, and there are only so many roads they can take."

"Pisa's on the coast, boss. They could be going by boat. Naples airport is a possible, too," Brady pointed out.

"The airports are already being watched, but get onto them and make sure they beef up their surveillance. Sea is a possibility, but too many variables. Unless it's a powerful boat, they wouldn't make it in the timeframe. Best put an alert out for their navy to do a stop 'n search on anything powerful on the western coast north of Naples." His personal problems were forced to the back of his mind for the moment. The immediate preparations to react to this unforeseen information had to take precedence.

As it happened, Maddox was right, and he was wrong, all at the same time. Right in the fact that there were two terrorist cells, but wrong in assuming they were both travelling north to their target. The four terrorists who had carried out the motorway bombing were at this moment holed up in a small motel outside of Foggia, near the eastern coast, and their travel plans did not include Pisa. The other four terrorists who made up Torquemada's second cell were now travelling south from Bologna, and would be in Pisa tomorrow, to plan and prepare for Tuesday's extravaganza. Neither group had been responsible for the firebombing at La Scala opera house.

*   *   *

It was early in the morning in Tel Aviv, and Alexi Davidovich answered the phone personally. Only a few people had a direct line to his office. "Alexi?" he recognized the voice.

"James. It's been quite a while," he commented, as he accepted a strong cup of black coffee from one of his aides.

"We go back a long way, Alexi. Your Spetznatz unit was one of the first the Regiment had us train up in anti-terrorist techniques in the mid-eighties," he reminded Davidovich of his former career. "Mossad's been holding back on us," Maddox stated. "You owe me an explanation. Rebekah Weisz. You must know of my involvement, and yet you've said nothing whilst you've got her involved in this Al Qaeda business."

"James, she involved herself, and she specifically asked me not to advise you of events," he explained, as he sipped at his coffee. "She was only supposed to contact you if she deemed it necessary."

"How long has she been working for you, Alexi? I haven't heard from her since Oman, but I know she and her husband moved to Israel in 1985."

"She moved here with her husband and son in 1985, true." Maddox was momentarily taken aback by the news of a son. "Both of them were killed by a suicide bomber who blew himself up in a supermarket, in 1990, and she's been working for Mossad ever since. One of our best operatives, she's been involved in one of our special units, living, breathing amongst the Palestinians in the Gaza Strip, working undercover. A dangerous job, and she did it well. When we found out the name and location of one of the female terrorists, she volunteered to take on her identity, and infiltrate the cell."

"There's more than one," Maddox admitted.

"Obviously, or she would have completed her mission by now," Davidovich revealed.

"Which is?" Maddox asked.

"Find and kill this Torquemada. The rest are relatively unimportant. He himself must be eliminated."

"What's so special about him?"

"He came to the notice of the Taliban in Afghanistan. Fanatic yet bright, educated. He was a rising star, far more intelligent than most of their recruits. One more thing which may be of interest to you . . . ."

"What's that?"

"He's British."

"What? How do you reckon that?"

Davidovich chuckled at the other end of the phone line. "Sources I'm not at liberty to reveal, you know how it is, James. Unfortunately, that's all we have on him so far. An avenue you might wish to pursue with your own Special Branch?" he mused, planting the seed in Maddox's mind.

"I'll get my people on it," he promised.

"Rebekah joined up with one of the Al Qaeda cells in southern Italy, after we apprehended the real Fatima Khalid. She is being interrogated now, as we speak, though so far she has revealed little. I will pass on any information we do get out of her, though I am not immediately hopeful. We may have to use chemicals on her, and they are not that reliable as you know." Maddox remembered his own training to resist such interrogation techniques.

"Rebekah's note said that they were hitting Pisa on Tuesday. I've got things moving to try and counter that, but without hard information, there's no way we can close down an entire city."

"I agree. Terrorists just act, whilst we can only react. The initiative is always theirs. It's not a conventional war any more, is it James?"

"So if there's more than one cell, we must assume Torquemada is connected to the other cell?" Maddox mused.

"Either that or Rebekah has not yet discovered his real identity. He may not be known by that name amongst his own men. He's a new kid on the block. Most were just roped in for this campaign. I don't think any of them know him personally. If we had a real name, we could track him down. I wish you luck there."

*   *   *

Fatima grunted as she exercised, doing ab-crunches on the stone floor. They had kept her in this stinking jail for just over a month now, in solitary of course. This cellblock was kept empty apart from herself, so her identity remained secret from the other prisoners who must be held here, though she couldn't hear them through the walls. Her everyday clothes had been removed for analysis, and a simple prison shift was all she was allowed, with thin slippers. The bunk was plain, uncomfortable even, and the cell's single toilet stunk, in need of some disinfectant. She fumed as she surveyed her surroundings. Her capture would cause a severe setback to the Italian Campaign, but Torquemada was resourceful. He would find another way to achieve his objective. She had taught him well.

Her stomach rumbled, reminding her that her captors had yet to feed her today. The bottle of water on the floor was plastic, and nearly empty. She unscrewed the top to take another sip, just a small one. They might take it away from her at any moment. She knew how these interrogations worked. There had been an informant, and they must know the importance of her capture.

In her favour was the fact that Hamas would also know of her capture, if not her mission, and the Jews may have made a mistake by deciding not to transport her directly to Mossad's HQ. Holding her here in this small nondescript police station might have fooled some people, but Hamas were organized and thorough, a lot more thorough than the Jews gave them credit for. If she could hold out, there might be a chance if Hamas attacked the station. She must be ready for that moment.

*   *   *

Gabriel and Laura went straight to the hospital direct from Leonardo Da Vinci airport, which was a short enough drive considering the airport was almost in the centre of the city. Donatello's BMW collected them from the airport, and the Italian was full of apologies for the injuries Belle had suffered in his country. After initial treatment in Milan, Donatello's private jet had been recruited to fly her back to Rome to undergo recuperation closer to home.

"Forget it, Donatello. Nothing to do with you. It's just fortunate you were there to help her," Gabriel smiled. Laura agreed.

"Yes, if you hadn't pulled her from the fire as you did, her injuries might have been a lot worse," she pointed out.

"It was nothing, I assure you. My Marianne, and others all helped," he explained. The BMW drew up right outside the hospital entrance, where Grimaldi had had his personal physicians take Belle, and Gabriel and Laura went directly inside with Grimaldi whilst his chauffeur parked the vehicle.

Grimaldi waited outside as both Gabriel and Laura went in to visit their daughter. That overbearing matron would not allow more than two visitors to a room, despite his protestations. Belle looked quite cheerful, considering her right leg was strung up in front of her, heavily plastered. Laura went straight to her and embraced her. Gabriel was slightly more reserved, but hugged her nonetheless.

"You're looking well," he commented, trying to lighten the situation.

"No I'm not, I look like shit!" she announced, scowling. "My leg is broken in three places, and my hair is absolutely ruined!" she complained, pulling out one side of her hair which was all frazzled from the fire.

"Nice to see you can still look on the bright side of things," joked Laura, relieved that her daughter's injuries weren't any worse. Belle scowled.

"Do they know who's responsible for the bomb?" she asked.

"There's quite a bit of terrorist activity going on in Italy at the moment, Belle," Gabriel started to explain.

"The Red Brigades? I thought they were quiet these day?"

"No, not the Red Brigades. This present trouble is apparently being caused by Al Qaeda."

"What the hell are the Arabs doing in Italy? I thought they only attacked American interests?" she asked, puzzled.

"Looks like they've changed targets, for whatever reason," he suggested.

"Those crazy fanatics!" Laura shook her head.

"Actually, I don't see that much difference between them and the organisation the two of you used to work for," Gabriel pointed out. "They're all extremists." Before she could open her mouth to protest, he continued, "One man's beliefs don't necessarily make another's wrong," he insisted. "A person can believe in God, Allah, Satan even, I don't care. So long as he doesn't try and force his beliefs on me, he can believe what he wants. But that's what organised religions do," he explained. "They just have to spread 'the word'. It's all about power, and power-hungry individuals always seem to end up controlling religions. People are so willing to be controlled, it's frightening."

"Fucking scumbags!" Belle swore. "Just you wait till I get out of here," she promised. "I'll make them wish they were never born."

"No," promised Gabriel. "That's *my* job. You're going to rest and recuperate, and your Mother is going to make sure that's all you do." Laura started to say something, but Gabriel stared her down. This was one time when she was *not* going to have the last word. He knew it, and hoped she knew it too.

"Whatever," she eventually smiled, promising herself some future payback. This wasn't the time for an argument.

"Okay, now I'm glad that's settled. I'll leave you two here, and I'll meet up with you at the hotel later. We booked two rooms there, and your Mother will be arranging for you to be transferred later today, as soon as your doctor can sign your release papers. She'll be looking after you herself."

"Where are you going?" Laura asked.

"I have a confession to make," he replied, as he slipped out the door, allowing Grimaldi inside. As he left, Belle and Laura exchanged glances. Each seemed to know what the other was thinking.

*   *   *

Donatello got a call on his cellphone from Marianne, while he was at the hospital, to advise him that she and Lesya were just about finished with their shopping, and he had to leave to pick the two of them up in his BMW. Laura gave him a peck on the cheek as he left.

After Lesya's help in the aftermath at the firebombing, Grimaldi had invited the girl to stay at his villa in Latina, and Marianne was delighted to have her there. A newfound companion to ease the boredom she sometimes felt during Grimaldi's absences. She was enjoying showing Lesya around Rome, the oldest of cities. The company was good for her, and there wasn't that much in their ages. Marianne wanted to make the rest of her holiday enjoyable, and not take back with her any unpleasant memories of Italy.

*   *   *

Gabriel slipped into the church of St Bartoleme, and took a seat in one of the hard wooden pews. There was a small queue of plaintiffs waiting to have their confession heard in the small discreet Confessional booth.

Ten minutes later, Gabriel slipped inside the booth himself, and took his seat. "Yes, my son?" asked Father Falcone.

"People will talk if you keep making blasé statements like that, Father," Gabriel pointed out, and noted the shadowy outline of the priest stiffen momentarily, though he did not make out the sudden smug smile that crossed the good Father's face.

"Gabriel," he stated.

"In the flesh, Father. Achille Ratti wanted my help. I'm now offering it, but I'll deal with you, and you only," he insisted. "Tell the rest of your people to keep the hell out of my way," he warned. "I'll need all the information your people have gotten on the outrages that have taken place so far, and then once I've digested that, I'll decide how best to handle this. I might call on you for assistance, or I might call on some of my other friends. Whatever, I want no interference, regardless of how I decide to handle things. Is that clear?" he asked.

"Very clear," Falcone nodded. "Come back to the church in an hour, and I will admit you to my private rooms. I can give you all the information you require at that time."

"Very well." Gabriel stood up, and left the Confessional, allowing the next plaintiff to enter, and Father Falcone continued to take Confession as though nothing had happened.

*　　*　　*

Gabriel watched St Bartolome's from a distance, wandering around and checking on the other entrances for the next hour. He saw no one suspicious coming or going. Gradually, the stream of people entering and leaving the church thinned, and the doors were finally closed.

He went around to the side entrance to the priest's living quarters, and briefly knocked on the door. Falcone's elderly housekeeper opened the door and admitted him, showing him to where the priest had his study. An oak table was covered in a large map of Italy, and notes and post-its had been attached in various places on the map. Falcone was studying a notebook, which Gabriel could see was half-filled with his personal observations and insights into the present situation.

Falcone got up to greet him, and Gabriel shook hands less than enthusiastically. "Ratti has charged me with investigating these outrages, and so I have a good deal of preliminary data to share with you," he explained, and bade Gabriel take a seat at the table while he explained things.

Gabriel scanned the map closely. "This was the first incident last week?" he pointed to the post-it near the city of Naples, and Falcone nodded.

"Yes, the schoolyard attack, carried out mid-morning. No witnesses. The surviving children are too traumatised for the police to even think of questioning them," he stated. "Two days later, the attack just south of Modena, here. The authorities are still officially maintaining it was driver error which caused the crash, though we know the front end of the coach was riddled with bullets."

"Both pointedly religious targets," Gabriel noted, "as if making a point, and yet then they switch to ordinary members of the public in subsequent attacks. If I had to guess, I would probably assume that the terrorists have switched targets intentionally, to avoid us second-guessing their targets. It also helps their cause if more people think themselves in the firing-line and it's not just the clergy."

Falcone nodded. "From what we can gather, this unholy crusade is aimed not so much at our religion itself, but what is seen as the home of our religion, for Catholicism is spread worldwide, in much the same manner as Islam." Falcone shrugged his shoulder. "The authorities have not released the two recordings received from this Torquemada, and until the motorway carnage, the general public was only aware of an isolated case of terrorism which would likely be blamed on the Red Brigade maniacs. Now the public knows there is a campaign of terror underway, and this Torquemada is getting the publicity he seeks," Falcone agreed.

"I'd like to listen to those tapes," Gabriel asked.

"I have them here," Falcone replied, them from the top of a bookcase, and he inserted the first into a small tape recorder, and pressed PLAY. Torquemada's cultured voice spoke, and Gabriel listened to both the voice and the words intently. Falcone played the first two tapes one after the other. Then he produced the third tape. "This was the latest, received yesterday evening. Like the other two, it is being witheld from general release by the authorities, but the newspapers have leaked details, refusing to co-operate with the police. The general public is now aware that a terrorist cell or cells is operating in Italy." Falcone put the third tape into the machine, and Gabriel listened once more.

"Today's attack should prove you are helpless against us. We can attack anytime, anywhere. Sooner or later, your whole country will realise how helpless you are against our wrath. Enjoy the days of terror, my friends. They are far from over." The tape ended, and Gabriel pondered as Falcone studied him.

"No fanatic, despite his rhetoric. Speaks English fluently with only a slight accent," was his first assessment of the man known as Torquemada. "No demands, either. I'd say you've got trouble on your hands, Falcone."

"These outrages will continue until he is stopped."

"Oh yes, as he said, it's far from over. The man is most definitely out to make a point!"

Gabriel studied the maps, and the position of the post-its. Naples in the south, Modena in the north, then back to southern Italy once more for the attack on the motorway, yet simultaneously carrying out the attack on the fashion show in Rome itself. Having worked with ETA in the past, Gabriel had to agree that at least two cells were operating on the mainland. Keeping one step ahead of the police was one thing, but travelling extensively had it's own complications, and without a lot of pre-planning and resources, too many things could go wrong.

Yet terrorists, however zealous, knew that an extended campaign only increased their chances of getting caught. Single targets were usually preferable. In and out before the authorities managed to track you down, and he knew the anti-terrorist units would be actively at work on tracking down the people responsible for these attacks.

The campaign had to have an ultimate agenda, therefore. Each attack was more spectacular than the one before it. What then was intended for the climax?

"This isn't a spur of the moment attack," Gabriel stated, as he considered the events so far. "It's been well-planned in advance. I suppose the authorities are looking for rental car details?" he surmised. Falcone inclined his head. "It's not how I'd do it. I'd arrange to purchase the vehicles in advance, second-hand, nothing too flashy, but powerful enough. If they have a pre-mapped plan, they'll switch the cars around if they have any sense. We know at least one of them knows what he's doing. The rest might just be there to make the numbers up, if we're lucky. A lot of Arabs are light-skinned enough to pass for Italians. If their papers are good enough, you're going to have a hard time finding them. I wish you luck."

"Is that all the help you can offer us?" Falcone asked, disappointed, He had already figured out much of Gabriel's revelations himself.

"From a logistics point of view, yes. Your own organisation will doubtless be assisting the authorities in their investigation. My own enquiries will lead down darker paths, and its best you know little about them. The only way I can see us getting anywhere is to get a man on the inside, and I think I can manage that. As I said, keep your people away from me. I haven't time to differentiate between friend and foe. Doubtless you'll see my name in the papers in a day or two, and I'd rather not publicise my movements, but it's the only way. Despite what you may read, remember why I'm doing this. If they can be stopped, I'll stop them," he insisted. "You asked my help because of my former terrorist links, and I'll have to use them to arrange a suitable introduction to the Al Qaeda people. Then I'll have to see what I can do about this Torquemada." Gabriel stood up from the table.

Falcone rose also. "Here is my cellphone number," he offered, writing it down on a scrap of paper. "Memorise it, and I or my organisation will be on hand to offer any assistance you require, anywhere in the country," he promised.

Gabriel took the piece of paper, scanned the number and consigned it to memory. He had an almost photographic memory. "Done," he said, handing the piece of paper back to the perplexed Falcone. "Time to go," he announced. "I have a lot to do in a short space of time."

* * *

As Gabriel left, Falcone picked up the phone and dialled through to the quarters of Achille Ratti, now head of the Sword of Solomon organisation.

"Yes?" asked an old rasping voice.

"He took the bait," Falcone informed him. He heard a chuckle down the other end of the phone.

"Very good, Marco. Looks like your Plan B worked well. No fatalities, and the Arabs take the blame. Very well done. Now how is our Knight-Errant going to play this game, do you think?" he asked.

"He'll use his friends in ETA. The network of terror across the world is well-informed. I suggest we let him run with it. It's what we asked his help for. We'll keep a watching brief, and see what develops. We will offer assistance as required. It's in all our interests to end this bloodshed," Falcone advised.

"Indeed so, Marco. Gabriel has dealt with these people before, but if he needs help then give him everything he wants. Our agendas are the same here." Ratti confirmed. Falcone nodded silently to himself. His own agenda did not necessarily match Gabriel's, or even Ratti's for that matter.

Chapter Nine

June 9th

Gabriel went directly to the hotel, where he found Laura in the process of directing the hotel staff to prepare the adjoining room for Belle to join her as soon as she was permitted to be discharged from the hospital.

She wouldn't need private medical care, just rest and relaxation while the leg healed. Laura had arranged for one of the doctors to call every other day to check on her condition. From past experience, Gabriel was expecting Belle to be on her feet within the next two weeks, if her regenerative powers were as good as his own. Which meant he had two weeks to sort this mess out, otherwise knowing how pedantic she could be, he'd have the two women sticking their noses into things, and he had enough to worry about as it was.

Laura broke off her conversation with the hotel staff as she noticed him enter their suite, and came over to give him a hug and a quick peck on the cheek. "How'd it go?" she asked.

"As expected. They don't know much. This isn't the sort of campaign which Al Qaeda is known for. Sounds like they've got themselves some smarts. It means I'm going to have to get my hands dirty."

"How dirty?" she asked, concerned.

"As dirty as it takes," he confirmed her fears. "You might see my face in a few newspapers over the next few days," he warned. "I have to get them to come to me. It's the only way. Believe me, I don't want the publicity I'm likely to get."

"That's going to be dangerous." Laura bit her lip, and embraced him. Gabriel held her close to him.

"I plan on having a few people watch my back for me," he tried to allay her fears. "I'm going to have to move out of here. Too dangerous to have any close contact. I won't know where I'll be for the next few days."

"Then let's make the most of the evening," Laura smiled, and she closed the door to the adjoining room, and locked it. Gabriel smiled as she came over to him once more. "You're not leaving too early I hope?" she began to unfasten his tie.

"No," he confirmed. "Not too early," his leaned forward to kiss the nape of her neck, moving up to nuzzle her ear as she pressed against him. He let his jacket fall to the floor as she pulled at his belt, eagerly dragging down his trousers. He laughed as her hand grasped his manhood, working him, and together they moved awkwardly to the luxurious sofa, the bedroom was too far away in the heat of their passion, and Laura drew him down on top of her, kissing him hungrily. Not even bothering to remove her underwear, Laura simply pulled the gusset to one side, so eager was she to feel him inside of her. She needed release from the worry and anxiety of the last few hours.

Gabriel moved between her thighs, moaning as her wet heat enveloped him, buttocks clenching as she gasped, and clung to him. His mouth covered hers, kissing passionately as they made love. Passion needed release, and both of them worked at it, hips thrusting as they gasped and moaned.

*   *   *

Later, in the early hours of the morning, Gabriel rose from the bed where they had eventually retired, trying not to wake Laura. He went into the other room to use the phone.

He called a number he had not used in many years, one known to only a few people. It rang four times, before a sleepy voice answered. "Si?"

"Rosa?" he enquired, and there was a pause on the other end of the line, and then a slight intake of breath, before the woman answered.

"It's been a long time, Gabriel," the voice responded, finally.

"How did you know it was me?" he chuckled softly.

"Ah, but how could I forget such a charmer. Bastardo!" she cursed, laughing softly. "This number is known to few, and only one of them ever spoke English as eloquently as you."

"Would you prefer we spoke in Spanish?" he asked.

"My English is good enough, as you know, my darling. But why now, after so many years? You left suddenly, and without word. That was not polite."

"You know why I left, Rosa. Your bomb-makers learned their skills from me, but were not so discreet about how they used them. I never signed on to slaughter innocents." There was a sigh at the other end of the phone.

"Poor little Gabriel, those precious sensibilities of yours," she teased. "Sometimes innocents do get hurt, but you know we try and avoid that," she accused.

"I know you killed Montoya after his bomb blew up the public assembly in Pamplona. You have your scruples too."

"As I said, we try and avoid civilian casualties in our campaigns. His death served to reduce the risk of future such incidents. They do not serve our campaign well. Montoya did not share our concerns there," Rosa admitted. "One must maintain discipline."

"I need your help, Rosa," Gabriel admitted.

"I figured as much by the phonecall. You have never contacted me in all the years since your disappearance."

"I have never betrayed you or any of your organisation either, over the years. I honour my friends," Gabriel reminded her.

"We know this, Gabriel. That is why we have left you alone in your self-imposed exile for so many years."

"What do you mean, Rosa?"

"I know where you live, Gabriel," she stated plainly, and Gabriel pondered for a moment, as the full impact of that statement sunk in. "It took us a long time, and a lot of money, but eventually we tracked you down. I spent a holiday in Buenos Aires a few years ago, and I drove past your villa," she laughed. "Almost knocked on the door. It would have been worth it just to see the look on your face, but alas, I respected your decision and your behaviour since. Friends are friends, and we were a little more than friends," she reminded him. "I keep your secret, as you keep ours."

"Yes, we were more than friends, Rosa," he finally spoke.

"So what can a friend do for a friend?" she asked.

"I'm calling from Italy. I take it you have been following recent events out here?"

"Hmmm, yes. Those fanatics of Al Qaeda. Torquemada he calls himself," Rosa chuckled.

"I don't think these particular people are fanatics. This Torquemada knows his stuff. So far he's made no mistakes and has gotten the security forces chasing shadows. This isn't a casual campaign of terror against American or even business targets, Rosa. The guy has declared a Jihad against the world's religions."

"That bit of information was not known to us," she revealed. "Can he really do this?" she asked.

"Italy seems to be a testing-ground. Phase One in the grand master plan. Home of Catholicism," Gabriel affirmed. "Succeed here and then move on to another country, another religion."

"Spain is predominantly Catholic too," Rosa commented. "Despite our differences with the present government, our religion is common ground."

"I want to infiltrate these Arab cells, Rosa. Can you help me?" There was a long pause on the other end of the phone.

"Why would you do this, Gabriel?" Rosa wondered. "You have no love for the Church. Why get involved at all? These people are far more ruthless than my own. They trust no one not of their own race or religion."

"Like Madrid, they have made this personal," he revealed.

"Ah, Madrid, such a beautiful city. I remember Madrid only too well," she reflected. "So now you fight on the side of the righteous, eh?" she chuckled. "What help do you need? These people are no friends of ours, and as I said, religion is a common ground, for those of us who believe, anyway."

"Put out the word, that I am back in business, as it were. I'll be contacting other friends of mine to help gain a little notoriety, but if you can, get word to Al Qaeda that I have something that they will want. You'll read about it in the newspapers in a day or so. Tell them I'll be staying at the Rialto Hotel."

"From what I remember, darling, you were always the shy retiring type. Why go to all this trouble to stir up a hornet's nest and remind the authorities that you still exist?"

"I don't have much time. If I don't make contact soon, more people could die needlessly. The atrocities are getting bigger and obviously designed to get maximum media coverage. This bastard wants people to know he's here, and he's a long way from finished if I'm reading him right."

"Very well, I can do this for you. But take care, my darling. These Arabs are a different breed, not at all what you are used to."

"I know their mentality well enough, Rosa. I lived there for a time, oh a long time ago," he revealed.

"As you wish. I will say a prayer for you, Gabriel. Don't make this the last call I ever receive from you, and one day, I might actually decide to knock on that door of yours. Now I need my beauty-sleep." She blew a kiss down the phone, and then put the receiver down.

Gabriel did the same, and then turned as he caught sight of Laura, standing in the open doorway to the bedroom, naked and leaning, arms folded against the door-jamb.

"Who's Rosa? You've got about five seconds, so make it good!" She was not smiling.

*　　*　　*

Later that day, after seeing Belle installed in the suite, Gabriel took his leave from both women. He needed to make himself invisible to all but the people he wanted to find him.

*　　*　　*

Early that morning, a cordon was forming around Pisa, and every vehicle coming into the city was stopped and checked, grave-faced police studied faces and papers, before letting anyone through. Similar checks had been carried out on the motorways leading up from the south.

Torquemada's men however, were already within that cordon, and they had not been idle. The bomb was secreted within an ordinary backpack, and fully thirty pounds of gelignite was wired up to the detonator. It would be a big bang, but more important than the explosion itself was the target, and the publicity that would ensue from it.

*　　*　　*

Maddox was still in The Hague, kept upto date with events going down in Pisa by radio, where he was in touch with the local field-commander for the operation. Nothing. Not a trace. Every car and vehicle that had been stopped had checked out, and a gridlock was forming around the city. When the motorway barriers had proved ineffective, he had tightened the cordon around the city itself. The terrorists may well have been put off by the heightened security, but he couldn't take the chance. He'd rather scare them off than let another atrocity take place.

He hadn't slept well in the camp bed he and Brady shared, one taking a couple of hours sleep while the other kept in contact with the security forces working around the clock. He also had Nick Turnbull's little piece of news preying on his mind, and that was taking up too much of his thoughts at the moment. He needed a clear mind for this.

He snatched at the phone when it rang. "Maddox."

"Hello, Jim," Maddox gasped as he recognised the voice at the other end of the phone. He shook his head, checking that Brady was still out of the office, and he shrank down in his seat as though worried someone might see him.

"Two calls in less than a year. Haven't you got any sense, man?" Maddox was furious. "Calling me here, of all places. Let well enough alone, Gabe, and don't draw attention to yourself like this. The Regiment has left you alone because you've kept a low profile. It's not low enough, obviously. Now what do you want, and make it quick? I'm upto my neck in shit here, and the tide's coming in."

"I might be able to offer you a shovel, Jim. I'm in Italy," Gabriel revealed.

"Oh Christ!" he looked to the heavens. "Don't tell me you're involved in all this?" He had enough worries.

"Not yet, but I'm going to be. That's why the call. I need your help," he revealed.

"I don't have time, Gabe. There's another attack planned for today in Pisa. We have the place crawling, but I've got a real bad feeling about this one," he explained.

Gabriel let the news sink in. Falcone had said nothing about Pisa, therefore he didn't know about it. So how did Maddox know? Mentally, he reviewed the distance from Pisa to Naples. "You agree, then, it's more than one cell we're dealing with? But that this Torquemada is co-ordinating things?"

"Has to be more than one cell. No way could they hit the targets so far apart as they're doing."

"This is one cool customer in charge of things. Not your usual hothead, Jim. How did you know in advance about Pisa?" Maddox didn't answer, which revealed a lot. "Very well. Listen Jim, I'm getting involved in this thing whether you want me to or not. I'll be less likely to interfere with your own operations if you give me a little help and a little direction."

"Stay out of it!" Maddox warned. "You raise your head and it's likely to get shot off. Don't say I didn't warn you."

"No can do, Jim. I'm in, like it or not, I have a personal stake in this." Maddox froze. Did Gabriel know? But then how could he?

"I want to see you, then," he insisted. "No help without a face to face. Young Turnbull told me about Wales. You left an awful lot of questions unanswered, Gabe. You want my help, you meet me. That's it," he insisted.

"I can get a flight to Schiphol tonight," Gabriel confirmed, resignedly. "I can be there around 10pm."

"Okay. There's a bar, De Bierkelder, on Buitenhof. A lot of students use it, but it's okay. Sit in the back and I'll find you. Now get off the line. I've got a lot to do before tonight." Gabriel put the phone down, and Maddox breathed a sigh of relief. Gabriel knew. He had to know. What other personal stake could it be?

*   *   *

Gabriel was airborne by the time the announcement was made and the police began clearing the area around the Leaning Tower Of Pisa. The Via Roma and Via Cardinale P Malfi were crowded as usual, and pushing people back, even using a bomb-threat, was a slow and arduous task. People would only move so far, keen to see what was happening. One of many sightseers had reported finding a suspicious backpack inside the tower, and the terrorists themselves had phoned the police and the media.

Before long, everyone in the city knew of the bomb in the tower, and police cordons heaved with the crush of spectators and paparazzi eager to see what was happening.

Torquemada wanted publicity to aid his campaign of terror. He had stage-managed this one well, arranging the bomb, and making sure the whole world was watching. He was watching it himself from behind the barricades, camera in hand and mingling with the rest of the paparazzi, only his camera wasn't really a camera at all. Inside was a short wave transmitter, and he was just waiting for the right moment to use it.

A police bomb-squad wagon pulled up as they cleared a way through the barriers for it, and two men got out wearing heavy armour. Robot drones couldn't be used, as the bomb was a third of the way up inside the ancient structure.

Torquemada had planted the bomb himself, and he knew exactly where it was, and exactly how long it would take the men to reach it. He had made bombs himself, and he knew the many precautions the men would need to take to disarm the device. They were not going to get enough time. Planted against the re-enforcing columns installed years previously to stop the tower finally keeling over altogether, the blast was designed to bring the whole tower down.

He counted off mentally, as the two men slowly walked into the tower and started climbing those many steps. Torquemada looked casually around, grinning as he saw the TV vans and live broadcasts, all focused on the unfolding drama.

The two bomb-squad officers would be seeing the bomb for the first time right about now. The rucksack was big enough and brightly coloured. They could hardly miss it. He had even hand-scrawled the word BOMB on it himself, to keep the curious away until the stage had been set.

It was time! His finger depressed the trigger on the disguised transmitter, and bricks and mortar were pulverised as the mighty explosion deafened everyone behind the barricades. A huge cloud of dust rose into the air, obscuring the view of the tower itself as the tremendous force of thirty pounds of exploding gelignite dissipated itself in a terrific roar.

Everyone ducked down. People screamed and held their hands over their faces as the dust-clouds billowed out, and many of them coughed and spluttered amid their shock, and disbelief. When the clouds of dust finally settled, the Leaning Tower of Pisa, one of the Seven Modern Wonders of the World was no more. It lay broken in pieces, scattered across the square. Only the two bomb-squad men were casualties this time, but then Torquemada had not gone for bloodshed with this strike. Just for the publicity. Gabriel had been right. He had wanted to make a statement. This was the exclamation mark.

*   *   *

Maddox watched it all unfold on TV alongside Tom Brady and some of his other support crew in the watch-room. Gabriel was right. This Torquemada was a cool customer. He had stage-managed the whole thing. He'd gotten the media's attention at last and given them a spectacle they'd be replaying and talking about for years to come. He'd either been there to trigger the device himself, or close enough to watch it on television and still be able to set it off. "I want Pisa closed down. Nothing in or out. He's there. I know the bastard's there. I want every hotel checked, every hostel, every house that's just been rented. I want to see photocopies of the passports of every tourist registered at the local hotels. Move it, people!" he demanded. He knew he was asking for the moon, but the attempt had to be made. Short of declaring martial law and restricting peoples' movements, democracies worked against themselves where terrorism was concerned. Their own freedoms were too often used against them.

*   *   *

By the time 10pm came around, Maddox was drained, both physically and emotionally. He was in no state to handle the shock of seeing a ghost as he walked into the bar, and upto the booth in the rear. Gabriel was studying one of the evening papers, reading of the latest terrorist atrocity in Pisa. Torquemada was finally getting the world's attention.

He looked up from his paper as Maddox stood there, his face a mixture of emotions. "I thought Nick was taking the piss," he said, exasperated. "It's been over twenty years, and you don't look one fucking day older!" he accused. "No wonder your face doesn't flag up on the computers these days. Europol uses a computer-enhanced image to age you to around your mid-fifties, as it was the only photo we had of you on file." Gabriel could only smile. "That's more than Grecian 2000 you're using to maintain your good looks. No scars from plastic surgery that I can see, either," he commented, studying his face carefully. "Care to tell me how it's done?" Maddox slid into the booth alongside Gabriel, who caught the attention of the barman to order another beer.

"Let's just say I look after myself well," he answered, "and leave it at that. It's good to see you again, Jim," he smiled and shook Maddox's hand. The barman brought over a fresh glass of beer for Maddox, who took it gratefully, and downed a good portion of it in one go. He wiped his hand across his mouth as he put the glass down on the table.

"That's better. I needed something like that after the day I've had," he admitted.

"He's certainly got everyone's attention. No way that the authorities could cover up something like that," Gabriel pointed at the front page of the paper.

"Tell me what you want," Maddox insisted. "You realise I'm not supposed to socialise with wanted men?" he joked. "I'd say the shorter we keep this meeting the better."

"The only way we're going to stop this, is to get someone on the inside," Gabriel began, and then paused at the look that crossed Maddox's eyes. His suspicions were right about the advance info Maddox had received about Pisa. "But then you've already got someone inside, haven't you? Am I stepping on your toes, here, Jim?" he asked.

"You mean you don't know?" Maddox asked. "You said this was personal, I thought you knew," he explained.

"Knew what? Now you're confusing me," Gabriel took a drink from his own glass. Maddox hesitated before saying any more, and then he suddenly seemed to make a decision, and continued his explanation.

"There was a fourth bomb on that motorway. It was found by the police bomb-squad after they'd searched the scene. The bomb was fixed so it wouldn't explode. Inside the traffic cone, attached to the disarmed claymore-mine, there was a note warning us about Pisa," he paused. "It was addressed to me personally, and it was signed 'Rebel'!" The name triggered Gabriel's memory.

Rebekah!

Chapter Ten

1980: The oilfields of Oman were not the prettiest place in the world. In fact, they were not pretty at all. Barren, flat, mostly shale and rock, like an alien landscape on one of the old Doctor Who's which was still re-run on the BBC from time to time. If you can imagine a quarry, that's been stretched for more than a couple of thousand miles in every direction, you'll get the idea.

Most of the year it was extremely hot and dry, with plenty of dust kicking up to parch the throat every time the hot shamal winds blew. An ideal place for 22SAS to gain experience in desert warfare, the British Army had had a presence in Oman ever since they were asked to aid in the Jebel Akhdar Green Mountain War in the Fifties, fighting against the Yemeni incursionists.

On their way back from a long campaign in Malaya, D-Squadron 22SAS were diverted to assist in Mid November 1958, and saw action within days of their arrival. So successful were they, backed up by reinforcements from Hereford, that they were allowed to maintain a permanent presence thereafter, after they had helped young Sultan Qaboos overthrow his tyrant of a father in 1970. They were based at Um al Quarif in the southern reaches of Oman

After the Battle of Mirbat in 1972, when the Adoo rebels were repelled, the incursions were reduced to a trickle, and officially, the Dhofar Rebellion was ended in 1975, but PFLO marxist infiltrators still caused problems from over the border in South Yemen.

Gabriel had come to Oman fresh from Wales in 1976 where he had been responsible for supervising the mountain training of the British

Army's elite fighting troops in the Brecon Beacons and Black Mountains, with an occasional stint in the Norwegian Fjords. There were mountains here in Oman, too, from the aforementioned Green Mountain in the south, to the Jebel Mardar range near Muscat in the north.

Based south of Salalah, the SAS ranged far and wide across Oman, practising desert warfare acclimatisation. Their presence was a known but not publicised fact. Although they disguised their own landrovers to look like the normal oilfield vehicles, even going to the trouble of displaying numbers and departmental colour codes to match the main government oil company PDO, Petroleum Development Oman, most of the oilfield workers gave a sly grin whenever they passed one of the army vehicles. Colour codes and numbers didn't always match, and the mostly British workforce wasn't dumb.

Gabriel and Jim Maddox waved casually to one such company vehicle they passed along the road. The back of their landrover was filled with surveying gear, whilst they had a plethora of maps within the vehicle itself. Truth be told, they were indeed on a survey mission, though not for the oil company.

The majority of middle-east countries were always rather vague when it came to giving any accurate information about its oilfields, and the facilities rarely appeared on any published maps. A threat-assessment study was underway, and with the backing of the Omani government, the SAS were given the job of accurately mapping the gathering stations, and manifolds which would be a likely target of any terrorist or military assault.

The blacktop ran all the way from Salalah in the south to Muscat in the north, meandering this way and that as it sweltered in the hot sun. It was a long thirsty drive, and watering points and wadis were few and far between.

One such unofficial watering-hole, which was used regularly by the SAS, though remained unknown to the head-shed, was Fahud, in the northern reaches, between the salt marshes and the Saudi border. Fahud was an industrial complex, comprising a gathering station which governed the pumping of oil and gas to the coast, a few satellite pumping stations, and housed a large ex-pat community. It was located north of Qarn Alam, and south-west of the oasis village of Nizwa, where the main blacktop road passed to within a few miles.

The Sultanate of Oman was not a dry Muslim state, and alcohol was on sale openly at licensed premises. One such was the Oryx Bar, in Fahud itself, a veritable oasis in the middle of the desert. The main foyer was filled with rock pools, and waterfalls decorated with fake flowers, instantly cooling and relaxing as you came in out of the hot desert sun. Once through the games room, you had a choice of the bar, cinema, reading room or video room to while away your leisure time. There were limited sports facilities there, too, such as squash-courts, tennis-courts and even a swimming-pool.

SAS personnel would often masquerade as contract workers 'just passing through', and frequent the bar for a few cold ones. There was no restriction on outside contractors using the bar and even the local police chief frequented the place. Strangely the bar opened at lunchtime, halfway through the working day. Bar-books could be purchased over the bar, for a few riyals, and the two indian barmen, Tony and Tom were quite affable and happy to serve any strangers. Those weren't their real names, but were the closest to pronunciation most of the workforce got after a few beers. No company ID was needed to drink there.

Lots of ex-army types frequented the bar, and Dicky Webb, Roddy Valentine and the like, soon recognised the imposters in their midst for what they were, but a knowing wink was all that passed between them.

There was never any trouble, just a few friendly drinks and a bit of chat, which made the lads feel human again after a long tour out in the desert. The only time things almost got heated was when one of the contractors, a young plastic paddy from Wisconsin, called Denis Turnock, began to drunkenly proclaim his support for the I.R.A. and boasted of giving money to NORAID, the American fundraising arm of that terrorist organisation, and he started an argument with one of the undercover troopers.

Quickly for a man of obvious girth, Dicky Webb was quick to intervene, and Big Roddy towered over the little shit. "No problem lads. You two finish your drinks," and with that the pair of them frogmarched the obnoxious American out of the bar, never to be seen in there again.

His future absence in the bar wasn't commented on by any of the regulars. They had heard too many tales of people turning up inside flowlines, when a more expensive 'pig' hadn't been made available.

Americans were cheaper, more readily available, and less likely to be missed, some of the lads joked. Oil-workers were no pushovers, and took no prisoners.

There was an extensive Rogue's Gallery of past and present workers pinned up on the walls surrounding the main bar, as occasionally the Shell resident senior engineer would come round with a polaroid camera, and top up the montage. Little did he know that at least six of the photos on the wall worked for 22-SAS and not Petroleum Development Oman.

The engineers didn't frequent the bar that often, fortunately, for they weren't that popular, often having a habit of coming into the bar late, after most people were bevvied-up, and then drinking soft drinks, whilst steering the conversation around to work, in the hope of loosened tongues saying things they perhaps shouldn't.

One obnoxious P4 was named Ian Reid, and he was a jumped-up little shit, full of his own importance, with a nose that must have been surgically altered so he could look down it at people. He only lived a short walking distance away from the bar, which was just as well, as there was a long queue of people hoping to bump into him one dark night.

As well as the bar, the camp boasted a swimming pool, which a few of the ex-pat workers used on their rest days. The normal rotation was 63/28, but 3 of those 63 days could be taken as rest-days, and you had the opportunity of spending them down on the coast in Muscat, or staying in camp.

The cool water of the pool was a luxury and a welcome relief from the heat of the summer, which could get well over a hundred degrees Fahrenheit. The pool wasn't locked, and Gabriel and Jim had made use of it on more than one occasion.

The only downside was having to camp out in the desert overnight. Some of the ex-pats had offered spare keys for some of the empty rooms, but neither man was willing to take a chance on camp security, as lax as it was, catching them out. The local militia which manned the security fences around the camp probably weren't even allowed bullets in their rifles, but best to take no chances.

When Gabriel and the rest of the squadron were given rest days, they had a choice of spending time in Salalah, which had some good beaches, or Muscat in the north, which had a bit more nightlife. There was always a bit of wadi-bashing somewhere in between for the more adventurous, as if they didn't get enough of that sort of thing in real life.

Gabriel liked to go off through the Jebel Mardar range by himself, doing a little freestyle climbing, which the army frowned upon, but then he was an excellent climber. Maddox sometimes joined him, and the two of them usually ended up in the Ruwi Hotel, where the Regiment had arranged rooms for them. The bar there was quite comfortable and the surroundings luxurious like most of the hotels in the middle-east, for the one thing the oil had given the Arabs was wealth, and all the trappings associated with it.

A lot of the Omani Arabs lived a more or less western lifestyle, for they were not as devout as a lot of the other middle eastern regimes. They drank alcohol, indulged in soft drugs like Hashish and Marijuana, and had secret drying-out clinics, more like prisons, in the mountains, far away from the public eye. Anyone sent there was not likely to want to visit again, but it all depended upon how much money you had. The more wealthy often just paid their 'fines' when their indiscretions were revealed.

The Ruwi Hotel was a regular honey trap for the Arabs, with a lot of the stopover airline stewardesses prepared to lower their morals along with their knickers if the price was right, and the Arabs always had a lot of money to throw about. Some of the Air France stewardesses were gorgeous, long legs and big tits, and they knew they were prime pussy in a place like this.

Despite her conservative dress, both Gabriel and Maddox took Rebekah for such a stewardess when they first caught sight of her having dinner with the Omani Oil Minister in the restaurant.

At subsequent evening dinners at the British Embassy, where sometimes Gabriel, Jim and one or two others from his squadron were occasionally invited, as a perk, but nominally to beef up security, they later found that the delightful Miss Weisz was the personal secretary assigned to the Cultural Attache at the American Embassy.

Cultural Attache usually meant C.I.A. which was an unusual posting overseas for a young woman in an Arab country, even one as pro-western as the Sultanate of Oman. She looked to only be in her mid to late twenties. Raven black hair hung down shoulder lengths, curled in ringlets. She was gorgeous, and she knew it, as did most of the good-looking women out here, who were busily making catty-remarks behind her back, and ensuring their husbands didn't stray too far out of their sight.

A lot of the diplomatic staff had a free run of the PDO-owned Ras al Hamra Recreational Club, which contained the tennis courts and a large swimming pool and bar. The wives and children of the ex-pats on married-status normally used the facilities on a daily basis, and it was quite crowded on the few occasions that Gabriel and Maddox were invited.

They made the most of their days off, soaking up the sun, sinking a few beers, and relaxing in the cool waters of the pool. "This is the life, eh Gabe?" Jim sighed, leaning back against the side of the pool after being narrowly beaten in a ten length race by his friend. Both men were aware that most of the women around the pool were eyeing them up, some discreetly, and some not so discreetly. Their husbands worked in the interior, eight days on, and six days off, which left them a lot of time on their hands. Some were quite obviously available to the right man, and single unattached men were a rarity in Oman.

"Let's grab a beer," suggested Gabriel.

"You go, old son. Think I'd better stay in the pool a bit longer. That blonde over there has been eyeing me up, and she's having an effect on me." He nodded down beneath the water, where Gabriel laughed as he saw the bulge in his friend's trunks.

"I don't think she'd blush." Gabriel laughed. "The way she's been parading in and out of the water in that white swimsuit, she knows damn well it's transparent when it's wet. Must have taken the lining out on purpose, just to give us poor blokes a hard-on," he joked. "She knows what she's doing all right."

"Hey, look at that!" Jim exclaimed, his gaze turned toward the bar, where a tall leggy figure was striding out into the hot sun. it was Rebekah Weisz, wearing a button-down pale blue cotton dress, and carrying a beach towel. Both men watched from the pool as she chose a sun-bed, and lay her towel down. Then she slowly unbuttoned the front of her dress and stripped it off, revealing a dark blue one-piece swimsuit that clung to her body. She was stunning.

"Wonder if she'd like a drink?" Gabriel mused, and started to get out of the pool.

"Bastard! I saw her first," complained Jim. Gabriel laughed.

"Better wait till that goes down before you get out of the water," he laughed, indicating Maddox's erection, and set off towards the bar. Maddox could only watch as he reappeared with a glass of iced lemonade and took a seat on the next sun-bed to Rebekah. Score one for Gabriel, but Maddox was still in the chase, and he eventually joined the twosome.

"Hope I'm not interrupting," he lied, "but I don't think we've met? Miss?" he held out his hand.

"Weisz. Rebekah Weisz. I'm with the American Embassy, but then you already know that by my accent," she smiled, and Maddox was head over heels in lust already.

She took of her sunglasses, throwing back that oiled black hair, as she took a sip from the drink Gabriel had brought her. "Jim Maddox," he introduced himself.

"I know who you both are. You were at the Embassy party the other week. I get briefed on all the guests. I have a good memory for faces," she revealed. "You're with the British Army. Special Forces, right?" she smiled, revealing gleaming white teeth which caught the sun.

"And you're a spook for the CIA," Gabriel grinned in response, proving their own intel was just as good. She laughed amusedly, Maddox eyes were glued to that jiggling bosom, and he sighed.

"Put your tongue away, Maddox," she suggested. "Be good boys and behave yourselves, at least until we get to know each other a little better," she smiled, as if taunting them, which she indeed was. The two men fussed over her all afternoon.

"So what's a nice American girl like you doing over here?" Maddox asked her, a short while later as they relaxed by the pool.

"I got in the Diplomatic Service a few years ago back in Washington, and then the chance of an overseas assignment came and I jumped at it. My folks didn't want me to take it, but then I suppose I've always been a bit of a rebel."

"What's it like working for the C.I.A.?" Gabriel asked.

"What's it like in the S.A.S.?" she countered, and then all three smiled.

"Okay, no more shop-talk," Maddox insisted. "Let's just enjoy ourselves on our time off."

* * *

In the weeks that followed, whenever duties would permit, the three of them saw a lot of each other, the two men constantly vying for her affections, as they chaperoned her everywhere. She understood the game that was being played, and played her own part in it well, first favouring one and then the other. The game turned slightly more serious however once Maddox admitted he was in love with her.

"Are you sure it's love and not just a lump in your pants?" Gabriel asked his friend, who was agonizing over a cold beer. Maddox shook his head.

"All I know is that I've never felt like this over any other bird before. I just can't get her out of my mind, Gabe. Fucking hurts not having her here with me, now." He took another swig of beer.

"Look Jim, she hasn't said anything to me, but I know she likes you. I haven't tried it on with her, well at least since I realized she didn't fancy me. But she does fancy you. I've seen it in her eyes. So go for it while you've got a chance. It's an old cliché, but this time tomorrow you could be dead. Live life while you can," he advised his friend.

*   *   *

Rebekah alternated her time between the Embassies in both Muscat and Salalah, and so Maddox and Gabriel saw her quite frequently. The beaches of Salalah were more remote, and public bathing was not frowned upon so much away from the city. The only downside was the isolation. Yemeni incursions were still an occasional possibility, and a few years previously, two of the oil workers had been machine-gunned on one of the lonely beaches by persons unknown.

Patrols had been stepped up, but the shoreline was a long one, and the Yemenis often came in small boats which couldn't be picked up on radar. Whenever Rebekah would visit the beach, either Gabriel or Maddox would accompany her, depending on who could get off-duty at the time. They made a point of always carrying weapons, either side-arms, or automatic rifles in the back of their jeeps. It may have looked like Paradise, but they weren't fooled by appearances. The Yemenis were a constant thorn in the Sultan's side, always chipping away at the fringes of his empire.

One day, as Rebekah and Gabriel were strolling barefoot along the beach, she turned to Gabriel, and caught him off-guard with a very pointed question. "Jim's in love with me, isn't he?" she said, more as a statement than a question. Gabriel paused before replying.

"Yes, he is. I've never seen him like this over any woman," he admitted, "and I've known him a few years now." Rebekah smiled sadly.

"I love both of you in my own way," she said, sadly. "You're like the big brothers I've never had. We've had some marvelous times together," she admitted. "Lately, Jim's had these silent awkward pauses when we've talked, as if he hasn't known what to say to me. Now I realise why."

"Is that a problem?" Gabriel asked, concerned for both her and his friend. He didn't want to see either of them hurt.

"I'm afraid it is," she admitted. "You see, I'm already married," she revealed, with a pained look in her eyes. Gabriel took a deep breath, the revelation coming as a surprise. "I don't wear a ring, as I find men's tongues become looser around a woman they think might be available. I'm not listed as married in the Embassy Personnel Lists either, for that same reason. You've both come to mean an awful lot to me in the months I've been out here," she said, with a hint of sadness in her voice. "I've asked to be transferred back home to Washington. I leave next week." She hung her head guiltily.

Gabriel kept walking, letting it all sink in. "What about Jim?" he asked. "What do I tell him?"

"I'm going to tell him, myself. I owe him that much at least. I'm seeing him tonight. I'll tell him then." Head bowed, Rebekah walked along the sand, carrying her shoes, in one hand and holding Gabriel's hand with the other. On an impulse, she suddenly threw herself into Gabriel's arms, and Gabriel saw her eyes were moist, as she hugged him to her. "I didn't mean to hurt him, Gabe. Please believe me," she pleaded, and Gabriel planted a soft kiss on her brow.

"I know, Reb. Sometimes relationships sort of run away with you." He comforted her as best he could, stroking her hair lightly, for he could see she was struggling with some inner conflict. The three of them had been inseparable friends these last few months, yet he had realised that Rebekah's own feelings for Maddox were a lot stronger than just mere friendship, married or not.

* * *

That evening, Maddox left for his date with Rebekah with a smile on his face, and Gabriel said nothing, just gave his usual wave as his friend took off in the jeep. The evening wasn't going to turn out too well, and he hoped Jim wouldn't take the bad news too much to heart. He didn't envy him.

The intimate dinner in one of the local restaurants was rather strained as Rebekah wasn't in her usual ebullient mood, and soon Maddox picked up on this. "Reb, are you okay. Is it something I've done? Not done, then? Offended you in any way? Give me a break here, I just can't understand a woman's mood swings," he finally admitted.

"No, it's not you, Jim. You're lovely, as you always are." Smiling sadly, she put up a hand to stroke his face, and Maddox took it in his own, kissing the back of it lightly.

"Then tell me, how can I bring you out of this funk you've gotten into? Let me put a smile on your face again, eh?" he offered.

"Take me to the beach," she suggested. "Let's go for a moonlight stroll on the beach."

The night air was warm, and the slipstream pulled Rebekah's long curled hair out behind her as Maddox drove. It wasn't far out of town to the long stretch of beach they often frequented. The sea here was friendly enough, and there were no treacherous currents.

He parked the jeep just above the tideline, and the two of them got out and began to slowly walk along the beach. Rebekah took off her shoes and so did Maddox, and they wandered along the shore, letting the incoming waters lap at their feet.

As Rebekah gripped his hand tightly, she broke the news. "I'm leaving at the end of the week, Jim." Maddox stopped, letting her hand slip from his own. He was lost for words momentarily.

"This is rather sudden isn't it?" he asked, trying to hide his shock and slight annoyance. A thousand thoughts were suddenly rushing through his mind, as he struggled for words. Rebekah avoided his eyes, guiltily.

"I'm being posted back home to Washington," she admitted. "This will be our last night together." Maddox bit his lip, stunned by the news. There was so much he wanted to say to her, but under the circumstances, he knew it wouldn't be right. He couldn't reveal his true feelings for her like this, just as she was going away, out of his life. His face revealed his sadness, and Rebekah took his hand once more.

"Don't be sad, Jim," she pleaded. "These last few months have been really special to me, and I know they have been to you, too." She put up a hand to forestall his interruption, pressing a finger to his lips. "You and Gabe have come to mean an awful lot to me, since we've met. I'm going to miss you both terribly."

"Reb, I don't want you to leave," he admitted, anguished and tongue-tied. "Isn't there some way you could stay on here?" he asked, softly, though inside his heart was breaking. Maddox wanted to scream, to shout, to kick someone's head in. This just wasn't fair! Rebekah simply smiled resignedly, and slowly shook her head.

"I can't, Jim. Believe me when I say, if I could, I would stay with you. But no more sad words tonight. It's going to be our last, so let's not waste it," she leaned forward and lightly kissed his lips. "I'm going swimming," she announced with a small grin.

"What?" Maddox asked, puzzled. "But you haven't a costume." Her laughter echoed above the surf as she began to remove her dress.

"I won't tell if you won't," she taunted, and in a flash, she was out of that dress, skin all white and dazzling in the moonlight as she ran for the surf, splashing out through the shallows. Maddox stood for a moment, stunned by the sudden strange impulsive behaviour, and then he too tore at his own clothes, and was soon running into the water after her. He heard her splashing ahead of him, and swam after her, through the breaking surf, and into the deeper, cooler water. She wasn't trying to get away from him, and he easily caught upto her. "You really are nuts, you know," he laughed, and Rebekah giggled. They swam together, enjoying the flow of water on their naked skin, before eventually heading back to the shallows again, and as they waded out of the water, Maddox found himself looking down at the length of Rebekah's naked body all wet and glistening in the light of the moon.

Rebekah looked down at Maddox's body, and smiled as she saw his stiffening cock. She reached down for it, fingers closing around the still cold, hard flesh, and Maddox gasped at the heat of her hand, before pulling her against him and kissing her hungrily.

She writhed against him, feeling his hardness against her wet belly now, as they clung to each other. "Our one and only time, Jim," she moaned between kisses. "One I'll remember all my life," she promised, and the two of them sank down on the sand, limbs intertwining as the surf lightly crashed over them.

*   *   *

In the afterglow of their lovemaking, a little higher up on the shoreline now, on the dry sand, Rebekah clung to Maddox, crying softly against his shoulder, as he tried to console her. Women were just so damn complex. He had no idea why she was crying now. Should he try for a posting to Washington? He didn't know if it was possible, or in what capacity it might be allowed. Certainly the Regiment had no reason to be there, but if he actually resigned his commission?

"It doesn't have to end like this, Reb," he spoke softly into her damp hair.

"Oh, but it does," she admitted sadly. "I have to leave and you mustn't follow. Promise me?" She looked up into his eyes, and he saw the sadness in her own. "There's a lot you don't know about me, Jim Maddox," she warned. "Let's just remember what we had tonight?" she suggested. "Please?"

Maddox was about to reply, when his eye caught sight of something out on the water, and he jerked his head around to study it more closely. The moon dipped back behind the clouds, and for a second he thought he had seen nothing, imagining, but then it came out momentarily again, and the dark shadows stood out against the brighter waves. "Christ!" he cursed as quietly as he could. He grabbed for his shorts and began pulling them up his legs. He then pushed her own clothes into her arms. "Keep low, and move as fast as you can. Find cover." He began pushing her away from him and up towards the treeline.

"What is it?" she turned to ask, scanning the sea herself. Then she caught sight of what Maddox had been alarmed about, two boats, low in the water, filled with men, coming in slowly with the tide, letting the waves bring them ashore instead of using their engines. Yemenis!

Maddox was already scurrying like a crab along the sand to where they had left the jeep, which stood exposed in the open. His weapons were in the jeep and so was the radio. He had to get on that radio and warn of the impending raid.

The two boats were heading for shore two hundred yards away, and they hadn't seen the jeep yet. Putting the vehicle fully between himself and the two boats, Maddox got to his feet and ran the rest of the way, feet kicking up sand behind him.

Breathing hard, he grabbed for his pistol, slinging the belt of webbing around his neck. Then he pulled the Sterling sub-machine gun from out of his satchel in the rear. Cocked and loaded. He had only two spare magazines in the satchel, and one spare clip of ammo for the small handgun.

Grabbing the radio, he pressed the transmit button and held it down as he spoke in hushed tones. "This is Maddox, come back," he waited for a response. "I repeat, this is Maddox, come back." *Pick it up somebody* he pleaded mentally.

After what seemed like an eternity, the radio crackled back at him. "Philips here. Go ahead, Jim," the response came finally.

"Get the boys out, fast! Full alert. No drill! Repeat! No fucking drill! We have two boats landing north of the village, maybe a mile along the shoreline. About twenty men, and I'm stuck out here with one piddling little Sterling. If you want to see me still here when you arrive, get a fucking move on. Confirm!"

"Watch your arse, Jim. Cavalry's on its way. Stay low and avoid contact till we get there."

"Might be harder than you think, sonny-boy. Don't spare the horses!" He dropped the radio, and started backing slowly away from the jeep. The first boat was landing some distance away in the surf. He looked up. The clouds were starting to clear away from the moon. When they saw the jeep, the shit was going to hit the fan! *Why now? Why fucking now?* he cursed as he scuttled back up towards the tree-line.

*   *   *

Back at HQ, Philips sounded the alarm, relaying Maddox's call to his C.O. who ordered a full turn-out. Checking the roster, Gabriel had filled in his expected destination for the evening, and he called the restaurant urgently.

*   *   *

Gabriel was enjoying a meal on the south side of the town, just about to start his main course of Lobster Thermidore, which was a rare treat. He left the table at the manager's behest, and went over to the public phone in the lobby, to find out what the call was about. Less than a minute later, he dropped the phone, and ran from the restaurant, heading for where he had left his jeep.

It would take at least fifteen minutes for any help to come from base. That was fifteen minutes Maddox might not have. He could get to the beach in five, and he flung himself behind the wheel, pausing only to unlock the welded container in the rear, where he stowed his weapons. He put the Sterling SMG and spare magazines on the passenger seat beside him, put the key in the ignition, and fired up the engine.

*   *   *

Maddox handed Rebekah the automatic and the spare magazine. "Can you use one of these?" She nodded affirmatively. He steadied the Sterling, resting the perforated barrel across his forearm as he lay down, offering the minimum target, and noted Rebekah was doing the same. It wouldn't be long now.

The two of them lay there in silence, watching and waiting. At last the moon cleared the clouds fully, and as the incursionists dragged their boats up onto the beach, one of them pointed to the jeep. Four of them began immediately running towards it to check it out. The rest of them fanned out into defensive positions.

One man approached the jeep cautiously, as the other three held back till they made sure no one was inside or hidden behind it, then they joined the first and began a rapid search of the surrounding sand, one of them signalling as he spotted Maddox's tracks.

"Let them come," he whispered to Rebekah. "We don't have much ammo, so let's take these four out nice and quick, and then run like Hell before the rest of them can get a fix on us." Rebekah nodded silently. "When we get up, run towards the town. It means going past them as they come at us, but if help's coming, that's the direction it'll come from. The more noise they make closer to the town the better. It'll wake people up and take away the element of surprise."

They watched as the four men approached, scanning the soft tracks in the sand by moonlight wasn't easy. Maddox let them get within ten yards, before he opened up with the Sterling, using short controlled bursts, trying his damnedest to hold it down as it kicked up at him.

It was hard to be accurate with the Sterling, and anything over thirty yards was chancey. The first burst took out the closest two Yemenis. The second took out the third man as he wheeled around to target Maddox. Rebekah took out the fourth man with a single shot from the hand-gun, holding it ball & cup style to steady her aim. "Now run!" Maddox hissed, as the night erupted with gunfire aimed in their direction, and he pushed her out in front of him. "Head for the main road," he ordered, pausing to fire another warning burst over the heads of the rapidly approaching group of men.

The Yemenis returned fire, and bullets sprayed through the air, hitting mainly the trees as the man and the woman ran as fast as they could parallel to the beach, using what cover there was, and firing back from the hip. They had more targets to aim at, and three more terrorists went down.

Maddox cried out and went down as a bullet tore through his calf, and Rebekah wheeled around as he cried out. "Leave me! Get the hell out of here," he ordered, pulling himself up and then taking refuge behind one of the palm trees. He fired off another burst as the shadowy figures advanced, trying to outflank him. "Go on, I'll cover you," he ordered.

"Fuck you, Jim Maddox!" Rebekah swore at him, and she crawled back alongside him, firing back at the fleeting shadows.

"You're gonna get yourself killed, woman."

"Then I die here with you. Now shut up and keep firing," Rebekah replied, firing off another couple of shots, teeth gleaming in the moonlight as she heard the cry of pain as one of the terrorists went down.

"Always the rebel, eh? Well, this last word might just be your last, if help doesn't get here soon," he warned. Maddox fired another burst, and then cursed as the magazine was empty. It took forever to discard the empty one and fit the second. Two against possibly fourteen or fifteen men. They hadn't enough ammunition to last more than another five minutes. He knew how far away the camp was. They weren't going to make it in time.

*   *   *

Gabriel heard the gunfire over the noise of his engine as he drove along the main highway. He steered one-handed as he readied his own

Sterling across the top of the dashboard. He was driving lights out, with only the moon to steer by, wanting to give no warning of his arrival.

It wasn't long before he could see the muzzle flashes in the distance, and he quickly pulled over, not wanting to present too much of a target. He switched the engine off, and let the car coast, over the last few hundred yards. He was out of the jeep and running before the wheels had stopped turning. Speed now was everything. Sterling in one hand and a satchel full of magazines in the other. The gunfire proved Maddox was still alive.

Gabriel circled wide of the action, keeping to the far side of the road, with the darkness of the desert at his back, not wanting to get caught in any crossfire. If he tried to come upon Maddox from behind, his friend might shoot first and ask questions later. He counted the muzzle-flashes. Two against twelve possibly, which meant Rebekah was still alive, too.

He fired his first burst into the rear of the attacking force, taking them completely by surprise, firing as he ran, and taking out three, then four of their number who shook and shuddered in a dance of death as the bullets hit them. He hated the Sterling, for it took almost all his strength to hold the damn thing down. He hadn't the body-mass for prolonged use of automatic weapons. But he'd rather be behind it than in front of it.

"Coming through!" he cried out as he charged for Maddox's position, and letting them know help was arriving. He slid in behind the tree, shaking out the ammunition as he did so. Maddox grabbed for another magazine, and rammed it home into his own weapon.

"Couldn't keep away from the party, eh?" he grinned. "Always cutting in on my dates."

"Let you keep this pretty girl all to yourself? You know me better than that, Jimbo!" and he leaned out to fire another burst into the trees. Rebekah fired again on the other side. "Your leg looks bad," he observed, noting the blood-flow.

"It'll keep. Play nursemaid later, after we've cleared out these scumbags," he offered, and fired a burst off himself. Gabriel rolled off to one side, taking a position behind another of the trees, and attracting fire as he did so. Rebekah whirled around as movement caught her eye, and she fired off two quick rounds as two of the Yemenis had managed to track back up the beach and come in through the tree-line to try and take them unawares. Gabriel fired the Sterling from the ground, taking out the second man as he fired back at Rebekah. More shots were fired, thudding into the tree-trunks, or whizzing past over their heads. The standoff continued for a few more minutes, bullets being traded from both sides, with the gunfire diminishing gradually.

At the sight of headlights approaching from the main highway, the group of surviving Yemenis suddenly broke off contact, and headed back to the beach. Gabriel broke cover, and started a hesitant pursuit, till he observed the nine survivors pushing their boat out to sea, and a powerful outboard motor started up. They were retreating.

He went back to where Rebekah was tending Jim's leg, making a tourniquet with a strip torn off the hem of her dress. At the roar of engines, Gabriel looked up and saw three Land-rovers full of troops pull up. Instantly, they scattered, guns already out and seeking to secure the perimeters. Maddox cursed them good-naturedly as he lay there, enjoying being fussed-over.

"And where the fuck do you lot think you've been?" he berated, sarcastically. "What took you so long? Been sticking to the speed-limits like good little boys?" he taunted. "Good job this wasn't a drill or I'd have the lot of you on jankers for a week!" he promised.

*　　*　　*

Maddox was there at Seeb Airport to see Rebekah off at the end of the week, bad leg or no bad leg. He discharged himself from Koola Hospital, and to hell with the doctors. It was a sad farewell. She had her reasons he was sure, but damned if he knew what they were. She had turned and waved from the top of the airplane steps, and that had been the last time he had seen her. There had been no contact whatsoever from her over the years.

He had made enquiries about her in the years since, but had received no response from the Americans. It was only when he had gotten this job here in The Hague, that he heard she had left America. Rebekah had moved to Israel, and he guessed from her C.I.A. past that she was now involved with Mossad.

Then had come the mysterious letter, addressed personally to him, courtesy of the Arab terrorist Torquemada.

Chapter Eleven

im, I had no idea Rebekah was involved," he revealed, truthfully. "It's a shock. She disappeared from sight years ago. You saw her off yourself when she left Oman. I haven't seen or spoken to her since those days. How is she involved here, can you tell me?"

Maddox took another swig of his beer, as he decided how much of this he could tell Gabriel. "I learned years ago, when they moved me upstairs and I joined the ranks of the Green Slime, that Rebekah had moved to Israel," he began. "Her previous affiliation with the C.I.A. meant she was soon tapped up for a job with the Mossad. It was they who got us our first lead on this campaign, when they tracked down one of the Al Qaeda mullahs for the septics in Northern Pakistan. Looks like they never handed over all their intel, and decided to mount an operation of their own. We think she's a ringer, working deep undercover. She risked blowing her cover to try and get a warning out about Pisa. She's obviously after the head man himself," he speculated.

"That makes two of us, then. I've got a bone to pick with him myself. One of his bombs put my daughter in hospital," he finally admitted. Maddox's eyes widened.

"Your daughter? You never struck me as the type who'd settle down, Gabe."

"It's a long story," he shrugged. "Anyway, I've been asked by certain parties to do something about these terrorists, and I've already taken steps towards getting an introduction to our Arab friends. Now I need your help to take things a step further, and personally get inside their organisation."

Maddox looked curious. "How so?"

"I want you to put my name and my face in the newspapers. As you said, not many people know me these days since I've lead a rather sheltered lifestyle lately. That needs to change if I want these people to contact me."

"You realise what that could mean? You've built up a steady list of enemies over the years, man."

"I know what I'm doing, Jim. It's the quickest way of getting a result. If I get to meet up with Rebekah, perhaps the two of us will stand a better chance than one."

"You might also get her killed," he warned.

"More likely myself. I need to have something they want. I can pass for an Arab at a pinch, and at a distance, but real Arabs would suss me out in no time. I'm a westerner, and therefore not to be trusted, only tolerated. Unless I am useful to them in some way, they'll have no use keeping me around, now will they? They're in for the long haul, here, and the campaign is picking up speed. I think they might try and take out the Pope," he admitted. Maddox raised his eyebrows.

"What did you have in mind?" Maddox asked.

"I need a story in the newspapers, and circulated at high level among the security agencies, that I'm back in business and with a supply of a suitable nerve agent to the highest bidder. That should prove too tempting for them to pass up."

"Christ, you're mad!" Maddox exclaimed.

"It's got to be something they can't afford to ignore, Jim. Biologicals or Nuclear. You can't fake radioactivity, but what I have in mind will work with your help."

"You're going to be walking around in the cross-hairs, you know that, don't you?"

"That's why I need your help, Jimbo. You have to cover my back, just like the old days, till I get a chance to take a shot at Mr Torquemada. He's the brains behind this campaign. Al Qaeda have never done anything like this before. He's obviously a rising star, a new player in the game. It's his show, and if he gets away with it, some other country is going to suffer. We need to take him out at the first opportunity."

"It's not my decision to make, Gabe. Wish it was. I'll have to consult the head-shed in Whitehall. You know what they're like."

"We don't have much time. If Torquemada is running true to form, they'll strike again in a day or so," he warned.

"Maybe not. I have Pisa locked up tighter than a drum. Anyone leaving the city is getting all their papers checked thoroughly and we're photographing or videoing everybody. If they do pass the checkpoints at least somewhere we'll have their faces on film." Gabriel nodded silently, but did not share Maddox's optimism. Checkpoints were stationary, whereas terrorists were not. "I'll put your proposal to my bosses tonight. I'll try and have an answer for you by tomorrow." Maddox promised.

"Let's meet here again for lunch, then?"

"Okay. Best be going. You've given me another busy night," Maddox complained as he drained his glass. "Your round, if I remember right," he grinned, and got up from the booth. Gabriel watched him leave, and reached for his wallet.

*   *   *

In Pisa, the four terrorists were becoming uneasy. The police were everywhere, and all major routes out of the city were subject to roadblocks and checkpoints. You couldn't even get on a train without showing your passport and being fingerprinted.

"We've walked into a trap! How did they know and react so quickly?" said Abdul.

"Can the Algerian help us further?" asked Omar.

"Keep calm. We just need to wait," Anwar Rahman assured them.

"Wait? They close the circle by the hour," Mophammed complained.

"Once the next attack takes place, they will switch their attentions away from Pisa, thinking we have already left, leaving us free to move once more. This strategy has worked well so far. They can't be everywhere. They don't know where we will strike."

"They knew, here!" accused Abdul. "Their reaction time was too quick. I say we were betrayed."

"If we were betrayed, we would not be here having this conversation. The police would already have us or we would be dead. Perhaps we were just unlucky for once?"

"Very well, I will step up the next strike. I guarantee you the authorities will be kept guessing. Be patient," Anwar talked persuasively, trying to settle raw nerves. Campaigns got riskier the longer they went on, and this one was far from finished.

*   *   *

Gabriel phoned Falcone's private number from his cell-phone as soon as Maddox left. "Yes?" came a cultured voice on the other end of the line.

"It's me. I have some information for your people. Listen carefully. Mossad have a woman on the inside of one of these cells. I know her. Rebekah Weisz. She's tall, very good-looking woman, black hair, aged in her early fifties. The only female name we have for any of the terrorists is Fatima Khalid, but she may have papers or passports using another identity. Can your organisation tap into Mossad or Europol and get her data? I don't want any harm coming to her. If you can track her down, you should be able to run down her current associates too. Just make sure no one shoots at her by mistake," he insisted.

"We have the necessary contacts. I'll instigate a trace and see what data we can pull up on her. I'll circulate photos among my people," Falcone assured him.

"From the way they're operating, we've had attacks up and down the country, but I have a feeling they're heading for Rome." Gabriel revealed. "If I was our friend Torquemada and I wanted to make a statement against the Catholic Church, I'd aim for the Vatican City. Whatever he's planning, the crescendo is going to be big. You'd best tell your top boy to keep his head down, and a quick overseas tour may be advisable." There was a momentary silence on the other end of the line.

"This thought had occurred to us, too. His eminence has been advised, but he stubbornly refuses to keep a lower profile while all this is going on, insisting his visible presence is a stabilising one to a worried nation. He will stay in Rome."

"Italy is too big a nation to track down individuals like this, so I suggest you pull back all your available manpower and stake them out in Rome. I'm heading back that way myself," confirmed Gabriel.

*   *   *

Maddox was on the phone to Whitehall as soon as he got back into the office, and it took some time to get a Minister Responsible enough to come to the phone at that hour of the night. Maddox related the evening's meeting with Gabriel and his proposition.

"Your suggestion will take a lot of resources, Maddox. Can this man Gabriel do what he says he can do? I'd rather have our own man in there than one of Mossad's," he admitted.

"He used to be one of ours, sir. Left the Regiment over twenty years ago but I'd trust him with my life." The Minister hummed and hahh'ed on the other end of the phone, not really interested in the man's former life. It was his present activities that now concerned him.

"Very well, I'll put this before the Cabinet. You'll have an answer by morning," he promised, and hung up. Maddox did the same. Brady brought him a mug of coffee.

"Ta, Tom. It's going to be a long night."

"Tell me about it. Cordon is tightening around Pisa, and the public is kicking up a fuss. Politicians over there are screaming for action, and we can't give them jack shit!"

"This Torquemada is good. Thinks he's covered all the angles," Maddox admitted.

"Can your old mate take him?" Maddox ruminated on that one for a minute, before answering.

"He's a sneaky little fucker is Gabriel. He just might!" he grinned.

*   *   *

Fatima Khalid tasted the blood in her mouth, as she rocked in her bolted-down chair. Lev Ashif, her interrogator, was losing his patience. She had told them nothing. They had starved her, beaten her even, but not a word had slipped from her lips concerning the terrorist campaign underway in Italy. Ashif had slipped up though, revealing to her that they had an agent in place, impersonating her. That was a secret she found hard not to smile at, for she had a further secret of her own. Of all the cell-members currently on active-service in Italy, she was the only one who knew Torquemada personally, and when this impersonator turned up in her place, Torquemada would kill her.

They were holding her here in a small town jail, under regular security, not wanting to publicise her capture by moving her to one of the major cities, and this was to her benefit. Hamas by now would know she been taken by the Jews, as she did not make the promised phonecall for final arrangements on passage to Italy. They would be actively seeking her whereabouts, and would doubtless try and secure her release. It was only a matter of time. She just had to hold out until they came for her. They would use the truth drugs on her before long. They were effective only inasmuch as you had the right person asking the right questions.

A young physician accompanied her interrogator, when they came to collect her from her cell, and two soldiers frogmarched her back out into the cell-block. It was pointless resisting as they shoved her back down in the bolted-down chair, and ropes were used to secure her.

The physician unpacked a small amount of medical equipment, swabs, syringes, and some small ampoules of liquid which Fatima eyed with interest. Ashif was setting up a tape-recorder to record the questioning so that her answers might be disected in detail later, and passed on to higher command.

The young man tapped the barrel of the syringe, as he slightly depressed the plunger, removing all trace of air bubbles, and then he moved alongside her and Fatima steeled herself against the bite of the needle as he plunged it into a vein. She could feel the liquid being injected, surprisingly gently, and then the physician stepped back, swabbing her arm. He then moved off to one side of the cell to observe, as Lev Ashif just sat there, watching coldly, and waiting for the effect of the drug to kick in.

He watched with cold disinterest as her body relaxed and then slumped in the chair. Her eyes lost focus and became glazed. Her breathing became shallower, slower. Now the questioning would begin.

*   *   *

Lev Ashif was furious with the results of the drugs-session. The bitch hadn't revealed anything other than the code-names of the personnel she was dealing with, this Torquemada, and some minor league members of Hamas who were already wanted in connection for various terrorist acts, and currently being hunted by Israeli Special Units. She was tied to the chair again, held upright by the rope across her chest, as she was still under the influence of the powerful narcotic.

Though drugged, she smiled drunkenly up at him, with a wild look in her eyes. She knew she had beaten the chemicals.

*   *   *

In London, a COBR meeting was held in emergency session as they debated Maddox's suggestions. Colonel Alex Danning of 22SAS was called to reveal what he knew about this Gabriel, and his past association with the Regiment.

"Colonel Danning is with the Regiment, and will give a brief history of this colourful chappie who has offered to assist in the matter of these Al Qaeda terrorists running loose in Italy. Colonel Danning, if you'd be so kind?" he relinquished the floor, and all eyes turned to the Colonel, who sat up ramrod straight, reading briefly from an Eyes Only file.

"Gabriel Angell. He was attached on special secondment to 22SAS from 1974 through 1978. Specifically, he was an instructor with the corps, an excellent climber and mountaineer. He served in Wales, Norway, and saw active service in Oman," he spoke to his assembled peers in government. "After 1978, he left the service, and nothing was heard from him for some years. In August of 1983 ETA began a resurgence in their terror campaigns in Northern Spain. Angell was found to be part of that campaign." He paused for effect. "He stayed with them briefly, before dropping from sight again. He has remained out of sight until present day."

"Another bad apple from the SAS, eh?" scoffed one of the ministers. Danning puffed up.

"Bad apples can come from many different sources, Minister. Angell was decorated with the George Cross for his actions in Oman, though he never collected the medal. I don't know what turned him to ETA, only that reports say it was for undisclosed personal reasons, and his notoriety was short-lived. He has stayed out of the limelight ever since."

"Who knows what he was upto, though, eh?" his detractor butted in once more. "And why is he involving himself with yet another set of terrorists? Wants an introduction to them, indeed," he scoffed in disbelief.

"According to Maddox, more personal reasons, yet this time he states he wants to help us catch the bastards."

"Do we believe him, though?"

"We need someone with inside knowledge. At the moment we're chasing shadows. Italy is in a panic. God help us if this lunatic brings a similar campaign of terror to Britain!" He looked around the table to see many heads nodding in agreement.

"Very well, then. But we must maintain some deniability here. If this all goes tits-up and this laddy's past association with the Regiment is touted around in the tabloid Press we'll never hear the end of it."

"I agree. We must have a contingency clean-up operation to remove all traces of our involvement in this exercise. Good God, if it became public knowledge that we were actively supporting someone with known terrorist links, and not only supporting but supplying him with Biological weapons, it would probably bring this Government down."

"Let's be fair, Minister. We wouldn't be supplying him with any such thing, just a carefully prepared placebo, in effect," Colonel Danning interrupted.

"The story we'll be putting out won't say anything about placeboes, Colonel," warned the minister. "Deliberately misinforming the media is not advisable. The Press can make or break Governments. They've done so before, remember?" he reminded him.

"Yes, and to make this story believable, we're going to have to fake a break-in at Porton Down, and mobilise a fake manhunt in this country, all for nothing. It could cost the taxpayer millions."

"Whether this succeeds or whether it fails then, we seem to be agreed. This operation must maintain deniability. It would seem to be in everyone's interests if this Gabriel were removed with the rest of the terrorists."

"What if he's successful? Do you want him rewarded with a bullet for risking his life?" Danning asked coldly.

"You said it yourself, Colonel. He volunteered for ETA. That and his association with the SAS is more than cause enough for a bit of internal 'housekeeping' don't you think? Dogs of War are meant to be kept on a leash in peacetime, not running around loose and savageing people. Time this particular mad dog was put down, and out of everyone's misery. When he's outlived his usefulness of course," he chuckled.

"Until then, we support him as he requires. Agreed?" Heads nodded around the table. "Put a team on him to watch his back, and then if the Arabs don't kill him, we will!"

*   *   *

In the small hours of the morning, Danning himself phoned to break the news to Maddox, who listened carefully and patiently, weighing up what he was being asked to do to one of his oldest friends. "I see, sir," he said, flatly, when Danning had finished speaking.

"I realise there's a history between the two of you, Maddox. But I hope you can put that to one side here. Whitehall has made its mind up."

"I want to pick the squad myself, sir, if that's okay?" he asked. Danning considered for a moment, and then agreed.

"I'll authorise anything you want, within reason, Maddox. I'm as pissed-off about this as you sound yourself. Putting down our own is never pleasant, but sometimes necessary. I'll fax the necessary authorities across to you first thing in the morning. I'll leave it to you to smooth things with the Italians."

"Yes, sir. One thing about the EEC, sovereign nations give up all individual rights once they join. They'll do what they're told," he assured. Danning then hung up, and Maddox played with the handset, deep in thought.

*   *   *

Nick Turnbull was fast asleep when the phone rang in his private quarters. He wasn't due to report back to Stirling Lines till midday. When the phone rang, he picked it up on the third ring, ever a light sleeper. "Yes?" he squinted as he put the bedside lamp on.

"Nick, I've got a job for you." Maddox's voice came down the line. "I want you, Dixon, Palmer and Coverdale on the next available flight to Rome. I'm flying out there myself first thing tomorrow to take personal charge of this operation," he affirmed.

"Rome? Not anything to do with our little chat, guvnor? Or is it recent events?" Nick asked, cagily.

"Both, but not on an open line, Nick. I'll brief you personally when I meet up with you in Rome. I'll have someone meet you at Leonardo Da Vinci," he promised.

"Wet work, guv?"

"Maybe later," he confirmed. "I'll arrange equipment with the Italian authorities once I get out there. Sorry for disturbing your sleep, Nick. Better get back to it."

"Best of luck, guv." Nick put the phone down, and then lay back on the pillow, with a thousand thoughts running through his mind. Rome and Maddox's present assignment could only mean Al Qaeda's latest bunch of lunatics. Maddox had just requested the four of them, himself and those other three shits. Very strange bedfellows indeed, considering. What was Maddox upto? Not a big operation, or there'd be more manpower.

Four man teams usually meant quick incursions, in and out, or surveillance. If they knew where those ragheads were, they wouldn't be just watching them. They'd have already either killed them or roped them in for interrogation. He was sure the Italians wouldn't need any help in interrogating the bastards. Nix on the old in and out, as well. Not possible unless you had a target, and if they had the target, the Italians wouldn't wait for help. They'd want to go in and do the job themselves. Gung-ho fuckers they were these days, keen to dispel the old cowardy-custard rep they'd had since the Second World War.

Chapter Twelve

June 11th

*N*ick Turnbull woke up after completing a restless night's sleep. He felt shitty, and still half asleep, He didn't like getting his sleep disturbed, but it was something you had to put up with in his job. He came wide awake in a hurry as Sky News broke the story during the 8am news broadcast the next morning. Kay Burley came in as her co-presenter concluded a report on the latest economic trends in the housing market.

"News just in: Reports are just coming in of a Home Office enquiry going on at the Government Research Facility at Porton Down. Police forces in the area have been put on alert and are believed to be conducting a search of the surrounding area. We'll bring you more on that story as the day goes on. Now here's Jacqui Levy with the Sports Headlines . . . ."

*   *   *

It was too late for the first editions, but the later editions of the morning newspapers carried suitably edited details of a supposed theft from the facility.

'Bio-Hazard Material Goes Missing From Porton Down' was echoed across three or four of the tabloids. An undisclosed cabinet leak was blamed for the unconfirmed report, but as the day went on, tv crews recorded footage of the police search that was indeed being carried out in the countryside surrounding the facility, and zoom lenses from helicopter news teams showed numerous police vehicles parked up at the remote secure facility to add weight to the story that was being planted in the news media.

The Official Secrets Act was conveniently used to avoid answering any direct questions by reporters or the news media. Just enough information leaked by various vague sources was often pounced on by unscrupulous journalists, and it wouldn't be the first time that governments had used their need for an exclusive story against them.

The article was soon picked up by CNN and FOX News, and syndicated around the world, ensuring the 'right' people saw the story, and were suitably convinced of its veracity. The size of the police search, hastily mobilised and still manning-up as the news cameras watched, added the only visible evidence, but it's scale proved that the authorities were treating the matter with due respect. The tabloid press could be relied upon to sensationalise anything, and they were doing a good job.

*   *   *

Luke studied the news articles with interest. He had access to some sophisticated equipment at the college, while he worked on his Cisco Certification Course, and he was well ahead with both classwork as well as coursework. He had plenty of time to browse the Internet using the broadband modem. He had logged onto the CNN site, and found the UK based story repeated there.

As he read the article, he was astonished to find mention of Gabriel's name in connection with the theft. 'A fake security badge, used to gain access to the establishment, was found in the grounds of the facility. The man in the photograph, has since been positively identified as Gabriel Angell, formerly with the British Army, and having links to the known terrorist organisation E.T.A.' Luke's mouth dropped open wide. No fucking way! The photo accompanying the article showed a blond man, with a short beard, but looking closer, Luke could see that it looked like Gabriel behind that growth, presumably dyeing his hair.

This was not the Gabriel that Luke had known, albeit briefly, but that man couldn't be responsible for something like this. It bore further investigation, and Luke decided it was time to let Rover out for a walk again.

Rover was a search-engine of his own design, and it was the best there was. Just a shame that it was also highly illegal, and he would never get a patent for it, for the encryption routines it used to screen and transmit its data were prohibited by recent Government legislation on privacy of information. Only fitting then that he used it quite frequently to snoop on what the government was doing, just out of curiosity, and it wasn't as if he did anything with the information.

He had refined the program since Gabriel had first come across it, tightening up the code, and making it harder to track and better at hiding it's own existence within other operating systems. It operated like a worm virus, insinuating itself within another system and searching for data. It was cleverly coded to use an anti-virus against itself, indeed was dependant upon one being present in order to operate. Anyone not having an antivirus had nothing to hide, was the logic behind it, and the mere recognition triggered executable code, as it fooled the anti-virus into thinking it was detected, quarantined or deleted. If it didn't find that data it was looking for, it simply stayed there, dormant. If eventually, that information did get entered into the machine's memory, then Rover would reactivate itself and bring home the bone. If it didn't find out anything within 30 days, Rover would self-destruct in effect, removing all traces of itself from the infected system.

Luke programmed Rover to do a cross search of Gabriel's name with the terrorist organisation ETA, and sat back to wait for the results.

*   *   *

Chapter Thirteen

MADRID 1983

Alonso Borgia took the news badly. He crumpled the fax he had received from the research facility in Madrid in his hand, fuming. Those idiots hadn't even dared phone him to break the news personally, just an anonymous fax informing him of the termination of Project Icarus.

He called an impromptu Council Meeting to break the news to the others, and he smoothed out the crumpled fax on the table in front of them, to emphasise his anger over what had happened.

"Those bunglers, Giuseppi and Annibale, in Madrid, have terminated the project prematurely," he announced, handing the fax over to be read and passed around. "This now limits our options. Our only other remaining test-subject is too valuable to risk by handing him over to their tender mercies."

"Can we not use this as a means to snare Gabriel and Lucifer once more?" asked one of the avid hawks around the large table. Inwardly, Alonso smiled, though he gave no outward appearance of doing so. He had hoped one of the others around the table would realise the opportunity, and had wanted someone other than just himself to suggest the idea.

"By this, I take it you mean leak details of Project Icarus to Gabriel?" he suggested, feigning surprise at the idea. He had hoped one of the others would suggest it. "It's a possibility, I suppose. But details would have to be both vague and at the same time specific enough to assure his interest." Borgia played these word-games well.

"Yes," another of them quickly agreed. "If it was stage-managed efficiently enough, he would take the bait. He couldn't afford not to." They were beginning to see the opportunities as though he had unveiled the plan right there in front of them.

"A suitable conduit is needed. Gabriel would not take the bait if he knew it came directly from us," the frail Silvester argued.

"We know of his Mafia contacts, and his friends in the Grimaldi Family. The Mafia also know some of our own dealings and of Gabriel's enmity towards us. If they became aware of the sort of information we would make available, then they would certainly draw his attention to it. We merely allow them to access the information on our terms, in a manner designed no to arouse any suspicion."

"A pawn-sacrifice is called for, I think. Let one of our messengers be compromised, and make sure he is carrying the information we decide upon at the time. Once they realise its significance, they are bound to inform Gabriel. Then it will only be a matter of time before he acts to verify that information for himself. He can't afford not to under the circumstance."

"Very well. I will contact Madrid, and ensure that certain carefully worded documents and photographs are despatched by courier. We merely have to ensure that the Mafia intercept him before he gets here. I have a contact in the Police Department." Some of them chuckled at his reference to his paramour, the lovely Eve Maggio, otherwise known as Sister Angelica. "She can see that news of our courier's route is brought to the attention of the right people."

* * *

Donatello Grimaldi, recently made head of the Grimaldi clan, recognised the importance of the information his men had retrieved from the Solomon Courier. In a sealed package, which he had opened himself, were progress reports, backed up with various photographs, of a variety of experiments carried out on a winged human. Admittedly the wings could hardly be called such anymore, for they were all withered and wasted, but wings they undoubtedly were. The photos were clear enough. He did not understand the significance of the find, for he himself knew nothing of Gabriel's origins, but he knew of Gabriel's interest in anything the Sword of Solomon organisation got upto.

He arranged for the information to be copied, and then he had it mailed to a PO Box address in Lexington, Kentucky, North America, which Gabriel used as a filter for all his mail. He then sent a coded fax, to a special phone number, informing Gabriel that a package was on the way to him.

*　　*　　*

It took nearly a week, before Gabriel had his hands on the documents himself, and Lucifer watched as he opened the package and began pouring through the computer printouts and many typed pages, before he came to the first photograph of Matthias.

"Is it really him?" Lucifer asked, hardly able to believe that one of their brethren was still alive after all this time. Gabriel's pulse quickened as he nodded, studying the photos intensely.

"That's Matthias alright," he agreed, handing over some of the photos to Lucifer. "I don't know how they found him, or how long they've had him in their power, but the bastards are using him like a lab-rat by the looks of things. Even worse than what they did to you in Rome." Lucifer nodded, grimly. Memories of what was done to him in the catacombs still gave him nightmares, and he had odd panic attacks at times these days. His health was no longer as good as it should be, for some damage had been done to his blood system by the Church's scientists whilst they had him in their power.

"We can't leave him there," Lucifer insisted. Gabriel looked up from the photographs.

"Don't worry. We won't," he said simply. The documentation contained headings from a medical facility called the Munez Institute, and the address given was in Madrid, Spain. Another Catholic stronghold where he had no friends. Mentally he was reviewing his options. If this was being run by Solomon, it would not be easy getting in and out of the place. In Rome he had the Mafia helping him, but they had no presence in Spain that he knew of.

Calling his new manservant Manuel, Gabriel arranged for a substantial transfer of funds to a bank in Spain, in preparation for the forthcoming trip. He would need access to money to finance what was even now germinating in the back of his mind. A lot of money.

*   *   *

Over the next couple of days, arrangements were made by phone, and Gabriel and Lucifer flew into Madrid. With hastily dyed blonde hair, Gabriel and Lucifer could easily be mistaken as the brothers their passports now claimed them to be. Even with his swarthy skin, such a mix of hair-colours was not uncommon these days, with the mixing of races across the world.

His tour of duty with the SAS had served him well, teaching him methods of travel and educating him in the ways of modern world politics. Spain was nominally a kingdom, in the same way as the UK. Juan Carlos remained on the throne, as a figurehead, while a parliament actually handled the running of the country. It had changed much since his days here in the Spanish Civil War.

No organised crime to speak of, but Spain was beleagured by poltical groups, some of which resorted to force to try and achieve their aims, and E.T.A. was just such an organisation. Gabriel had no time to win friends here in Spain, but he had brought money enough to buy some, and the sort of paramilitary aid they could supply was just what he needed. The Guardia Civil all carried firearms, and they seemed to be on every street corner in Spain, a legacy from Franco's days.

A locally purchased map showed that the Munez Institute backed onto the Parque De Breogan, on the east side of the city, on the Avenida de Brasilia. The nearby M30 motorway also backed onto the park, and would provide a convenient escape route out of the city, assuming of course that the planned raid could first be successfully achieved. Lucifer would scout the terrain and come up with a plan of attack while Gabriel flew north to Zaragoza, to try and recruit some help and hardware.

*   *   *

Most of the people here in Basque Country spoke Spanish, but one or two still conversed in Romantic, which was one of the oldest dialects in Europe. Gabriel found the people friendly, once they found his passport claimed him to be American. Some of them seemed to follow him with their eyes as he walked about, and a taxi driver took him to a hotel in the centre of the city.

He spent the first couple of days behaving as a tourist was expected to, going out and about and familiarising himself with the city. He also made a point of befriending the barman at the hotel where he was staying, and on the third day, he let it be known that he was looking to buy some weapons, and explosives. "You know many people, I'm sure, Carlos. If you can think of anyone who might be able to help me, please ask them to get in touch with me."

The waiter looked guiltily up and down the bar, and spoke in hushed tones. "It would not do for you to ask too many people that question, Senhor Angell. The Guardia frown upon this sort of thing. I will give it some thought, and if I can think of anyone, I will let you know." Gabriel decided to let it rest for a while. He had seen some of the clandestine meetings that were held in a corner booth in the hotel bar, and thought it might purely be coincidence, but he had the feeling that Carlos knew exactly who to talk to about his request.

He phoned Lucifer from his hotel room, asking in vague terms how he was enjoying his stay in Madrid. "Oh, getting about, and seeing the sights, you know how it is," Lucifer answered, all too aware that the Spanish Police often eavesdropped on telephone conversations. "I've been out looking at a few vineyards in the country and talking to a few export/import merchants about the possibility of handling one or two of their best vintages. Negotiations are still going on, but it looks like being a hard bargain to be struck. We may need some extra collateral to swing the deal."

"Well, keep at it. I may be back in a day or so. I'm sourcing some additional resources right now. I may have good news in a couple of days." He put the phone down, thinking on what Lucifer had just said. He had been tasked with mapping the place out, and drawing up the actual plan of attack, whilst Gabriel had agreed to try and make contact with ETA. Lucifer's inoccuous comments had revealed that he thought it was going to be difficult. Gabriel decided to sleep on it.

Early the next morning, the phone rang, and Gabriel assumed it was Room Service confirming his breakfast order, but the voice was a different one. "There is a dark blue fiat parked outside your hotel with its engine running. It will remain there for the next five minutes, whereupon it will leave and will not return. I suggest you get into the car, Senhor Angell." The man hung up on him.

Gabriel flung back the sheets and went quickly over to the window, pulling back the drapes. He saw the car waiting two floors below, and hastily began to dress.

He left his room running. They had given him no time to make any arrangements for anyone to follow the car. If he didn't make it, the car would leave and all chance of any contact would be lost. Worse, they now knew him and his purpose here. It was up to them what they did about it. He was an easy target should they decide he was a threat, or likely to draw attention to them.

He slowed down somewhat as he went through the lobby, dropping his key on the desk, and he left the hotel, turning right to where the car waited. The rear-door opened as he approached, and he slid into the back seat, closing the door behind him. The car pulled away from the kerb as the woman sitting alongside him levelled the gun at his midriff.

He had hardly gotten over his shock when she threw him a pair of glasses. "Put these on," she ordered. Gabriel looked at them, ostensibly a pair of sunglasses, though they were in fact safety-glasses, like worn on construction site, with the lenses and side-glasses painted black. Wearing them, he wouldn't be able to see a thing, yet to anyone looking into the car from outside, he would simply appear to be wearing sunglasses, and not attract any undue attention.

Gabriel put them on, and settled back into the seat, making himself comfortable as the journey continued. He was not under immediate threat from these people. He had sparked their curiousity, and once he had satisfied it, they would decide whether to help him or not. The woman then frisked him, quickly, and professionally, though vanity persuaded him that her hands did linger overlong around his crotch, or was it his imagination?

The car turned this way and that. In the centre of the city, the taller buildings blocked the sun, so he couldn't even use that as a guide to which direction they were taking him. He was blind in the glasses, but his nose enjoyed the delightful perfume the woman was wearing.

The journey lasted just over twenty minutes, and they were still within the city, though Gabriel had no idea just where. The car pulled up, and the woman spoke softly to him. "You may remove the glasses now." Gabriel did so, eyes squinting slightly as he readjusted his vision.

High-rise apartment buildings, in sorry need of repair, towered above either side of the street. It was a long street, and Gabriel could see no indication of its name. The driver exited and opened the rear door, indicating that he should get out. Gabriel did so, glancing behind momentarily to see the woman put the gun into her handbag, and then a flash of white thigh as she moved over to exit the vehicle on his side.

Between the big oaf of a driver and the gun in her handbag, the two of them obviously felt well-assured that they were in command of the situation. From the bulge under the driver's jacket, he was also carrying a weapon too. Gabriel was unarmed, but far from helpless. He wasn't intimidated at all, but merely gave the impression for now. His curiousity was about to be resolved.

"Stefan will lead the way, Senhor Angell. Please follow him," she indicated. Gabriel smiled in return, noting a pleasing response from the woman, his eyes pointedly roaming up and then down her body. The white floral-print dress clung in all the right places. She was obviously well-used to such stares, and followed behind him as he went up the stairs after Stefan.

After two flights of stairs, Stefan lead the way down a corridor, stopping at the third door on the left, whereupon he knocked sharply twice, and stood back so that the occupants could see him clearly through the spy-hole in the door.

It opened suddenly, and Stefan stood back, beckoning Gabriel forward. He accepted the invitation and entered the flat, followed closely by the woman. Stefan closed the door behind them, remaining outside in the corridor.

There were four men in the room waiting for him. One of them stood, offering his hand, whilst the other three were sat around, two of them drinking coffee, the other reading the morning paper. The others all looked up to stare at the visitor, as if sizing him up.

"My name is Carlos. This is Juan, Jose and Manuel. Rosa, you have already met." Carlos wore what was left of his hair combed over, to hide his bald spot, and his white shirtsleeves were rolled up. Sweat marks under his arms was evidence of the lack of any working AC in the room. Juan was a lot younger, with black curly permed hair. Manuel looked of an age with Juan, though had a full head of hair, and he chain smoked by the look of his stained teeth. Washed out jeans looked a bit young on him.

Gabriel smiled as the introductions were made, and nodded briefly, pleased to see the smile on Rosa's face as she moved over to the sofa and sat down next to Jose. The white print dress with the red roses she was wearing rode up her thighs as she sat down, and she demurely adjusted her hem, aware of his eyes on her legs. His interest amused her, obviously, for she smiled deliberately up at him.

"You have been making enquiries, Senhor Angell, about weapons and men." It was more of a statement than a question. "We have such, and they are available at a price, to the right people. But how do we know you are the right people, eh? You could be a government spy, sent to infiltrate our ranks. It has been tried before," he revealed.

"I'm no spy, just a man with a mission in a foreign land. I can't complete that mission without help, and I don't have much time to get that help. My mission involves the Spanish Authorities, and you are already fighting against them. I thought you would look kindly upon my little venture and assist me with the right incentive," Gabriel explained. "Just name your price."

Juan sneered. "We fight for a cause, Senhor Angell. Money is but a means to an end. We want a totally independent homeland, and we do what we must to force the authorities to grant us that. Money is welcome, but available from many sympathetic sources. Why then should we align ourselves with you? We need a better reason," he stated.

"A friend of mine is being held at a government facility in Madrid. They are subjecting him to medical and chemical experiments, torturing him as we speak. I have only recently found out about this, and I intend putting a stop to it as soon as I am able. Your help will mean this will happen sooner, rather than later," he explained.

"Your friend's plight is a sorry one. We have had our own people taken away by the government, tortured and then killed, without the need for any trial. You have our sympathies, but not yet our assistance. The money you offer, by itself, is not enough," explained Carlos.

"What then? What can I do to persuade you to help me? If I attempt this on my own, I will more than likely end up in the next cell to my friend," Gabriel admitted.

The woman, Rosa, swung around to face him once more. "Gabriel Angell, recently with the British Special Forces, is that correct?" she asked. Gabriel nodded, silently. Their intel was obviously first class, as such information was not readily handed out. "I am familiar with your service history," she revealed. "You specialised in mountain climbing techniques, I believe?"

"Yes, that why they hired me on special secondment."

"You also excelled at munitions," she smiled coldly. Gabriel said nothing for a moment.

"Just how did you get this information?" he asked. Rosa smiled.

"Not important for now," she smiled. "But what is important is that your skills in this area can be of use to us. The Guardia last month captured our last skilled bomb-maker. We want you to teach your skills to a few of our best technicians."

"You expect me to help you bomb the populace? You can't be serious," he scoffed momentarily. Rosa shook her head.

"Senhor Angell, do not believe everything you read about us in the Press. The present government of this country deliberately sets out to sensationalise everything we do. They paint us in the blackest possible light. Yes we bomb public buildings, and yes sometimes innocents do get accidentally injured or killed, but we do our best to ensure that doesn't happen. Our enemy is the government, and you admit yourself that they are your enemy too at the moment. I will give you my word that our bombing campaign will restrict itself to only buildings instead of civilians. I will oversee this personally, if you agree to help us."

For some reason, Gabriel found himself believing her words, lost in the beauty and passion of her ideals for the moment. "I am afraid I don't have time to do any training for you. My friend's plight is urgent, and I must act soon."

"Then I will take you at your word, Senhor Angell," Rosa suggested. "Agree to do this, and we will help you first. When your friend is rescued, and safe, then we will expect you to honour your word. Is this agreed?" she asked. It seemed that she was making Gabriel an offer he could not refuse.

"Very well," he agreed.

"Good," said Jose, pleased the negotiations had been settled so quickly. "Now let us talk logistics. How many men will you need, and what do you need in the way of weapons and explosives? This all will cost money, and may take time to obtain. Of course, we will need to approve whatever plan you have for this rescue attempt. I will not risk my men on any fool suicide mission," he added. Gabriel nodded.

*   *   *

Two days later, Gabriel sat down with Lucifer, who had been busy in his absence. He opened up an A4 notebook, on which he had been making sketches of the layout of the Munez Institute. The two of them studied the rough plans together as Lucifer explained his findings.

"It backs onto the public park here to the East," he pointed. "Double wire fence around the perimeter. Lower half of both fences patrolled by dogs, usually two at any one time. Higher up and insulated from the lower part, the top is electrified, so if you manage to get past the dogs, you risk getting fried," he smiled grimly. "Two guards on the main gates, both carrying semi-autos, as well as pistols, and they are changed every six hours. They check passes on every one that goes in, and they phone someone in the building to verify they are expected."

"We either kill the dogs, or lose the power to the fence. But if we do that, someone inside is going to know about it. There are other ways we can cross, but Matthias is not likely to be able to do anything other than walk out of there, if he's still that mobile," Gabriel pointed out. Lucifer nodded.

"We have to get him out through the fence. That means the dogs go, and we'll need a large enough hole to maybe carry him out. If we use poisoned meat, they might start whining before they die. Best just to kill them quick and easy with a silenced handgun." Gabriel nodded in agreement, though he was loath to kill animals, even though these would likely be trained killers. "Once we get him out we need to get him away. There's a parking area, just across the park, where the motorway passes. We can have a transit van parked up, ready to whisk him off. The motorway should provide a quick escape route, as long as we don't take too long in the extraction."

"Yes, that's going to be the problem. I don't suppose you've been able to find much about the internals of the place?" Lucifer shook his head.

"Only what I've seen from outside." Gabriel took out the blueprints from his inside jacket pocket.

"Our new friends from ETA have contacts. They plan their bombings thoroughly, at least that's what I've been assured," he explained, as he laid out the map on the table. The two of them studied it, though Gabriel had had a good explanation from the sympathetic town clerk who had delivered the map. "This is the main research area," he pointed. "Here are the laboratories, and this is what they call a secure area meant for test-subjects, animals, monkeys . . ."

". . . and Angels?" Lucifer asked, grim-faced. Gabriel noticed the tightening of his friend's knuckles as he gripped the table.

"Easy, now," he tried to calm Lucifer down. He had seen him like this on a few occasions now, when the memories kept flooding back. He could go months with no hint of any physical or mental problems, and then all of a sudden something would set him off, and he would become unstable. "You need to calm down, Lucifer. I need you to keep focused here. Matthias is going to need us to break him free of this place." Lucifer nodded, still gripping the table edge, fighting to calm himself against this sudden panic attack. It was easing, as he concentrated. As long as he had Gabriel with him to help him focus, to reassure him. Gabriel knew what he had gone through, what Matthias was probably going through. They had to get him out of that place.

"What . . . what help will our new friends provide?" Lucifer asked, getting himself together again.

"Explosives, weapons, vehicles, a safe house and medical assistance should Matthias or any of us need it. They will also assist with the extraction. Two of them will be coming inside the facility with us. Experienced people," he assured his friend, who nodded in agreement. Four was a good number, not too many and not too few. It wasn't a big facility, and there shouldn't be too many armed guards to get past. It was just the response-time from the Guardia after the alarm went up that they had to worry about. They had to get clear within fifteen minutes. After that, they'd be chancing their luck. By-passing the alarms required accurate wiring diagrams, and such things were not easily come-by. They could get into the grounds quietly enough at night, but entering the buildings would set off the alarms for sure. That was when the countdown would begin. Fifteen minutes to find Matthias, free him and get the hell out to the waiting van in the park, and God help anyone who got in their way.

* * *

The next day, Lucifer was introduced to Rosa and Manuel, the two ETA members who would accompany them inside the facility. Stefan was also there. He would wait in the park with the transit van, ready to whisk them all away once they had carried out their objective.

They had brought the munitions with them, in a number of small suitcases. Fifteen pounds of semtex, with detonators and timers. Hand guns only, as requested, for portability. This was intended to be a quick operation, in and out as fast as they could, so they intended to travel light. The only armed resistance they expected would come from the two guards at the gate, and possibly more within the facility, if they remained on the premises during changeovers. Rosa had agreed with Carlos, that a diversion on the other side of the city would be arranged to divert the Guardia as far away from the facility as possible, and thus lengthen any reponse time once the alarms went off.

Gabriel made the bomb himself, as Manuel watched intently. A simple enough device, consisting of five pounds of explosive, packed into a cake tin, which was thin enough to transmit radiant heat and yet secure enough to be fastened to the engine block of a car. Without the use of any sophisticated timing device, a simple thermocouple was used, preheated so that the metal completed the electrical circuit to the small battery. As the thermocouple cooled, so the circuit would be broken, and the bomb would explode.

Once attached to the engine block, as long as the engine was running, the bomb would remain stable. The simple idea being that someone parked the car up outside a target building and then just walked away. As the engine cooled down, the thermocouple would cool too, and begin to retract, eventually breaking the circuit, and BOOOOM. Manuel would plant the bomb in one vehicle, before immediately returning to aid in the assault. He should have ample time during the light evening traffic.

*   *   *

Inside the Munez Institute, the two Council members Giuseppi Sarto and Annibale Della Genga, were reviewing security operations. It had been over 2 weeks since the news of Matthias' incarceration was made available to the Mafia. Gabriel must be in Madrid by now, and making his plans. The Sword of Solomon had also made its plans, and they were put into place even before Gabriel set foot in Spain.

159

Using temporary facilities in the basement of the Institute, the full contingent of guards was now permanently on site, rotating at 6 hour intervals. They could all be called upon within minutes of any announced breach of security. Each man was issued with a dart-gun, instead of his usual live ammo weapons. They wanted Gabriel alive. Dead, he was as much use as Matthias.

*   *   *

Gabriel cased the place for himself the next morning, as Lucifer did a slow drive-past in their hire-car. Two big black powerful dobermans patrolled between the fences, set about eight feet apart. Ceramic blocks insulated the lower part of the fence from the parts above, more for the dogs' protection than any thought given to intruders.

The front of the place looked normal enough, with barrier and control-booth, as you would see at the entrances to most firms. The hinged steel ramp behind the barrier would admit only, unless a switch was thrown to allow vehicles to exit. Two men in the Control Booth, one of whom was talking into a radio, which meant more men alert inside the facility. "Take me round again," Gabriel ordered, suddenly alert as one of the men stepped out from the booth to check documents on a delivery van that had just pulled up.

Lucifer took the corner slowly, then accelerating to make the circuit in the shortest possible time. They came past again, Gabriel this time using the small pair of binoculars and zooming in on the holster on the guard's belt. He was fairly knowledgeable on firearms, and that did not look like the butt of any gun he knew. Even the holster itself looked to be of a new design, such that it would break away, rather than permit the gun to be withdrawn in the normal fashion. "They know we're coming," he announced, grimly. "Dart-guns. It's been a setup from the start. Bait we couldn't afford not to take."

"We can't call it off," Lucifer complained. "We can't leave him in there."

"He might not be in there, Lucifer. But you're right, we have to go ahead with it. It's our only lead as to what's happened to Matthias. We go tonight."

*   *   *

It was just after nine o'clock when Manuel parked the car outside the Municipal Offices. Rosa was with him, to ensure that the target was secure enough. Montoya was a little rash at times, and Rosa wanted to be sure he followed orders. A diversion was all that was called for.

There were a few lights on in the upper floors of the building, but most employees had long since gone home. He locked the door, and eagerly climbed into the second vehicle that Rosa drove, and they set off for the other side of the city, Rosa driving as Carlos readied their equipment in the rear of the car.

Gabriel wanted the raid carried out, not in the early hours of the morning, but late evening when there were still enough cars on the roads and motorways so as not to attract too much attention to themselves as they made good their escape. Nothing worse than being the only car on the road for the Guardia to target. If they were expected, then they would know the soundest strategy would be to wait for them to sleep, and that was when they would be awake waiting for him. Chances are they would try and catch an early nap, and not expect him to make his assault so early in the evening.

Stefan parked the van in the car-park of the public park. One or two other vehicles were also parked up, but the courting couples therein were too busy to notice what was going on in the transit van, as Gabriel and Lucifer dressed in their assault gear, all black and armed to the teeth. Adrenaline was pumping, and Gabriel knew that he needed to keep Lucifer occupied to keep his mind off things. He couldn't afford to let him have one of his blackouts while this operation was underway.

Rosa's car pulled up about 9.15pm, and at a signal from Gabriel, four shadowy figures slipped silently across the car-park and vanished into the shrubbery, heading west toward the floodlight fence.

They stopped short, still hiding within the bushes, some yards from the fence, at the closest point, and Gabriel looked at his watch as they waited. Rosa couldn't be distinguished from a man from a distance, wearing the same all-black attire, face blacked and beret pulled down over her face, with her hair tied into a bun underneath it. She looked no stranger to this type of operation, and needed no prompting. It was obvious she was the senior hand in this ETA partnership.

They saw the flash in the night sky, even across the city's nightlights, and moments before the dull thud of the explosion could be heard. They had agreed on five minutes, and so counted down, giving the authorities time to respond to the alert. The waiting was tense, crouched down as they were in the shadows, eager to begin their assault.

All four figures finally moved as one, and Gabriel used the bolt-cutters on the links of the fence. Carlos helped peel the section of fence back as Lucifer and Rosa remained on alert for the dogs.

The first one came bounding along out of the distance, as it's sharp ears picked up the sound of the snipping of the links, it's black short-haired coat gleaming in the light of the floodlights. Trained, it didn't bark out a warning to any intruder, which meant it also didn't bark to warn the guards.

Lucifer took it down with two silenced shots in the chest, and the animal crumpled silently to the ground. In they went, moving quickly to the internal fence, and once more using the bolt-cutters. Rosa took the second dog as it came at them from the other side, despatching it just as efficiently as Lucifer had the first.

Lucifer also used his silenced gun to put out the two nearest floodlights now the threat of the dogs was over, resting the barrel across the wrist of his left hand as he took aim and fired. Unless the guards came round to check on the whereabouts of the dogs, the lack of lights wouldn't be noticed.

Using the hand-signals with which they were both familiar, the two friends moved quickly to the side door they had located earlier as their best entry point. Once inside, they would have to move quickly. Rosa and Carlos followed their lead, alert, and guns ready.

Gabriel had already prepared the charges, and he slapped one against the lock, moulding it into place, and depressing the timer. All four hastily retreated around the corner and waited for the explosion, which was surprisingly muted in the night air, with the sounds from the nearby motorway still loud enough to help mask the noise. They were under no illusions, though. Alarms would now be going off in the control room. It all depended on how fast they reacted, whether they thought it was a real alarm or not.

In they went, route already memorised, and clear enough to follow by the dim emergency lighting which was kept on inside the building. Lucifer led the way, with Rosa and Carlos behind, and Gabriel bringing up the rear.

*   *   *

The men in the control-booth used the radio to alert the men in the basement about the loss of circuit-signal at the rear of the facility. Sleepy bodies roused themselves slowly, and as Gabriel had suspected they were slow to react. Two of the additional guards decided to check it out, whilst the rest tried to get back to sleep. One of the men from the control booth went into the fenceline, walking back along the perimeter, and using a shrill high-pitched dog-whistle to attract the doberman dogs.

He walked almost to the first corner, when he realised the dogs should have answered the call by now, and he ran the rest of the way, swearing as he spotted the darkened floodlights at the rear. He unclipped the radio from his belt and put out a general alert to everyone on the facility.

He cursed as he found the first of the dead dogs, and then spotted the holes through the fence. He reported that as well. "Rear door blown off its hinges. Holes in the perimeter fence, and they've shot both the dogs. Do you want me to hold here, or follow them in?" he asked.

"Maintain position. Main force now moving to intercept. If by any chance they retreat, Gabriel is your only target. Forget the rest, just make sure you dart him."

"Understood." He put the radio back on his belt, and left through the hole in the outer fence. He took up a position hidden in the bushes, close to where the assault team had been hidden previously.

The remaining guard in the control booth alerted the two Council Members as well as the security guards in the basement. He did not, however, alert the Guardia Civil. This was meant to be a private party, and now Gabriel had accepted the invitation, they were going to ensure a hearty welcome for him.

*   *   *

Inside the complex, Gabriel was working on the lock of a closed door, using his lockpicks as he did not want to create too much noise inside the buildings. Lucifer, Rosa and Carlos were watching his back. Lucifer's sharp ears picked up the approaching footsteps around the corner of the corridor, and he dropped the first man as soon as he appeared. A single shot in the centre of his chest knocked him back against the man following, who cried out in alarm. Carlos ran quickly down the corridor, and two shots rang out as he shot the man before he could get back to his feet.

"So much for the subtle approach. Better get a move on," Lucifer advised his friend, and Gabriel felt nimbly for the tumblers to click into place. He was rewarded by the door swinging open, and they were into the secure area, filled with numerous cages full of dogs, monkeys, rats etcetera which were all used for a variety of medical experiments. The chatter and screeching increased as the humans milled about. They went in quickly, scanning the larger cages where they expected to find Matthias imprisoned.

Look as they might, they found no sign of their old friend. Frustrated, they turned their attention to the main research area, returning along the corridor, and stepping over the two dead bodies.

Gunfire opened up around them as they ran down the next corridor. Bullets ricocheted off the walls, and one or two slammed into the heavy bullet-proof vests that Gabriel and his friends were all wearing under their black sweaters. "So much for dart-guns. Looks like you were wrong, for once." Lucifer returned fire, and so did Rosa and Carlos.

"I'm the one they want to dart, not you," Gabriel pointedly reminded him, firing himself at the bunched group of guards. Lucifer swore as a bullet tugged at his pants leg, before dropping the guard with a double-tap in the chest, and then Gabriel shoved him aside, offering his own body as a human-shield whilst his friend reloaded.

Momentary confusion reigned amongst the guards, as they tried to change weapons, aware that they could not use live ammunition on Gabriel, but he was under no restrictions, firing away whenever they stuck a head out from around the corner.

Quickly, they forced their way into the research area, barricading the door behind them, with desks jammed up against it. "We'll use the explosives to blow our way out through the back wall," Gabriel announced, and then as he swung around to review the room, his jaw dropped as he took in the charts and photographs that adorned the walls. Anatomical sketches and diagrams. The main computer was still switched on, and the screen displayed a similar 3D model of an angel skeleton, with it's unique musculature and wings.

Against the rear wall of the place, were a series of large glass jars, each filled with what could only be formaldehyde, and containing human tissue of some sort. The barricaded door began to surge as the guards tried to break through. Carlos sent a couple of bullets through the door panel to dissuade them from trying too hard.

"My God, look at those things!" Rosa cried out in disgust, as she examined one of the jars and its contents. Lucifer was too busy studying the cctv camera high on the wall, which was now swivelling around to look at them, and instantly deciding to conserve his ammunition rather than blow it away.

Gabriel was speechless, stood over by one corner, staring into one of the glass jars. Inside the glass jar, Matthias's vacant eyes stared back out at him. The jar contained his head, resting limply on the bottom of the jar, and lolled to one side. The mouth was open, and Gabriel could see inside. Black hair hung limply in the clear liquid.

Lucifer went over to his friend, and then cried out, turning away in disgust, and trying hard not to vomit. Rosa and Carlos were also disgusted, but not to the same extent as the two men who were now realising that the jars on the shelves contained all that was left of their former friend.

"If that is your friend, then I am sorry, but we have risked our lives for nothing. We have to get out of here," Rosa insisted. Lucifer nodded. Gabriel said nothing. He just stood there meeting Matthias' dead gaze as though holding a mental conversation with his dead friend. "Gabriel, come on." Rosa tried to pull at his shoulder, but it was like trying to move iron. Every muscle in Gabriel's body was locked rigid, as though he had had a seizure of some sort.

"Gabriel, she's right. We must go. We can't help him now," Lucifer insisted, wiping his mouth. "They'll be coming through that door any minute, and who knows how many others have been alerted."

"Dismantle the computer. We can't take it with us, but we can take the hard-drive." Gabriel finally spoke. Grim-faced and ashen, he turned and took off his rucksack. He began taking out one of the explosive charges, and adjusting it.

Carlos gave Lucifer a hand in dismantling the computer. He quickly had it unplugged and the casing screws loosened to get at the guts of the thing, and he disconnected the heavy hard-drive, shoving it in his own pack. He turned as Rosa gasped, and found Gabriel attaching the explosive charge to the barricaded door.

"What the hell are you doing?" he asked. "We need to go through the rear wall to get into the grounds." Gabriel moulded the charge against the doorframe which still bulged as the guards outside applied their weight to it. He could hear their cries of frustrated rage as they tried to force their way in.

"I'm going out the same way I came in." Gabriel announced grimly, and he triggered the timer. "Ten second fuse. I'd take cover behind the other desks if I were you," he warned.

Lucifer, pushed Rosa down, and Carlos eagerly followed. "You fucking madman! You'll kill us all," he complained. Gabriel strode slowly, grim-faced over to the side of the room, and then crouched down. He took out his gun, and slowly cocked the hammer.

The charge went off with a large BOOOMMM, and the men outside the door didn't even have time to scream, taken completely unawares, and they were still trying to break down the door even as it exploded. Torn off its hinges, the frame of the metal door killed three, and flattened the rest of them, who now lay coughing and screaming in the corridor outside the room.

While the smoke was still billowing, Gabriel got to his feet, and slowly, deliberately, walked over to and through the doorway. He levelled the gun at the first face he saw and pulled the trigger, the loud gunshot echoed in the confines of the corridors, and red blood and grey brains splattered messily on the floor behind. He moved the gun slowly from side to side, his finger squeezing slowly, deliberately. Shot after shot after shot, stepping slowly between them. Every one of the guards who was still alive, looked the Angel of Death full in the face, and saw no mercy in those cold eyes. He executed them one after the other.

Behind him, Lucifer and the two ETA members stood looking on horrified at the cold-bloodedness of Gabriel's actions. Only Lucifer really understood what was happening here. For so many years, Gabriel had kept himself believing that there might be others of their kind alive in the world, and now to have their hopes dashed so finally. It was Gabriel who had snapped, not Lucifer.

Coming to the two wizened old men who had fallen at the rear of the party of guards, Gabriel didn't know their names, but he guessed who they were. He reloaded, calmly, as they coughed and tried to rise. He beckoned with the gun, and they got to their feet, fearful of their fate, and only too aware of the fate of their own underlings who lay at their feet in a messy pool of red. "Back inside," he ordered, and the two frightened men moved as directed back into the research laboratory.

Rosa pulled Carlos back out of the way, as he was about to intercede with Gabriel. Lucifer agreed, that now was not the time. There was no stopping what Gabriel was about to do, and part of him wanted to do the same.

"He was dead all the time, wasn't he?" Gabriel asked the question, knowing it was rhetorical. "When did he die?"

"Weeks ago," answered Annibale, drawing himself up to a height once more, as he tried to compose himself. "We were informed that some form of septicaemia had set in from the filtration process. His regenerative system had weakened from so many years of the process, and our scientists could no longer keep him alive."

"And then you butchered him," Gabriel accused.

"He was dead, damn you! We didn't intend to kill him, but he died, and in his body could lie the key to so many miracles," Giuseppi tried to defend their actions. "We were so close to synthesising your blood. Do you realise what that would mean to the rest of humanity?"

"Do you realise what 'Humanity' has done to my kind?" asked Gabriel, in return. "You killed every fucking one of us!" he accused, his voice raising. "You think that's a cheap price to pay for your fucking 'Humanity'?" He levelled the gun once more. "This place isn't a scientific establishment. Look around, it's an abattoir!" he looked up into the lens of the cctv camera. "This is your doing, Borgia!" he accused the lens. "Only you could be so cruel. Some day you'll see this. Some day you and I will meet again. Till then, remember this . . . ." and he pulled the trigger twice. Giuseppi flinched as the showering blood splattered his face, and then he too joined his fellow Council-member in death. Rosa shuddered. Lucifer and Carlos looked grimly at one another, not wanting to look at the two bodies slumping lifeless to the floor.

"Are we finished here?" Carlos finally asked. Gabriel looked slowly around, his eyes were strangely vacant, matching those of Matthias in the jar.

"Not quite. I want to leave nothing here but rubble," he spoke coldly, with no trace of emotion left in his voice. He went back over to his rucksack and pulled out the rest of the explosive charges, setting them one after the other, and then positioning them about the room. "Ten minutes from now, this place will go up in smoke. Now I'm finished." He followed silently as Lucifer and the two ETA members hastened from the room.

*   *   *

Lucifer led the way back out through the fence, holding open the links as they all filed through. None of them saw the security guard cowering in the bushes, and he made sure things stayed that way. Hearing the gunfire and explosions inside, and then seeing them come out of the building, he could only assume that all his fellow guards were now dead, and they expected him to try and capture one armed terrorist out of four with just a piddling dart-gun? Fuck them!

Chapter Fourteen

Luke watched the mpeg three times. It was grainy, and black and white. No sound made it all the more realistic. Gabriel's face was identifiable even under the blacking he had on his face, talking quite animatedly into the camera lens. He knew he was being filmed, and yet he had cold-bloodedly executed those two men. Two bullets, less than a second apart. Gabriel shot them both in the head. The black jets of blood seemed horribly more real than if they had been in technicolour.

He knew Gabriel, or at least he thought he did. What would make him do such a thing? Gabriel was his friend, yet did he really know him? People changed over the years. If everything he believed about him was true, then Gabriel could have led an entirely different life in years gone by. Still, he could only give him the benefit of the doubt, at least until he talked to him about it.

He played it back again and again. There was something not right with the footage. The tracking static only appeared when Gabriel appeared to speak, and obscured his lips. There was no sound on the mpeg. Very strange, as though someone had induced the static deliberately in an attempt to prevent Gabriel's words from being lip-read.

More worrying than the video he had found on the web, were the Minutes of the COBR Meeting on Operation Osprey. Whatever Gabriel was upto these days, obviously in collusion with the British Authorities, they were planning to stab him in the back. The SAS didn't fuck about, and if they were told to take him out along with

169

these terrorists, then that was what they would do. Gabriel had to be warned.

Luke tried the mobile number Gabriel had given him. In fact he had tried it four times now, leaving a message, but no one got back to him. He decided to attach everything to an e-mail, and he sent it off with a Priority Heading, hoping that Gabriel would read it in time. It was all he could do.

*   *   *

In Buenos Aires, Manuel collected the hard-copies of his Master's e-mail, and he remembered the boy's name from the unfortunate affair that ended in Master Lucifer's death a few years previously.

He read through the e-mail with alarm, printing out the attachments and going through the Minutes of Meeting himself. He grabbed the phone immediately, and speed-dialled his Master's cell-phone number, but the recorded message told him that Gabriel was now 'in-country'. He always left his personal effects behind on such missions. A cell-phone ringing at the wrong time, or in the wrong hands, could spell disaster if he was working under-cover. Manuel changed numbers, and phoned Madame Laura.

*   *   *

Belle noticed the colour drain from Laura's face as she took the call from Manuel. "What is it?" she asked, pulling herself upto a sitting position in the bed, the harness jingling as her leg moved.

Laura waved her to silence.

"Yes, Manuel, I understand. He hasn't been in contact for a few days, and I don't know whether he will risk a phone call. They might be watching him." Belle gathered the call was about her father, and was puzzled by her obvious concern. She waited impatiently for her mother to finish the phone call. "The bastards are going to doublecross him!" she fumed, "I knew it was a mistake to call attention to himself."

"What do you mean?" Belle asked, puzzled.

"The British Government are helping him make contact with these Al Qaeda people, but they class Gabriel as a terrorist himself. He dies with the rest of them once they can safely round them all up. They're using him as a stalking-horse to draw them out, and then the SAS are going to take them all out, your father included."

"Get me the fuck out of this thing!" Belle began struggling with the hoist that was elevating her leg. "We need to help him." Laura shook her head.

"Don't be silly. It's been less than a week since you broke it."

"My bones aren't hollow like his. I'm a fast-healer," Belle complained.

"We wouldn't know how to contact him anyway, and I doubt he'd risk contacting us. He's working with the Church on this, so they're our best hope of contacting him. I'll ring Falcone," Laura decided, and speed-dialled his number on her mobile. Belle was left pondering just how her mother had Falcone's phone number. She knew the drill once an operative was taken, all phones were changed. How did she have his current number? After a pause, Laura heard the pickup at the other end. "Marco, its Laura. Listen, the British are out to doublecross Gabriel. They plan to kill him with the rest of the Arab Terrorists. We need to get a warning to him. Has he been in touch?" she asked.

"Not in the last day or so, but I am expecting him to maintain contact. I will do what I can to alert him of their treachery when he calls," he assured her.

*   *   *

Falcone cradled the phone against his cheek after Laura had hung up. Interesting news indeed. Typical of the British Security Forces. They never liked unfinished business, and he and Gabriel were also unfinished business, both rivals for the same woman's love was how he saw it. If Gabriel was killed by the SAS, then Laura was free to return to him, perhaps not immediately, but in the fullness of time, something they both had a lot of since imbibing Blood of Christ. Falcone was nothing if not a patient man.

*   *   *

Rosa Velasquez carried out her promise to Gabriel. After making suitable enquiries amongst her terrorist network, a fax eventually arrived on Yusef Abdullah's pc at the University, containing a photograph of

Gabriel and a young woman, Rosa herself in her younger days. The woman's face was cut out of the photograph, but Gabriel's was plain to see. Attached to the photograph was a brief note, asking 'Have you seen the News today?' and gave the name and address of the hotel Gabriel had said he was using in Rome.

Yusef Abdullah, the Algerian studying the fax, was aware of the source of the material he had received, and he tuned into CNN and soon found the story being replayed, and as the disguised photo-ID was displayed, he had little difficulty in recognising the wanted man as this Gabriel, formerly of E.T.A.

Chapter Fifteen

Gabriel and Maddox flew into Leonardo Da Vinci together on the same early morning FN5867 flight, though they sat apart and gave no signs of acknowledging the other's presence. Getting in around 9am, after clearing Customs and Immigration, they each went their separate ways. Maddox was picked up by one the Embassy's cars, whilst Gabriel used a taxi to take him to the Rialto.

Maddox had many arrangements to make with the Italian authorities and had a busy morning ahead of him. The British government had been quick to support the game-plan and now Operation Osprey, as it was being called, was well under way.

Jennings, one of the Embassy 'staffers' was in the car which collected him to give him an update on things. "The suitcase you ordered is being delivered by Diplomatic Bag on the afternoon plane, sir."

"Good, Jennings. We don't want any delays on this. I have to get that case planted in Termini Station, and then pass on a 'free sample' no later than tonight. No idea when our friends are going to make contact," he mused. "What flight is the surveillance team on?"

"The same one, sir. Should be here mid-afternoon."

"Good, I want them in place no later than this evening. Those Al Qaeda people can be quite ruthless, and our stalking-horse may need all the backup he can get. Have we arranged delivery for their equipment?" he asked, euphemistically. Jennings gave a tired grin. He didn't really like getting too involved with all this cloak 'n dagger stuff.

"Yes sir, 9mm Brownings, two spare clips each. You'll have to sign for them, I'm afraid."

"What about the heavier munitions? Automatic weapons?"

"Stun grenades and explosives are being arranged through the Italian military. Semi-Automatic machine pistols, uzi's etc I've had to try more unconvential sources," Jennings revealed. "The Italians aren't too keen about us going around mob-handed, I'm afraid."

"Good man, I can't see us needing much more hardware on an operation of this size. What about the radios?"

"Personal comms equipment being sent out from Hereford, their normal gear, sir. Everything should be here today except for the semi-autos and explosives. Those are promised for tomorrow," he affirmed.

"Good job, Jennings," Maddox complimented him. "Now, take me to the Embassy, I have a few phone calls to make if we're going to pull this off."

*   *   *

Nick Turnbull arrived at Heathrow bleary-eyed and dressed casually in a polo shirt, slacks, and carrying a light jacket over his arm. He had one suitcase which was packed with a week's supply of clothing, long enough for whatever mission he was now embarking on.

Dixon was already waiting in line at the check-in, and a small nod was all that passed between them. Slightly shorter, and stockier than Nick, he wore his hair slightly long, but generally close cropped.

After Dixon was checked through, and Turnbull got closer to the counter, he noticed Coverdale and Palmer joining the queue behind him. They travelled individually, and all looked just as nondescript as he himself, wanting to draw no attention to themselves.

Coverdale slouched to disguise his taller height, and attempt to blend in more, but at five foot ten, he found that difficult. The blond hair was short and curly, like his pubes. Palmer was a dark eyed, dark haired, shifty so and so. About Nick's height, little ferret moustache disguising the thin top lip. He rarely smiled, and when he did, he looked like a rat with an excess gas problem.

"Any particular seat, sir? Aisle or window?" smiled a rather bored looking attendant.

"Why don't you just stick me next to the screaming kid, like you usually do, love?" he smiled, causing her to look up and raise her eyebrows. "Only joking, love. Anywhere will do," he smiled, mischieviously, and got a welcoming half-smile in return, charmer that he was.

Once they got through to the lounge, they sat apart. Palmer went into the bar, whilst Coverdale went to sample a little bit of the cuisine in the Italian restaurant along the concourse. Dixon took out a book, and sat down to read. Turnbull busied himself looking through WH Smith's and then the Virgin shop. He shook his head at the prices of some of the CD's. *Duty free my arse*! He mentally cursed. *Cheaper at my local supermarket*. Finally, flight BA548 was called, and Turnbull queued up to enjoy the delights of Economy Class travel once more. No chance of the tight bastards at the MOD authorising a bit of comfort.

When they finally got on the plane, he had to laugh as they asked him to play close attention to the flight stewardess (*sorry, much too fat for my taste-if she'd been anything like decent, I'd have already been paying her close attention*) as she then demonstrated the safety equipment. As for the safety instructions in the pocket of the seat in front, and their diagram of the correct crash position to be adopted, he took a close look at the proximity of his body to the seat in front. Jammed in like bloody sardines. Obviously, the only people intended to survive a crash were the nobs up front in First Class. They were the only ones who had sufficient room to adopt the crash position as shown on that card. All he could hope for was an aisle seat, so he didn't get stuck in against the fuselage, also basic as regards anti-hijack procedures, which he himself had helped tighten up for the Regiment recently.

* * *

The railway line ran up the western coast of Italy towards Rome, following a mainly northern route. It ran through valleys and hills, and crossed rivers and gorges. Where it ran through built-up areas, access to the tracks was usually fenced off in some fashion, but out in the countryside, access to the tracks was a lot less controlled. South of Formia, it ran along the coast, and where the sea cut into the coastline, a huge iron structure spanned the gap over the waves below.

Mustafa Rachid and Achmed al Wali eyed the railway bridge as they crossed via the road which ran close by. The bridge was a masterpiece of engineering, slender yet strong steelwork, interknit together to form a solid and stable platform on which the train could cross high above the water. It would take days of expert munitions-placing to bring it down, but there were far easier ways of achieving their objective.

Achmed studied the railway timetable. The express train to Rome would cross that bridge in just over an hour. Plenty of time. After they crossed the road-bridge, Mustafa pulled the car over into a lay-by, and the two men got out and went around to open the boot of the car. Achmed began taking out the spare wheel, while Mustafa took out a small, but heavy rucksack, and he backed off from the road, slipping behind the shrubbery, out of sight.

As Achmed began changing the wheel, as though he had had a puncture, Mustafa was already making his way cross-country, out of sight of the road, over the nearby hillock to the defile where the tracks ran towards the bridge. He smiled as he half-slipped down the muddy bank, for the tracks were easy to access. He didn't even need the wire-cutters. This remote area was of little interest even to ramblers.

Opening the rucksack, he took out the small but heavy limpet mine, and carefully positioned it on one of the iron tracks, lowering it slowly and energizing the electromagnet in its base to anchor it in place. Then he armed the device, and stepped back respectfully, with a grin to admire his handiwork. Today's express would be a little late.

*   *   *

The train was filled with the usual commuters, most of whom recognized each other with polite nods on their daily journey, though most were anonymous. People often preferred it that way.

Paolo was a young student on his way back to Rome after a short holiday with his Aunt after a family birthday. He had enjoyed the celebrations and meeting family and friends who managed to attend. Now it was back to the hectic life of the campus again. He had a thesis to finish by the weekend, and it was going to be hard work catching up.

As he sat there, half-reading a magazine for the second time, he couldn't help but glance at the thighs of the pretty redhead opposite him. She was engrossed in a crossword in her newspaper, and her concentration was more on that than on the hemline of her short skirt and the way she was sitting, which caused the hem of that skirt to ride up more than she would have wanted.

Paolo could see that the men sat on either side of him had noticed, too, though none of them made any move to say anything. All were too interested in the view, which was improving every time she moved around on the seat. He found it hard not to smile, or to be too obvious, and he deliberately held his magazine down to cover his crotch which had started to react of its own accord.

Stockings, she was wearing stockings. He almost moaned aloud as the darker bands at the tops of her nylons began to appear. *Go on, go on*, he willed her, fantasizing deliciously about what was waiting at the tops of those thighs.

People looked up at the sound of the explosion, startled, yet unsure of what had just happened. Then the train lurched violently to one side, and people began to scream as they were thrown from their seats.

The driver of the train was helpless, staring ahead blindly as he realized he had been de-railed, and the momentum of the train was carrying it helplessly forward towards the steel bridge. They were too close to stop in time. The brakes squealed, but did nothing with no traction. There was no stopping it, and the driver opened the cab, crossing himself and muttering a short prayer. He had only seconds to act, and he leapt from the out of control train, bouncing and rolling, before finally coming to a halt, unconscious. Everyone else on the train wasn't as lucky.

The train hit the structure still doing 80kph, and shattered the steelwork as it ploughed forward, hardly stopping. It ran forward for almost sixty meters, before the front end of the train tore through the framing structure, and toppled into space, dragging the rest of the carriages with it, one after the other, to fall the three hundred and fifty meters into the sea below, and landing with a tremendous crash, roar and spitting of steam as the boiler split open with the sudden coldness of the water enveloping it. Screams followed the carriages down, then all too suddenly ceased.

Traffic on the nearby road-bridge began to slow, and some vehicles stopped to watch in horror as the churning waters below swirled around the wreckage. Achmed slowed as well, and then kept driving right through, grinning at a job well done.

*　　*　　*

All through the afternoon, Emergency Services were swarming over the area. Police divers, helicopters and ambulance crews were standing by, but it was simply an exercise in filling body-bags. The only survivor was the driver, who was treated for shock, and gave a statement to the police about the explosion while on his way to the hospital to be X-rayed.

Railway officials examined the track, and soon confirmed suspicions. Sabotage with an explosive device. Torquemada's fifth tape was delivered to the syndicated news by early evening, and the authorities had no choice but to call off their cordon around Pisa to concentrate their efforts around where they thought the terrorists where now operating. The northern cell was now free to move South once more.

*   *   *

The flight to Rome was uneventful and Nick managed to get an hour's kip, foregoing the inflight meal as he never liked airline food. As they cleared Customs at Leonardo da Vinci, there was an Embassy guy holding a placard with their names printed on in black marker ink. Nick and the other three converged on him, and he escorted them out to the main car-park as though they were ordinary businessmen, though on a special sort of business.

Jennings told them nothing, as he knew nothing, and drove them to a hotel where they all booked in. Turnbull was to return with Jennings to the Embassy, where Maddox was waiting to brief him on the mission. The other three were left to unpack, and enjoy a few cold beers.

Maddox was waiting for him in a reserved office in the basement of the Embassy, where most of the spook operations were ran from. Secure comms were set up down there, and they were reasonably secure from prying electronics, even allowing for the fact that the Italians were considered as friends. "Nick, you look like shit. You should have taken the time to get a shower." He got up out of his chair and moved to take Turnbull's hand, shaking it. "Good to see you again, though, son."

"I'll get a shower later, Boss. You've got my curiousity all fired up with this lark. What the fuck's going on?" he asked.

"Sit down and pour yourself a cuppa," he indicated the tea trolley next to the desk. "I'll give you the real lowdown on what's happening with Al Qaeda, an old friend of mine, and your mission here in Italy."

Over the next hour, Turnbull absorbed the details of the mission, codenamed Operation Osprey. Basically to protect their stalking-horse, draw out the terrorists, and then, possibly in concert with the eyetie security services, take them out. That's all that Maddox told him, but Turnbull knew Maddox, and knew there was something being held back.

"What's the real story, Boss?" he asked. "Why 'this' team? What have you got planned?"

Maddox smiled. "Don't get too curious too soon, Nick. You might not like what I have planned, but you'll be told what you need to know when you need to know it, rest assured." That wasn't the answer Nick wanted to hear. "For now, watch Gabriel's back. He's at the Rialto, and I want at least two men with him at all times. Your comms and personal weapons will be delivered to you tonight, and your other gear should be here by tomorrow, so get things moving no later than a.m. first thing, whether it's here or not. We can't afford any slip-ups."

"I'll brief the others tonight, and we'll work out a box to keep him in. Has he been told to expect us? I wouldn't want to piss him off and let him think we're the opposition." Maddox smiled ruefully at that last remark, and Nick caught the change in the expression. "Boss?"

"Not now, Nick." Maddox cut him short, lost in his own thoughts. He knew Whitehall's orders, and he also knew Turnbull wouldn't like them. Gabriel was his friend, and he knew that Turnbull having met him only briefly, had felt a comradeship towards him, as did most ex-SAS amongst their own. Turnbull stared him down, waiting there silently. "Nothing is set in stone, Nick. Allegiances can change, depending upon how this operation pans out. Let's wait and see, eh?"

Turnbull accepted the answer reluctantly and took the offered documentation that Maddox had prepared, photos of Gabriel, maps of the area, with Gabriel's present location marked. Copies of bus and train timetables, phone numbers of taxi-ranks etc. Four mobile phones

"Keyed in to each other, as a back-up in case you have problems with your comm-gear" explained Maddox. Turnbull smiled. It made a change for someone to think of backups. Most ops went wrong at some stage. You could never second-guess everything, and the Regiment had had its fair share of bad luck on some operations. "One more thing," Maddox went on, and pulled two more photos out from a folder on his desk. One photo was recent, and grainey, the other was old and a bit dog-eared, but showed a similarly dark-haired beauty. He handed them to Turnbull. "The first photo is the only terrorist we have positively been able to identify as yet. Her name is Fatima Khalid. She is currently being held incommunicado by the Israelis. The second photo is of the Mossad agent who is impersonating her, working undercover currently with one of the Al-Qaeda cells. If spotted, make sure she comes to no harm."

Turnbull studied the photos well. Physically similar, though one a bit younger than the other, maybe not if the photo was as old as he guessed. Processing had improved over the years, and this one could be a few years old from the state of it. It was nice to know they might have a bit of inside help. Mossad were good. He had worked undercover in Ireland for a couple of tours, and knew what that sort of stress could do to you.

*   *   *

That night, back in their hotel, which was on the next street to the Rialto, Turnbull, Dixon, Palmer and Coverdale met for Turnbull to relay the mission stats. "Heavy stuff should arrive tomorrow, if we need it, so S.O.P. We'll have him in a box whenever he's on the street. I'll direct movements from the rear. Two of us will hang about in the lobby of the hotel, while he's inside. I'll arrange a meet with him myself to make sure he's on ball with what's going down around him."

"Piece of cake," said Dixon, confidently. "These ragheads won't know what's hit them."

"We've got to find them first," cautioned Coverdale. "Without those rags on their heads, they all look the fucking same."

*   *   *

Gabriel had checked into the Rialto under the alias of Aguila, a nom de plume he often used, and with assorted false papers to back up that identity. He had nothing with him apart from the clothes he was wearing and some which he had transferred from the rental car, when he had changed that. His knives were discreetly hidden within the clothing, as was a small Beretta .25 and three clips of ammunition.

A small package was delivered to him that evening by the concierge, and he found it contained a small padded box, with a vial of pale yellow liquid, carefully stoppered and hermetically sealed. With it came a key, and a brief note identifying which left-luggage locker in the Termini Station it would open. He would wait in the hotel until contacted by the Al-Qaeda terrorists themselves if Rosa had done her job effectively.

He took the phone-call as he relaxed on the bed, watching a movie. "Yes?"

"Turnbull. We met in Wales. I'll be knocking on your door in a few minutes." The phone disconnected. Gabriel hung up the receiver. Yes, he remembered the younger man. Jim held him in high regard. It would make sense that Maddox would do his best to look out for him and watch his back.

He got up, and put the small box with the vial of supposed nerve-agent out of sight. Turnbull knocked on the door a couple of minutes later, and Gabriel opened it cautiously. Turnbull smiled as he held out his hand. "Nice to meet you again, Guv." Gabriel shook the hand warmly.

"Come on in. I guess Jim's got his best team on the job, eh?" He closed and locked the door behind Turnbull. The younger man frowned as he replied.

"Not what I'd call his best team, personally, but good enough to get the job done. We're here to watch your back, so I just want to go over a few things with you to make sure we can cover you adequately, and you know where not to go and what not to do, to get away from us."

"I suppose things have changed a bit since my time with the Regiment," Gabriel mused, and then they sat down and he listened as Turnbull updated him on surveillance procedures. Effectively two men ahead, and two behind at all times, one on either side of the street, controlled by secure-comms from behind, with Turnbull in charge. He fished out a set from his jacket pocket for Gabriel himself to use, and Gabriel was surprised at how compact they'd made it these days.

"Just wear it when you can. If you think you might be heading for a contact, then ditch it. We don't want them finding you wearing any sort of wire," he warned. Gabriel nodded.

*   *   *

Torquemada took the news from Yusef Abdullah in one of his scheduled calls. Yes, he had heard of the raid in the British Germ Warfare Research Centre. Was it coincidental that the man responsible was here in Italy? Maybe not, as Italy was a central location for most of Europe and the Mediterranean countries. "What word do you have of the shipment we are expecting?"

"There were problems," Abdullah reported truthfully. "Our first attempt at delivery was compromised by the Italian Coast-Guard, but we are now sending a second consignment overland, hopefully with more success. It is difficult to transport such materials, as you know," he reminded.

"So, it may be best to consider alternatives. Is that what you are saying?"

"Indeed." Abdullah did not believe the promises of these people when it came to his own safety, and he planned to be far away from Rome when the operation reached its inevitable climax.

"Very well, we will adjust our plans accordingly, and make preparations to take advantage of fortunate circumstances. You have contact information for this man, I take it?"

"Yes. A contact of mine in ETA passed this information on to me. He is staying at the Rialto Hotel in Rome, under the name of Aguila."

"Very well, I will arrange to make contact with this man, and see if these 'goods' of his can be of use to us."

*   *   *

The next day, Turnbull and his men set up shop around the Rialto. He and Dixon milled around the lobby, one or the other going out to take refreshment in a nearby coffee-bar. Palmer and Coverdale were acting similarly out on the streets, pretending to shop, yet staying close by should the need for movement or response be required.

Nothing happened until that evening, when two men came in off the street, and Turnbull overheard them talking at the desk, enquiring about a Mr Aguila. Dixon was out on the street. He was on his own. His call. The two men nodded politely, and made to move away from the desk. Turnbull was ready to move, but the two men walked back towards the entrance to the hotel. Nick keyed in his throat mike. "Dixon, two men coming out the front of the hotel. I want photos. Don't blow it. Don't alarm them in any way, and let them walk. Just get the photos, okay? They'll be back, and we'll be waiting."

"You got it, Nick. See them coming now. Dixon out," came the response. For all of his personal dislike for the man, Dixon was a good soldier.

*   *   *

Abdul Aziz and Mohammad al Shair had driven down the autostrada through the afternoon and early evening, and had paused at the hotel to confirm their man was inside. They would spend the night at the villa booked for them by the Algerian, and make contact with this Aguila tomorrow. It had been a long drive, and they wanted to relax and refresh themselves. He was going nowhere, and would wait until they were more wide awake.

Dixon walked on the opposite side of the street, the small low-light camera held in his hand at waist height, but the wide angle lens would ensure he got the shots he needed of the two men. The camera had been used before on surveillance stakeouts with good results. By tomorrow, they would have photos to circulate among the security forces, and someone somewhere would put names to these two faces.

As Gabriel slept, the film was delivered to the Embassy and developed on the premises. Maddox scanned the blow-ups himself and e-mailed them back to The Hague, Hereford and to all his contacts Europe-wide and especially to Alexi Davidovich in Jerusalem. He wanted names and known affiliates by morning. The jigsaw was starting to take recogniseable shape.

*   *   *

Kovacs and Grechko were managing to stay one step ahead of pursuit. Rival factions of Mafiya as well as the authorities in Kazakhstan, were now actively trying to hunt them down. A safe house was no longer as safe as it used to be. The two men traveled less inconspicuously these days, no more fancy cars and fancy suits, lest they draw too much attention to themselves. They were being forced to move at least once a week, as the authorities (more familiarly known as the old KGB Mafiya) kept hot on their trail and the reward offered for information leading to their arrest was substantial. Kazakhstan was a big place to hide in, with little, if underdeveloped, infrastructure.

All the physical evidence had been shredded, once Kovacs had realized Lesya had gone to ground. She had obviously had contacts, and one of those contacts was in collusion with the KND. He had beaten a hasty retreat just before the special task force had arrived to engage his own men in a gun-battle. All they had was photographic evidence, which being digital could not be relied upon, and the testimony of the young woman who had taken the photos. Remove her from the equation, and Kovacs was virtually home free. He had his informants working very hard to find that young woman.

The dacha they were living in was a small one, used as a country retreat by one of Kovacs' business acquaintances, and loaned to them under duress. It should be safe there for a while. Grechko was unpacking the groceries in the kitchen, when he heard Kovacs' cellphone go off in the living room. He didn't mean to overhear the conversation, but Kovacs had a particularly gruff voice.

"Yes? That's good news, at last," he sounded relieved. "Where are they hiding her? What? What the fuck is she doing there?" He sounded half-amused. "It would seem as though the authorities don't really know what's going on. In trying to hide her, they've put her right where I can get to her. I already have people there I can use for this. She shouldn't be too hard to find, a lonely Kazakh in Rome. One more tourist won't make much difference with everything else going down over there at the moment," he chuckled. "Thank you for the news, Ilya. I will remember you, my friend," he promised. Grechko was frozen for a moment as he realized that by getting out of Kazakhstan Lesya had jumped from the frying-pan into the fire. He knew details of the operation, and knew Kovacs had loaned Russian Mafia assistance to Al-Qaeda through their Muslim Chechnyan connections. It would be a simple enough favour to ask of them to help eliminate the girl. "Good news at last, Pyotr," Kovacs called out, and then came into the kitchen as Grechko continued to store away the groceries. He had always been used to catering for himself, whereas Kovacs had grown too used to having people pander to his whims.

"Oh, what is that?" Grechko pretended not to have overheard the conversation.

"Your little friend is in Italy, probably Rome, though I'll get my associates over there to make enquires and verify her whereabouts. Then we need to arrange a little accident for Miss Romanova. A fatal one," he smiled, coldly.

*   *   *

After dinner that evening, as Kovacs settled down in front of the television to enjoy a cigar and a large brandy, Grechko excused himself, on the premise of checking the grounds. He took his cellphone with him as he went out of the rear door. The evening air was crisp, though the breeze and wind-chill were fortunately light. His sweater was warmth enough against the cold. He speed-dialled the number of Lesya's mobile phone, hoping against hope that he could make the international connection. He held it upto his ear, and listened to it beep annoyingly.

'The mobile number you have tried to reach, is currently unavailable. The party is either not switched on, or outside our network area. Please leave your message after the tone.' Grechko swore under his breath. Nothing for it. "Lesya, it's me, Pyotr. Kovacs knows where you are. He's sending people after you. Get to the nearest police station, or the embassy. They'll know how to advise you from there."

"That's not very clever, Pyotr!" came a cold gruff voice from behind him, and Grechko slowly turned to see Kovacs stood there, pointing a gun at his mid-section. Pyotr dropped the cellphone, guiltily. "You're a fool, Pyotr, and I have no time for fools." Kovacs pulled the trigger before Grechko could move, hitting him once in the chest, and sending him spinning to the ground with the close-range impact of the bullet. He fell hard, rolling once, and then, groaning in pain, slowly tried to raise himself up off the ground. Kovacs stepped up behind him, pressed the muzzle of the gun against the back of his head, and pulled the trigger a second time. This time Grechko did not get up.

*   *   *

The next morning, Gabriel was slightly nonplussed when he saw that Nick Turnbull was sat across the hotel restaurant reading a newspaper, as he came down for breakfast. He looked up momentarily, catching Gabriel's eye, and then pointedly changed his grip on the periodical, holding it up with two fingers splayed in a Victory-V. Fuck off or Fuck you? Gabriel puzzled for a moment. Then he flourished the paper again, to make sure he caught Gabriel's attention, still using the same odd grip, and Gabriel took a slow casual look around the restaurant, noticing as his eyes passed them by, the two men sat at one of the other tables, who were taking an unusual amount of interest in him. Good to know that Jim was covering his back. He was carrying, and he expected Turnbull to have at least one weapon on him, also. Jim was a good judge, and he rated young Turnbull highly, so he felt in safe hands.

The two men were eating breakfast, as he expected, though the larger, older man had a number of side-dishes filling up his table. He obviously enjoyed his food. Ignoring them, Gabriel made his way to a table towards the rear of the restaurant, close to the kitchen doors, and proceeded to order his own breakfast. As he ate, his eyes casually scanned the restaurant, absorbing details of the other occupants, besides Turnbull and the two probable terrorists. He was confident that there were only the two men to worry about, and between him and Turnbull, they seemed to have things under control.

It was whilst Gabriel was starting on his coffee that the two men stepped away from their table and finally approached him. They moved normally, adopting no threatening pose. Gabriel allowed himself to look up at their approach. "Signor Aguila? Do you mind if we join you?" the older man spoke, smiling affably. Gabriel acted non-plussed, and shrugged his shoulders, as they pulled out chairs and sat at his table. "We believe you are in Rome to negotiate the sale of certain pharmaceuticals?" the older man spoke again.

"You seem to know more about me than I do about you," Gabriel commented, and beckoned the waiter over to order more coffee. "Two more cups, please, for my friends."

"Oh, we are most assuredly your friends, Signor Aguila," the younger man spoke this time. "My name is Mohammed, and my friend's name is Abdul. We are interested in this product you have for sale," he smiled. Somehow Gabriel didn't believe they could ever be friends, but he went along with the charade of talking around the real purpose of this meeting, as Arabs tended to do out of politeness.

"If you have heard of this 'product', I take it you know its value? Ten million, US dollars not lira. Not a penny less," he smiled smugly.

"That is ridiculous!" protested Abdul. "Where can we raise that amount of money?"

"The fact that you are sitting down here with me discussing it, means that you already have access to those funds, or you wouldn't be wasting my time," Gabriel smiled affably. "The product is airborne, virulent, and very effective. It is well worth the money, and I took considerable risks to get it here."

"How virulent?" asked the younger man. Gabriel smiled.

"The stock currently in my possession could take out a sizeable part of a large city, if released in the right place. Of course that would depend upon the weather and wind-strength. Rain would of course dilute it and prevent it's delivery over so great a distance." He could see the gleam in the mens' eyes as he spoke, and they imagined the effects of the nerve-agent he was offering.

"It is still a great sum of money," Abdul complained still. "We will need to consult with our superiors, and I am sure they will want to see some sort of demonstration."

"I am sure something suitable can be arranged," Gabriel smiled confidently.

"We will be in touch." Mohammed spoke, as both men stood up and stepped back away from the table. They nodded politely as they turned to leave. Gabriel made a hand-signal to Turnbull as they walked towards the exit, and Turnbull let them go. Then he got up and slowly moved into the corridor. After signing the receipt, billing his room for the breakfast, Gabriel left the restaurant too, and found Turnbull waiting by the lift. It came, and they both got in. Turnbull spoke as the doors closed.

"The big guy is Abdul Aziz. Yemeni. His sidekick is Mohammed al Shair. Saudi. Both nasty pieces of work," Turnbull confirmed.

"Glad to know Maddox is still as good as ever. If you know them, then they're not the real targets. Our boy is a newcomer, I'm sure. A dangerous newcomer. He might be new to the game, but he's playing it damn well, and we'd better find him before he hones his skills," Gabriel warned.

"Give them some rope, then?" suggested Turnbull.

"Yes, until we can nab more of them. Take them out now, and you would just alert the others. I'm offering them something they can't resist. They'll be back, and hopefully Torquemada will be with them. They won't trust that amount of money to just any underling."

"The Italian coast-guard intercepted a boat the other day," Turnbull mentioned. "It was registered in Sofia, and supposedly with an illegal shipment of gold bars on board. They got a tip-off from one of the spooks operating on the ground over the water." Gabriel looked up, a bit bemused at the comment. "When they boarded, turned out it wasn't gold at all, just gold paint covering lead, shaped to look like ingots. Guess what was under the lead?" Turnbull asked, and Gabriel made the connection. "Maddox was alerted some time ago to a possible illegal shipment of nuclear waste material out of Kazakhstan, via Chechnya. Seems like someone is trying to get it into Italy. I wonder what for?" he mused, though both men knew the reason why.

Gabriel's earlier reasoning was right. This was no ordinary terror-strike. It was a planned campaign, and it looked like climaxing in one big bang!

Chapter Sixteen

Gabriel took the call in his hotel room later that night. "Yes?"

"This is Abdul. We met this morning," he reminded Gabriel, before continuing. "My superiors have agreed the fee. One million US dollars paid up front tomorrow, as a token of good faith. You will then provide evidence of the effectiveness of your 'product', and if successful, we will arrange payment of the balance within the week. Is this acceptable?" Gabriel pretended to consider.

"Very well. I will give the demonstration some thought overnight. Pick me up at 10am tomorrow outside the hotel." He put the phone down as the other party hung up. Taking the secure-comms from beneath the mattress, he fastened the throat mike and keyed the send button. "Our friends have been in touch. They want a demonstration arranging for tomorrow. You'll need wheels. I hope Maddox has been moving behind the scenes."

*   *   *

Belle gritted her teeth as she forced herself to move, dressing herself under protest from her mother. "I'm okay. The leg's just a bit sore. I'll manage," she insisted.

"You're as stubborn as he is." Laura complained.

"I thought I got it from you," Belle smiled, antagonizing deliberately.

"Keep it up and I'll break the other one for you," Laura warned, only half in jest. It was still awkward dealing with an adult when you found she was suddenly your child. They were both still adjusting to their newfound relationship.

"Stop bickering, mother. He's in trouble and he doesn't know it. His allies are limited. He needs our help," Belle insisted.

"Are you going to use the crutches, or not?" Laura asked. Belle glowered at her in return. Laura shrugged, and rested them against the wall, though she really wanted to insert them somewhere where they would hurt her daughter a lot. "Okay, be vain then."

"Honestly, my leg is okay. I can walk on it. Look," and she crossed the room, slowly but steadily.

"Okay, but don't overdo it. You're healing fast because it's in your blood, from your father, but bones knit better when you let them take their time. You don't want to end up with a deformed leg," Laura cautioned her.

"Falcone hasn't responded to that call you made, mother. Does Grimaldi know anything?" Belle asked, changing the subject and immediately putting Laura on the defensive, which was Belle's aim.

"I haven't been in touch with him, yet," she answered. "I thought the Church might have a better handle on this, as Gabriel is supposedly working closely with them." Laura watched her grown-up daughter sit down in front of the dresser-mirror to start tidying her hair. Laura helped, using scissors and comb, to try and get the hair cut into a style she liked, much shorter than she was used to, as a result of the fire-damage.

Under protest, Laura finally called Donatello Grimaldi, as Belle went into the bathroom to wash her hair out. "Donatello, it's me, Laura. I was wondering if Gabriel had been in touch over the last few days. I haven't heard from him and I need to get an urgent message to him. Very urgent," she stressed.

"I am sorry, Madame Laura," Donatello apologized, "but I also have heard nothing. I understood that he was relying on older acquaintances to gain access to these terrorist cells, someone from E.T.A." Laura remembered the conversation she had had with Gabriel the last night she had spent with him. Rosa. Who the hell was she and how could she find her? She couldn't very well contact Maddox, because he was in on the plot to kill Gabriel. Keep your friends close and your enemies closer. Wasn't that what they said? Bastards! She heard feminine laughter in the background, and remembered the houseguest that was staying with

Donatello and Marianne. "I need to find him, Donatello. Please, do what you can. Get him to contact me urgently."

"Very well. I will have my people search, but if they spot him, there is a chance that other people may spot my people. You see how it is? That is why Gabriel wanted me to keep clear."

"I understand Donatello, but his life may depend upon the information I have for him, so he's at risk either way," she insisted. She hung up as Donatello replaced the receiver at his end. She called Falcone once more, and waited for him to pick up. In the bathroom, she could hear Belle using the hairdryer. "Marco?" she queried, as the phone was answered.

"Si?"

"Marco, its Laura. Have you heard from him? I have to warn him of what they're planning to do to him."

"Laura, I have promised to do what I can, but I have my limits. Gabriel gave me little details about what he was planning to do, and he warned me, quite explicitly, to stay out of his way. He is working in areas where the Church is weak, and that is why we sought his aid. With his previous terrorist associations, I am sure he will be in a better position than we to understand the mindset of this Torquemada. I have no idea if he is even still in Rome. All I can do is alert my people to watch for him and report back if sighted. Unless he contacts me, or we get lucky, there is little else I can do."

"Try, Marco. Try hard," Laura pleaded. "As soon as he gets in touch, he must know of their plans. He can't afford to trust his so-called allies." She hung up, reluctantly.

*　*　*

"No, my dear Laura. He certainly cannot," Falcone chuckled softly to himself, as he put down the receiver.

*　*　*

"I take it your boyfriend can't help?" asked Belle as she reappeared from the bathroom as Laura was hanging up the phone, just in time to catch the end of the conversation. Laura flushed.

"Ex-boyfriend. Get it right." Her hackles were rising. It was a touchy subject.

"You never did explain how you came to have his new phone number, mother," Belle pointed out. "I was one of the inner circle for a time. I know how regularly those numbers get changed. Borgia could be paranoid on security issues."

"We keep in touch, that's all," she answered defensively. Belle smirked.

"Does my father know?"

"What? That we keep in touch, or that we used to be lovers?" There, she had admitted it to her.

"Both. I doubt he'd be pleased to find out."

"Is that a threat?" Laura stood firm.

"Hardly. I don't want him hurt, and I don't want you hurt either. Are you having second thoughts about him? You spent the last 50 odd years apart, remember. Most of that time you hated him. People do change with time."

"No, certainly not. At least I don't think so. I know Marco is still sweet on me, and I don't hate him, now we're no longer together, so I don't see any reason why not to stay in touch. He was loving, tender once. Then either he or I changed, and I just wasn't attracted to him anymore. I went through a lot of changes myself in those fifty odd years," she admitted, a shadow coming across her face momentarily. "We still talk sometimes, though. He always was a good sounding-board for me, whereas Gabriel too often goes off into his moody silences," she explained.

"I've known Falcone a while myself, as you know. He always struck me as cold and calculating. I wouldn't put too much faith in him. He always did have his own agendas, and even Borgia and Ratti never knew what they were. He liked to think of himself as the power behind the throne. He always seemed to come up trumps though, I'll give him that. Always came up with the goods. So let's hope he's genuine when he says he wants to help." Belle left Laura to think that one through. As for herself, she had her contacts in the Red Brigades. Perhaps they would be able to offer some assistance here.

*   *   *

The pickup was prompt. A black audi came to a halt outside Gabriel's hotel as he came out from reception into the hot sunshine. Abdul was driving, and Mohammed opened the rear door to let him climb inside. Across the street, Turnbull keyed his throat mike, and a white fiat, with Dixon driving, picked him up. They set off in pursuit of the black audi. "He's heading north, now changing east at the intersection," Turnbull spoke into the throat-mike, letting Palmer and Coverdale know which way the terrorist's car was traveling. "Look's like Gabriel is giving them directions. Keep an ear out. If he changes again I'll shout. Try and get in front of him if you can, but keep well clear. We don't want this going sour at this stage."

*   *   *

Inside the black audi, Mohammed stared at the little insulated box that Gabriel had on his lap as he gave directions. Gabriel had thought about this demonstration a lot, knowing it would be required, and wondering how he could pull it off. He opened the box carefully, revealing the single vial of lemon colored liquid. "Is that it?" asked Mohammed. "Such a small thing can do so much damage?" he asked, incredulous. Gabriel nodded.

"In a confined space, this stuff is as deadly as they come. It turns into a clear odourless gas upon exposure to the atmosphere. I don't know how they worked that one out, as you don't have time to smell it anyway if you're too close," he added. "Effects are almost instantaneous. The body's nervous system goes into shock, spasming uncontrollably, and the lungs shut down. Death in minutes. Quite painful I believe. Fortunately, its effects get diluted in a strong wind. Best application is in a building with a sealed ventilation system, but beggars can't be choosers. This little demonstration will be public, and we'll need to get away quickly before we get a whiff of the stuff ourselves," he warned. Mohammed nodded, as if understanding. In the front driver's seat, Abdul was sweating, understanding only too well just how virulent the contents of that single small test-tube could be. He had had experience of chemical weapons, and seen their effects.

"Where do you plan to show us this demonstration?" Mohammed asked.

"As I said, better in a confined space, but as we need to do this outdoors, I thought it best to do it somewhere there will be crowds for maximum effect, regardless of the weather. Keep going east, then take a left at the big roundabout at the end of the street. That should take us to the museum. They have daily bus trips of tourists at this time of the day," he explained, and Mohammed smiled.

*   *   *

The Museum of Antiquities was set on one side of a one way street, where a lay-by existed to drop off tourists. The road was too narrow for parking, and there was a slip-road which led to a car-park at the rear, where the buses waited for pick-up, leaving by a separate street entirely. One such bus was just disembarking its load of tourists as the black audi slowly came down the street. Behind them, Turnbull's fiat turned off. "It's going down. Repeat. It's going down. Regroup north at the crossroads and we'll pick them up as they come out of the one-way system," he instructed Palmer and Coverdale in the other car currently running parallel to their own down an adjacent street.

*   *   *

The group of tourists milled around a tour-guide, as the bus pulled away and turned off towards the car-park at the rear. The guide was obviously explaining the various architectural features of the old and weathered building, and some of them were avidly pouring through their guide books.

The black audi approached slowly, and Gabriel rolled down the rear window, readying the fragile glass test-tube in his hand. "Get ready. We won't have much time," he warned Abdul, driving. Abdul nodded nervously. Closer, closer, less than ten yards now, and one of the tourists looked up as Gabriel's arm came out, throwing the yellow tube high in the air. Two of three others also caught the action, and then someone cried out.

Gabriel was already winding the window furiously up, before the fragile glass shattered on the pavement next to the throng, leaving a dark wet splash, such a simple thing, and yet all at once people began panicking, throwing themselves on the floor, shuddering, spasming, screaming, their arms and legs threshing wildly, like ants sprayed with insecticide. Mohammed had seen nothing like it, as he stared out of the rear window as the audi passed the stricken throng. "Drive." Gabriel instructed Abdul, who floored it, terrified at what little he had seen out of his rearview mirror, and keen to get away from any possible contamination himself. "Put a couple of miles between us and the museum, before you change direction. Give the wind plenty of time to clear the air," Gabriel advised.

*   *   *

The museum became the centre of a media circus by lunchtime, with a widespread cordon around it to keep the public and the press at a distance. Government vehicles and men in strange white chemical suits were snapped by eager Paparazzi, desperate for an exclusive for tonight's news. Evening papers circulated the story of a massive chemical spillage, in line with what was visible outside and inside the police cordon. A number of deaths were reported. Investigations ongoing, it claimed.

Torquemada smiled as he watched the story unfold on the television. That would work, he mused. That would work nicely, thinking ahead.

*   *   *

Gabriel had been dropped off back at his hotel later that morning, with a briefcase filled with newly laundered American currency to the tune of one million dollars. He had remained there, waiting for Turnbull or Maddox to report back in. He was still watching the re-runs on the television of the 'chemical-spillage' outside the museum. Twenty three deaths reported, and six people on respirators, conditions described as 'serious'. The day's events had gone well, and by now Turnbull and his men should have a handle on the Arabs' base of operations. It was a place that would be immediately put under surveillance. Now that they were impressed with the goods he had to offer, and considered him more or less trustworthy, he expected to be contacted further. The bigger fish would start to swarm. The bait had been dangled, and the hook was set. He just needed to land his catch.

The stage for today's performance had been arranged a few days ago, after Gabriel had had word from Maddox that the Italian authorities were prepared to play ball. Their own people were eager to be seen to be getting involved in this operation, even if all they had to do was play-act. Realising the need for a realistic and dramatic demonstration of the supposed nerve-agent, the museum had been chosen as a place they could effectively control and easily cordon off to create the right effect with the news media.

Operatives from the Italian armed forces had played the part of the tourists, warned what to expect, and held in abeyance until Turnbull and his men had radioed ahead to arrange their 'arrival' at the museum, just ahead of the terrorists' car, so everything looked natural enough. No one had known the supposed effects of the substance supposedly being thrown at them, so some of the performances were a bit over-dramatic, but it had had the desired effect. When the test-tube had shattered on the pavement, they had all reacted instantaneously, as though really exposed to some sort of nerve-gas, and the two Arabs had been convinced of its potency. All then that remained was to ham it up for the media, cordon the area off and let enough people in chemical suits be seen and photographed. The authorities would be expected to play down the incident, and not admit to an act of terrorism, and that was the official line, just a 'chemical spill'.

Maddox phoned him early in the evening. "Okay, we've located their base. It's a small villa in its own grounds, to the north of the city. So far, just the two men there as far as we can see. Palmer and Coverdale are staying there till we can get the Italian Security services to take over under cover of darkness, nothing too obvious, don't worry. But we need wire-taps and monitoring equipment in place by daylight. Turnbull and Dixon are now back covering you at your hotel, just in case."

"Your concern for my welfare is touching, Jim," Gabriel joked, though Maddox paused before replying.

"We'll take good care of you while this operation is underway, Gabe. Turnbull is a younger version of you, just not as sarky!" he chuckled. "You can trust him. As regards the villa, it's set in its own grounds, with an underground garage, and a security system in place that we'll need to breach should there be a need to go in. We're finding out about it as we speak, who leased it, plans lodged with the authorities by the builder, that sort of thing. You know the drill," he reminded him.

"Someone has thrown plenty of money at this operation, arranging all this. It would be nice to find out who was working away behind the scenes," Gabriel agreed. "Always follow the money. Have someone collect this down-payment tomorrow, and put your lab boys onto tracing it if you can," he suggested.

"My thoughts, exactly. We need a clean sweep, to not only prevent this, but to set an example to Al Qaeda not to fuck with us. The face of the world is changing. It's time they came out of the Dark Ages and accepted that. I respect another man's beliefs and religions, even when I don't agree with them. Time they learned a bit of tolerance, too."

"And on that sobering thought, I think I'll turn in for the night," Gabriel yawned. "Goodnight then. Tell Turnbull I'll be awake by eight am, no later."

"Goodnight, Gabe." Maddox put down the phone.

Gabriel undressed and got into bed. He would put the briefcase in the hotel safe tomorrow morning, until Maddox could send someone to collect it. They might be able to trace the serial numbers of the notes. He was thinking of Laura, wondering if he should chance phoning her, but then he smiled as he thought of the 'fun' she would be having in trying to make Belle behave herself and recuperate properly. 'Headstrong' hardly did her justice. Their daughter was quite a willful woman. Might be too much of a risk to do it from the hotel, just in case those Arabs had managed to arrange to have his calls monitored, but he could possibly ask Turnbull to do it for him, via the secure-comms link? He would give it some thought, overnight.

*   *   *

As Gabriel settled down for the night, the two women uppermost on his mind were out and about. Laura had finally agreed that they needed to take action themselves, and so the two of them were out visiting old contacts, both with the Sword of Solomon organization and the more seedy side of the underworld, where members of the dormant Red Brigades still hung out.

They met up back at the hotel suite, shortly before midnight, where Belle had a confident smile on her face. "You obviously had better luck than me. What did you find out?" Laura asked impatiently.

"I couldn't ask too many questions, as I've been out of touch with the organization for quite a while. Whilst they've been quiet, there was no need for the Church to keep tabs on them. However, I did find out that a former member now runs a club in the inner city, and he still keeps his hand in with the Brigade. Some of them frequent the club. So he's our likeliest starting point. He was an activist with the Brigades in the eighties. We'll have to go back to my apartment for a change of wardrobe. We're not exactly dressed for a night out like this," she pointed out.

"What's the catch?" Laura asked. She was learning to read her daughter well. Belle grinned.

"The club is called Mondo Bondage, it's an S&M club run by a slimeball called Gianni Varadi. He and I aren't exactly friends. You'll need to catch his eye and get me in there."

*　　*　　*

"You have such a suprising wardrobe, Belle dear," Laura said, sarcastically, going through some of the interesting articles in Belle's wardrobe. Leather, latex, you name it, it was in there. Belle smiled back.

"Choose something more sexy than stylish. The bastard has no taste whatsoever," she grinned. Laura picked out one of the latex outfits, holding it up against her body and checking herself in the mirror.

"How do you get into one of these things anyway?" she asked, feeling how clingy the latex could be.

"Talcum powder helps," Belle offered, chuckling at the expression on her Mother's face.

"You couldn't wear anything under this," Laura protested.

"That's the whole idea."

"Why me, anyway?"

"Because he likes blondes with big tits, and because last time I saw him, I put him in hospital, traction too, if I remember correctly," Belle smiled in fond remembrance.

*　　*　　*

The taxi driver hardly batted an eye as he picked up the two women outside Belle's apartment. Nightlife in the Eternal City was getting wilder. The long-haired blonde wore black leather, a single short piece, slit up her right thigh, and zipped up her back. A studded collar and thigh-length black leather boots finished the ensemble, with a small Gucci black purse, just big enough to keep a small handgun in. Belle had gone for the red latex, and high heels, and the soft rubber clung to her body like a second-skin, especially her ass, which the taxi driver almost couldn't resist reaching out and caressing, as she stooped to get into the rear of the vehicle. Her own purse contained nothing more deadly than a small pocket knife, but it was deadly enough in her hands. He wasn't surprised by the address of the club they wanted to go to, and he knew the way.

The club was noisy and well-patronised, with the usual long queue waiting outside to get in, but like most clubs, gorgeous girls were always ushered to the front by the bouncers, and both women got a friendly goose as they were allowed in, as the hopeful bouncers tried their latest chat-up lines on them. Laura and Belle laughed and joked, and left them wanting more, as they vanished into the noisy throng.

"Creeps," complained Laura, as the two of them worked their way towards the bar to order drinks. She was looking around at the décor, garish lighting, chains, a few torture devices on display, scattered about the place. One almost naked man was bound in some stocks, while his girlfriend was lashing his back and buttocks with a cat o' nine tails, but not hard enough to draw blood. Amused onlookers watched avidly as the flogging continued.

"Mother, you'd have been offended if it had only been my ass they grabbed, so quit bitching," she chuckled, and ordered some drinks from the crowded bar, after elbowing her way in.

"You're right. He has absolutely no taste at all, if this is anything to go by," Laura added, continuing to 'admire' the scenery. She accepted the drink, and they milled around, mixing with the other partygoers and doing their best to blend in. The building was three-storey, with the centre section one big room, with a ceiling that went all the way upto the roof, to where a big skylight let in the stars, and let out the smoke. Balconies ran around the periphery at each floor, leading onto private rooms and office on the upper floors.

The two women watched the antics of the crowd as the evening wore on, and also watched the bouncers patrolling around, and occasionally checking the upstairs rooms, as patrons entered and left. From the noises, the rooms contained a variety of jaded amusements. A couple of video screens showed various people participating in sado-masochistic games, and neither women were sure if they were watching pre-recorded tapes, or live video footage from some of those private rooms. "It never ceases to amaze me, just how some people get their amusement," Laura commented, as she watched some of the antics. Belle chuckled.

"Come now, Mother. You've been around longer than me. Haven't you done your own share of experimentation in your time?" she mused. Laura snorted indignantly.

"For me to know, not you. Trying it and liking it aren't necessarily the same thing," she added. Belle suddenly stared hard up at the higher levels, and Laura followed her gaze to see a short portly man descending the stairs from the upper levels, nodding to the big bouncer who stood guard on the uppermost landing. Belle turned away.

"That's him, Varadi. He's older but just as ugly. I need to stay out of his way. What you need to do is get him interested enough to invite you upstairs for playtime. Then you ask if you can bring a friend, and that should get us past that big bastard on the top landing. Once we get Varadi alone, we can make him talk."

"A simple enough plan," Laura agreed.

"Most men are that simple. They usually think with their dicks." Belle smiled. "Sometimes all it takes is a smile, or a beckoning finger." Laura nodded, agreeing.

"Why would he think I'd be interested in him, as short an as ugly as he is?" Laura asked,

"People come here looking for the thrills, not perfect bodies. Some want control, others want to be controlled, and then there's the pain and humiliation element. Whatever turns you on, as they say. I'm sure you'll find some common ground," she smiled. Belle faded away into the crowd as Varadi stepped onto the dance-floor, looking around at the thrill-seekers, nodding to a few acquaintances. Laura was slowly angling her way towards him as he moved towards the bar.

The 'accidental' collision spilled Laura's drink, and some of it splashed on Varadi's jacket. "Oh, I'm so sorry. How clumsy of me," she apologized, as Varadi put up his hands, trying to make light of the incident.

"These things happen. Don't worry about it."

"I wasn't looking too well," she explained. "I thought I'd leave my glasses at home tonight and I can't wear contacts too well. Here, let me help you," she offered, dipping into her purse for a napkin, which she started using on the front of his jacket, leaning forward to display her low-cut bodice. Varadi let her rub the material of his jacket, watching the jiggling bodice as her hand moved rhythmically.

"It's not a problem, honestly. It will wash off later. I'll have one of my assistants clean it for me."

"Oh?" Laura looked up, as though seeing him for the first time. "Are you the owner of this club?" she batted her eyelids, as though impressed. "My girlfriend comes here all the time, and tonight she finally persuaded me to come along. You must be Mr Varadi?" He smiled in acknowledgement.

"Yes that's me, and you are?"

"Maria." She held out her hand, and Varadi took it, raising it to his lips, and kissing the back of it gallantly. "My friend Theresa loves this place, and she thought I would too, as our interests are, shall we say, similar," she giggled, and Varadi chuckled.

"Yes, I know what you mean. As you are new here, why don't you join me, and let me show you around the place? If there is anything particular you would like to see or to experience, then I am at your disposal."

"Oh, how kind." Laura appeared both impressed and grateful, and Varadi took her arm, escorting her to the bar to get her a fresh drink and one for himself. Belle watched from a distance, as he began giving Laura the ten cent tour.

Varadi took her around the ground floor, explaining some of the torture devices, their use and how they worked, explaining which ones were the most popular. As he began walking her up the first flight of stairs, his guiding hand moved from her elbow to her waist, as Laura walked alongside him.

Laura's eyes were really opened, more with amazement than outright shock, at some of the things she saw when Varadi started opening the doors to the private rooms.

One woman was hung naked from a reinforced beam by her wrists, with a target painted on her bottom, whilst two men, also naked, played a game of darts with her. Laura could see the many puncture marks on her buttocks, some still fresh and bleeding. They showed unconcern at the appearance of spectators, obviously used to an audience.

Another room featured a naked bound man, tethered and on his knees, being made to orally satisfy one naked woman, whilst another was behind him, sodomising him slowly with a plastic strap-on cock, while she reached around him to manually stimulate his own. The woman enjoying the cunnilingus smiled at Varadi and Laura, and reached down to grab the back of the man's head, grinding her loins into his face as she groaned in pleasure.

Other rooms just featured couples and groups having sex, straight or weird, it varied, and a few had even more extreme fetishes being played out. Varadi's hand had slipped now from her waist to her ass, fondling it familiarly, and Laura had hardly noticed, so engrossed had she been in the sights he was showing her. "Which excites you the most?" he asked her, nuzzling her ear through her long blonde hair. "This? Something you've seen earlier? Tell me what is is, and I'll do it to you," he suggested, and Laura allowed him to draw her closer.

"My friend and I like to play together," she giggled, and Varadi smiled.

"The more the merrier," he suggested. "Why not collect her, and we can all have some fun together? I like to watch, if not participate too much, these days" he explained.

"It may take some time to find her down there," Laura warned. "Why don't you prepare one of the upper rooms and I'll bring her up?" she suggested. Varadi smiled.

"Very well. I'll prepare something special, while you bring your girlfriend up to play." He patted her bottom affectionately, and Laura leaned forward to kiss him on the lips. She blew him another kiss as she started back down the stairs and looked back to see him talking to the big bouncer, advising him to let the two women up to the upper levels.

Laura made her way across the room, to where she had spotted Belle waiting amidst the crowd. "We got us a hot date, Daughter." Laura chuckled. "Men are so fucking easy."

The big guy on the stairs nodded to Laura as she reappeared with her friend, even more gorgeous than the blonde, in that figure-hugging red latex number. Varadi was going to have a good night tonight. "Room 23," he offered, pointing down the landing. Laura and Belle smiled at him, and wiggled their way along the landing towards the waiting room.

Laura turned the handle and the heavy door opened inwards. The walls were thick and obviously soundproofed, which would make their interrogation of Varadi all the easier, or so she thought. He was stood waiting for her by the bed, dressed in a tight, but overstretched black leather jacket, and a small black leather pouch holding in his manhood beneath his bulging belly. An Alsatian dog was curled up by the foot of the bed. Laura smiled as she moved into the room, and Varadi moved towards her, then froze as Belle appeared behind her, closing the door quickly. "Hello, Gianni," she grinned coldly.

"My God! Belladonna. It's you, isn't it? Still you. You haven't changed one bit. Are you a vampire?" he crossed himself.

"No, but I do know a couple," Belle smiled menacingly. Sensing his master's alarm, the dog began to stir and got to its feet. Laura fished the gun from her purse, pointing it in the animal's direction.

"Tell Fido to be a 'good doggie', otherwise he's going to be a dead doggie," she warned, and Varadi spoke to the dog, reaching down to stroke its fur as he placated it.

"After all these years, our paths cross again. I doubt its coincidence, so what is it you want?" he asked, calmer than she imagined he'd be.

"Information about your terrorist friends," Belle admitted. Varadi scoffed.

"The Brigades are not active these days, and I have few current contacts. There is nothing of note I could tell you there."

"I'm more interested in your links with Arab terrorists," she said, and watched his reaction. Yes, he knew something.

"Again, my contacts are few. But why should I give this information away? Are you going to pay me to tell you?" he asked, humourously.

"I was thinking more along the lines of beating the shit out of you again, till you told me," Belle smiled menacingly. Varadi just sneered.

"Yes, you enjoyed that, didn't you? You bitch, I was in hospital for months because of you," he accused, gesticulating wildly. Belle shrugged.

"Nothing you didn't deserve, Varadi. You were trying to get the Brigades actively into the drugs trade. Too many terror organizations fund themselves through drugs for us to allow you to start something like that here in Italy. You were taught a lesson, a non-fatal one, so be thankful for that."

"I suffered nerve-damage, you cunt! I still suffer nerve damage. To the extent that I can hardly feel a thing. I don't feel pain any more. You can beat me, but it won't do you any good. I can barely feel the wind or the sun on my face when I walk in the street," he revealed. "I can still get a hard-on, but I can't use it for long. I just don't feel anything. That's what you did to me, bitch!" Belle was still unrepentant, though Laura was showing slight signs of sympathy. "The result is I don't feel pain too well. Comes in handy, though, like now for instance. You can't make me feel pain, you can only kill me, and if you kill me, you don't get any information out of me," he chuckled. "So the question is now, not what I can do for you, but what you two girls can do for me, to persuade me to give you that information," he leered. Belle and Laura looked at each other, then back to the grinning lowlife.

"What information do you have?" Laura asked. Varadi turned to her.

"You're after Al Qaeda, right? I'm not stupid. I read the papers, watch the news. They're Arab and they're active now in Italy. They should stick to their own countries or go blow up some fucking Americans." Laura tried not to react to that last remark. "I know one guy. He's Arab too. He's the main organizer for their cells, has been for years. The Brigades had some contact with him in the past. He's still the main man, the Mr Fix-It. You get him, you'll get them. So what's it worth to you?" he chuckled, and sat back down on the bed, patting the mattress beside him.

"You can't be serious?" Laura asked. "I thought you said you couldn't feel anything?"

"I can't, but I get my enjoyment more through watching these days," he explained. "Once I get my rocks off, you'll get your information," he promised. "You know what I like, Belle," he leered.

Belle deliberated, as Laura looked at her, puzzled. "Not her, just me," she stated, looking to Varadi for confirmation. He grinned widely. "Half an hour, no more. I'll do whatever you want."

"Okay. We got a deal," he confirmed. Laura still looked puzzled.

"Belle?" she turned around.

"I do know what he likes. Why don't you wait outside?" she suggested. Laura wasn't too sure what was going on, or that she liked the idea of her daughter agreeing to Varadi's proposal, but Belle was a big girl, and their options to get him to talk seemed to be limited. Reluctantly, she put the gun away back in her purse, and opened the door onto the landing. She went outside and closed the door behind her.

Back on the landing, Laura nodded to the bouncer, who looked once in her direction, and then she turned her attention on the crowd below, and checking the time on her watch. Half an hour.

$$*\quad*\quad*$$

"You agree to do anything I tell you to do, for the next half-hour, and I'll give you the name you're looking for, and no repercussions from you afterwards. That was the deal, right?" Belle nodded. "I have a new little gadget, one I'm sure you'll like," he promised, pulling it out from beneath the bed. It consisted of a small padded seat, which sprung up to lock the short legs in place, as he manipulated it. Steel handcuffs were attached to all four legs. No keyed locks, just a push-button release, which would be impossible to reach if you were the one fastened into them. "A real best-seller that came onto the market last year. I think you can see how it's meant to work," he chuckled. "Get into it," he ordered.

Belle began to undress, reaching behind her to unfasten the zip. She began to slither out of the clinging red latex. She had nothing underneath it, and Varadi chuckled as he admired her naked body. She put the dress with her purse on the small sofa where Varadi had left his own clothes, and then went over to the side of the bed where the bondage stool waited for her. She knelt down behind it, with her ankles lined-up with the rear legs. She put the steel bracelets around her ankles, and clicked them shut. She leaned forward, resting her breasts and ribcage on the padded surface, and put one wrist into another handcuff, and fastened it shut herself. Varadi helped fasten her other wrist into the last steel bracelet, and that was it. She was now securely fastened. She would only get out of the device with someone else's help. Varadi walked around, admiring her as she posed on all fours for him.

"I like that nice white ass of yours. Like a nice pale peach." He admired Belle's posterior, running his hands over the damp buttocks and making Belle cringe as he moved his hands lovingly over her bottom. He patted one cheek lovingly. "I think it would look better in a shade of pink, don't you?" he chuckled, and went over to where he had left his street-clothes. Unfastening his belt and pulling it out of his trousers, he came back over to her. The leather belt hung down to the floor as he swished it from side to side. Belle watched him as he walked around behind her once more.

"Stick that ass up a bit higher," he ordered. Belle did so, and waited for what she knew was coming. WHACKKKK, the broad leather struck her hard across both buttocks, stinging and making her jump, at least as far as her handcuffs would allow her to move, which wasn't far. Varadi chuckled, watching the livid strap-mark begin to appear.

WHACKKKK . . . WHACKKKKK . . . WHACKKKK . . . . Belle gasped and grunted, gritting her teeth against the pain. "Scream for me, bitch!" WHACKKK . . . . WHACKKKK . . . . "I want to hear you scream!" WHACKKK . . . WHACKKK . . . . the belt rained down upon her bottom again and again, this way and that, sometimes missing and hitting her back, and eventually it had the effect Varadi wanted. Belle began to scream. It didn't make him stop, only encouraged him. The bedroom was soundproofed for good reason, but Gianni liked to hear them scream. Belle knew this and tried to hold back as the leather belt fell again and again, landing on her back and buttocks, crisscrossing her white flesh with pink stripes. Gianni worked up a good sweat, and really layed into her. The more she screamed, the harder he got. "That's it baby, you know you like it. Scream louder for me. Louder!" he taunted as the leather belt struck her flesh remorselessly. WHACKKK . . . WHACKKK . . .

Gasping for breath, she still held back the tears. She wasn't going to give him that satisfaction. At last, the blows stopped raining down, and Varadi came round in front of her, kneeling down. "Now suck for your supper, bitch!" Varadi ordered, pulling on her hair to raise her head, and then forcing his stiff erection into her mouth and ramming it in to the back of her throat while he held her head there. "Suck it or choke, I don't really care," he laughed, pinching her nose shut. "I can't feel it, but I'll still come down your throat regardless," he promised.

Varadi grunted as he face-fucked Belle. She had agreed to be his plaything and he intended to get full value for money out of her before his half-hour was up. The enforced fellatio wasn't to give himself any physical pleasure, as he could hardly feel her mouth's suction. It was done merely for the humiliation value. Putting the bitch in her place, and making her suffer for what she had done to him, what he had been forced to live with ever since.

*　*　*

Out on the landing, Laura was checking her watch. Still ten more minutes to go. She couldn't hear any noises coming from the soundproofed room, so had no idea what was happening in there. The only noise came from the heaving throng below. It was boring watching them milling about, people queuing-up to take a turn in the stocks. She found her attention drifting to some of the action in the video screens scattered around the place, all showing different kinky behaviour.

Varadi and her daughter's face was suddenly visible on screen, which jolted her back to full awareness. That was live, and it was happening right there in that room behind her.

*　*　*

The bedroom door suddenly opened, and Varadi whirled around. "Don't shoot him. I promised." Belle pleaded, from her bound position. Varadi looked ridiculous, caught in the process of strapping on a hollow dildo around his waist.

"Guess my watch is fast, but your half-hour is over, Varadi. Let her loose and get dressed," she orders.

"Damn. What a shame. Still I mustn't complain. A deal's a deal. It's been fun," he gloated. "We'll call that even for the six months I spent in hospital," he chuckled as he unfastened the handcuffs one by one, and then stood up, grinning.

"It's okay," Belle tries to reassure Laura, as she stands up and examines the strap marks on her buttocks. "I've had worse. I'm a fast-healer, remember?"

Varadi gloated, grinning at Laura. "It excites you, doesn't it? I can tell. You want some?" he chuckled, handling his softening penis.

"You disgust me, you animal," Laura remonstrated with him. "Now give me the name of this Arab go-between, and if it's false, I'll be back." Varadi shrugged.

"His name is Yusef Abdullah. An Algerian. He works in the University. He has no great love for Italy ever since we occupied his country many years ago. I think his parents got badly treated or something. Anyway, he uses his position to smuggle arms and launder money for a number of Arab organizations." Belle got back into her pvc dress, wincing as she wriggled this way and that. Laura helped her zip it up. The two women left Varadi's room, and went back downstairs, exiting through the front foyer.

"How could you let him do that to you?" Laura asks, as they walked along the pavement. Belle shrugged.

"I'm practical. He got what he wanted, and we got what we wanted. I had worse beatings in my childhood on the farm," she revealed. "Let's make the information count. I'm hoping either Donatello or Falcone can get us a handle on this Abdullah." Laura flagged down another taxi, and the two women went back to the hotel, where Laura left Belle soaking in a hot tub while she relayed the information about Abdullah to Falcone.

*   *   *

The border crossing was watched intently, ever since the discovery of the sinking boat off the eastern coastline. If Croatia was the source, then this was the way the hgv would come. The team of experts was assembled and waiting, dressed the same as the normal border guards. Their equipment was hidden away from prying eyes, but instantly accessible. Portable enough to be wheeled out, used and returned in the half hour the customs people could be expected to distract the driver.

Two teams of six, rotating every four hours, they checked every hgv, van, truck or tanker discreetly, wondering just how the attempt would be made. More and more checks were made on vehicles these days because of the economic refugee problem all over Europe. Customs were more thorough in their approach. The Russian Mafia or the Chechnyans, individually or in collaboration, whoever was really behind it, would know all this, yet how would they try and beat the system?

The Geiger counter needle swung finally as they checked out one big 18-wheeler truck which was carrying frozen meat. It didn't swing much, but it was sensitive enough so that only the thickest of shielding would defeat it. The operator hadn't intended to switch it on till he got to the back of the truck where they were even now opening the sealed refrigerated doors, but the needle had swung towards the front of the truck, near the cab, and, away from prying eyes, two of the inspectors paid this part of the vehicle very close attention.

On inspection of the two large chrome exhausts, running up each side of the cab, one was hot as expected, but the other was cold. The mountings looked slightly more solid on the cold one than for the other exhaust, and on examining under the cab, they found a modification which routed all the exhaust fumes up through the one exhaust, obviously so that the heat of them didn't start to melt through the lead shielding. Not as large a shipment as they'd tried to get in by boat, but still worrying enough. Once a decision had been made, one of the two men installed a tracking device underneath the cab, and the other man radioed his superiors to report success.

The truck would be allowed through. Monitored by radio and occasional airborne fly-pasts by helicopter, thought not often enough to attract the driver's attention, if indeed he knew anything about his illicit cargo.

Chapter Seventeen

June 19th

Yusef Abdullah took the call from Kazakhstan, recognizing the cellphone number immediately. "My dear Feliks, what can I do for you? I trust the shipment is progressing nicely?" he asked innocently enough. The other voice was more gruff and hurried, with little time for the niceties which Yusef liked so much in his conversations with other races.

"I need someone killed, Yusef." He came out with it bluntly. "She can give evidence against me, and I can give evidence against you. So it's in all our interests to see she doesn't talk." Yusef's curiousity was piqued by this revelation.

"How can I be of assistance here?"

"Not you. Our mutual friends," he stated simply. "The woman is in Rome on holiday, and whilst Al Qaeda is on its current rampage, one more tourist won't be noticeable among the body count," he added simply. "My contacts in the Security forces have finally given me information on where she is hiding out, and once she is dead, they have nothing personally on me. The original evidence is destroyed, and they have no proof. I cover my tracks well. I'm sure you do the same, and with your thoroughness, you should have little trouble in tracking her down and eliminating her. The sooner the better, for both our sakes."

*   *   *

Lesya stepped out from the changing cubicle into the massage-area, looking around at the sumptuous décor. Incense smelling of sandalwood burned in a bowl on a table over by the other door. Thick carpet underfoot tickled the soles of her bare feet as she walked towards the massage-table where the slim young Thai man waited for her. He was stripped to the waist already, wirey torso already oiled, and he grinned amiably and bowed towards her as she came towards him. She would have returned the bow herself, but holding onto her towel would have been difficult. She smiled and nodded instead.

"Welcome, Missy. Me Pak Dong, your masseur," he introduced himself. Lesya looked about the sumptuous room, a little puzzled. It was hard to tell the age of someone of Asian origin. He looked in his teens, slightly effeminate, as did a lot of asian men.

"Pleased to meet you, Pak Dong, but I ordered a 'special' massage." The man smiled, knowingly.

"Is in stages, your massage," he explained. "First we give full-body muscular massage, and then perfumed oil massage and then final massage. Missy will not be disappointed," he grinned in reassurance.

"Very well. I put myself into your hands," Lesya giggled, and sat on the massage-table, before swiveling round and laying face down on the table. Pak Dong came around the table and gently unfastened the towel, baring her back as he worked it down to around her hips. Lesya, had enjoyed many massages from her male yoga instructor in Kazakhstan, and she appreciated the skill with which he used his hands. As soon as Pak-Dong started, she knew he was skilled, hard stiff fingers kneading her flesh and her joints as she groaned in a mixture of pain and pleasure, eyes closing in contentment.

The Thai looked at her young white body with an appreciative eye, running his hands slowly and methodically up and down her spine, kneading and manipulating each verterbrae in turn.

Lesya moaned and sighed, relaxed and contented as she surrendered herself to his skillful manipulations. So deft were his fingers, she hardly noticed the towel being loosened from around her waist until she felt the cooler air on her buttocks, and then his hands were there too, kneading and manipulating the base of her spine and gluteal muscles.

She was naked under the towel, and had not expected a male masseur, and so gasped as she realized his hands were now allowed free reign over her nude body. They felt good though, for he obviously had many years' experience.

Pak Dong always enjoyed this part of his job, massaging attractive naked women, particularly western women, and his skilled fingers knew all of the pleasure centres of the human body. She was moaning under his manipulations even now as he stroked and applied pressure here and there. He was actually the son of the owner of this establishment, and he always liked to 'keep his hand in' when there was a pretty western woman requiring a massage.

Her buttocks felt soft in his hands as he squeezed them lovingly, manipulating, separating them slightly as he enjoyed looking at her anus and then looked down further still to her puffy vaginal lips. It was hard to remain detached with a woman as pretty as this in his hands. She would be getting moist now as he worked her buttocks back and forth in slow circular movements. He looked up to the concealed lens of the video camera, and smiled a knowing smile. Lesya moaned once more, pressing her tummy down flat against the table. The feel of his hands, and what he was doing to her, felt so good.

She rolled over instinctively at his indication, the towel remaining where it was underneath her on the table, and Pak Dong feasted his eyes on the woman's body. Small perfectly formed breasts like set-jellies, quivering deliciously as she breathed, with her nipples already aroused. Tummy all flat and a trimmed black bush covered her pubic mound. Lesya laid there, eyes half-closed, breathing deeply, her rib-cage rising and falling and her breasts seeming to lift up towards his fingers, as if saying 'squeeze me, squeeze me.'

Pak Dong took the fur massage-glove from the side-table and put it on, and then Lesya gasped as he lightly ran it over her chest, stimulating her already aroused nipples, before running it down across the sleek tummy to her hairy mound, and lightly caressing her black hairs. He covered every square inch of her body with the glove, allowing her to turn over once more, caressing the nape of her neck and her flanks, the backs of her thighs, the soles of her feet, before making her turn over once more. She lay there, eyes gently closed, allowing the sensuous intimacy.

He couldn't repress a smile as he took off the glove, and then lifted the small bottle of perfumed oil and lightly began to pour it from her neck, down over each breast, her tummy, and finally let a trickle drip down into her dark jungle as she gasped in surprise. As well as the scent, the oil itself was impregnated with a stimulant, not aphrodisiac in itself, but it would soon get her tender areas enflamed and aroused, as he was himself at the moment, stiff erection pushing out the front of the towel, which was his only clothing too.

Putting the bottle back on the table, he flexed his fingers, like a virtuouso pianist, finally deciding which note to play next. Lesya groaned as his skeletal fingers slid over her ripe breasts, his coarse palms rubbing her already aroused nipples this way and that. She opened her eyes partially, as she gasped, and looked up into the young man's grinning face as he continued to caress her.

She was becoming aroused, no question about it, her body shuddered occasionally under his hands as they slid over her oiled skin, fingers kneading and stroking her flesh softly, yet firmly, down over her flat sleek tummy, and his fingertips dared to penetrate the hirsute undergrowth, just tentatively at first, as she gasped, and then delving deeper, as they stroked and rubbed the oiled mound. A long educated finger found the moistened groove and slid down it to where her swollen nub of a clitoris awaited, and she shuddered violently as he manipulated it.

Pak Dong grinned and manipulated his own aching erection with one hand as he used his other to masturbate the woman. Lesya gasped, helpless beneath his skilled fingers. Her nipples were on fire, and she began stroking them herself, as the Thai stroked her pussy. He was good at it, from many years' practice, and he brought her to the threshold of an orgasm, more than once as she cried out, before moving his fingers away, and stroking her inner-thighs instead. Lesya found her legs opening almost automatically as the charismatic young man stimulated her. His eyes were gazing down between them now, at her oiled bush and oiled lips, so sensitive now and swollen after his manipulation. She found one of her own hands going down there, not to cover herself from his gaze, but to caress herself with her own fingers. Gasping, she stared brazenly up at him, meeting his gaze as she began to pleasure herself.

*   *   *

Turnbull was walking about 50 yards behind Gabriel, and within a few yards of the two Arabs following him. Dixon was on the other side of the street, and Palmer and Coverdale were further ahead, being controlled this time by Dixon, out of earshot of the two Arabs. Turnbull could hear his secure comms as Dixon gave advice on progress. Suddenly, one of Arabs dipped into the inside pocket of his jacket, and Turnbull gasped momentarily, reaching inside his own for the gun that nestled there as he thought one of the men had rumbled him and was reaching for a similar weapon. No, just a cell-phone. Someone was calling him. He moved closer, trying to overhear the conversation.

The Arab repeated a name a couple of times, something foreign. 'Roman'? something. It sounded Russian, and then another name, some massage parlour he hadn't heard of. The man put the phone away, and this time he was definitely checking his weapon, talking hurriedly to his friend, who also checked his. Something was about to go down, but he had no idea what. He began to drop back, and let the two men peel off down one of the adjacent streets, now no longer interested in Gabriel's movements.

*   *   *

Hardly had Lesya got her breath back from the Pak Dong's ministrations, than two Thai girls entered the room from the rear door. The two Thai girls were twins, that much was obvious. Long silky black hair hung down almost to their waists as they walked into the room together. They wore silk thongs, one of red, the other of blue, and that was the only clothing they had on, and the only way to tell them apart, for the bodies were otherwise identical. Small pert breasts, with hard nipples, sleek stomachs, and legs even longer than Lesya's own. One of them carried a plastic carrier-bag. Lesya felt a flutter in her stomach as Pak Dong left the room and closed the door behind him, leaving her alone with the two women. This was what she had come here for, to 'examine her feminine side', and she had heard a lot about the special massages Thai women give.

The two women smiled at Lesya, lying now propped up on one elbow, quite naked, oiled and sweating from her earlier exertions. They giggled, nodding to each other, and approached Lesya where she lay on the massage table.

One of them leaned forward and kissed Lesya slowly on her full lips. Lesya was quite surprised at the nature of the kiss, expecting either tongues or a faint lip-press, but the woman's teeth fastened onto her bottom lip, chewing lightly, as she pressed her back down onto the massage table.

The other woman put down the carrier-bag, and took from within it what looked like a long pink snake, crafted in a lifelike manner, only this snake was made of pink latex, and battery-operated internals gave it life, as she pressed a small switch at the end of its serpentine body. It began to wriggle and undulate, and the woman pressed it down onto Lesya's oiled tummy and ribcage, letting it wriggle and delight, as Lesya gasped at the many simultaneous feelings they were making her feel.

*   *   *

In the video-room, Pak Dong felt himself getting hard again as he watched his two girls seduce the attractive brunette in a slightly different manner to that which he had used himself. Their tongues fluttered over every inch of Lesya's body, licking and laving. Women knew their own bodies far better than a man, and so knew exactly how to stimulate each others. Lesya kissed one of the women back in the same manner as she herself had just been kissed, and the woman giggled as her hands fondled her oiled breasts.

*   *   *

Blue's thong was now on the floor, and she climbed up onto the table with Lesya, lowering herself onto her oiled body, and Lesya groaned at the feel of her naked skin pressed against her own, with the wriggling latex snake in between. The woman's crotch was hairless, but rubbing impatiently against Lesya's own hairy mound, and she gasped at the intense and expert stimulation of her clitoris by the woman's deliberate actions.

The wriggling snake was now between their breasts, undulating wildly with its buzzing internals, and Blue pushed the snake's head up to Lesya's face, where she found a stabbing latex tongue slowly going in and out of its well-sculpted head. She stuck out her own tongue, licking the snake's forked tongue, mischievously, as Blue giggled. "Get it good and wet," she suggested, and Lesya licked and laved her tongue lovingly all over the head of the snake.

Red was already between Lesya's legs, using her fingers to stroke and tease the lubricated lips of both her sister and the female client, who wriggled and squealed alternately on the tabletop.

* * *

Pak Dong zoomed in with the remote camera on the brunette's crotch as the bulbous snake-head was pushed into it. Her squeals and moans of delight could be heard quite clearly through the adjoining wall as the latex head vanished inside her, stabbing tongue probing her innermost depths. He used one hand to masturbate his revived erection as he watched the intimate lesbian acts.

* * *

Lesya gasped and threshed, as Blue shoved the latex length into her oiled vagina. It went in deep and easily. Its vibrations and undulations were soon driving her wild. Eager to get in on the act now, Red slipped off her thong, and climbed up on the table, straddling Lesya's face, and reversing, before pressing her oiled vaginal lips down onto Lesya's gasping mouth. This was what Lesya had been waiting for, and her tongue stabbed up, tasting the other woman's sex for the first time, even as she felt Red lean forward and apply her own tongue to Lesya's aroused clitoral bud. Blue's tongue joined her sisters, teasing and tormenting the threshing woman, and stuffing her repeatedly full of the undulating length of vibrating latex as they took turns lapping at her aroused sex.

* * *

Pak Dong chuckled, his camera screen full of his two girls' dancing tongues and the brunette's swollen clitoris, as she shuddered deliciously under their joint oral ministrations. The two girls were extremely good at their double-act. The footage would be sold to the various porno establishments in Rome, and maybe exported, depending on how good and how long the session was. That horny little brunette looked like she could go on all afternoon, and he was already thinking of going back in there and rejoining in the fun. He moved the camera up to where that mischievious tongue of hers was lapping away at Red's bald pussy, lifting up to stab at the girl's puckered asshole occasionally, too. She liked it alright.

She had said she had wanted to experience everything possible, on her application form, and Pak Dong was notorious for catering to every whim of his more jaded clientele. Five of them were in private booths right now, as he was, watching the live action footage of the naked brunette being transmitted direct to their own televisions from the hidden camera.

*   *   *

Gabriel was well-covered by the four-man SAS team, who flanked him front and back on opposite sides of the street. The discreet coms-link earpiece kept him informed of their observations as they followed the two Arabs who in turn were following Gabriel. "Hang on a minute, Guv. Something's up." Turnbull's voice in Gabriel's earpiece made him pause, pretending to look into a shop window, though using the reflection in the glass to peer back down the street. "Tweedledum and Tweedledee have just taken a call on their cellphone, and their priorities seem to have changed. Someone called Roman something was mentioned. A Russian I think. They're heading off back the way we've just come. One of them reached into his jacket to check his gun."

"What's your view, Turnbull? Give me a quick assessment," Gabriel ordered. His own mind was whirling, remembering the houseguest staying with Donatello, a woman called Romanova, and she was Kazakh, former Russian satellite state. It was too much of a coincidence considering the recent nuclear connection that had recently been made. Somehow she was involved in all this.

"More urgent priorities, Guv, and if they're checking guns it doesn't bode well for somebody."

Gabriel made an instant decision. "Okay, turnabout is fair play. Let's follow them and see what they're upto." He didn't want any unnecessary blood on his hands, and this woman might be able to cast some light on things. He caught the signals from Turnbull to the other three SAS men who were now rushing back in an attempt to follow the two Arabs.

Using the comm-links, two of them rushed ahead, and formed the box, being guided by the men at the rear. Gabriel kept back out of sight, in case either of the two men turned around and spotted him.

The two Arabs were leading them back across the city towards the west, away from the main streets, and finally vanished into a massage parlour. "What do we do?" Turnbull asked Gabriel, as he directed the other three men into a holding position across the street.

"You do nothing. I'm going inside. Be prepared to come running if I call." Gabriel started across the road before Turnbull could protest. This was bang out of order, and Maddox would have his guts if he knew he had let Gabriel expose himself like this.

"Dixon. Get round the back. I'll take the front. Palmer, Coverdale, either end of the street, but get ready to move at a second's notice," Turnbull warned. Gabriel was already inside the building now. "You take it careful in there, okay?" he warned.

"I've done this sort of thing before, Nick. Don't worry too much," came Gabriel's response, calm and controlled, over the secure comms.

Inside the building, things were stirring like a hornet's nest. The two Arabs were leaving behind a bit of panic in their wake. As Gabriel entered, he found one girl screaming at the sight of the receptionist laid out on the floor, though still breathing. He half-raised her into a sitting position, slumped against the wall. "She'll be okay," he reassured the girl, and then quickly checked out the registry on the desk. He spotted the name quickly, recognising it. Romanova, Red & Blue, Room 27. "Where is Room 27?" he asked the other girl as she quietened down.

"Th . . . Third floor . . . . on the left at the top of the stairs . . . ." she stuttered, still in shock. Gabriel keyed his throat mike again.

"Nick, I need help. Get someone up the fire-escape if there is one. They're going up to the third floor. I'm heading up the stairs now."

Outside, Turnbull relayed orders. "Dixon, get your arse up there, and prepare to give covering fire if required. I think it is going to be required, so don't fuck about. They so much as look in his direction, slot the fuckers! I'm heading in there, after him now. Palmer, Coverdale, get back down here, front and back, and watch for a firefight. This one's going down the pan all too rapidly!" he cursed, walking briskly into the building, one hand already reaching for his gun under his jacket.

The receptionist was coming around, attended to by the other woman, as Turnbull went by them, heading for the stairs. He keyed his throat-mike again. "Coming up behind you. Don't rush it. Wait for back-up," he warned, alerting Gabriel of his presence. Looking, up he saw a vague shadow, but heard nothing, as Gabriel clung to the wall as he went up the stairs. Nothing else, which meant the Arabs were already on the third floor. They may already be too late.

*   *   *

Mohammed and Abdul were screwing silencers onto the barrels of their guns as they checked the room numbers along the third floor corridor. Strange scents and stranger noises were coming from behind some of the closed doors. Grinning, they pushed open a few doors, peeking inside momentarily, and chuckling to each other like naughty schoolboys peeking in on the girls' changing-rooms, at some of the more 'exotic' massages being given in this establishment.

Despite the thick carpeting, they began to tiptoe as they approached the door to Room 27, and slowly turned the handle of the door.

*   *   *

Outside, Dixon wasn't having much luck with the fire-escape. Rusted and corroded, he had a job getting the bottom section ladder down, and then found it was hanging off the brickwork in places, meaning he had to take it slow or chance making too much noise, and the whole thing coming away alltogether. He relayed the bad news to Turnbull via his throat-mike.

"Shit!" was Turnbull's only response and he started running up the stairs. No time for stealth now. He just caught sight of Gabriel on the third landing as he entered the upper corridor. Turnbull didn't chance the comms now, in case the Arabs were close enough to hear. He had to catch Gabriel up quick to give him some backup.

*   *   *

Inside Room 27, the two Arabs were stood dumbfounded, as they watched the antics of the 3 naked women, slithering all over each other like snakes, covered in massage-oil. They were way too intent on their own pleasures to realize the door had opened, and were continuing to pleasure each other with hands, fingers, and tongues.

Abdul grinned to Mohammed, who also seemed content to let things continue, enjoying the show. When the women saw them and screamed, the two men would begin shooting.

*   *   *

Gabriel saw the open door at the end of the corridor, and began walking cautiously along the thick carpet towards it, listening intently as he got closer. He heard sounds of pleasure from within, female moans of delight, and then the door closed when he was within ten feet or so. That was when the first scream sounded.

*   *   *

Red looked up and saw the two men standing there, watching them. She was no stranger to an audience, and so it didn't register to her immediately, but then she saw the guns in their hands, and she screamed long and loud. The two guns raised and began to spit out death.

Red's body shook and splattered as bloody holes appeared in her chest. The other two women also began screaming at the sudden violence and blood, and naked bodies flew off the couch as the guns moved, firing this way and that. It was hard to tell their target, with all the women being naked and oiled. One of them screamed as she took a bullet in the leg, and then in her stomach.

Suddenly the door crashed open, and a third man was stood there. Raising his gun, he fired at one of the Arabs, this gun not silenced like theirs, and sounding loud in the confines of the room. Abdul and Mohammed whirled at the intrusion, the movement saving Abdul's life and giving him only a flesh wound in his upper arm. They returned fire, and Gabriel darted back behind the door jamb, still firing with one hand, and this time hitting Mohammed in the chest. He went down, blood already frothing at the mouth. Far away, screams could be heard from the other rooms in the establishment, particularly those with a videolink to Room 27 who had witnessed the firefight erupt.

Abdul started to back away, still firing, gun still spitting, until it ran out. No time to change magazines, he dropped his own weapon, and grabbed for the dropped gun of his friend Mohammed, turning and firing once more. The woman was now of secondary importance, for he had now recognized Gabriel, and realised he was a plant. Torquemada must be told.

He quickly went through the rear adjoining door to the next room, and Gabriel dashed into the main room to check on the girl. Lesya was crouched down behind the sofa, blood splattered her oiled body, as she tried to regain her composure. Her eyes were wide, glazed even, though he wasn't sure it was from fright, shock, or the sexual pleasures she had been enjoying before the firefight started. Red was lying limp and naked on the carpet, whilst Blue's body adorned the sofa, just as dead as her sister.

Abdul opened the other door to the landing from the adjoining room, just as Nick Turnbull ran past, and Abdul shot him in the back at point-blank range. Turnbull cried out and dropped with the impact, and the Arab dashed past him towards the window and the fire escape. He had to get away. Behind him, Turnbull groaned as he rolled back over, onto his side, just managing one shot which ripped through Abdul's jacket between his arm and his body, and then he was gone through the window, his footsteps rattling the fire-escape.

Turnbull heard a cry, and then gunshots. "Got him, Nick." Dixon's call came through on the comms. Nick forced himself to his knees, back still aching, though the Kevlar had done it's job. Luckily the bullet had struck to one side of his spine, and so he would get away with just some nasty bruising. He looked inside the room, and saw Gabriel ripping down one of the velour curtains to cover a very attractive and very naked young woman. Lesya took the green material eagerly, wrapping it around herself, and using the sash to tie it under her bosom. From a distance it would pass as a dress.

"What is happening? Who are these men and why are they shooting everyone?" she asked, still pale and still a bit shocked.

"We need wheels, Turnbull. Let's get out of here before the police get involved." Gabriel ushered the girl out along the corridor. Tamely, she went with him, eager to get out of the scene of this bloodbath.

Turnbull keyed his throat-mike as they went down the stairs, guns still out and visible. He was taking no more chances. "Palmer, we need a car."

"Get real, Nick. We left the cars miles away." Palmer complained.

"Well fucking steal one then! You've got about two minutes till we hit the street," he cautioned. "Make it happen!"

"Where are we going? Who were those other men?" Lesya was starting to recover her composure as they hustled her along.

"They were sent to kill you. You know too much about what they are doing here. Best you come with us and we'll keep you safe, till we figure out why this all just happened." Lesya didn't understand, but Gabriel kept her moving, Time to think later.

As they hustled her out of the building, they pulled up sharply, as a police-car pulled up in front of them. For a second, they thought they'd blown it, and then Palmer's cheeky face appeared in the window as he opened the door for them.

"A fucking cop car? Are you nuts?" berated Turnbull, as he got in the front, moaning as he eased his back into the seat, and Gabriel and the girl climbed into the back.

"Oh shut it, at least the siren will be useful for getting us away from here in a hurry," Palmer grinned, and switched it on, the wailing siren audible enough to clear the traffic ahead of them as he pulled away sharply. "Always wanted to drive one of these things. Kojack eat your heart out!" he laughed insanely as he weaved in and out of the slowing traffic who were making way for him, driving like a real Italian for once.

*   *   *

Palmer dropped Gabriel and Lesya off along the street from the Rialto, and as Turnbull took up position outside the hotel, he drove off to get rid of the vehicle. Gabriel and Lesya walked through Reception, pausing just briefly to pick up his room key. No one batted an eye at her bare feet. Lesya spoke hardly a word until they were up in his hotel room. Then she asked for an explanation. "So who are you, and what was all that about? You said they were sent to kill me."

"Donatello Grimaldi is a friend of mine. He mentioned your name to me in conversation, and when I heard what those two men had planned for you, I had to step in and foil their plans. They're part of a large terrorist cell currently on the loose in mainland Italy," he started to explain. "At this moment, there's a shipment of nuclear material being smuggled out of Kazakhstan and headed here, to Rome we think. You are connected with it all somehow, and someone obviously doesn't want you around." Lesya's mind was whirling.

"Kovacs! It can only be Kovacs," she answered. "I came here to keep safe till he was behind bars. It must be him who has arranged this." It was the only explanation she could think of. "He is a big wheel in the Russian Mafiya, and it spreads throughout the whole of Kazakhstan like a plague," she explained. Gabriel was thinking now. Russian Mafiya in league with Al Qaeda, and working against the Italian Mafia's interests? What would Grimaldi think about all this? Lesya explained further. "I recently discovered Mafiya involvement in smuggling in the company I work for in Kazakhstan. The more I looked, the more I found out, and they began to watch me. I had to get evidence on Kovacs to try and bargain for my life, and an old friend of mine helped me get out of the country till Kovacs could be caught or killed."

He looked at the girl, still a smudge of blood on her chin, and wrapped up in a green velour curtain. She looked damned attractive, nevertheless, one of those women who could wear a sack as though it were a Christian Dior creation. "You can give me all the details later. For now, why don't you go clean up in the bathroom, and I'll phone down to get you some clothes? Better still, I'll call Donatello, and have him send some of your clothes through from his villa? There are some complimentary bathrobes in there for you to wear in the meantime." Lesya liked his smile, and his latin looks. She smiled in return as she went into the bathroom to run herself a hot bath.

Gabriel rang Grimaldi's mansion, listening as the phone rang three, four times, before being answered. "Si?"

"Signor Donatello, grazi," The manservant recognized his voice, and he waited until Donatello came to the phone.

"Gabriel, my friend. I was getting worried at not hearing from you. I trust all is going well?" he asked.

"Better than I first thought, Donatello, but there are a few complications. I have your house guest here with me, Miss Romanova." He waited a few seconds to let the news sink in.

"I do not understand, my friend. What is Lesya doing with you? I only spoke of her in passing. I did not introduce you to her." Donatello was trying to figure it out, and failing, so he waited for Gabriel's explanation.

"She's Kazakh, and somehow involved in this current campaign. Some of Al-Qaeda's supplies seem to be coming out of Kazakhstan, and she has evidence against someone called Feliks Kovacs, a bigshot in the Russian Mafiya. She was taking a holiday over here till they had him behind bars." He heard Grimaldi swear on the other end of the line.

"I've never heard of him," he admitted. "You must realize, Gabriel, that the Russian Mafiya, though modeling themselves on the Cosa Nostra, are not connected with ourselves, and are far more ruthless than even some of the oldest of the Families. Whereas the Cosa Nostra started out as a means of protecting the peasants from the rich aristocracy, and grew into a worldwide criminal empire, these days clampdowns by law enforcement agencies are forcing it to legitimize its operations. I myself saw the wisdom of this many years ago as you know, and your help in legitimizing my own operations was invaluable. The rest of the Families are gradually seeing the wisdom in this. The more loosely-knit Russian Mafiya are more powerful than the law agencies in their own fledging economies, and they are an emerging force in the criminal fraternities of the world. Money is all they care about, and with the breakup of the soviet blocks, there is much to be made."

"Well, this Kovacs is obviously connected with our terrorists directly, as he had two of them try and kill your houseguest. It was pure chance that some friends of mine overheard the plot, and even luckier that I recognized the name when they told me. We managed to stop them, and she's now here with me at the Rialto. She's in need of some clothes, though. We had to leave the scene in rather a hurry and her clothes sort of got left behind. Can you arrange for Marianne to come out and collect her in the morning, and bring some suitable clothing for her to wear?" Grimaldi chuckled.

"This I can do," he laughed, and made a mental decision not to tell Gabriel to contact Laura. Under the circumstances, it was best if Laura knew nothing of Gabriel's hotel assignation with a naked woman. They were both men of the world, and whereas such things seemed reasonable enough to explain to each other, trying to explain such an event to another woman was doomed to failure. Best keep quiet about it till things resolved themselves. "I will make my own enquiries about this Kovacs, and have Marianne come through with some clothes in the morning. In the meantime, have a very pleasant evening my friend. Lesya is indeed a very beautiful young woman," he chuckled.

Gabriel smiled to himself as he heard Donatello jumping to conclusions again. The old rake always assumed that others enjoyed the same hedonistic lifestyle as himself. He was surprised that Marianne had stayed so long with him in a way, and wondered if Donatello had finally found a woman he could be happy with. "Goodnight, my friend," he put down the receiver, and turned as Lesya came out of the bathroom, toweling her short dark hair, and looking almost lost in that large white fluffy bathrobe which was cinched around her waist. "I just spoke to Donatello. He's having Marianne come over to fetch you in the morning, and she will bring out some of your clothes," he explained.

"Oh, well I guess we won't be going out to dinner then?" she smiled. Gabriel smiled back.

"I'll get room service to send up something. There's a menu over there on top of the television. Just let me know what you prefer, and we'll eat in. I'll order some wine, or would you prefer champagne?"

"Wine will be fine. Can they serve it warm? I like it 'mulled' I think is the expression?" Gabriel nodded.

"That should be no problem," he confirmed. Lesya ruffled through the menu, trying to remember her Italian.

"Pollo Cacciatore sounds nice. I like Italian food so far, though I'm not that keen on pasta. It's looked upon as a cheap meal in my country," she explained.

"Pasta is pasta," Gabriel agreed. "It's the sauce that makes the dish," he explained. He phoned Room Service, to order their meal for two. "It'll take about an hour. Italians are very serious about their cooking," he explained. "So tell me about yourself while we're waiting," he suggested. "I know Kazakhstan's broad history, but nothing much about the place since it became more autonomous. I take it the oil investment is helping your country develop better these days?"

"Oh, for sure," Lesya admitted, sitting on the edge of one of the twin beds, one bare thigh sticking out from under the fluffy white robe. "The money is there, and our government are spending some of it to build up the infrastructure. But Kazakhstan is a big country, the seventh largest in the world, and its people are scattered even more than the Americans in their country, with only isolated pockets of civilization here and there. All the oil and gas are in the west of the country, in what is called the Caspian Depression, and there are rumours of unrest amongst our people. More of the money seems to be getting spent on the west, in Atyrau and the other towns, than elsewhere in our country, and most of us have to commute west to work. Sometimes these trips are a couple of days each way. Some day, the infrastructure will be there. Right now, it isn't and people are impatient," she continued as Gabriel listened patiently. "I work for one of the big oil companies, and I stumbled on a plot to smuggle items out of the country. I didn't know what I was getting involved in. My poking around caused the Russian Mafiya to start spying on me, and I was frightened, unsure of what to do. They could easily have killed me. Yet, suddenly I had the opportunity to get some evidence on their operations, and so I took it, and then I went to a friend. He tried to have Kovacs arrested, but he got away, and until they catch him, I am the only witness that can give evidence against him. That's why I got out of the country. I don't even know if I still have a job any more," she mused, sadly. "I was scared to phone even my parents, in case Kovacs somehow tracked me down, which he obviously has anyway."

"Don't worry on that score. His resources are more limited here, and now reduced after this afternoon. Donatello has some influence himself, and I'm sure he will do what he can to help now he knows your real situation. Once Marianne comes to collect you tomorrow, I'll make sure he gives you 24 hour a day protection," he assured her. "I'm investigating the Italian end of this little smuggling operation, as you might have guessed, and I'm working in concert with the Italian security forces, among others. The operation is going well, and hopefully will be resolved in a few more days, and then you can continue to enjoy Italy as you intended to do." He only told her part of the truth, as he didn't want to divulge too much or scare her unnecessarily.

They talked a little more, and Lesya drank some mineral water out of the refrigerator. She liked to talk, and found Gabriel a good listener. For his part, he found her charming, friendly, and very beautiful. He was also very aware of how naked she was under that robe. Not ideal circumstances, but nothing he could do about it till morning. If he tried to arrange another room at short notice, it might be remembered if any more of the Arabs came checking up on him. Fortunately both men had been killed, and Gabriel's role in their deaths was unknown. He wanted it to stay that way. Torquemada wanted the nerve-agent, and he wouldn't entrust such a large amount of money to his underlings. He would bring it himself, and that was how Gabriel hoped to draw him out.

Lesya told him about her life in Kazakhstan, partly educated abroad, which was good for the language skills she had picked up and on which he complimented her, though she insisted she was 'not natural English speaker' as though deliberately giving the impression that her knowledge of the language was less than it was. Her Italian was understandable, though far from perfect like Gabriel's own, but apart from a slight accent, and sometimes strange turn of phrase, her use of English was as good as his own. Gabriel was fluent in many languages, so much so that it was hard for him to remember which was his native tongue after all these centuries. He realized, with some amusement, that he had forgotten having a native tongue after all these years, centuries in fact.

Room Service finally arrived as Gabriel was in the bathroom himself, freshening up, and he came out to sign for the meal, stripped to his waist, foam still on his face, as he had been busy shaving. Lesya was impressed with his physique. Being athletic herself, she knew the effort and work needed to stay that way. The feint scars on his shoulderblades were almost, but not quite identical, and she gathered he had had some sort of back surgery at some time.

Gabriel went back into the bathroom and resumed shaving whilst Lesya began to lay out the food on the small table out on the balcony. Up here she could see the bright lights and listen to the noise of the city, and the evening air was warm enough not to feel a chill. Dressed again, he came out to join her, and they continued their conversation over their meal.

The mulled wine was relaxing, after her bath, and Lesya was finally coming to terms with her near-death experience earlier in the day. The shock was starting to wear off, and like her experience with her Russian Mafiya boyfriend years ago, it had certainly had a stimulating effect on her, adding to that already experienced in the massage-parlour earlier.

Her rescuer had appeared out of nowhere, charging into the room just when she thought the bullets couldn't miss any more, and saving her life, as he and his friend fought with the two gunmen. He could easily have been killed himself, and she was grateful. Just how grateful, he had yet to find out, she smiled to herself.

But as the meal progressed, and Lesya employed her considerable charm, it was obvious that Gabriel wasn't interested. He didn't appear to be gay, so that left only one conclusion. "Do you love her?" she asked simply, as she swirled the last remnants of her wine around the rim of the glass, holding it up to catch the bright city-lights as she looked through it.

"Do I love who?" Gabriel asked.

"Your wife,"Lesya chuckled. "I take it, you are married?" she mused, half-smiling. She didn't mind that her seduction technique had failed, as she really didn't want to get involved with married men any more.

Gabriel looked at her for a moment, realizing what this conversation was about, and he answered simply. "Laura and I aren't exactly what you call married," he admitted. "We're not exactly your average couple." He wondered just how much to tell her. "We've loved each other for a long time, but never got around to formalizing it in any sort of official ceremony. It might complicate things. As it is, we both enjoy each other, live together, everything that a married couple enjoy, we enjoy. Legalities mean little to either of us, particularly as we often find ourselves at odds with the authorities," he admitted. "It's an open relationship. We spend time together and time apart from each other, as we each see fit."

"Like now?" Lesya asked, curious. Gabriel smiled.

"Oh, Laura is here in Rome too. We flew over together when we heard about the firebomb at La Scala. Belle is our daughter." Lesya's eyes widened at the sudden news.

"But you don't look old enough to have a daughter her age," she blurted out, suddenly noticing the resemblance, the features, skin-tone, same dark eyes.

"I'm older than I look," was the only explanation Gabriel gave her. "Laura is staying with Belle to supervise her recuperation, whilst I do what I can in concert with the authorities to help catch these terrorists. Knowing Belle, Laura will have her hands full," he chuckled.

Chapter Eighteen

June 22nd

Hamas used a six man team to carry out the raid on the police station. One of them had been held there before and knew the internal layout well enough to place the explosive charges. The wall almost disintegrated under the force of the explosion, killing one of the Israeli guards unfortunate enough to be walking past on his rounds at the time. Dust billowed out inside the station cell-block, as hooded men stepped over the rubble, firing sporadic rounds from their AK-47's blindly.

Fatima Khalid was woken up by the explosion, and she grinned at the sound of gunfire. Her people were coming for her, and she was instantly up off her bunk, hands on the bars in expectation. She heard the sound of the soldiers returning fire, and cries from the wounded as they went down under the Arab assault. There was normally only a skeleton staff here overnight, in this quiet suburb where little normally happened, and the Israelis tried to keep it that way to attract no undue attention to what was going on inside, but Hamas knew, and when Hamas knew, they acted!

After a minute's deafening gunfire, all was silent, and the door to the corridor was shoved open, clanging on the brick wall behind. Her interrogator, Lev Ashif, was frogmarched into the corridor, his shoulder bleeding from a bullet-wound. Pained and yet furious, he was forced to unlock Fatima's cell. She smiled as she walked coldly towards him, and as she drew close, before he could react, she grabbed for him and drove her knee hard up into his balls.

Ashif screamed and went down, hands clutching at his squashed testicles, as the Arabs laughed around him. "Give me a gun," Fatima ordered, and one of the men pressed an old Webley revolver into her hands, a souvenir of the British occupation after the War. It was oiled and loaded, and Fatima handled it familiarly. She looked down at the groaning Ashif, who was now staring back up at her with fear in his eyes. "The tables are turned now, Jew!" she smiled cruelly. "Now you are at my mercy, and I have none for your kind!" she spat at him. She cocked the hammer and aimed the gun down into the pit of his stomach. Before he had time to beg, she pulled the trigger, and Ashif screamed as the bullet ripped through his vitals. The men around her smiled as they watched his agony, but none more so than Fatima herself. "Die slowly and in great pain, Jew!" she sneered, and with that she turned on her heel and allowed herself to be escorted by the men of Hamas out of the police station. Italy awaited.

*   *   *

The phone rang shrilly on Maddox's desk, in the Embassy, as if sounding a warning, which indeed it was. He picked it up. "Jim?" sounded a worried voice, which Maddox recognised as belonging to Alexi Davidovich.

"Yes Alexi, it's me," he confirmed.

"Thank God I got through to you."

"This sounds urgent, so spit it out," he suggested.

"Fatima Khalid is loose and I can only assume on her way to Italy," he broke the bad news simply.

"Shit!" Maddox explained. "What the hell happened? You were supposedly interrogating her," he accused.

"Hamas attacked the local police station where she was being held, sometime during the night. Everyone was killed in the raid, and there was no sign of the woman when troops came to relieve the guards this morning." The news was sinking in, and Maddox was thinking furiously.

"How long do we have?" he asked. "What route will she take? Once she gets there and makes contact, Rebekah is blown sky-high."

"My sentiments exactly, Jim. We estimate two to three days, depending on her route. She'll no doubt be aware we'll be looking for her. Your assets are already in place. Can you do anything to help? I don't have time to set up an operation like this before she gets there."

"I'll call in what markers I can, Alexi. This isn't going to be easy."

* * *

Maddox decided to call at the Rialto himself to break the news, and once being cleared by Turnbull, met Gabriel in the restaurant. "Mossad's lost the real Fatima Khalid. We have less than three days to find and extricate Rebel before the Arabs find out she's a ringer!" Gabriel's jaw dropped.

"Who the hell screwed this one up?" was all he could think to say.

"Hamas sprung her from the detention cell. No good crying over spilt milk. It's happened and we'll have to deal with it." He fished in his pocket and came up with a computer diskette. "Mossad e-mailed me with latest photos of Rebekah and copies of all the forged travel documents she'll be using. I've got my own people on this right now, trying to track her down, but I thought you might have more success using your own people." He offered the diskette to Gabriel, who took it eagerly.

"Where's the nearest Internet Café?" he asked. Maddox indicated down the street. "Give me half an hour, and I'll be back." He put the diskette in his pocket, turned his collar up against the rain, and went out into the street. Maddox ordered a beer, then changed his mind and asked for a rum and coke. A large rum and coke.

* * *

Gabriel was restricted in his use of 'his own people'. As he sat down at the terminal and logged on to his secure web-site, all sorts of thoughts were going through his mind. He e-mailed first Donatello Grimaldi, and then Falcone, flagging up the messages as Priority, and enclosing all the attachments from the diskette that Maddox had given him. Furiously, his fingers began to fly across the keyboard as he typed. Between the Mafia and the Sword of Solomon organisations, surely one of them would be able to track her down in time? He looked at the image of Rebekah on screen, older now than when he had last seen her, but still as beautiful, with that wild faraway look in her eyes. No wonder Jim had fallen for her. What must be going through his mind just now?

* * *

Falcone downloaded the e-mail from Gabriel in his private office at St Bartoleme's. He read avidly the news of the Mossad agent working undercover, and he agreed that the escape of the terrorist she was masquerading as, now put her in immediate danger if she knew how to contact the cell. If, as they believed, she was now on her way to Italy, they had only a day or two to make contact with her, and extract her, or to find the real Fatima Khalid. He pondered telling Gabriel about the earlier call he had received from Laura. He had thought hard over the matter, and decided to let God make his own mind up on Gabriel's fate. He would not aid his rival for Laura's affections.

Falcone began making phonecalls, and sending e-mails of his own, spreading the news of the Mossad agent to his network of people, who would begin checking Customs and Immigration channels, and then would start contacting the hotels and police stations, to see if anyone had checked in to any accommodation using the passport and identification known. It might take time.

The phone-taps he had set up on the Algerian Language Professor were being monitored 24 hours a day since Laura's tip-off about the man. His movements were followed closely. It was he, Yusef Abdullah, who held the key to this thing. The phone taps were illegal of course, for Falcone had no qualms about operating outside of the Law. The Church was powerful in these matters should such indiscretions come to light. If the phone-taps didn't provide the required information, and soon, then Falcone had already decided to take further illegal steps. He would do what he could to remove this threat to the Catholic Church, even to the extent of helping a man he found himself hating. This Mossad agent, though a Jew, was also an ally in this cause, and so she would be helped too. Alliance and strange-bedfellows were not unknown where the Church was concerned, if transient.

* * *

Yusef Abdullah took possession of the balance of Gabriel's money. Innoccuous padlocked suitcases, which were transferred over to him by courier and had to be signed for. Abdullah knew what was in them, having received the 'smaller' deposit of one million dollars the other day. He had to get these under lock and key quickly. Robbery was not unknown here in Italy and should these funds go missing, before being collected, his life would be forfeit. He drove straight to Rome's Termini Station, and used two left-luggage lockers side by side, depositing coins and pocketing the keys. Two inconspicuous lockers, amongst hundreds of others. What could be simpler and safer? All he had to do now was get the keys to Torquemada.

He had found the only parking space close to the train station, by the time his Solomon tail had legally parked and rushed in after him, Abdullah was already out. The man could only guess at what had happened to the two suitcases the Algerian had been carrying. Either passed on to some unknown person at the busy station, or locked in one of the many hundreds of left luggage lockers, where they might never be found without a major security operation. Getting back into his car, Abdullah drove off, leaving a frustrated Solomon tail to rush back to his car, and hope to pick him up again on the road back to the Embassy.

Once back at the University, Yusef listened to a message on his answerphone, which had already been listened to by the Solomon agents manning the phone-tap. It was confirmation that the latest shipment of ordnance had been received and put into it's hiding place. He would have to contact the southern cell and advise them to collect the weapons. Tomorrow would do. He had had a busy day.

*　　*　　*

The lobby clerk was just putting the passports back in the cubbyholes for colleciton by the residents, after photocopying the main pages for forwarding to the local police, as he did every week. Actually he was supposed to do it every day, but it was too much of a chore to do it every day. Once a week was easier to manage.

It was the woman's photo that alerted him, having received a similar photo from the Sword of Solomon the day before, he had been checking female passports as he had been putting them back in the cubbyholes. He checked it again to be sure, and then called the phone number listed on the communique. A voice verified the identity of the woman, as stated on her passport, took the address of the hotel, and then instructed him to do nothing except wait. If the woman went out, he was to phone the number once more.

*   *   *

The woman known as Fatima Khalid tried to hide her surprise as they unpacked the latest ordnance that the Algerian had had delivered. Their contact, Yusef Abdullah, had already established a chain of supply with various arms dealers across Europe. They had a lot less trouble than Maddox in getting the weapons they wanted. The large suitcase opened to reveal a rocket launcher, broken down into two pieces for transport, but easily assembled. It came with two rockets. It could be held and fired by one man, and as she wasn't party to the phone conversation with the Algerian earlier in the day, or the conversation that Achmed had had with Torquemada the night before, Rebekah had no idea of the intended target.

Ali grinned, revealing two gold teeth as he caressed the long length of the launcher, in obvious penis-envy. Mustafa hefted one of the two rockets, though handling it carefully enough. It was light enough, but contained enough explosive to cause severe damage to anything it hit.

"We move out in half an hour," Achmed revealed. "Two cars, myself and Ali in the first with the launcher. Mustafa and Fatima in the second car, just behind. You will run 'interference' for us, slowing or hindering any pursuit, enabling us to get clear once we strike our target."

"Which is?" asked 'Fatima' as casually as she could.

"We don't have specific instructions," Achmed smiled. "Torquemada is happy for me to select a suitable target at random. He has specified the time and the place. The actual target is to be chosen by me at the time. I will have plenty to choose from," he promised. Rebekah had a bad feeling about this.

She had checked into their hotel, south of Latina, along with the three men, expecting the long awaited meeting with Torquemada. Rome was supposed to be the culmination of their campaign, striking a decisive blow against Catholicism, and then getting out of the country in the aftermath of the atrocity. This latest operation was not leaving her much room to maneouvre. If she was involved, there might be a way to forestall another attack if the opportunity presented itself, but her priority was to get Torquemada, and if innocents had to die to give her that opportunity, then the sacrifice would have to be made.

The rocket launcher was taken out to the first car still inside the large suitcase it had been delivered in. Ali sat in the rear of the car to unpack and assemble it once more, and Achmed got behind the wheel. Rebekah took the wheel of the second car, and Mustafa slid into the passenger seat alongside her.

*   *   *

The lobby clerk hastily phoned to report her movements, and was relayed to the same voice, though this time it seemed to be a weaker connection, on a mobile phone. "We're almost there now. Can you stall them at all?"

"No, I don't see how. They're pulling out of the car park now. Two cars, and they look to be taking the motorway towards Capodichino Airport."

"Describe the cars quickly, and give me the license numbers." Falcone cursed his luck as he took down the details, relaying them to his driver. Another ten minutes and they would have cornered this particular cell at their hotel. No time to set up surveillance. He had to play this one by ear.

*   *   *

Mustafa eyed Rebekah's knee which was now exposed as her skirt slid back up her thigh as she settled into the driver's seat, and adjusted it so that her feet could reach the pedals easily. All four of them had been dressed in western style clothing for their time in Italy, and all three of the men had enjoyed looking at Rebekah. It was a luxury they were not normally afforded in public in their homelands. Older than most of them, she was still a very attractive woman. He reached down, and put his hand on her knee, grinning at her. Rebekah pushed his hand away, concentrating on starting the car, and revving it up slightly. It was heavy and powerful, and would be able to maneouvre well enough to slow any pursuit down.

She could feel things building to a head as she followed the lead car. The route they were taking was south, heading back towards the main airport of Naples. The use of the rocket launcher was now becoming more noticeable, for the airport was on the outskirts of the city, and the runways were visible from some of the surrounding roads. Events were running away from her, and she wondered desperately how she was going to sabotage this latest terrorist act. If an aircraft was involved, the death-toll would be horrendous, and she could not stand by and let it happen. It felt like her whole life was just a prelude to the events that were about to unfold.

Rebekah had volunteered for the Ya'mas faction of the Mista'arvim, Israel's elite undercover unit, which operated amongst and within the Arab communities in Jerusalem, shortly after it was formed in 1990. The two existing Durvdevan and Shimson units were deemed insufficient with the upsurge in the Intifadah, which resulted in the death of her husband and son in a suicide bombing incident in the West Bank. Since then her life had been solely devoted to getting some payback from the fanatic Arabs who opposed peace on any terms with the Israelis.

Her looks were not typically Jewish, as her father had reportedly been an Arab, but once the romance with her mother had been discovered, he had been killed by his own people and her mother forced to leave Israel for the United States, and she would never discuss her father with Rebekah. As a result of her mixed parentage, she could pass for an Arab quite easily.

Her intelligence training for the CIA had stood her in good stead in the new life she had sworn to lead, working undercover, and living among the people she hated, posing as one of their own. She had to learn to live and breathe like an Arab, knowing that exposure would lead to possible torture, rape and mutilation, or death by the people she was spying on.

Her odd snippets of information were useful in a variety of snatch and execution operations, targeting members of Hamas, Fatah and the other outlawed organisations. She had participated in a number of these raids herself.

Her resemblance to the terrorist Fatima Khalid meant she was pulled from her regular duties as soon as her capture was completed.

The real Fatima was even now undergoing intensive interrogation in Tel Aviv, at least that was what she was led to believe.

*   *   *

Falcone followed the two terrorist cars at a close distance on the drive south. He had two other cars with him, each filled with four agents of the Sword of Solomon organisation. Since he had had word of the escape of the real Fatima Khalid, he knew that time was of the essence in freeing the Mossad agent from Al Qaeda's clutches before her cover was blown. He had no way of contacting or warning her, and surveillance had only just been set up when he had received the urgent call from his agent in place that the terrorists were on the move, and he had hastened to mobilize his people to play catch-up.

The real Fatima was expected to head for Rome herself, and they had no idea of how or when she would make contact with Torquemada's cell. Time was of the essence. A simple snatch effort was possible if they could get close enough in the traffic. Only the woman, and a single terrorist, in the rear car. It should be a simple enough job to fake an accident and achieve his objective before the lead car realised what had happened. Where were they all heading? Where could he stage the accident?

*   *   *

Rebekah's hands were starting to get sweaty and slipping a little on the steering wheel as they neared the Naples airport. She had to do something, and do it quickly. Changing her position in the seat slightly, she allowed the hemline of her dress to ride more up her thigh, revealing a lot of bare skin which attracted the Arab's eyes like flies round candy. Mustafah, sitting next to her, was more concerned with her hemline than what was happening around him, and the throat-strike caught him completely by surprise as the edge of Rebekah's right hand smashed into his adam's apple.

The car veered dangerously to one side as she made the blow, and the terrorist reacted, flailing about and choking. Rebekah hit him again, this time on the back of the neck, trying to push him away from her and speed up to overtake the lead car. She intended to ram it if necessary, to prevent it firing the rocket at any of the planes. Torquemada wasn't worth so many deaths on her conscience.

* * *

Behind her, Falcone mistook the movement of her car for something else. "They've spotted us. Move in quickly, and ram her car," he ordered the driver.

Tyres squealed as both Rebekah's car and Falcone's made sudden violent changes in both speed and direction, both trying to catch up to the cars in front of them. The Solomon driver was the more skilfull, and before Rebekah could see him coming, he smashed into her rear nearside wing, crumpling the bodywork down onto the rear tyre expertly, and slewing her car around as she fought for control. The tyre shredded and blew out, and the car bounced off the central reservation as she fought to control the skid. Cars around her braked, horns blared, and tyres squealed as they tried to get out of the way of the out of control car.

Falcone's three cars boxed her in quickly as the car finally came to a rest, and men surrounded the vehicle, guns drawn, as she slumped over the steering-column, momentarily stunned. They moved in quickly, and strong hands pulled her out of the car. The man was found to be dead at the scene, with a broken neck. They left him there in the car as Rebekah was quickly trussed with twist-ties, blindfolded, and eagerly thrown into the back of one of their cars, sandwiched between experienced agents. The Solomon cars then sped off quickly, before the other traffic had time to realise what was going on, taking the next sliproad exit. The whole scene had lasted less than two minutes.

* * *

Ahead, the two terrorists in the lead car, Ali and Achmed, were not unduly worried about losing sight of Fatima in the heavy traffic. They trusted her to do her job. They had seen nothing of the scene behind them in the heavy traffic.

The road ran parallel to the main runway of the airport, and the flight traffic was heavy. He weighed up the possible targets, all within range of the rocket launcher. A plane taking off would have the maximum loading of fuel, and that is what made his mind up in the end. A spectacular kill.

He opened both rear windows of the car, one for the rocket and one for the exhaust as he fired. He readied the rocket launcher, sticking it out and resting it on the lip of the rear window as he took aim.

On the runway an Alitalia jet was taxiing into position, taking its slot on the main runway and building up speed for take-off. As it neared the end of the runway, the experienced pilot pulled back on the yoke, and felt the landing wheels leave the ground as it took to the air, effectively baring its throat to the watching terrorists.

*   *   *

"Mamma, are you nervous?" asked the young boy, sitting with his mother, as the stewardesses took their seats and buckled in. The woman was sweating, very nervous of flying, though not wanting to alarm her young son. The boy held her hand reassuringly, and she squeezed his hand in gratitude for his support.

"Not with you beside me, Claudio. Keep holding my hand, and I'll be fine," she forced a smile. The plane was moving down the runway now, gathering speed as it prepared for flight. The runway flew past the small windows, as the woman and child peered out. There was a loud rumble as the wheels cleared the tarmac, and the plane took flight, rising steeply, and leaving her stomach behind on the ground as she tried to control her fear and nausea. The boy was more concerned with the view of the rapidly receding ground.

"Mamma, look at the fireworks!" The boy pointed, excited. The bright flash of the igniting rocket, and trail of smoke from it's trajectory was noted by a few of the passengers, who had only time for a brief scream as they realised what was happening.

*   *   *

The rocket hit the underside of the port wing, exploding close to the main fuselage, and rupturing and igniting the main fuel-tanks. The large explosion flipped the plane over, snapping the other wing to release more fuel and a secondary explosion broke the plane in two in mid-air, lighting up the sky with a bright fireball which could be seen for miles in every direction. A third explosion shattered the aft section of the plane, and debris and bodies rained down upon airport runways.

The two terrorists smiled with grim satisfaction at the sight, and calmly rolled up the car windows and continued on their way as though nothing had happened, as other cars slowed and some even stopped, gaping in awe at the unfolding carnage. Black smoke filled the sky behind them as they enjoyed the view in the rearview mirror.

*   *   *

Rebekah was stunned at the sudden intervention of these strange men. Professionals, they had taken out her car clinically before she had had a chance to react, and while she was stunned from the impact, had her out of the car, tagged and bagged before she knew what was happening around her. Now tied and gagged, she had no choice but to wait and see what these unknown men intended doing with her.

Falcone caught the mid-air explosion in the rearview mirror of his car as he drove, and flinched, crossing himself as he realized it must be something to do with the terrorists, but did not yet realize how close he had come to stopping the atrocity, and his unknowing assistance in letting them carry out the attack by making his move before Rebekah could make hers.

The cars drove north to a small villa off the highway between Latina and Naples. Set back in its own grounds, it was one of many safe-houses operated by the Sword of Solomon. Rebekah was helped from the car, and taken inside the building, where her blindfold and gag were then removed. Her hands were also unfastened as she squinted against the light, and she then rubbed the circulation back into her limbs as Falcone himself regarded her.

Some of the men who had brought her, now left, though two stayed in attendance, and obviously deferring to this man who now stood in front of her. "I am sorry for the rough treatment you received, but my men and I had to move quickly. We needed to get you out of there before the second car could react and interfere. We only had time to mount a very small operation before you were mobile," he started to explain.

"Who are you, and why did you interfere at all?" she asked, wondering what it was she had gotten mixed up in now.

"My name is Falcone, Marco Falcone, and I 'work' for the Church, and am currently assisting efforts to capture this terrorist cell that is operating on the Italian mainland. We know you work for Mossad," he revealed. "The real Khalid has escaped with the aid of Hamas, and is now on her way here. Your life was thought to be in danger, and so we were asked to extract you," he explained.

"Did Alexi contact you? Maddox?" she asked. "You don't understand the situation. I can't stop now. Torquemada is due in Rome tomorrow, and I'm too close to let this one go now. I have to be there when he arrives. It's the only time we know where he'll be. Both our cells are to rendezvous together there tomorrow. You have to let me go back," she pleaded.

"Gabriel contacted me," Falcone explained, and then he watched the colour drain from Rebekah's face, and the look of absolute astonishment in her eyes. "I believe you know him?"

"Gabriel? Gabriel contacted you?" she asked, trying to work out just how in the world he could be involved. Falcone saved her the trouble.

"I believe he is working with the Security Forces of Europol, trying to track down these terrorists," he revealed. "Both he and Maddox are currently in Rome." Rebekah gasped at the revelation. The two of them, together, so many memories came flooding back all at once. "Sit down, please. I'll have drinks brought," and he snapped his fingers to one of his aides as he helped Rebekah sit down on a padded sofa. He sat down next to her.

Rebekah was frustrated. She wanted to see them both . . . so near, yet her mission had to come first. They would not let her put herself back in danger by continuing with the charade, as long as they knew the real Khalid was on her way, yet tomorrow was just one more day, the best chance she would have to take out Torquemada. "Do they know I'm here?" she asked Falcone. He shrugged.

"As yet, we have had no time to tell them your whereabouts. We made contact with your cell only this morning, thanks to an informant of ours. By the time we got people organized, you were already on the move and we had to react as best as we could under the circumstances.

Would you like to talk to either of them?" he asked, offering the phone on the nearby table.

Rebekah shook her head. "No. I mean, yes, but not now. I can't, now. I have to see this thing through," she stated resolutely. "One more day. When is Khalid expected?" she asked.

"She escaped two days ago. You might only have one day left before she arrives, maybe longer if she is arranging entry herself. We have people at the airports, but Italy is a country that is very easy to access. If she knows what she is doing, she will arrive soon," he admitted.

What to do? Rebekah agonized. Jim and Gabriel, two of her best friends in her former life. She had never stopped loving Jim Maddox, yet she couldn't, daren't get close to him over this. It was something she had to see through, and he could never know the reason why. Gabriel. Why was he here? Had Jim involved him? Was it something to do with ETA that had brought him? She had heard the tales about his involvement with them, and struggled to understand them. Could she trust Gabriel to help her, and yet keep her involvement secret from Jim, one of his own closest friends back in Oman?

"I have to get back to Rome to make that rendezvous at the Villa. Torquemada is due to contact us there tomorrow. Once he does, we will all meet up for the final phase of our mission, which will be explained by Torquemada himself in person. That's when I'll get a crack at him. I just need one more day. I have to chance it," she insisted. "What happened back there can be made to look like an accident, and I can turn up pretending I was forced to avoid the authorities, and they'll believe me." Falcone was considering his options as she spoke. She was already on the inside, whilst Gabriel remained on the fringes. She would have the greater chance of getting to Torquemada, and so he had to help her. It was her risk, and she was prepared to take it.

"Very well," he agreed. "If that is your wish, we will help you get to Rome. If you do not wish us to contact either Gabriel or his friend Maddox, we also will refrain from doing so. But I know Gabriel is staying at the Rialto, should you feel the need to contact him," he offered. "You can stay here overnight, and my men will drive you to a nearby station early in the morning to take the first train into Rome."

*   *   *

Chapter Nineteen

June 24th

Fatima Khalid was well-used to men staring at her body, as these lusty Greek sailors did now as she perched on the side of the boat in her dark blue bikini. She accepted the swimming fins from one of them, and fastened them to her feet. Spitting into the mask, she washed it out with seawater before fitting it over her head, and putting the snorkel into her mouth. The boat rocked gently in the water, about a mile out from shore. She had assumed the identity of a sick seaman, confined to bed, as the Italian Coast Guard had come on board to check papers and manifests, but all was found to be in order, and the vessel allowed to enter Italian waters.

She slid over the side, plunging beneath the cooling waves which had not yet had time to warm in the morning sun. Surfacing, she blew out through the snorkel, and took in a lungful of air, and then started swimming leisurely with the tide, in towards the shore where a line of deckchairs could be made out all ready for the daily influx of tourists on the beach. By the time she reached shore, those deckchairs would be filled, and no one would think anything unusual of a bikini-clad woman emerging from the sea.

The beach was filling up nicely as she waited, just beyond the breaking surf, timing her arrival as she checked her waterproof watch. She shook off the fins and let them sink, did the same with the facemask, and started swimming up the shore till she was opposite one of the beach cafes where her contact was to meet her with clothing and transportation.

No one gave her a second glance except a couple of spotty adolescents who wolf-whistled her as she walked dripping out of the surf. Smiling, she let them stare at her jiggling rump, and deliberately accentuated her walk as she moved past and away from them. Piece of cake.

The small beachside coffee-bar was easily spotted, and she took her place alongside the Algerian, who had a towel waiting for her, and a strong black coffee, which she sipped at. To all intents and purposes they were a happy couple, though they had never before met in their lives. After taking her time with the coffee, and indulging in innocuous small-talk with her 'boyfriend' the two of them got up and she tied the towel around her waist as she walked with him along the beachfront towards the nearby car-park.

Once they were far enough away, their small-talk became more businesslike. "Did the shipment arrive?" she asked as she checked through the suitcase on the backseat of the parked audi. It contained documents, a map, and some clothing, all in her size, though not necessarily to her taste. There was also a small automatic handgun, and three clips of ammunition.

"The Italians got lucky, and intercepted the boat. But we made arrangements for a second shipment to be despatched by road." Fatima went behind the car to change, as the Algerian made his explanations. "Is the target still the same?" he couldn't help but raise his head, and saw Fatima pulling on a silk blouse. She was non-plussed.

"Don't worry, it will not be a nuclear explosion. My training has not extended that far at this time, but I can still make a manageable portable device which will irradiate most of the Vatican City, provided you have enough regular explosives," she assured him. "I can fit it into the trunk of the car. A protective suit to help me assemble the device is all I will need. I will place the device, arm it, drive it into position and then just walk away. There will be no stopping it once armed. Then we just have to park the car close enough to the Vatican City. No way will we be able to get the car inside. Those Swiss Guards take their job a lot more seriously than they do their dress sense," she sneered. She finished dressing as he watched, and tidied her wet clothing away in the suitcase. "When is Torquemada due in Rome?" she asked.

"Tomorrow. I have hired a villa for him to use. It's marked there on the map, plus a backup for contingencies. I thought it best to avoid hotels as the police are stepping up their searches."

"Have you managed to contact any of the cells yet to warn them of the viper in their midst?"

"They are not due to make contact with me again until tomorrow. They know my number, but I don't know theirs while they're on the move," he explained. "They use a variety of different cellphones, and I only know the stationary number in the accommodation I arrange for them. Unfortunately, this building is of recent construction, and I have not had time to get a secure phoneline installed. Unless Torquemada contacts me, he will remain out of contact for the time being."

"Very well, then. I have a long drive ahead of me." Fatima bade him farewell, and he stood back while she closed the car door, started up the engine, and drove off.

*   *   *

Abdullah returned to his own car, intending to drive back to Rome himself, though by a different route. He had a villa himself to the east of the Eternal City, and he spent little time there. If things were going to heat up in Rome, then perhaps now would be a time best spent out of the city. If he believed her, the damage to the city itself would be minimal, but devastating for the Vatican City, the home of Catholicism.

Preoccupied with his thoughts, he didn't notice the tall man walking gingerly up behind him, until the crunch of gravel under his feet alerted him to sudden movement, and as he whirled, excruciating pain burst out behind his left ear, and everything went black as he felt himself falling.

Abdullah's limp body was bundled into his car, and propped up on the passenger seat. His assailant fastened a seat belt around him, and then climbed into the driver's seat himself. Out of sight completely from the road, he pulled a small flat container from his inside pocket, and opened it to reveal an already prepared syringe. He plunged it into Abdullah's arm, and depressed the plunger slowly.

*   *   *

Fatima drove north on the coast road, her black audi indistinguishable from the rest of the innocuous traffic, at least while she was close to the seaside town. Once the road opened out and stretched north, traffic became scarcer, and she spotted the white car behind her after fifty miles or so. It stayed back there, not closing up or overtaking her, though she was making an effort not to speed. She even slowed down, to see if it would overtake her, but it kept its distance. Somehow Abdullah had compromised the mission. She cursed under her breath, and considered her options. It wasn't a police car back there, but someone was certainly interested in her movements.

The audi wasn't the fastest thing in the world, and she had only the one small handgun. The further north she led them, the closer she was leading them to Torquemada. She couldn't let this chase continue. She had to do something, but what?

* * *

The two Solomon agents in the car had orders to follow anyone Abdullah met, and report back when stationary. Falcone hadn't yet been informed of the contact. They kept a respectful distance behind the black audi, though keeping it in sight, closing up when coming near signs of civilization, then dropping back on the open roads. Suddenly, as they watched, the black dot began to slide into a spin, taking a long turn possibly too fast, and churning up dust as it went off the road. There was nothing else they could do, but keep going, and they could see the car's crumpled front wing as it lay hard up against a big boulder.

The woman had gotten out of the car, and then apparently collapsed by the side of the road. They pulled up just behind the crashed vehicle, and one of them ran to help the unconscious woman, gently rolling her over onto her back. As he did so, her eyes opened suddenly, and the hand holding onto the automatic came out from under her body. She shot him twice at point blank range in the chest, pushing him savagely away from her, as the second man panicked and went for his gun.

He managed just the one shot, before Fatima emptied the rest of the magazine into him, and he too dropped lifeless to the floor. Fatima looked around. The road was clear in both directions but she would have to be quick about this.

She dragged the two men into her crashed car, forcing them into the front seats and putting on their seat belts. She took her things from the audi and transferred everything of value into the white fiat, then took the spare container of petrol out of the boot of the audi, and began pouring it over the audi's bodywork and the two dead men. She put it back into the boot, and closed it once more. Satisfied, she went to the fiat and depressed the cigarette lighter. When it glowed cherry red and popped out, she took it and threw it into the audi, where the saturated clothes of the two dead men quickly caught fire, and the flames spread quickly. This wouldn't fool a proper autopsy, but would be enough to delay any serious investigation until she was well clear.

As the flames rose higher, she got into the fiat, started the engine and pulled away, to continue her journey north. Behind her, black smoke rose into the sky.

*   *   *

Falcone had driven through the night, and was feeling drained, even after a couple of cups of coffee, but he needed to interrogate the Arab. Abdullah came round slowly, groaning in pain from the blow to the head he had suffered, and he opened eyes to find himself in a scene from some obscure horror movie. He was in some sort of medieval dungeon, and as he looked around, he could see all manner of strange and obviously ancient devices. He himself was strapped into something vaguely human shaped, and made of iron, like a coffin which had been propped up on it's end, and leather straps held him there by his wrists and his ankles.

To his right, he heard the creak of rusted metal, and slow footsteps approached, crunching dust under leather soles on the stone floor. Typically, Falcone was dressed in black, though he wore no Executioner's hood. The white dog-collar around his neck gave him away, and Abdullah knew he was in the hands of his religious rivals.

"Yusef Abdullah. Welcome to the REAL Inquisition." Falcone smiled menacingly. "Before I am through with you, you will understand what really happened to the heretics of Spain, and you will tell me everything I need to know about this 'Torquemada'." He used the name derisively.

"I will tell you nothing, Christian." Abdullah spat at the priest. "I owe your people nothing, and it is my pleasure to bring them pain and death. It is my duty," he insisted. Falcone simply smiled, not wishing to listen to the usual mindless rhetoric and began closing the door on the front of the device Abdullah was strapped into, another human-shaped door, only this time the inside of it was filled with gleaming sharp knives. The device was known in medieval times as the Iron Maiden, and screws on the outside controlled the penetration of the actual blades themselves. They were set high at the moment, but that would change as the questioning continued. He slammed the door shut as Abdullah realized his fate. He gave out a loud feminine scream, which was cut off suddenly as the lid closed, and the points of the knives bit home in many places.

Falcone turned, and left Abdullah there, wailing in pain, yet realizing he was still alive, though bleeding from many wounds. He wasn't going anywhere. Time to catch up on a little sleep. He would return in an hour or so to see if the Algerian was feeling more talkative.

* * *

Torquemada and the remaining terrorist looked at the two suitcases as they stood there on the floor, next to the coffee table. He had inspected the contents, the balance of the ten million dollars the man called Gabriel had asked for as the price for the stolen nerve toxin.

"That is a lot of money," the other man commented.

"I am aware of that. What he offers is worth it, if it completes our mission here." He added. "The authorities got lucky and intercepted the boat with the nuclear material. Abdullah has arranged for a second consignment by a different route, but no telling whether this one will get through either, and such material is hard to come by at such short notice. We must seize this opportunity while we can."

"Still, it is a lot of money," the other man commented again.

"Yes, it is," agreed Torquemada. The man known as Anwar Rachman was thinking back to his youth in Keighley, and how hard he had strived there to earn just a fraction of the money that was now in front of him.

Chapter Twenty

Gabriel hushed Turnbull to silence, as he picked up the ringing phone, and listened to a cultured voice in the earpiece. The same voice he had heard before, on the terrorist's audio-tapes.

"Your name is not Aguila, as mine is not Torquemada," he began, "but mutual friends highly recommend using your services. I have the balance of your money. We will make the exchange today at the Cemetary of Campo Verano in one hour. Enter by the main gate, and about two hundred metres on the left is a large tomb of the family Gandolfo. The entrance is in decay and broken. I will meet you there. Come alone." Torquemada hung up.

"Did you hear all that?" Gabriel asked, as Turnbull put down the second earpiece. He nodded, already opening up the map of Rome that Maddox had given him.

"We'll be hard-pushed to get that covered in the short time he's given us. It's a big place. Nice and open, with lots of exits."

"I could just go alone as he asked."

"Fuck off! Maddox would have my balls if anything went wrong. Besides, we both know how cagey this clown is. All sounds too simple. I don't like it."

"Neither do I, but we're playing by his rules for the moment."

"Why not change the rules?" Turnbull mused, grinning slightly.

"What do you have in mind?" Gabriel asked.

"We're both roughly alike, and the only two who have seen you close up are both dead. I go in your place," he suggested.

"Torquemada won't go there alone either, but he will be there. He won't trust any underlings with that amount of money. He'll see to it himself." Gabriel was sure.

"All the more reason to nab the bastard while we can, then," Turnbull grinned.

"The cemetery will be a hard place to cover. Too open, and there'll be other members of the public there too. We don't have time for any subterfuge. Your boys will be spread thin. I'd rather go myself. You'd be better at controlling your own men, and have more chance to do it. Torquemada is probably already in place. I would be, if it were me making that call. He'll have whoever turns up in plain sight as soon as we get there. He's too cagey to do otherwise." Turnbull frowned, realising Gabriel was probably right.

"This is my call. I go, not you. I'll be wired and still in control of my men. You go with Dixon. Understood?"

"Perfectly," Gabriel smiled. He was starting to like Turnbull, but the man could be a pain at times, just like himself.

*   *   *

The Piazzale San Lorenzo was busy with traffic, and pedestrians. People filtered in and out of the cemetery gates, some pausing to pay their respects at the small chapel of San Lorenzo fueri le Muri. It was a large cemetery, with both old and new graves. It's only unusual feature was a cemetery within a cemetery for the Jewish community, to the north of the grounds.

Turnbull arrived by taxi, carrying the suitcase full of pseudo nerve-agent, as Torquemada would expect. Gabriel and Dixon, and Palmer and Coverdale arrived in pairs, on foot, one or the other carrying a small bouquet of flowers as did most of the visitors to the cemetery, mixing with the throng and pretending to search for the graves of loved ones. "Turnbull, live. Going in through the main gates," they all heard on their ear-pieces. The two pairs split up, one going south of the main path, the other pair going north, whilst trying to keep Turnbull in sight without being to obvious about it.

Torquemada was already here, Gabriel knew it. His backup would be here too, somewhere, and their whereabouts would be unknown, even though they knew the rough position of the rendezvous Torquemada would keep.

Turnbull walked slowly, sticking to the path. Up ahead he could see the various family crypts, all in various stages of repair, some modern, and some older, the stonework crumbling or sadly vandalised as so often happens with the wild youth of today. The graffiti was somehow reminiscent of his youth in Keighley.

His skin crawled as he approached the crypt in question, for he could feel the unseen eyes on him. As instructed, he went over to the broken entrance, and stood there, studying the engraving on the stonework, and a cultured voice bid him enter. "Come in slowly, and stand there in the light. No sudden moves," the voice warned.

Turnbull looked forward, eyes trying to pierce the black interior, but the only light fell in a short semi-circle just inside the tomb, where he walked forward, and stopped as instructed. His breathing was heavy, framed against the light, he was an easy target, a black silhouette, whilst he could see nothing of Torquemada. Worse, the darkness and echoing of the man's voice meant he couldn't even roughly place him within the dark interior. His eyes would need a few minutes to get used to the gloom. He hoped the radio broadcast would still penetrate the stone of the crypt so that his men would hear what was happening.

*   *   *

Gabriel and Dixon looked at each other, listening intently with their earpieces. They had seen Turnbull enter the crypt. Their eyes scanned around, trying to locate Torquemada's backup. He wouldn't be fool enough to come alone.

Palmer and Coverdale were looking too, and they thought they'd found one of them, a dark-skinned individual sat on the side of the grass with a sketchbook, scribbling away in a rather poor attempt at artwork, trying to copy one of the tombs. They walked past slowly, giving no indication they had paid him undue attention. "One possible, south of the main path," Coverdale whispered into the mike, on a frequency only the other watchers would hear. None of them dare broadcast on Turnbull's frequency in case Torquemada overheard.

*   *   *

"Open the suitcase. Show me what I'm buying." The hidden voice instructed. Turnbull knelt down, putting the suitcase on the ground, and slowly releasing the catches. He opened it slowly, letting the light fall on the golden ampoules of liquid, twelve of them, all nestled in padded recesses.

"How about showing me the money?" Turnbull asked. As he gestured, he turned slightly, and the side of his face caught the light. He heard a small sharp intake of breath.

"Turn around slowly. All the way around," the voice instructed. Turnbull did as he was told, turning in a small circle, the light from the entrance falling this way and that on his features. A small chuckle could be heard. "You've come a long way to die, Turnbull," the voice spoke with menace, and Turnbull's blood froze. The man knew who he was, but how? He flung himself sideways as the first shot rang out in the confines of the tomb. A second quickly followed, and he cried out as the vest saved his life a second time. But his head slammed into one of the stone projections near the entrance, and he saw stars, going down, sinking to his knees, vision blurring, as Torquemada came forward into the light, standing over him and aiming the gun down directly into his face.

Turnbull looked up into the face of the man who was going to kill him. Seeing the grinning face look down over the barrel of the gun, features slowly coming into pained focus. "You!" he gasped, as recognition finally dawned.

"Me," the grinning face nodded, and his finger tightened on the trigger.

*   *   *

Gabriel and Dixon began to run as soon as they heard the first shot. Palmer and Coverdale did the same, closing down the suspect artist, who was alerted by the shot and also their movement. He pulled a Spectre machine pistol from under his sweater, and unleashed a deadly salvo in their direction, the whole magazine of 50 shots peppered the two SAS men, stopping them in their tracks as they dove for cover.

Cursing and swearing, both men dropped behind tombstones, trying to ignore the screams from the innocent passersby, who were now running screaming from the site. Palmer tried to return fire as the terrorist slammed a second magazine into the breach. Coverdale cursed as he nursed a wounded arm. Their Kevlar vests had saved them both from worse injury.

From a distance, Gabriel and Dixon saw Turnbull fall, and saw the dark figure who now stood over him, saw the gun being levelled point-blank at Turnbull's face, and knew they would not get there in time.

Gabriel stopped, and levelled his gun, though he knew the range was too far with this light Beretta. Bracing his gun-hand, he rattled off the full magazine at the standing figure, seeing the bullets raise splinters off the surrounding stonework, though all missing their target.

The distraction was all Turnbull needed, though, and he kicked up, catching Torquemada in the crotch, just as his gun went off, and Turnbull screamed once, trying to throw himself to one side, feeling the heat of the discharge, and the hot flow of blood as the bullet creased his cheek. When he rolled back, Torquemada was gone, and so was the suitcase full of pseudo nerve-agent.

More gunshots could be heard outside, as Palmer and Coverdale both swapped fire with Torquemada's henchman. Dixon was first to the scene, checking that Turnbull was still alive, though luckily. The bloodied face looked worse than it was. Gabriel, having paused to reload, went past the crypt, pursuing Torquemada. He couldn't afford to let him go.

The tall dark figure ran north through the tombstones, towards the Jewish cemetery, clutching the suitcase to his chest as he ran. Gabriel followed, unleashing two quick shots, then realising he needed to get closer. "Going North," he panted into his comms mike, hoping the others could join in the pursuit.

Screaming figures ran from the tall running man and his pursuer, already alarmed by the sound of gunfire, they could see that something serious was going on. Gabriel hoped Torquemada would just keep running, and keep it man to man, before he took advantage of the situation around him, for more and more groups of grieving relatives were to hand. Hostages for the taking.

*   *   *

Turnbull staggered out of the crypt, head still ringing, and helped by Dixon. "He's getting away," he heard Palmer cry, and another burst of machine-pistol fire. There wasn't much they could do against that sort of firepower with revolvers. Everything was going tits-up again.

"Follow Gabriel. I'll try and help the other two," he ordered, though part of him was hoping the other Arab was a bit more accurate with his aim. Dixon took off north towards the screaming, running fast to try and play catch-up. Gabriel had a good head-start on him now.

*   *   *

Gabriel's worst fears were about to be realised. Looking back and seeing his undaunted pursuer, Torquemada took a hostage. Grabbing one wailing woman, he held the gun to her head as Gabriel pulled up short. "Throw the gun away!" he ordered, finding it hard to hold onto the now-hysterical woman. "Throw it away or she dies," he warned. Gabriel had little choice. He threw the Beretta to one side. Torquemada smiled, and levelled the gun once more, this time at Gabriel.

He dropped and rolled as Torquemada fired, trying for the gun, but coming up short, and he cried out as the bullet struck his lower leg. Torquemada threw the woman from him, and ran off through the tombstones, out of sight.

Dixon found Gabriel sat up in the grass, trying to staunch the bloodflow from his leg. Dixon pulled out a handkerchief, and made a makeshift tourniquet, pulling it tight above Gabriel's calf.

Torquemada had gotten away, and from the comms broadcasts, so had his single accomplice. No other suitcases were found in the crypt. Torquemada had intended a doublecross all along. Dixon helped the limping Gabriel back through the cemetery to where Turnbull and Palmer where attending to Coverdale's arm-wound. "He got away, but at least we both got a look at him. We now have a description to work on." Gabriel assured Turnbull, who snort laconically.

"Oh, I can go you one better there, Guvnor. Him and me are old friends," he revealed. Everyone's eyebrows raised at that piece of news, as Turnbull paused for effect. "His name is Masoud al Asmi. The cunt was two years above me in school in Keighley!"

Chapter Twenty One

Keighley, 1982: Masoud al Asmi counted his money on the kitchen table. £347 in bills and coins. He tied a rubber band around the three hundred, and tossed it into the small safe, closing it and spinning the tumbler. He didn't trust banks. He had a lot of money in the safe already, well over Ten Thousand. He had plans. He didn't intend to stay in this shit-hole for the rest of his life.

University beckoned, but needed to be paid for, and so he was working on building up his funds, by dealing in drugs, and getting some of the local girls hooked, and peddling their asses off on a streetcorner to earn him money. He had six girls in his current stable. One cute little black thing, called Jemma, who was even now asleep in his bed upstairs, and five white girls.

They had all started off young and beautiful, but a few months on drugs and on the game and they were starting to look a bit rough, and had to be beaten occasionally to get them to look after their appearance better. No punter was going to go with a scrubber. Give them the appearance of beauty and refinement in their whores. That's what they all wanted when they were banging away on top of them, before they went back to their plain, prim and proper wives. Just a little excitement in their lives, that was all they craved.

A knock at the door required an answer. He opened it calmly, aware that his bodyguards out in the street would not let anyone suspicious approach his door. It was sweet Sally, who was stood there, sniffing and using her cuff to wipe her nose, as she looked up at him, strung out. Masoud chuckled and smiled as he looked down at her.

"I need a fix real bad, Masoud," she explained. Masoud nodded.

"Yes, I can see that," he smiled. He had enjoyed getting the girl addicted, giving her free drugs until she simply had to have more.

"I don't have any money, but I'll get some. I promise," she pleaded. Masoud smiled and held the door open as she stepped inside.

"There is more than one way to pay for your drugs, Sally. Why don't we go upstairs, eh?" Sally looked at him for a moment, then nodded obediently, and started climbing the stairs. Masoud closed the door and began to follow her, eyes on her jiggling rump which the short jacket and skirt didn't quite cover.

She stopped short when she opened the bedroom door and saw the sleeping black girl already in Masoud's bed. "There's a girl in your bed," she turned, and told him.

"Yes I know. Let's join her," he smiled. "Take your clothes off and get in there with her," he ordered. Sally hesitated, and Masoud slapped her viciously, making her cry out and recoil against the wall. "Do as you're told, Sally. You want the drugs, I want paying, and you can pay with your pussy!" he explained. Whimpering, the frightened girl began to undress, watched by the leering Masoud. He was going to enjoy this.

Sally shivered as she took off her clothes, all too aware that Masoud was also undressing. Masoud was thinking more of her brother than he was of her, if truth be told. Her brother had been a thorn in his side for a long time, and fucking his sister would only be the start of the payback he had planned.

He pulled back the quilt, and pushed Sally onto the bed. "She's asleep," she complained.

"Well, use your tongue to wake her up!" Masoud leered. "Get lapping away at her pussy!" he ordered, forcing her head down into the sleeping black girl's crotch. Sally tried to recoil, but Masoud was too strong, and he forced her face into the other girl's sex. "Lick it, you bitch! Do as I say!" Masoud pressed up behind her, and she could feel his hard cock against her buttocks. She forced herself to lick, performing cunnilingus on the sleeping girl, as she felt him positioning himself behind her, the hard end of his prick stabbing between her thighs. She stiffened as she felt it going in, but didn't dare stop what she was doing, and Masoud grunted as he thrust home. The black girl, Jemma, woke finally, and looked down her body at the blonde head at her crotch, and she sighed pleasantly in post drug-stupour, reaching out a hand to gently stroke Sally's blonde hair.

*　　*　　*

Later, Sally lay on the bed, enjoying her fix, wrapped in the arms of the black girl, while Masoud took a shower, and put on some fresh clothes. Sally would be a nice addition to his stable, and he would make damn sure her brother knew all about it. He hated that man with a vengeance.

Chapter Twenty Two

*T*urnbull's face was still red above the dressing on his cheek, one eye slightly swollen, and Gabriel limped heavily across the room to accept the brandy that Maddox poured, as the two of them were getting debriefed at the British Embassy. The other three SAS men were being attended to downstairs, where medical aid was already being offered to Coverdale's light arm wound.

Turnbull groaned, his ribs aching, as he turned in his seat. "Not exactly best mates at this school of yours, then, I assume?" Maddox asked him, sarcastically. Gabriel took a refreshing sip of the brandy, and waited for Turnbull to continue the tale as well as Maddox, who was sifting through intelligence reports just received from Mossad.

"You have to understand the place I was brought up, to understand Masoud, or Torquemada as he's calling himself right now. With the influx of Arabs and Asians into our local community, and all the political correctness going on and making sure the ethnic communities got all the grants and looked-after at the expense of the white indigenous population, there was a lot of racial tension there. Still is, to this day," he added. "You couldn't look the guy in the eye without being accused of racism, and the authorities would always believe the coloreds. Couldn't afford not to with the way the media presented things. You wouldn't believe some of the things that guy and his gang got away with back then. It was no surprise that gang warfare broke out unofficially. Whites were a minority. We took the law into our own hands, as we knew their hands were being tied by the establishment. Everyone knew where the no-go areas were. Gangs didn't care, and we went looking for trouble. I gave Masoud the kicking of his miserable life one day," he chuckled, reminiscing. "It didn't solve anything. They had the law on their side, even the local MP's. Scumbags, bent and on the take, all of the fuckers." He pulled a face, and took another slug of brandy. "I joined the Army to get away from all that, a simpler life, as it were," he chuckled. "All bosses are bastards!" he winked at Maddox as he said it, and Jim chuckled wryly.

"You make it sound a bit one-sided," Gabriel noted.

"From my point of view, it was. I was there, mate. You weren't. It's happening in a lot more places than Keighley. I've never considered myself a racist. But this is sort of racism in reverse. Look at the world today. Black this, Black that. How many things do you know that start off with the word 'White'? Not fucking many. It's as though 'white' is a dirty word these days. They're even dumbing down the English language, and we just accept it, use their own bastardised words ourselves as though it's 'cool'. I see white guys performing rap songs, singing and dancing as though they were black. Makes me puke. The only thing missing is the face-paint," he chuckled. "Bring back the Black and White Minstrels, eh? Sure slavery existed, and sure, we whites exploited that at the time, but it was the blacks themselves that started the slave-trade, selling each other off to the white traders. Why is it always painted as something only the whites should feel guilty for?" he asked. "Its history, and best learned from if not forgotten," he added. "Everyone today should just get on with their lives and get on with everyone else, regardless of colour or religion. Most do, but some extremists take advantage of western society's political correctness to foment unrest, and these cunts get protected by the very laws they argue against. They come over to UK claiming persecution in their own countries, and then start preaching unrest and about how unfair British society is, declaring open support for people like Bin Laden, and we just let them. How stupid is that? If they don't like our society, why come over in the first place?"

"What's your view on it, Jim?" Gabriel asked. Maddox shrugged.

"Can't argue with facts, Gabe. Britain is a little island, despite being a 'big' nation. Far too many immigrants and asylum seekers are allowed into the country, both legally and illegally. The government pays these people from taxpayers' money while their claims for asylum are being considered, sometimes more than most UK people earn from legitimate jobs. They get free housing, whilst some indigenous people are homeless. Of course they are not legally allowed to work until their case is heard, but they get that money regardless. Companies flout the law, and get a slave labour force, while paying no taxes. Whole system is riddled with bureaucracy, and open to abuse. Why do you think, with the whole of the EEC to choose from, asylum seekers travel all the way across Europe to get to England? The rest of the EEC helps them on their way, too. They don't want the problems England is prepared to make for itself by letting all these people in. We're being buried in a sea of people, political correctness and red tape. I may have to work in it and wade through it, but I don't like it," he admitted.

Turnbull continued his story. "Anyway, I joined the Army to get out of Keighley, and to further my education. My parents couldn't afford to put me through university. Masoud got plenty of help from the Government, as he's an 'ethnic minority', 'positive discrimination' etcetera," he scoffed. "Nationwide, he might still have been classed as such, but the whites were the ethnic minority in Keighley, and we got no fucking help from the Government." Turnbull ranted, bitterly. "He also bankrolled his education with a sideline in drugs and prostitution, which the police knew about but didn't care to do anything about. Look how he turned out. A fucking terrorist!" he shook his head. "Pieces of paper are so important these days in finding a worthwhile job. Doesn't matter how good you are, you need a piece of paper and you have to work for peanuts," he snorted. "That HSBC bank is only the thin end of the wedge. Sacking a load of Brits to give their jobs to people in India. Just answering a fucking phone, for God's sake. Their excuse was that the people now doing the jobs are not only cheaper than Brits, but are College Graduates. They have Degrees and work for peanuts, comparative to Brits. I ask you, the cost of living is so much cheaper over there that they can afford to, but it's Elitism. Sooner or later a Degree is going to be a minimum qualification for answering the fucking phone," he laughed and took another slug of brandy, enjoying the warmth in his stomach. "The world is going to hell in a handcart! Companies don't care about people, only profit. Maximum profit for minimum cost. They're not satisfied with a fair profit, it has to be maximum profit, as much as they can squeeze out of the marketplace. National minimum wage? Just an excuse to downgrade peoples' salaries to slave wage levels. More and more jobs are disappearing overseas like this. The UK workforce is being put on the dole more and more. Sooner or later it'll disappear altogether. Governments don't care. All politicians do when they're in power is milk the expenses, and cosy up to the big firms to assure themselves of board positions to fund their retirement. One day, countries like the UK will find they no longer have a workforce, and then how will they be able to support themselves? They won't be able to earn any money to spend on the products these fat-cat companies produce. Anarchy will reign, likely civil-war, yes even in a country like UK. We've let our Governments take us for a ride for too long. By that time all these unscrupulous politicians and company directors will be safely enjoying life on their private islands somewhere while the rest of the world goes up in flames."

"There speaks the voice of experience?" queried Gabriel, trying to raise the mood, but he'd obviously touched a nerve with Turnbull.

"I've seen your file, mate," he announced to Gabriel. "Some of things in it don't make obvious sense, and I'm not trying to pry, but humour me," he asked, before continuing. "You left the Regiment in the 80's, before getting mixed up with E.T.A. Then you disappeared, and have been keeping a low profile ever since. That takes money. Everything takes money these days. It's the one common denominator. I'd guess you're worth a few bob?"

Gabriel nodded in reply. "I made a few investments," he explained briefly. "They turned out quite nicely." He didn't want to give too much information away. Both Turnbull and Maddox were no mugs. Turnbull nodded.

"Luckier than me, then. All my dabbles into the Stock Market ended up in failure. All my insurance policies, endowments, went tits-up. Lost money instead of made any. All I got was a 'sorry'. Governments have screwed people with insurance and pensions for years. It's been a long time since you had to work for a living or even lived in UK, right?" Gabriel could only nod in agreement. "My divorce was inevitable under the circumstances. Not many people in the Regiment have good marriages. My wife got the house, and I got the policies, supposedly an equal split, but based on the expected maturity values of the policies. They didn't mature that well, as I said, so she ended up with a house worth £133,000 and I LOST £5000 on the two endowments before I cut my losses and cashed them in. Never made any money on them at all. Now my private pension currently looks like netting me £300 a YEAR, not a week, as it was supposed to. Where's the equal split, eh? Doesn't matter which lot you vote in, Governments don't give a fuck for the people. Society is degrading. Everything is about money. Those who have it and those who don't. All the adverts on tv are about money, insurance, loans, consolidation loans, credit cards. It's harder than ever to get a job that's secure. Staff jobs are a thing of the past. It's all contract work these days. You're always at the mercy of your bosses' whims. Doesn't matter if you're good at it, if they have a mate looking for a job, they'll give him yours without a second thought, and no protection at all from the Government. The Army is about the only place where you can feel reasonably secure, and that's why I ended up in it. Not because I'm a death or glory idealist. I just wanted a steady job," he snorted. "England's changed since the last time you lived there, Gabe, and Masoud and me we're children of the times. I found the Army, and he found the Al Qaeda. You did the right thing becoming an Ex-Pat and getting the fuck out of UK. It's a shithole these days," he grinned wryly at Gabriel.

"You always were a cheerful sod, Nick," Maddox chuckled, trying to raise the mood slightly. Gabriel was examining his leg, rolling up the torn trouserleg, as he mulled over Turnbull's words. He was insulated from a lot of modern life's current problems, because of his accumulated wealth, yet he could empathise. Jobs weren't guaranteed to last, and they were harder to find and to keep, as Technology marched on and needed less workers to march with it. In a modern society, everything depended upon the flow of money, and once employment wasn't there, you had none.

The flesh of his leg was still red and livid, but the bullet had gone straight through the calf-muscle, and was healing quite nicely already. Turnbull and Maddox both marvelled at the way the flesh had already knitted itself back together. There was a lot the two of them knew about Gabriel, and an awful lot more they didn't know.

Maddox was perusing the files he had finally persuaded Mossad to transmit. All they knew about Masoud al Asmi's time with Al Qaeda, and his training in the Middle East. "Well, this laddie's photo has now been circulated across Italy. If he sticks his head up, it'll get shot off."

"Any result from the stakeout at the villa?" Gabriel asked. Maddox shook his head.

"None. It seems as though he has alternate plans, now he knows we're onto him." Maddox admitted.

"First opportunity I get, that bastard's dead!" Turnbull swore. "Should have topped him back home, and then we wouldn't be in this present mess."

"I hope you get the opportunity, Nick, but we need to find him first. We're checking on similar properties on the outskirts of Rome. He must have had a backup plan in mind, but wasn't expecting his cover to be blown so soon. He'll try and change his appearance or just keep out of sight till it's over," Maddox surmised.

"Apart from the beard, he looked similar to the last time I saw him. Tall like that, he'll stick out. You can't change your height too well. The beard will probably go. Not much else he can do," he surmised.

"He'll also have a plan for getting out of Rome," Gabriel pointed out. "He's educated, and I doubt he'll be of a mind to make a martyr of himself. This Jihad isn't meant to end here in Rome, remember. The home of Catholicism first, then on to the rest of the world's religions. He has big plans, which entail getting out of here in one piece. Considering what could happen if he pulls off this hit on the Vatican, he must already have a way out of here. We need to find it."

"More importantly, we need to find Khalid. As well as the obvious threat to Mossad's agent in place, Alexi's files reveal she is the bomb-maker. She's had training in the Bekaah Valley in the handling of nuclear material. Without her they can't make a nuke, but if she manages to get through, then as well as killing Rebekah, she'll turn the nuclear material into a dirty bomb. Insufficient material for a proper nuke, it could still irradiate a substantial portion of Rome, including the Vatican, which is their obvious target."

*   *   *

Torture was a fine art, and Falcone had become an expert at it. Brutality had its uses, and combined with a few selective drugs, could be used, in different doses, to break most men. Abdullah had already given him the names of all the terrorists involved in these atrocities, and already his people in the Sword of Solomon organisation were carrying out enquiries.

The safe house he had disclosed was already under surveillance by the security forces, so Abdullah must still have a few secrets to sell. He was no longer strapped inside the Iron Maiden, though his body still bled from dozens of small puncture wounds. Falcone had no intention of killing him too quickly, till he had extracted all of Abdullah's secrets.

He was rambling now with the drugs coursing through his system, and a tape-recorder was taping everything for later analysis. The nuclear material was smuggled out of Kazakhstan and into Chechnya, where rebels and former nuclear plant workers helped package the material, first into lead encased ingots for further transportation by sea, which the Coast Guard had unfortunately intercepted, and then the second backup consignment which had been sent by road. That information was already on the way to the authorities, as his own organisation was ill-equipped to respond to that type of threat. Gabriel's offer of the bio-toxin was an obvious ruse, to him anyway, which they seemed to have fallen for as a result of the loss of the boat, and in this instance he hoped Gabriel was successful in contacting and eradicating the terrorists. His British allies would then eradicate Gabriel as well, and Falcone would shed no tears.

*   *   *

Masoud al Asmi fumed quietly as he shaved in the bathroom mirror of the hotel room he and his single compatriot were currently holed-up. The beard would have to go, but he would keep a moustache, changing the basic shape of his face just enough.

Turnbull! Half a world away and still that little man plagued the life out of him. When he'd heard Turnbull had left to join the army, Masoud had thought himself well rid of him. Now plainclothes and over here meant only one thing. Special Forces. Now they had his name, and photos would quickly follow. Time was running out. The suitcase full of the supposed bio-toxin stood there on the floor. He had no doubt it was all a set-up, and was glad he hadn't bothered to take the two suitcases of money to the rendezvous. He would have to do something with that money. No good letting it go to waste, and the Al Qaeda had more than enough money. They wouldn't miss it. It was time he started thinking of his future.

Omar and he were all that was left of the Northern Cell. A suitcase full of glass bottles of what was probably urine, and two suitcases full of an obscene amount of money there on the bedroom carpet. What to do now? Tomorrow he was due to rendezvous at the safe house in Rome, but if the authorities were onto him this early, just how safe was it? What should he do with the money? Return it to his masters? But his western upbringing had taught him the value of money. They had enough money, whilst he could find much better uses for it.

He had tried contacting the other terrorists in the Southern Cell, but Ali was not answering his mobile phone. Yusef Abdullah at the University was also unavailable, and that did not bode well. All he could do was hope Yusef would get back to him. There was a back-up plan for such eventuality involving another villa, but no guarantees that hadn't been compromised as well. How could he be sure? Without phone contact, he would have to get Omar to visit the second villa and wait to see who turned up, remaining in phone contact with him at all times. He would think of what to do with the money in the meantime. Best that Omar did not know what he did with it. The young idealist might have objections.

The phone rang, and Torquemada hoped it was Yusef Abdullah, but no such luck. It was the Russian, Kovacs. "Your shipment is due at the warehouse at 1800hrs, local time, tonight. I would expect the authorities to be interested in it. Best take no chances. Did Yusef get you the uniforms and passes?"

"Yes, he did, though the men who were to use them are no longer with us. We will manage, and proceed as planned." Torquemada confirmed.

Chapter Twenty Three

Rebekah took a taxi from Termini Station, attempting to reach the safe house at the address she had memorized, but on nearing the place, she suddenly spotted a familiar car parked up the street, some distance from the villa, and containing Achmed and Mustafa who were watching the place with interest. She quickly ordered the taxi-driver to go around the area, pretending to be lost, and taking in the surroundings herself. Her trained eye soon spotted the surveillance, parked vans, with darkened windows, or heavily laden suspension, revealing possible bodies hidden in the rear, as had Mustafa and Achmed. Finally, pretending to locate the address she wanted, Rebekah got dropped off further up the street, and slowly approached the Arabs's car, letting them see her in good time, so as not to startle them.

"You took your own sweet time, woman!" cursed Mustafa. "Where is Ali? The place is being watched by the Italian Security Forces," he explained. Rebekah nodded in agreement, and hastily climbed into the rear of the car as a door was opened for her.

"With all the panic at the airport, there was an accident, and our car went off the road. Ali was killed in the crash. His neck was broken, and I had to get away to prevent being questioned by the authorities. I checked into a hotel overnight, and came to Rome by train, and hoped to meet up with you here," she gave her explanation. Achmed cursed, slamming a fist into his palm.

"It was only a matter of time. Allah's will, I suppose. Still, there are three of us to make the rendezvous. Torquemada will not come here now. He will resort to the backup accommodation, the smaller villa with the underground garage, where they intend to build the bomb," Achmed revealed.

"Bomb?" asked Rebekah, for she had not been privy to Torquemada's plans, as had been the men. The two of them looked at her strangely for a moment.

"The nuclear material that the Algerian promised us. The bomb you are supposed to make." Rebekah fought to regain control of her surprise.

"I didn't think they'd be able to smuggle that material into Italy," she said simply.

"Let us hope they succeeded, and we can finish this mission and get the hell out of Italy. Our luck can't last forever," Mustafa admitted. Achmed started the engine, and pulled away from the kerb slowly, driving away from the villa and its watchers. Rebekah's stomach felt queasy. The stakes had just risen, and it felt like she was playing a blind hand.

*   *   *

The drive to the second villa took about twenty minutes, driving east, towards the outskirts of the city, and Achmed drove slowly around the property, taking note of the surroundings and the vehicles, as did Mustafa and Rebekah. Finally satisfied, they pulled up outside the walled property labeled Alton Apartments, and Mustafa entered a sequence of numbers into the keypad on the wall to operate the electric gates, which swung wide to admit the car as Achmed drove forward. Mustafa closed the gates once more, as Achmed drove down the ramp to the underground garage. Mustafa walked down the ramp to punch in more numbers on a second keypad, and Achmed drove into the roomy garage as the door swung up to admit him.

Rebekah noted no other vehicles in the garage, so Torquemada and the Northern Cell had not yet arrived. She got out of the vehicle as Mustafa closed the garage doors, and Achmed took two suitcases out of the boot of the car. There was easily room for another vehicle, and the rear wall was filled with a large workbench. A variety of tools were pinned up on the wall, and a heavy metal chest, presumably containing more tools, was against one end of the bench.

She and the two Arabs entered the villa from the adjoining door, which opened into a small laundry room, with a single flight of stairs upto the main house. Once up there, they took in their surroundings. A large lavishly furnished living area looked out onto a small rear garden with a medium sized swimming pool. There was a kitchenette, and a dining room separate from the rest. Mustafa went upstairs to check on the bedrooms. There were three of them, one master bedroom, and two others containing single beds, but convertible sofas gave the option to sleep more. A typical holiday villa, as used by many visiting families. Nothing to attract attention, which was the last thing they needed right now.

"I'll need new clothes," Rebekah announced. "All my things had to get left behind at the motorway. I had no time to grab anything," she explained. Mustafa grunted. "I noticed a small shopping complex a few streets away. I shouldn't be long," she explained, already on her way out. She wanted to let Mossad know what had happened to her.

"Just a minute," Mustafa called her back, and Rebekah paused, one hand on the doorknob. "You haven't much money," he pointed out. "I'd better go with you," he suggested, and Rebekah couldn't think of a reasonable argument against his suggestion.

"Food's okay. I checked the kitchen," confirmed Achmed. "Cupboards are stocked with enough food to last us a week. We should be out of here within that time."

"Very well, let's go," suggested Mustafa, and he and Rebekah left the villa. She watched him key the numbers into the keypad to operate the door, and memorized them for future reference. Then the two of them walked back along the tree-lined street in the direction of the small shopping complex. As they walked, Rebekah was puzzling how she was going to contact Mossad with Mustafa in tow.

*　　*　　*

Mustafa stuck close to Rebekah as they walked through the complex, playing the attentive husband, and Rebekah saw no opportunity to get to a phone while he was with her. That left only the toilets and the changing rooms. Excusing herself, she headed into the Ladies Toilet, hoping against hope that there was a phone inside. There wasn't. Cursing silently, she went into one of the cubicles and sat down for a few minutes. Only one thing left. She had to leave some sort of message, and so she pulled some sheets of toilet paper, folding them and putting them into her handbag. Then she got up and flushed the toilet. She walked out calmly, and Mustafa accompanied her as she selected a few dresses, blouses, and underwear to try on.

She went towards the changing rooms, while Mustafa remained behind. Going into one of the cubicles, she went through the motions of undressing and trying on a few items, and then, satisfied, she took out the tissue and a biro from her handbag, and scrawled a hasty note on the tissue, before folding it and stuffing it into one of the pockets of the jackets she had no intention of purchasing. She didn't dare speak to the assistant in case Mustafa overheard, but when she returned the clothes to the racks, she would hopefully notice and act on the note she was leaving for her.

The note said simply 'EMERGENCY . . . pls phone Gabriel Aguila at Hotel Rialto. Advise worst fears realized. 12 Alton Apartments.' That was all she could do. If she tried to get the woman to phone the authorities, who knows what she might do. Best not to frighten her, and Gabriel would know by now to contact Mossad if he was involved with Maddox again. She attached the largest denomination bill she had in her purse, in the hope that the small bribe would help persuade the woman to make the call. In the meantime, she had to see things through, and hopefully take out Torquemada as soon as she identified him.

Remaining calm, Rebekah came back out from the changing cubicles, with her purchases over one arm, and the other items she didn't want over the other. "Thank you, but I won't be needing these," she smiled at the assistant, and she handed over a skirt and jacket. The jacket was deliberately buttoned up wrong so as to draw the assistant's attention to it, and the tissue paper just poking out of the pocket, barely visible. She ran her hand over the pocket to draw the assistant's attention to it, and then turned before she could react, to link arms with her supposed husband, who escorted her to the checkout to pay for her other purchases.

*　　*　　*

The discarded items were left on top of a pile of other items, and eventually buried beneath others as the afternoon wore on. It was not until after the shop closed for the day, that items were returned to their racks and put on display once more. It was only then that the note was found by a puzzled assistant. She didn't know what to make of the note, but the money would come in handy. Her salary wasn't much. Feeling a slight obligation, she got the number of the Hotel Rialto from the phonebook and made the call, asking for a Gabriel Aguila.

*   *   *

By that evening, Achmed took a call from Torquemada, to tell them that the nuclear material had arrived, and to make the underground garage ready to receive their car. He intended to collect the raw materials and arrive that evening. He passed the information on to Rebekah and Mustafa on their return, and Rebekah considered her options. Alone against three, possibly more, Arabs. If help didn't arrive, she had no one else to rely on. She couldn't afford to take him out on sight without going up against considerable odds. Best to wait till they were all asleep. In the privacy of her room, she checked the pistol in her handbag. She would need to use a pillow or something as a silencer, make the hit, and then vacate the walled premises before the rest of them knew what had happened. Then get the authorities down here to mop up the rest before they got away. But Torquemada had to go down.

*   *   *

It was getting late, around 11pm when Mustafa answered another call on the cellphone. He went down to open up the garage and the compound gates, and Rebekah watched through the window as a dark car drove in and down the ramp. Mustafa locked the gates and went down into the garage. Achmed gave her a reassuring smile. "Don't worry. Now he's here, we can finish up our mission and get out of Italy. They won't catch us." Rebekah gave him a nondescript smile in return, not wanting to comment on details he knew but she obviously didn't. She turned as the door to the garage stairwell opened, and Mustafa came in, carrying a suitcase. A younger Arab followed, carrying another case, and then finally one more man, taller than the other two, hawk-nosed and with a pencil-moustache lining his upper. That had to be him!

His eyes locked on hers for a second, and in that second, Rebekah knew she was blown. "You are not Fatima Khalid!" he accused, and the other Arabs whirled around in shock, as Rebekah grabbed for her handbag. No alternative now but to go down fighting, she clawed open the clasp and plunged her hand inside to grab the automatic. Her fingers closed around the grip as the Arabs flung themselves at her, piling on to her, and overpowering her with force of numbers. The gun went off once, harmlessly, before being forced out of her hand, and then Rebekah was forced to fight with hands, elbows, knees, downing one Arab, before another smashed the butt of a pistol down on her head, and everything went black.

Chapter Twenty Four

June 25th

The big truck sat there in the garage. It had simply been parked there, after unloading its trailer, in the warehouse, and no one had returned to it since. It had been under surveillance by the Italian authorities overnight, as soon as they had gotten word of its arrival.

The truck had been shadowed on it's long journey south by the Security Forces, sometimes keeping visual track on it intermittently via other vehicles taking the same route, or being overflown by helicopter, though not close enough to attract undue attention from it's driver.

It had finally come to rest in a frozen food warehouse yesterday evening in the northern suburbs of Rome. It's container had been unloaded, and the vehicle parked at the far end of the long warehouse. The place had been under constant surveillance ever since, with a team of men ready to move at the first sign of anyone attempting to move the vehicle.

Nothing had happened since then, and time passed slowly. Too slowly. Something should have happened by now. Someone should have come to move the vehicle. The on-site controller was Marcello Calascio, and he had been pondering the situation ever since hearing of the debacle in the cemetery. Damn stupid foreigners! He understood the situation had developed quickly, with no time to call for support, but he disliked the idea of foreign security forces working within the Italian mainland.

Now the terrorists were free again, and he was looking at a potential target of their interest. Yet here it had stood, untouched. He decided to check things out, and after dark, once the place had closed for the night, two of his men went to the back of the property with scaling ladders and blankets, to get over the fence and barbed-wire, and enter the property from the rear.

The two men showed no lights, using night-vision goggles, and they entered silently, as though expecting trouble. Their weapons were holstered, but readily accessible should they be required, and backup was mere seconds away. Having studied the plans of the place, they knew where to go, and it took less than a minute to pick the lock of the rear door, which opened more noisily than they would have liked.

They closed the door behind them as they slipped inside, reporting their entrance over secure comm-link to Calascio. The truck still stood there, and they went over to examine it more closely. Switching on the Geiger-counter they had brought with them, the readings were decidedly less than what they expected to find.

Moving closer to the silencer on one side of the cab, they used it again. Only trace readings. The screws holding the big baffle to the exhaust looked new. Someone had swapped silencers while the container was being unloaded. The nuclear material had been removed. No one was coming for this truck now. There was no need. Using the unloading of the container as a cover, persons unknown had removed the truck's real cargo and substituted a real silencer in its place to fool anyone looking from a distance, which they had indeed done. It could only be assumed that the terrorists now had the nuclear material. Calascio muttered a silent prayer. Their worst dreams were coming true.

*　　*　　*

In the underground garage, Rebekah regained consciousness to find herself in blackness, hogtied with duct tape, hands behind her back, and ankles tied together, and she was quite helpless, she found, as she pulled at her bonds. She wondered whether to scream. Rolling around, she guessed she was in the trunk of one of the cars. The Arabs had left her alone, but they weren't stupid enough to leave her like this unless they were sure she wouldn't be found. The garage was underground, and the door to the ramp was substantial. The mere fact that she was still alive meant they wanted information out of her. That and the withholding of it, would be the only bargaining tool she had to stay alive. Once they had everything they wanted from her, she was dead. Her only hope was that somehow Gabriel would get that message she'd left in the store.

Her head hurt from the blow, and her scalp was sort of sticky with what was probably dried blood. She didn't know how much time had passed. The Arabs were probably still deciding how much their operation had been compromised.

Eventually, she heard the door to the stairwell open, and a crack of light appeared around the rim of the trunk. A key was put in the lock, and it opened, the light hurting her eyes, as strong hands hauled her out of the trunk, and she tried to keep her balance as they put her down, forcing her back against the body of the car. "Jew Bitch!" snorted Achmed, driving a punch into her solar plexus and driving the air from her lungs as she doubled-up. "Upstairs!" they dragged her as she was trying to catch her breath, offering no resistance.

In the kitchen, one of the dining room chairs was given place of honour, and Rebekah was forced down into it. Her hands went behind the wooden frame, and more duct tape used to tie them them. The same was done with her ankles, and she was securely fixed to the chair. The best she could hope to do was overturn it, but that wouldn't get her anywhere.

The man known as Torquemada was sitting at the dining table, regarding her. His eyes fixed her coldly, and it took all her willpower not to show her fear at her current situation. She didn't want to give them the satisfaction. Achmed and Mustafa regarded her just as coldly as Torquemada. Only the young one, Omar, seemed not wholly into the current situation.

Torquemada went over to the kitchen drawer, and he began taking out a selection of kitchen utensils. A large carving knife was first, and he placed it down on the table in her plain view. He returned to the drawer, and slowly made another selection. A small meat cleaver was next, and he placed that next to the carving knife. Rebekah looked from the two sharp objects to Torquemada, and caught the cold smile he flashed her. A third selection was a small wooden rolling-pin, and that too went onto the table next to the other two items. By now, Rebekah was sweating. She knew the likely outcome. Torquemada made a fourth selection, a stainless steel skewer, about twelve inches long. It joined the others on the table. He selected an orange, from the fruit bowl, and placed that too on the table, next to the other items. Finally, a box of freezer-bags made an unusual addition to the assortment on the table.

Torquemada sat down again, regarding her, and noting with satisfaction, the sheen of sweat which had appeared on her brow. "You are not Fatima Khalid. I know Fatima personally. She was my instructor in the Bekaah Valley," he explained, and Rebekah silently cursed the incompleteness of his Mossad file. "We do not have much time to spare for this, so you will forgive the lack of subtlety," he indicated the assortment of items on the table in front of him. "Innocuous in themselves, but I assure you, what I can do with them will not be pleasant," he warned. "Save yourself a great deal of pain, and tell us what we need to know. I swear by Allah, that if you do this, then we will not kill you. Our mission here is nearly over, and in a few days, we will no longer be in Italy, so your life is not important to us. Just tell me your name, who you are working for, what happened to the real Fatima Khalid, and how much you have told the authorities about our operation."

His, and all the Arab eyes in the room, were fixed on her. Rebekah struggled to control her breathing, control the mounting panic. Could she trust his word. Would they kill her, as they'd killed her people before? "Go to hell!" She managed enough saliva to spit on the floor in front of Torquemada. He motioned to Mustafa, who stood up and came over to stand in front of her. He slowly unzipped his trousers and exposed himself, leering openly at her grimace of repulsion. She feared they intended to rape her, but was surprised when Mustafa took one of the large freezer bags, put his dick inside it, and began to piss into it, slowly filling the bag with pale yellow urine.

When he finished, he handed the bag to Achmed, while he zipped up his pants once more, and then Achmed went slowly behind Rebekah. Before she guessed what was coming next, the bag was upended over her head, the warm fluid immersing her hair and face, as Mustafa struggled to seal the bag around her neck with more duct tape as she flailed helplessly, the plastic bag muting her screams.

Achmed held down the back of the chair, keeping her upright, as she struggled to breathe. There was scant air in the plastic freezer bag, just a lot of urine. She choked on some of it, threshing her head back and forth, no longer screaming, just fighting hopelessly for breath.

Gasping and gasping, the plastic clung to her face, and Rebekah was slowly suffocating as the Arabs watched her impassionately. Her eyes started to roll as her brain was starved of oxygen. She started to lose consciousness, slumping finally in the chair, when at a signal from Torquemada, Achmed tore the tape loose, and pulled the freezer-bag off her head.

Her lungs sucked in huge amounts of air, as she coughed and spluttered her way back to consciousness, wet hair plastered to her head and neck. "We'll start with your name," Torquemada suggested, "or we put the bag back on, and start getting a little more serious," he warned.

"Rebekah . . . . Rebekah Weisz . . . ." she gulped and gasped, needing to tell him something, needing to forestall against what was to come, to draw it out for as long as she could. She only had two ways to play this. To tell them nothing, or to persuade them that the authorities knew everything. How much would they believe, and what did they really intend for her once her information dried up? Did she dare give in to that belief of hope that the man would keep his word? He had sworn an oath against Allah, and that was normally unbreakable, but he was an Arab and she was a Jew, and their religion allowed them to lie to non-Muslims.

Just then, a bell rang, and all of them whirled around at the intrusion, seeing the blinking light on the wall that accompanied the bell. Someone was ringing the bell at the gate. Rebekah's mouth opened to scream, but Torquemada grabbed the orange and crammed it into her mouth before she could manage it. Too big to dislodge easily, a strip of duct tape completed the gag, leaving her to breathe painfully out of her nose. "What do we do now?" asked Achmed. "If it's the authorities . . . ."

"If it was the authorities, they would hardly knock on the door. Omar, go and see who it is. It may be Abdullah. The rest of us wait here and cover him from the windows." Omar shoved an automatic pistol down the back of his trousers, under his jacket, and went out into the drive, gravel crunching under his shoes. He paused to switch the floodlights on, and then walked down towards the high gates, and unlocked them.

A striking woman stood there, carrying a single suitcase, having abandoned the stolen car, and making the final leg of her journey by taxi. "Who are you?" asked Omar, but he had already guessed by the physical likeness.

"Fatima. Fatima Khalid," the woman smiled, as she identified herself. "The other villa is being watched, so I came here. Help me with my case, and let's get inside," she ordered.

Torquemada greeted the woman warmly, with an affectionate embrace, which she returned, and then she broke the embrace to gaze at Rebekah, tied and gagged in the chair, struggling to breathe, and her cheeks bloated with the fruit gag in her mouth.

"So that is the Jew bitch? Yusef told me about her. How much damage has she done?" Torquemada shrugged.

"I only met her a couple of hours ago. We were just starting to interrogate her when you arrived," he explained.

"I was betrayed, and the Jews held me in prison, days of questioning me, till Hamas broke me out. I told them nothing," she assured him. "They must have decided to replace me with one of their own. Not a bad plan, except they didn't know we knew each other." Fatima came closer. "A good resemblance to anyone who didn't know me, facially at least, but we can fix that," she purred slightly, and her hand came out to carress the side of Rebekah's face, then her nails dug in and she tore a bloody furrow down one cheek as Rebekah tried to scream and overturn the chair to escape the pain. Fatima laughed cruelly, and slowly licked the blood off her fingernails. "That is but the start, little Jew. The pain will stop only when you tell us everything we want to know," she promised. "I leave you in capable hands," she chuckled. "Find out what she and her bosses in Mossad know." She spoke to Achmed, Mustafa and Omar, then turning again to Torquemada, "If you have the radiation suits, we need to get started on the bomb. We don't have much time." She spoke with authority, and even though Torquemada was in charge of this operation, old habits died hard. She had been his tutor before, and he was used to following her lead. Besides, she was right. Leaving Rebekah to the not so tender mercies of Achmed, Mustafa, and Omar, the two of them headed down to the garage where the material was stored.

Torquemada opened the boot of the other car, to show her the silencer containing the nuclear material. Two lead-lined suits were in the metal chest under the workbench, and they got them out, and started to get into them. Not exactly a perfect fit, but they would do.

Everything else she had requested had been provided, the welding set, the sheets of perspex, switches, explosives. It was enough.

Together, the two of them pulled the large metal silencer out of the boot, and Torquemada started up the welding set. It was going to be a long night.

* * *

Omar had volunteered for this mission to revenge himself on the Jews for the death of his family. Whilst he didn't mind killing them, torture did not sit well with him. The woman's face reminded him vaguely of his mother, for it was not a typical Jewish face, bruised now and bloody, after Achmed had punched her a few times, so that she nearly choked on the orange. Then they took it out, for they needed to hear her speak.

"Rebekah Weisz. You work for Mossad, yes?" There was no point in denying it. If she revealed details of her special unit, she would only make things worse for herself.

"Yes, I work for Mossad," she spoke with difficulty as her lip began to swell up.

"You knew enough to make the rendezvous with Achmed and myself. What else did they tell you about this mission?" he asked. All three men waited for her to speak. Achmed was testing the edge of the big carving knife, and grinning at her. As she paused, he leaned forward, and used the knife to cut through the top button of her blouse.

"We have a file on your Khalid. Her whereabouts were recorded, and it was decided to replace her. We had monitored her cellphone for a few days to verify the rendezvous point, and her personal belongings and travel arrangements all confirmed her part in the operation. We knew the main object of the mission, and Mossad have been keeping in contact with me, off and on, throughout my time in Italy. They had your villa under surveillance with the Italians. They know you are in Rome. You won't get out," she said with finality. Mustafa sneered. Achmed cut a second button off her blouse. "By the end of today, if you don't show at the first villa, they'll be here. Whatever you have planned, you won't have time to carry it out."

"Torquemada has it all worked out. We'll be out of Italy by tomorrow. Everything reaches a climax today. Your friends in Mossad and the Italians will be too late," warned Achmed, and he cut a third button. Rebekah's blouse now hung open to the waist, revealing her ample breasts cupped by a lacy blue silk bra. The tops of her dark nipples could be seen through the gauze of the half-cups. Achmed enjoyed the view.

"How did you keep in contact with Mossad? You were with us all the time," Mustafa reminded her.

"They knew the first rendezvous, and it was easy to leave a note behind when we moved on. The bomb on the motorway that didn't go off, was mine, and it carried a note as well," though Rebekah let them think it had been addressed to Mossad or the Italian Authorities. "Ali was killed during a planned accident on the motorway. That's why I was really late in getting here. We knew the climax of this operation was planned for Rome. Time to cut down the odds a little," she advised. "I left another note in the store when we went to buy clothes. I'd cut your losses and run while you still can," she warned.

"I think she's telling the truth," said Omar, who had been watching her closely, fascinated with the resemblance, more her eyes than anything else.

"What does it matter?" asked Mustafa. "You know the plan. In less than two days we'll be gone."

"We may not have two days," Omar warned. "Torquemada and I were almost taken at the cemetary. Two others of our number just disappeared. Someone is picking us off. It's just like Mossad to whittle down our numbers like this. The Italians aren't good enough. Those men I faced in the cemetary were professionals. They didn't look Italian."

"If they knew, they'd be here, or at least watching. I saw no signs of surveillance here. We'll be on the move tomorrow, and we won't be coming back. She never knew the escape plan, so there's no way she could have let the authorities know."

"Let's just fuck the Jew bitch, and then kill her," suggested Achmed. He was about to slice through Rebekah's bra with the carving knife when Omar stopped him.

"Torquemada gave his word, she wouldn't be harmed. What does one more Jew matter? We are here to do a job. Let's just do it and get out of this country in one piece," he suggested. "Just lock her up in the garage when we leave. They won't find her before we leave, and once the bomb goes off they'll have a lot more to worry about," he pointed out.

*   *   *

Gabriel was still at the British Embassy, being briefed on the loss of the radioactive shipment from the warehouse. "They didn't waste any time. They must have been advised the second that shipment arrived in Rome. The eyeties were caught cold." Maddox was slightly downcast.

"They should have had the place staked out before it got there. That's how we would have done it," Turnbull pointed out.

"Nick, we're here as guests of the Italian Security Forces. Most of them don't want us here, so no use crying over spilt milk."

"Let's get someone into that villa. If no one has turned up there yet, then it doesn't look as if anyone will." Gabriel pointed out. "They must have a backup somewhere. We need to find it. Try checking out the rental agencies, and see if the same outfit rented out something similar round about the same time."

"I'll get two of the boys over the back fence tonight to do a recon. They might find something from those two we chopped at that Thai Massage Parlour," Turnbull reminded him.

"How many down, and how many left?" Maddox mused.

"Maybe down to a handful. They couldn't come over here mob-handed to start with. But then there's the Khalid factor," Gabriel pointed out. "Any sighting of her yet?" he asked. Maddox shook his head.

"It's not looking good," he admitted. Suddenly, Maddox's phone rang. He picked up the receiver and spoke into it. "Yes?"

"Switchboard here, Sir. We have a call for a Mr Angell."

"Very well. Put it through," he advised, and handed the receiver to Gabriel. "It's for you." Gabriel accepted the handset and held it to his ear.

"Yes?" he asked, tentatively.

"It's Marco. Has the Mossad woman been in touch yet?" Gabriel's eyebrows raised in surprise.

"No. You've seen her then?" Gabriel asked.

"Si, we helped her on her way to Rome after we killed one of their operatives, and snatched their contact at the University. He has been very forthcoming, albeit with a little persuasion."

"Rebekah first. What happened with her?" Gabriel asked.

"I told her you and Maddox were in Rome, even gave her your hotel address, but I had the feeling she thought you might try and talk her out of fulfilling her mission. She's set on taking out Torquemada. She was due to meet him last night or today. I take it you have heard nothing on this?"

"You take it right, Marco. It's just like her. Always was a bit of a rebel." Maddox had picked up the second extension and was listening in trying to restrain himself. "It's far too dangerous for her with Khalid at large."

"Indeed so, and that is more bad news I have for you. When we took the Algerian, there was a woman with him. She fit the description, but our main mission was to secure the Algerian Diplomat. She left separately, and two of my men followed. They were found dead at the scene of an automobile accident. A subsequent post-mortem revealed bullet-wounds."

"Then she's in Italy and on her way to Rome," Gabriel stated the obvious.

"Probably already here, I'm afraid. The only bit of good news I can offer is what the Algerian told us. The bomb they are making will only be 'dirty' not nuclear. They don't have the training or the resources to build one at the moment. Exploded in the right place, it will still irradiate the Vatican City."

"The clock is ticking, then. Thanks for the update, Marco. Keep in touch."

"Of course, my friend. Ciao." The connection was severed.

"Get someone into that villa now, and see what you can find, Nick. I'll try and talk the authorities into cordoning off the Vatican City, but I don't hold out much hope with it being tourist season and Il Papa being the stubborn old sod that he is." Maddox was trying to come to terms with the terrorist threat and the more immediate threat to Rebekah.

"I need to get back to the hotel, just on the offchance that she's there or has left a message," said Gabriel. Turnbull rose also.

"I'll supervise the infil myself boss, and God help those eyeties if they get in our way," he promised.

* * *

Falcone was left in a bit of a quandary after relating most of his news to Gabriel. He had expected the call to be monitored by the British. He had other information he didn't see a need to pass on just yet, for the Algerian had revealed details of their escape plan. No use in preventing the bomb going off, but it would ensure they didn't get away to do something similar in another country. Small consolation if the Vatican was irradiated.

Preparations couldn't be too heavy-handed, and the two women, Laura and Belle, were pestering him for information, so he was prepared to let them handle that end of it. He would give them sufficient warning only to get in place for the takedown, and prevent unnecessary loss of life. Gabriel's life was not his consideration, and he wanted to give them no opportunity of trying to contact him about the Arabs' escape route. The British SAS were quite ruthless in their operations, and he was looking forward to attending Gabriel's funeral, and also consoling the grieving Laura.

* * *

Gabriel asked at the front desk if a woman had tried to contact him or left a message, but the night-clerk replied in the negative. Rebekah's note was currently in the top pocket of the day-clerk, who had intended to give it to Gabriel, but neglected to hand it over to his night-shift compatriot when he had knocked off for the night. Gabriel, of course, didn't know this, and guessed incorrectly that Rebekah had decided not to contact him, just continue on with her mission as she was so close to completing it. Typical of her stubborness. He phoned Maddox to keep him posted.

* * *

Turnbull and Dixon shinnied up the ladder at the back of the property. Palmer and Coverdale were acting as liaison with the watching Italians, to ensure they knew who was in there and prevent any Friendly-Fire casualties. The Italians had come up with floorplans and the code for the alarm system, which Dixon took care of, promptly. Then they were inside and recceing by torchlight, keeping it discreet just in case other watchers were out there.

The two Arabs hadn't spent much time in the place, and their luggage didn't take much time to check out. Nothing incriminating, unfortunately. The coffee-table in the lounge held a pile of tourist information on coach-tours visiting many of Rome's ancient ruins. One such was ringed, and two bus-passes were enclosed in the name of the dead Arabs. They intended getting out in plain sight by joining up with a coach excursion party. This info would only be good after the main event, but Maddox would know best how to use it. Turnbull pocketed the tickets and brochures. Time to leave. They'd got what they came for.

*   *   *

Back at the Embassy, Maddox was examining the leaflets and tickets with Turnbull. "What do you think, Boss? Can the Italians cover it?"

"I don't think we'll tell them about this, Nick. They have enough on their minds trying to stop this bomb being planted. We need to handle this one ourselves," he warned, with a knowing look. Nick caught it and asked him outright.

"Any particular reason, Boss?"

"A bit of housework, Nick."

"Wet work ?" Maddox nodded.

"Yes, you got it in one," Maddox said, with finality. "The SAS takes care of its own dirty laundry."

Chapter Twenty Five

The sun was high in the sky now, and Fatima and the man known as Torquemada were still assembling the bomb. It was a relief when they transferred the nuclear material into another lead-lined container, and they could take off the radiation suits. From there, the assembly went a lot smoother. The perspex sheets were pre-drilled, and fitted together well. Fuses, wiring, switches and conventional explosives each had their places, and Fatima was well-used to assembling such devices.

When they were finished, they were left with a perspex box, slightly more than four feet long, by two feet in cross-section. A single red button protruded through one sheet of perspex, its purpose to arm the device and set the timer inside. Apart from that button, it was a sealed unit, with trembler switches set against the inside of the perspex sheets to prevent tampering. The sheets were glued together around the edges, as well as screwed with self-tapping screws. Fatima was proud of her handiwork. "Help me lift it into the boot of the car," she said to Torquemada, and the two of them carried it gingerly, placing it carefully within the boot of the car, and then closing the boot itself.

Torquemada gave a chuckle, and embraced Fatima, who returned his affections, kissing him hungrily. "Today marks the culmination of our first crusade against the rest of the world," he spoke with conviction. "By tomorrow, we will be gone from these heathen lands, free to regroup and plan our second campaign of terror. I'll finish off here. You can go and take a shower, and I'll join you later."

"The Catholic Church will be hard-pressed to survive this blow we are about to deal them," Fatima chuckled. "What about the Jew?" Fatima asked. Torquemada frowned.

"I gave my word, that she wouldn't be harmed," he reminded her. Fatima smiled enigmatically, and took off the radiation suit, before hanging it up on a hook on the wall. Torquemada shook his head. Sometimes she was headstrong, though generally deferred to him. She blew him a kiss, and then went up the stairs to the main house, where the others waited. Torquemada might well have given his word, but she hadn't.

* * *

Rebekah could tell by the woman's eyes that she was in trouble. There was a fanatical gleam behind them, far in excess of anything she had noticed from the male Arabs. Something else as well, pure hatred for her kind. "So you're the Jew bitch the Mossad sent to impersonate me?" Fatima sneered. Rebekah tensed on the bed, though tethered as she was by her own stockings fastening her wrists to the headboard of the bed, there wasn't much she could do. Her legs were free, but only of use if the psycho bitch came in close, and even then, Rebekah would not be able to get off the bed. "They tell me they didn't get much out of you. Perhaps they weren't as 'persuasive' as I can be," she chuckled, walking around to the side of the bed and looking out through the window, raising the blinds so she could admire the view and let in more light as the early morning sun rose over the houses in the distance.

Fatima turned again, and looked at her, running her eyes appraisingly up and down her body. Rebekah's face was still slightly swollen and a bruise was forming. The congealed blood on her cheek, hid the deep furrows caused by Fatima's fingernails. Her clothes were in disarray after the interrogation, and Fatima sneered as she took note of the older woman's body. Not a patch on her own.

"A poor choice to replace me. They could have picked someone with better looks," she said, in way of a mild insult. She moved around the bed, keeping deliberately out of reach of Rebekah's long legs, before moving closer to the bed, and placed the machine pistol on the bedside table, before sitting down on the edge of the bed next to Rebekah. She leaned forward to cup Rebekah's chin in her hand. She turned her face towards her, before suddenly spitting in it, taking Rebekah by surprise as she gasped and tried to turn her head away. Fatima laughed, cruelly. "Poor little Jew. You've come all this way to die," she taunted, running her hand down Rebekah's chest to grab and squeeze one of Rebekah's breasts. She squeezed hard, making Rebekah cry out, and start to shiver uncontrollably. The woman was a psychopath indeed, and she was tied up and at her mercy.

Fingernail and thumb dug into the fat nipple, worrying the tender flesh, as Rebekah screamed. Fatima's eyes were gleaming, and she was obviously enjoying herself. Suddenly the bedroom door opened, and the younger Arab, Omar, stuck his head sheepishly around the door. "What are you doing? Torquemada gave orders. The woman is not to be harmed," he warned.

Fatima turned to face him. "I am not Torquemada, but I am second in command here, and I am interrogating the woman further. I will continue to do so until I am satisfied. You may close the door," she dismissed him. Omar glared at her, but reluctantly did as he was told. Rebekah's screams of pain could still be heard through the closed door, as Fatima continued her ill-treatment. "Don't get your hopes up, my dear," she warned Rebekah. "Torquemada has always done what I want, and if you think your screams will bring that young idealist back in here to save you, well, there are ways we can make sure that doesn't happen," she smiled, running her hand up Rebekah's thigh, under her skirt, to her crotch. Her fingers fastened on the elastic of Rebekah's panties, and she suddenly ripped and tore, till they came free in her hand, and as Rebekah opened her mouth to scream once more, Fatima delightedly stuffed the bunched up material into her mouth, effectively gagging her.

As Rebekah tried to breathe, Fatima chuckled. "Now we're going to have some fun," she announced, unbuckling her own belt and sliding it out from her skirt. She took off one of her own stockings, and used it to bind the panty-gag in place, tying it back behind Rebekah's head. Then she picked up the belt in one hand, letting it swing slowly back and forth, the heavy metal buckle acting like a pendulum as Rebekah's wide eyes followed it, mesmerisingly. She guessed what was coming, but there was nothing she could do to stop it.

Fatima swung the belt over her head and down, to land with a satisfying thwackkk on Rebekah's exposed chest, and she threshed in pain, though the gag effectively silenced her so that her pain could not be heard outside the room. Fatima smiled broadly, pausing for effect, before bringing the heavy buckle down once again, and again, and again, enjoying the contortions Rebekah's body made as she flailed about, trying to escape the inescapable. Fatima was getting quite worked up as she enjoyed her work. "I'm going to make those big tits of yours bleed," she promised.

The beating continued for many long minutes, and Rebekah's breasts were now bleeding from gouges caused by the belt buckle. The sight of blood only incensed Fatima more, and a sexual frenzy seemed to overtake her. She let the belt fall, and came back to sit on the bed, running her hands over Rebekah's pained breasts, smearing the blood across them, as she shuddered herself, squeezing her thighs together, before leaning forward and starting to lick the blood off the tender flesh. Rebekah shuddered as that slimey tongue ran across her pained breasts, teasing the tenderised nipples.

Fatima's head raised finally, and Rebekah saw her own blood still on her lips and chin. "Do you want the pain to end, little Jew?" she asked, and Rebekah nodded her heard fearfully. Fatima smiled. "Well, first there is one little thing I want you to do for me, and then the pain will all be over." She stood up, and unzipped her skirt, letting it fall. Eagerly she slid her panties down also, revealing a thick black thatch between her legs.

Grinning insanely, she clambered up onto the bed, onto Rebekah's bloodied chest, pulling the stocking from around her head and pulling the panties out of her mouth as Rebekah eagerly spat them out, taking in great lungfuls of air. Fatima took up the machine pistol from the bedside table once more, and then moved forward, pressing her crotch down onto Rebekah's face. "Eat me, little Jew," she ordered, holding the cold barrel of the gun against Rebekah's head. "Eat me, and give me pleasure, or I will end your pain now," she promised. The woman's wet sex enveloped Rebekah's mouth, giving her little option. It was either lick, suffocate, or be shot, and so she began to use her tongue to please the other woman. Fatima gasped and moaned, riding Rebekah's face, as she enjoyed having the bound woman as her plaything.

*   *   *

Outside the room, Omar could hear Fatima, if not Rebekah's muffled screams, and he clenched his fists in frustration. Jew or not, he did not think of her as less than human, as Fatima obviously did. Torquemada himself had said she would come to no harm. He had seen her take the gun into the bedroom, and he had seen that same look in her eyes in the eyes of other fanatics who had lost all control. The other two men played cards, ignoring the noises from the bedroom, and he knew he could expect no help from them, or sympathy for the Jew. Only Torquemada could stop this, and so Omar went now downstairs and headed into the sub-garage, where the man himself was busy securing the plexiglass container into the boot of the car, so it wouldn't move about during transport.

"What is it, Omar. I need to get this finished before dawn."

"I think Fatima is going to kill the Jew." Torquemada looked up from his work.

"What makes you think that?" he asked. Omar noticed for the first time that he was still in his protective suit, and still had the hood on over his features. Momentarily, he worried about the exposure, but then Torquemada slipped the hood back over his head, and wiped his perspiring brow.

"She is beating the woman as we speak," Omar explained, "and I saw her take a gun into the bedroom with her. The Jew is tied up. What does she need the gun for?" he asked. Torquemada's face twisted in puzzlement.

"Help me out of this cursed suit," he ordered, and Omar hurried to comply.

*   *   *

In the bedroom, Rebekah's jaw ached, and she could take no more of the humiliation, and as those hairy loins moved to cover her face once more, she used her teeth instead of her tongue, biting the soft tender flesh as Fatima screamed, beating at her head with the barrel of the gun, and forcing the teeth out of her soft labia before they ripped through the tender flesh.

"You bitch!" she hurriedly inspected herself, fortunate there was no bleeding, as Rebekah lay there gasping on the bed, a lump rising on her temple quite visibly from the blow with the gun-barrel. "You're no more use to me, anyway. Time to die," she sneered, raising the gun in her outstretched hand.

As she did so, the bedroom door burst open, and Omar and Torquemada rushed in. Seeing the gun in her hand, Torquemada made to grab for her, while Omar threw himself in front of the helpless woman. "I said she's not to be harmed." Torquemada cried out, as he backhanded Fatima, and she clawed at him with one hand, raising the gun again with the other, and pulled the trigger.

The machine pistol was on semi-auto, and bullets stitched across Omar's body, throwing him back on the bed to land on top of the woman. Torquemada swore, struggling with her, as she continued to fire, her aim now deflected and shattering the window before he could force it from her hand.

"You stupid bitch!" he cursed her, as she fell back against the wall, as the other two Arabs finally made an appearance. "Get her out of here, and get things packed quickly. We have to leave in a hurry before someone reports the gunfire and shattered window." He pushed Fatima towards the two of them, turning his attention quickly to the bed, which was red with blood.

Omar's body lay across Rebekah's, blood oozing from numerous bulletholes. Rebekah stared blankly up at the ceiling, blood coming from a neck wound, and some of the bullets must have passed through Omar's body. Both looked quite lifeless. He had no time now. Cursing Fatima once more, he hurried back down to the sub-garage to finish bolting the mechanism in place. They had to leave within the next half hour. Any longer would be chancing fate. He couldn't be caught this close to completing his goal.

* * *

Gabriel came down to Reception shortly after 8.30 am, intending to take breakfast in the Restaurant, but had the foresight to enquire after Rebekah with the Day-Clerk. Slightly embarassed, the youth handed the note over, and Gabriel's breakfast plans were put to the back of his mind. He grabbed the desk phone, and called the British Embassy, eager to speak to Maddox.

Irritatingly, he was asked to wait, but was finally put through to Maddox. "Jim, the second safe-house is a place called Alton Apartments.

No 12. I just got a note left from Rebekah. Get someone over there quick as you can," he advised.

"I'll pull the team from the other place immediately. Get over here by lunchtime. We should have things in place by then, and we can make a decision on what to do when we know more." Maddox was thinking things through. Had Rebekah succeeded in her mission, or was she already dead? He didn't want to think such thoughts, but it was a grim possibility. He put the phone down, and began calling the Italian Security Forces.

*   *   *

Turnbull met Gabriel for breakfast in the Restaurant, in a slightly subdued mood, or so it seemed to Gabriel. He related the news about the note he'd received, and Turnbull then left him to use the public phonebooth to check in with his boss. He returned a few minutes later. "Things are moving. The eyeties are setting up shop around Alton Apartments. Give em a few hours, and we'll be able to assess the situation better. Maddox wants us to meet him at the Embassy."

"Yes, I know," Gabriel confirmed. There was something about Turnbull today. Not much in the way of eye-contact. Gabriel wasn't sure why, but something had changed. "Anything I should know?" he asked. Turnbull looked up.

"What? Oh, no, just a bit distracted. What we having, then? I take it it's on your tab? Expenses haven't improved much since your time with the Regiment," he changed the subject adroitly.

*   *   *

Kovacs was getting ready to leave the dacha, and he made a call on his cellphone to Grechko's chauffeur Nikolai to come and pick him up. He was the only one who knew where Kovacs was hiding out while the manhunt was in full swing. Kovacs didn't deem it wise to stay in any one place for more than a week, and he needed to get back in touch with his organisation to find out what was happening with the authorities and see if that bitch was dead yet.

Two hours after the call was made, a non-descript car drove up the uneven road towards the dacha. Kovacs watched it approach. BMWs were a thing of the past, at least for now. Nikolai parked the car and got out to approach the house. Kovacs went out to meet him.

"Time to move on, Nikolai. The bags are packed and in the hall. Bring them out to the car if you would," he ordered. Nikolai nodded obediently, and went to get them. When he went into the house, he noticed only one set of bags. Wandering around the rooms, there was no sign of his employer. Eventually, he picked up the bags, and took them out to the car.

"Where is Mr Grechko?" he asked, simply.

"Mr Grechko won't be coming with us, Nikolai. He betrayed me. I killed him," he said, matter-of-factedly. Nikolai stared at Kovacs for a long hard moment, and then nodded simply. He took the bags to the car and put them down to open the boot. Kovacs was lighting up a cigar, and taking in one last look at the place, when Nikolai pulled the snow-shovel out of the boot, hefted it in both hands, and swung it at the back of Kovacs' head.

*　　*　　*

It didn't take Nikolai long to find Grechko's body. The cold climate had preserved it quite well. Nikolai was strong for his age, and he had no trouble dragging it back to the car. Similarly, he dragged Kovacs' unconscious form out to the small bunch of trees, and left it lying there whilst he used the snow-shovel to dig into the hard earth. The dirt was easier once he got down past the first foot or so, yet he only dug down three of four feet. Kovacs was starting to stir, and Nikolai bent over him, removing his belt, which he used to tie his hands behind his back, and then his tie, which he bound his ankles together with.

Nikolai began dragging Kovacs' towards the freshly dug hole, and Kovacs finally regained consciousness, struggling. "Nikolai . . . What are you doing, man? What is the meaning of this? I'll have your family on the streets for this. Untie me at once!" Nikolai ignored his words, and his struggles.

"Mr Grechko was a far better man than you. He didn't deserve to die like this, but you do." He rolled Kovacs over into the hole, and Kovacs screamed as he realised what was to come. He managed to roll over onto his back as the first shovelful of dirt landed on him.

"Nikolai, don't be stupid. I can give you money. Make you rich," he spat as the next shovelful hit him in the face. "Nikolai, for the love of God, stop," he pleaded. Nikolai kept on shovelling, ignoring the screams and the struggles, which eventually stopped as the earth covered him.

Going back to the car, Nikolai put Grechko's body into the rear. He could at least see that his former master had a proper funeral. Kovacs had just had his.

*   *   *

Just after midday, the Italian Authorities moved in around Alton Apartments carefully and slowly. It was a large holiday complex, each with its own enclosed villa/apartment. Discreetly, they evacuated the nearest properties and set up their observation posts. A vantage point into the property was found from one of the larger villas. Both the Italians and Maddox were already studying floorplans provided by the estate agent. Maddox also had the video-feed from the surveillance fed directly into his office at the British Embassy, and he watched with Gabriel and Turnbull as they discussed plans.

"The door to the underground garage is open," Turnbull pointed out. "We need another vantage point." Maddox got onto the phone to the field-commander, and suggested a second video-feed from a different vantage point.

"How long can we afford to wait?" Gabriel asked. "If Torquemada turned up last night as planned, then either Rebekah killed him or she didn't." He didn't want to labour the obvious to Maddox. "My instinct tells me he'll move today. Have you got the Italians restricting movement around the Vatican?"

"Yes, as much as we can. The Swiss Guard has stepped up their operations, and no vehicles will be allowed inside the Vatican City for the time being. Surrounding roads are being monitored by cctv cameras, and the police presence has been increased in plain-clothes. If they're there, we don't want to scare them off," he confirmed.

Just then, the video link changed to a split-screen, now showing two views inside the compound, the second revealing a view down the ramp to the garage. It stood empty. There were no longer any cars inside. "Looks like we're too late," Turnbull shook his head. "They've already gone."

Maddox got on the phone to the Field Commander immediately. "Hold your positions. I'll be there myself as fast as I can," he advised. "Let's go." He got up quickly from his desk, and Gabriel and Turnbull followed him out of the room. "We need to get inside, but no telling if there's anyone left in there." Gabriel looked at Turnbull, who knew what was going through Maddox's mind. Would they find Rebekah inside, and if so, would she be alive or dead?

They got an update by phone on the way there. No signs of movement either within the building or within the compound. Their car pulled up next to one of the adjacent villas, with the Italians were using as a Forward Control Post. Maddox consulted with the Field Commander briefly, before returning to Gabriel and Turnbull.

"Okay, the three of us are going in, covertly, to see what we can find."

"That might not be a good idea, Jim," Gabriel cautioned. A look passed between the two men.

"We're still going in," Maddox insisted.

"You sure you're still up for these antics, Boss? You're no spring chicken anymore," Turnbull queried, trying to lighten the mood.

"Shut the fuck up, Nick. If he can do it, then so can I. Now let's move." Taking flak-jackets from the Italians, they hastily strapped them on, and then were led around to the rear of the property, to where there were the least amounts of windows. A ladder was thrown up against the wall, and a thick rubber mat over the broken glass that adorned the top of it, and one after the other they went over. Turnbull led the way, dropping down into a crouch, and covering the other two as they dropped down beside him. "As the garage is open, that's the way we go in," Maddox directed, and set off around the edge of the property, keeping an eye out for movement through the windows. Gabriel and Turnbull followed.

Once they headed down the underground ramp, the three men resorted to hand signals only. Gabriel pointed out the discarded radiation suits, and Maddox and Turnbull nodded. The remains of the silencer was strewn under the bench. The welding set was neatly hung back up next to the oxy-acetylene bottles. Bits of wiring and packing littered the top of the bench.

Turnbull tried the door leading into the stairwell, and it quietly opened under his hand. Cautiously, he moved into the stairwell, taking his time. He started up the stairs slowly, and Maddox and Gabriel followed, moving in silence. At the top of the stairs, a second door awaited, and they had no idea what to expect behind it. Turnbull made more hand-signals, and then slowly tested the handle. It moved easily, and as he threw open the door, Gabriel darted inside the room, gun out and quickly scanning for movement. Maddox followed suit, staying out of Gabriel's line of fire, each man covering one side of the room. It was a long time since Maddox had actively taken part in any such mission, but the old training was still there.

They moved from the lounge into the dining room, and noted the cut duct-tape on the single chair which was set out away from the others. Someone had obviously been bound into that chair. It didn't take a lot of brain-cells to figure out who that person had been. They also noted the grim assortment of kitchen implements which were neatly arranged on the table. A quick glance into the kitchenette showed no one there either. That left the upstairs rooms.

Maddox steeled himself for what he now expected to find at the top of those stairs, and he began to follow Turnbull and Gabriel up the staircase. Gabriel could smell the blood before he got to the head of the stairs, and he held Maddox back as he went to take the lead position. "Better let me go in there, Jim." Turnbull caught his eye, and knew something was up. He put himself between Maddox and Gabriel.

"We'll cover you," he suggested. Gabriel just nodded, though he didn't think there was any danger in the room, just death. There was no easy way to play this, except to try and protect Maddox from the worst of it. Maddox was impatient, and he would not be held back for long. Gabriel turned the door handle, and opened the door, stepping inside quickly and closing the door behind him before the bloodbath was visible to the other two men outside on the landing.

The carpet and bedding was soaked with blood. Flies from the broken window were buzzing about the corpse on the bed. One of the younger Arabs, lay sprawled across the bed, torso riddled with at least four bulletholes, eyes staring blankly up at the ceiling, in death. Underneath him was Rebekah, still tied spreadeagled across the bed. She too was covered in blood, but her eyes flickered weakly at the noise of the door opening and closing.

Gabriel was momentarily surprised and relieved, shoes squelching beneath him as he hastily moved over to the bed. "Gabe . . . ." She managed to blurt out through a parched throat.

"Don't speak. Save your energy," he advised, as he rolled the dead Arab off her as gently as he could. She was covered in mainly his blood, though there was a deep gouge across the side of her neck where one bullet had narrowly missed severing a major artery, and her cheek was scabbed from an earlier wound. The blood had congealed over the fresher wound. He gathered the bedclothes around her, discarding the worst of them, before he attempted to cut her free, using his sharp fingernails to pull and tear at the stockings binding her wrists. "Jim's outside. I'll let him in, if you're strong enough?" Rebekah huddled against him, still shivering and in shock at her ordeal and near-death. She nodded against his shoulder, and Gabriel gently stood up, letting her compose herself.

He crossed to the door, and opened it slowly, the slight smile on his lips was a joy for Maddox to behold, for he realised why Gabriel had insisted on entering the room ahead of them. Without words, he pushed past Gabriel, and then stood stock still, taking the bloody spectacle in. Behind him, Gabriel closed the door. Rebekah looked sheepishly up from her swath of blankets and sheets. "Hello, Jim," was all she could manage, and then he crossed the distance to the bed in two strides, and swept her into his arms.

"Becky . . . . Becky . . . . Oh my God, I'm so glad you're alive,"he was hugging the breath out of her, and trying to kiss her at the same time.

Outside the bedroom door, Turnbull looked pleased. "A result, Guv?" Gabriel gave a thumbs-up.

"Against the odds, Nick, but yes, a result." Gabriel confirmed, smiling.

*   *   *

After ten minutes or so, Rebekah and Maddox came out of the bedroom, and she excused herself to go into the bathroom, to shower and change. As the water ran behind the closed bathroom door, Maddox revealed what she'd gone through. "They rumbled her before Khalid turned up. Seems like our boy has known Khalid for years.

They questioned Rebekah. No real rough stuff, at least not until Khalid got here. Torquemada gave his word she'd be left alive, once they left the villa. Khalid had other ideas. The young lad in there tried to stop her from murdering Rebekah, and got in the way long enough for Torquemada to wrestle the gun from her. There was blood everywhere, and with him on top of her, Rebekah played dead. It worked. They hightailed out of here shortly afterwards, in case the noise of gunfire was reported. She's damn lucky to still be alive," he shook his head. "There's only four of the terrorists left. Torquemada and Khalid are off to plant the bomb. It's in the boot of a car. She's given me a description, so we'll put the word out and get people looking for it. The other two are off to the arranged rendezvous. All four are expecting to leave Italy tonight," he announced. "That means this thing is going off today. We don't have much time." All three looked from one to the other.

"We need eyes, Boss." Turnbull stated the obvious.

"I'll be getting onto the Italian Authorities. Everyone will be in on this one, militia, police, special forces. Finding that car is our top concern. Khalid was the bomb-maker, and a dirty bomb planted close enough, will irradiate the Vatican for centuries to come. You two get them moving on it, while I wait on Rebekah. I'll radio it all in, and then take her to the hospital to get her checked out and that wound treated. I'll keep in touch by cellphone, and catch up with you in an hour or so."

"Right, Boss. C'mon, Gabe, let's get cracking. Those eyeties have got their work cut out for them," he commented, and he and Gabriel left Maddox to wait for Rebekah. Jim would make sure she got medical treatment, whether she wanted it or not. She had just had a lucky escape, and was in no condition to stay on this case.

*　　*　　*

Torquemada and Fatima headed out into the centre of Rome, the boot of their car filled with the dirty-bomb they had spent the night constructing. He wasn't happy being too close to the radioactive material, but Fatima had assured him the shielding would be good enough to protect them. On the rear seats were two suitcases, filled with clothing and the remains of the $10 million that Al Qaeda had sanctioned paying Gabriel for the supposed nerve-agent. He couldn't very well leave the money behind, and what Al Qaeda didn't know, wouldn't hurt them. His only problem was getting the money out of Italy.

The tour-bus would take them back on board the cruise liner, using the forged identities of passengers who were already on board, in league with Al Qaeda, and who had today left the cruise liner after it docked. The physical descriptions were close enough, and they had been under orders to keep a low profile. It should be easy enough to slip out of the country with minimal checks. Various contacts were already working to ensure they could disembark safely in another country, and Torquemada hoped to take the money with him. It would set him and Fatima up for life, and give them the option of breaking ties with Al Qaeda at some time in the future, if plans didn't work out. He would use part of the money as bribes if need be.

Turnbull's presence here had unnerved him. Even taking the Mossad agent into account, Turnbull must have been here before she could contact the British of European authorities. They were better than he had thought. Either that or he had made mistakes in his planning which had led them to him. It worried him. Turnbull, of all people. Life was strange.

"Drive slower," Fatima warned, worrying that they might get pulled up for a minor traffic offence with the device in the car. Torquemada watched his speedometer. His concentration had been slipping. The car slowed slightly as he took his foot off the accelerator. Fatima was studying a streetmap of Rome and the Vatican City. They wouldn't get past the Swiss Guards to park the car inside the Vatican itself, but there were a number of roads around the periphery, which would serve the purpose. First she was guiding them to a car-park, where another car was waiting for them to transfer the suitcases, and once the device had been set and armed, they would take a taxi back to the car park, and vacate Rome with due haste in this second car. They needed to meet up with the other two at the ruins. Then, a leisurely drive south to board the cruise liner to catch the evening tide.

The coach party would arrive at the ruins on its last stop of the day, before traveling south to the waiting cruise-liner that would take them away from Italy. They would join the party, and sail on to the next port of call as part of the standard package holiday, taking their leave eventually, and regrouping once Torquemada made contact with the

Taliban once more. This was the most simple part of their mission. Just plant the bomb and leave. Then rendezvous with the tour-bus.

The other three men had one last task to perform, more as a distraction than anything else. If the authorities knew they were in Rome, they couldn't close the whole place down without mass panic ensuing, so a suitable diversion was required to clear the way for them to get close to the Vatican City.

*   *   *

The Stadio Olimpico was a huge 86,000 seater stadium which was home to Roma and Lazio football clubs, on the Via Foro Italico. Easy enough to approach on non-match days, yet high-profile enough that a bomb or even bomb-threat would be taken seriously enough to get the authorities attention.

As it was, the single car-bomb, planted by the other two terrorists, went off shortly after 2pm, killing three by-standers and causing the planned confusion amongst the authorities, who responded to the scene with their usual aplomb. A hastily made phonecall warned of other devices, timed to go off at intervals throughout the afternoon, thus diverting a lot of manpower to cordoning off streets and approaches to the stadium.

While the authorities were concentrating on this threat, it left the Vatican free for Torquemada and Fatima to plant their device.

*   *   *

The Italian police had eventually gotten lucky studying the cctv footage of the streets surrounding the Vatican City. One bright-eyed observer had noticed the man and the woman park and exit the car on Viale delle Mura Aurelie, which ran alongside the westernmost wall of the City-State. It was the woman's actions in quickly opening and closing the boot of the car, and the bright reflection of something inside that had caught his eye. Replaying and slowing down the footage, he zoomed in on the boot of the car for the few seconds it was open, and saw the shining surface of what appeared to be a large rectangular box, almost filling the interior of the boot. Instantly, he picked up the phone to report the matter to his superiors, and the message was passed along to the Security Forces as well as Maddox and his SAS team.

"It's in position. Police are securing the area now. Let's go!" Maddox waved Gabriel back towards the car, and their driver floored the accelerator, heading across the city, sirens wailing to clear the road in front of them. "Torquemada and Khalid have planted the bomb, and walked. Right now we're concentrating our efforts in clearing the area, just like a typical bomb-threat. No sense letting the public know what's coming. Too much panic otherwise." Gabriel agreed.

"Just hope we can get there in time, and we can defuse the thing before it goes off."

"Bomb-squad's already on its way. It'll be there before we arrive," Maddox assured him. He knew of Gabriel's expertise in such devices.

"Where's Turnbull?" Gabriel asked.

"Standing-by with the rest of his team, and making preparations for later on. We know now where and how they intend leaving the country. There's an excursion tour visiting some of the ancient Roman ruins at Lavinium. They intend hooking up with that tour-bus, which leaves south to join up with a Mediterranean Cruise liner which sails tonight. We checked with the tour company after we found tickets in the first villa belonging to those two Arabs that tried to kill your Russian girlfriend."

"She's not my girlfriend," Gabriel insisted, uncomfortably.

"More fool you, then," laughed Maddox. His mood had greatly improved since finding Rebekah alive, though there was still something about him. He was normally more chatty on these missions, from Gabriel's memory of their time together in Oman.

* * *

The Italian police had little difficulty clearing the surrounding streets once they'd identified and cordoned off the suspect vehicle. Suited-up members of the tactical bomb-squad approached the vehicle and used mirrors to check underneath the vehicle, and inside the boot once they had used skeleton-keys to open the boot's lock. Very slowly and carefully, they raised the boot an inch or so, using the mirrors again for further checks, till finally they opened it all the way and got a good look at what they were dealing with.

The perspex box contained electronics on one side. A single wire ran down from the projecting red button to a control box and battery-pack fixed to the base. A digital readout was slowly counting down, to reveal they had 43 minutes before the device exploded. From this control box, feeder wires ran out to trembler-switches resting up against the inner walls of the perspex, which would trip if any of the perspex sheets were removed. Other coloured wires ran to a large grey mass of C4 explosive which acted as a bed for a large rectangular box made of dull-grey lead, which contained the nuclear irradiated material.

Things were not looking good, as the officer reported his findings over his throat-mike. "The sheets of perspex are held with machine-screws, and glued around the seams, but if we loosen them, the trembler-switches will trip and activate the device. Similarly, if we try and drill through and inject liquid nitrogen, the vibration of the drill could set it off. We cannot move the vehicle either, for the same reasons. I am open to suggestion," he said forlornly.

"Stand by," was the only answer that came into his earpiece, and one he didn't want to hear. That meant they were just as clueless as himself as to how to proceed.

*   *   *

Maddox's BMW pulled up at the barrier, and was then waved through as his driver showed identification to the police on duty. It pulled up eventually behind the bomb-squad control van, parked some distance from the terrorist's car. Maddox stuck his head inside the van. "How long have we got?"

"Less than thirty minutes. My men cannot see how we can defuse this device in time."

"Call them back, and let us assess the situation," Maddox insisted. The officer relayed the orders by microphone, and the two suited-up officers returned towards the van.

"We do not have spare suits. You will have to take the protective gear from my men," the officer explained.

"No time," explained Gabriel, who was already walking forward towards the car. Maddox fell in behind him. The two of them crouched down beside the boot of the car, admiring Khalid's handiwork. The digital readout now said 27 minutes and counting. "A neat one, and no mistake," Maddox grudgingly admitted, for he had had the basic SAS bomb-course whilst on active service. It was mandatory for all personnel. They had to know how to recognise, rig and de-fuse such devices. Some were better at it than others, and he knew Gabriel's skill in this field. "Over to you, Gabe," he relinquished responsibility.

"You still remember your basic course-skills, Jim?" he mused, whilst studying the device. Maddox nodded in assent.

"My hands were a bit too big and my fingers too clumsy, though," he admitted.

"Well, the key to making such a device is simplicity. Too many bombers ended up dead as a result of trying to be too clever. Keep it simple, tried and trusted methods, and it goes bang when you want it to, not before," he pointed out. "This one is basic enough, blue, red and green wires running from the control box to the detonator in the C4 are all standard. All bombers like to test their devices, so they won't screw about with the wiring unnecessarily. What we don't know is if any of these wires are decoys. There could be another wire running under that baseplate," he pointed. "Can't see without looking underneath, and we can't do that without moving the device, which is what those trembler-switches are there for, to prevent us moving it, or even removing the panels to get at it." Maddox nodded, one eye on that digital readout. 26 minutes left. "I don't know how sensitive those switches are, so best leave them alone."

"So how do we disarm it if we can't get at it?" Maddox asked. Gabriel looked up. The sun, though past its zenith was still bearing down hotly.

"That officer in the van had a pair of binoculars. I need them, and a hammer of some sort. The bomb-disposal team should have something we can use in their toolkit," Gabriel suggested.

"Right," Maddox dashed off back towards the van, wondering what on earth Gabriel wanted with binoculars and a hammer, but he had learned to trust his friend's judgement. The officer in the van was also mystifed by the request, but handed over his binoculars, and a large hammer was obtained from the bomb-squad experts. He rushed back to the car. Twenty three minutes and counting. "Alright, now are you going to let me in on what you want these for, or do I just stand back in awe while you demonstrate your Godlike powers?"

Gabriel took the binoculars from him. "Khalid kept the bomb simple, and made sure we couldn't get at it to defuse it. Ordinarily she'd have succeeded, but one thing can penetrate this perspex at the moment. Light," he revealed, and placed the binoculars on the ground. Raising the hammer, he brought it down hard on the binoculars, once, twice, till the lenses popped free. "The one good and consistent thing about Italy is the sunshine. It's almost always bright, hot and sunny," he smiled, as he began picking up the lenses from the remains of the binoculars. A light dawned behind Maddox's eyes. "I'll need your help here, Jim. We'll need all four of these lenses holding just right to focus the sun's rays," he explained.

Holding the lenses betweens thumbs and forefingers, Gabriel placed the second lens where the focal point of the first lens ended. Maddox did the same with the third and then the fourth lens. In effect they were creating a mini-laser, focussing the sun's rays into an intense beam. "Now we burn through those wires, yes? Which one, the blue, red or green? I can never remember," he admitted.

"Just in case there is a second wire under that base plate, we ignore the wires alltogether. We cut off the power. The connection from the battery-pack, there on the left," he pointed. "See the soldered connection. Focus the beam there," Gabriel directed, and in concert, they slowly re-positioned their improvised laser so that the intense focal point of heat rested on the soldered section of wiring, and it wasn't long before they saw the solder melt and flow, breaking the connection. Maddox breathed a sigh of relief. The counter stopped dead at twenty one minutes fourteen seconds.

"Okay, that should hold things to let the bomb-disposal boys tidy things up. Pump liquid oxygen through one of the screw-holes to freeze the switches, just to be safe, then use solvent to help remove the panels and dismantle the guts of the thing."

"You're a fucking cool one and no mistake, Gabe. I was shitting bricks for a minute there."

"I've had a lot of practise, remember?" Gabriel reminded him, though Maddox needed no reminder. "If you like, I'll rig up a dummy of one of my own designs one day, and let you figure out how to stop that one going off," he joked, or did he? Maddox couldn't be sure. The two of them walked slowly back to the control van, giving the thumbs-up to the two suited-up experts. Gabriel stopped to advise them of what he had done, and what needed still to be done to secure the device. Maddox was already talking on the telephone in his car when Gabriel climbed back in with him.

"Okay Nick. That tour-bus is due any time, and scheduled to leave the ruins around 6pm. Are your men in position?"

"Yes, Boss. Hunkered down around the perimeter of the site. We've got major exits covered. Pity we can't invite anyone else to this party, but the four of us should be able to handle things."

"Good. We should arrive before 5pm. Just keep a watching brief till we get there, unless anything crops up to endanger any of the real tourists."

"Roger that, Boss. Out." Turnbull severed the connection. Maddox turned to Gabriel and gave him a smile. "Everything's going to plan. We should wrap this up tonight," he assured him. Somewhere in the back of Gabriel's mind, a little alarm-bell had just gone off, though for the life of him he couldn't understand why.

Chapter Twenty Six

Marco Falcone had reservations about letting the two women get involved with the clean-up operation, though they had both been quite insistent. Truth to tell, both women were highly competent, and few terrorists remained alive to deal with. If he flooded the site with Solomon personnel, it could get unnecessarily messy. There was only one way out of the site for that tour-bus to take, so he would locate a small backup squad of men there, in case somehow the bus managed to leave with the terrorists on board, but Laura and Belle knew better than to let that happen and chance more hostages being taken.

He was indeed relieved when his contacts within the Italian Security Forces had reported that the dirty-bomb had been successfully defused, and Achille Ratti passed on his congratulations. Everything was moving along to a reasonable conclusion. The Algerian remained to be disposed of, now that he had given them all the information he had. His mind was already wandering, so a simple increase in his dosage would stop his heart, no need for anything more brutal, however satisfying that might be. Marco was ever a practical man.

* * *

The ruins at Lavinium were spread across rolling hills to the south of Rome, the remains of what was once a fine Roman estate, and the buildings and columns, though broken and ravaged with time, were still in a well-preserved state. Money was being sourced to excavate further, and restore more of the ruins, though this work was not allowed to interfere with the tourist excursions. There was still money to be made out of the place, whatever its state of repair.

A small car-park held a few vehicles, and a couple of freelance tour-guides took people round the site, explaining the history of the place and its reputed owners. A small kiosk had been set up to help distribute information pamphlets with a rough map of the various archeological features excavated to date.

Turnbull and his team were spread out across the periphery of the site, hiding in plain view, using what terrain they could, and observing the main site through field binoculars. Their throat-mikes kept them all in contact. "Bingo," he said, more to himself, when he spotted Torquemada and Khalid get out of a parked car. "Tango One and Two have arrived. Keep an eye open for the others. We want them all before we move," he advised the other three of his team. They all acknowledged sight of the two main targets. The expected firefight would be brief if handled right, messy if not. The real tourists would be expected to run for it, either back onto the bus, or down the small road back to the main highway, and out of harm's way, once things started getting lively. That was best, as they didn't want to give the Arabs the chance to seize any hostages.

Torquemada and the woman must have stolen another car to get here, but what had happened to the other men? The news about the diversion atrocity wasn't clear about casualties. How were they going to show up? He wasn't happy going into a firefight with just handguns, but the Italian Authorities still wouldn't allow them anything like their normal gear on a covert op like this, so the MP5's were out. Basic cam-suits, vests and hand-guns were all they had going for them, apart from the comms gear. They needed a fast takedown, so the element of surprise was all-important. Would Torquemada chance bringing weapons, and if so, how heavily tooled-up? Some of those machine pistols were ridiculously small and easily concealed, yet lethal. He and his men had two spare clips each for their automatics, all the Italian's would allow them to carry. Still, it was all they should need, with the element of surprise on their side.

Torquemada would be expecting a smooth getaway now the Italians had made a radio announcement about a large bomb going off in the centre of Rome. They were too far away from the city to have seen the results of any explosion, but they were giving the effect that the atrocity had gone off as planned, though playing down its effects as would be expected. If it had gone off for real, the radiation effects would not be noticed for a few hours, until people started feeling ill. As far as Torquemada was concerned, things were still running to plan.

Maddox was bringing Gabriel here now, like a lamb to the slaughter. His presence here was all important if Maddox's plan was to come off. He wondered how Gabriel would react when he found out. Probably not too pleased, he chuckled to himself. It had come as a shock, hearing of the full brief of Operation Osprey. You couldn't trust Box one bit. Those bastards would shaft anyone. Gabriel's time had come, they'd decided, and this was to be his funeral as well as Torquemada's. So be it. Turnbull chuckled.

*　　*　　*

Belle and Laura had joined the bus-excursion at its last stop, as had a few other people, and they sat together on the bus, after having pretended immense interest in the last previous archeological site they'd visited. Their girl-talk was nothing to do with the wonders of ancient Roman architecture though, as they concentrated on their expected role at Lavinium, which was the bus's next port of call.

"Marco's men will be held in reserve down by the main road. Any firefight breaks out, and we try and get the real tourists moving in that direction. His men will advance and give us backup if we need it," Laura explained, in hushed tones.

"So why hasn't he still been able to get in touch with Dad? I know he likes to do things by himself, but this is bigger than one man alone can handle, and if the Brits are trying to shaft him, they can't be trusted." Belle expressed her concern.

"I'm frustrated too, but Gabriel has been spending more time at the British Embassy, and Marco said there was no way he could get a message to him without the Brits knowing about it. They won't do anything till they take care of these terrorists, and so if we take them out and hopefully take some of them prisoner here today, we have some bargaining power with them. We give them Torquemada as a prize, to haul before the court of World Opinion, and they give us Gabriel back, safe and sound".

"I trust Falcone about as much as I trust the Brits. He has his own agenda, particularly where you are concerned," Belle accused.

"You're being silly," Laura assured her. "Marco and I are history, just friends now."

"Does he know that?" she countered. The bus turned off the main road, and both Belle and Laura were pleased to see the small mini-bus that had apparently broken-down, with one of the occupants changing a wheel. Friendly faces peered out of the interior of the bus, sheltering from the hot sun. Marco's men were in position.

*   *   *

"Eyes up, boys. The bus is coming up the road." Dixon's voice came over the comms-link. "No sign of Tango Three Plus yet?" Neither Turnbull nor the rest of the men had spotted the other terrorists yet. They couldn't close-in without narrowing their field of view, so they needed clear sightings of targets before they could move.

Torquemada and Khalid wandered around the ruins as any other couple might be expected to do, pausing here and there to consult the site-map and pamphlet they had gotten at the kiosk. The woman was carrying a large shoulder bag, which hung suspiciously heavily from her shoulder. They were just biding their time, looking relaxed.

The tour-bus came up the small twisting road, negotiating the tight bends slowly, before finally pulling in and parking in the small car-park. Tourists began getting off the bus, and assembling with the aid of an elderly tour-guide who was trying to organise them whilst extolling the virtues of this ancient site. Turnbull counted them getting off the bus, aware of the potentiality for a tits-up situation once a firefight started. They didn't want any civilian casualties if they could help it.

The blonde and brunette would have caught his eye at the best of times, each of them striking in their own right, but paired together as they were, they brought back memories, and Turnbull twigged who they were in an instant, zeroing the binoculars in on their faces he verified their identities, and instantly tweaked frequencies on his throat-mike to one he knew Maddox would be monitoring. "Boss?"

In the approaching BMW, Maddox picked up the handset and held it to his ear. "Yes Nick, what is it?"

"Possible problem. Gabriel's two women have turned up at the site. Both of them carrying, too, by the weight of those handbags they've got with them. I'll assume they're here for the same reason we are, and treat them as friendlies, for now. Can't say how they're going to react later. Okay with you?"

"Affirmative, Nick. That's how I'd play the situation. We're still about half an hour away. How many targets have turned up so far?"

"Just the main two. About forty or so potential hostages, though. We can't afford to mess about."

"All you can do is use your best judgement, Nick. That's what you get paid for. Maddox out." He put down the phone and looked Gabriel in the eye. "Things are going according to plan," he assured him. "Torquemada and Khalid are there, and Nick's just waiting for the rest of them to turn up. We should be there an hour before that bus is due to leave, so plenty of time yet." Gabriel nodded.

*   *   *

Nick changed frequencies again, so that Dixon, Palmer and Coverdale could hear him. "I daresay you three have noticed the blonde and brunette in the red and blue dresses over by the tour bus. The Italians have decided to lend us a hand. They're on our side, so no one takes a pot-shot at them if they see them running around with a gun in their hand. Got that?" He got three affirmatives, in reply. "They may not know we're here, or where we are, so be careful they don't shoot at you instead of the targets once the fun starts, but I repeat, no one is to shoot at the women under any circumstances."

*   *   *

Belle and Laura mingled with the other tourists from the bus, scanning the site for signs of the two terrorists, Torquemada and Khalid, whose photos Falcone had shown them. They didn't know how many other terrorists would be turning up, but once they spotted Torquemada with the woman, they would assess who was congregating around him, and make their judgements accordingly. There couldn't be many of them left, and provided they got their shots in first, they were confident of taking them down, alive or dead.

One thing Laura hadn't shared with Falcone, was that she had her own suspicions the Brits may show up here as well. The SAS were not to be underestimated, particularly on anti-terrorist matters. "Keep your eyes open, Belle. Things are quiet." Laura, having grown up in Kentucky, was used to the sounds of wildlife, and although these ruins were set amidst rolling woodlands, there was far less noise than she would have expected. Something wasn't right.

*   *   *

The car carrying Achmed and Mustafa passed the supposedly broken-down mini-bus with barely a second-glance, and turned off up onto the winding road to the site. Mustafa parked the car amongst the rest of them, and he and Achmed got out to stretch their legs, idly scanning for signs of Torquemada and Khalid. Their movements caught Turnbull's eye, more interested in the people around them than in the ruins themselves.

"Looks like Tango Three and Four just arrived in the car-park. Is the party ready to start?" announced Palmer over the comms-link. Nick verified from his binoculars.

"Yes, that's them. Guess that's all that's coming. Start moving in. Wait till we can get them grouped together, and wait on my signal before taking any action." Nick then switched frequencies and called Maddox once more. "Four hostiles in total, Boss. We're moving in closer. Better hurry if you want in on the action. I want to move as soon as I get the four of them close together. I don't want any friendly-fire casualties if I can help it."

"Affirmative, Nick. Leave that sort of thing to the Septics. We're less than twenty minutes away," he confirmed. Gabriel turned to check on the following vehicles. Two unmarked police cars kept up with them, and their instructions were to secure the site from the main road, to prevent any more vehicles from turning up the access road. Their instructions were to leave the actual action to the SAS, who had far more experience in these matters.

Torquemada and Khalid had spotted the car as it entered the car-park, and had remained visible, though made no attempt to join up with the two other terrorists once they got out of the vehicle. The trick was going to be to catch all four of them grouped close enough together to minimise anyone else getting caught up in the crossfire.

Turnbull was also using his binoculars to check on the two women. They had also tagged Torquemada and the woman, though appeared to be taking no interest in the other two men as yet. Did they know how many they were dealing with, here?

He checked his watch. Maddox was still some minutes away. It would take maybe another five for his team to work in closer, and then it would be his call to either act or to wait. The three male terrorists looked slightly out of place, all wearing light suits, whereas the rest of the tour group was more casually dressed, in short sleeved-shirts, some wearing shorts and sandals etc. Despite the heat of the late afternoon sun, they kept their jackets buttoned, doubtless to conceal weapons.

The cam gear was good enough to get within a couple of hundred yards, but that might not be close enough. If they stripped it off, vests as well, and tried to mingle in as civilians, they might get closer, but once a firefight started, it would be harder to pick out targets, and would cause more panic amongst the civilians. They might be easier to control once they saw uniforms of some kind. Decisions, decisions.

He spoke into his throat-mike once more. "From the top, identify your targets. I have Tango-One."

"Tango-Two is good for me," announced Coverdale.

"Tango-Three is an ugly bastard. He'll do for me," said Palmer.

"Guess that leaves Tango-Four for me," agreed Dixon.

"Good. Once I give the signal, drop them, and follow in as fast as you can. The public will be screaming and running around. Show yourselves and try and herd them down the access road, out of the way. Then get down there and make sure of the kill. Orders are no prisoners," he verified.

"That works for me," agreed Dixon.

"Watch out for those two women," Turnbull reminded his team.

"It's hard to take my eyes off them. That wind keeps blowing the brunette's skirt up. Lovely legs," Coverdale chuckled.

"Keep your mind and your eyes on the target, Coverdale," Turnbull advised, then changed frequencies. "We're going in a few minutes, Boss. Four targets. Closing in now."

"Affirmative, Nick," replied Maddox from his BMW. We're coming up on the access road now. We'll stop short and come in on foot."

"There may be some foot-traffic heading your way. We'll try and herd the screaming punters down that way and away from the gunfire," Turnbull advised.

"We'll watch out for them," Maddox confirmed.

Nick Turnbull drew his gun, and lined it up on Torquemada. The range was more than fifty yards, and the wind was capricious, but he had made more difficult shots. If that tour guide would just move his little group over to one side.

"Get ready," he advised his team over the comms-link. "We go in Five, Four, Three, Two, One . . . ." Four shots rang out almost in unison, followed by four or five more, and then the screams and panic started as the tourists began running around wildly.

Turnbull saw Torquemada fall, before his body was obscured by the panicking tourists. Khalid too lay prone, her chest now all red and bloody. Dixon was up and amongst the crowd before he could get there, showing himself, and waving people off back down the access road. Turnbull joined him, and started doing the same, before Palmer gave a warning over the comms.

"Shit, Nick. They're wearing vests! They're wearing vests!" More gunfire, as Nick whirled around, seeking the source, and seeing his men now being fired on by the two male terrorists. He turned back, seeing Khalid on the ground, but there was no sight of Torquemada.

*   *   *

Laura and Belle had dropped down by the side of the bus as the first round of bullets had hit the terrorists. Belle had started to pull her gun from out of her shoulder-bag, when Laura had stopped her. "Not now. They might think we're with the terrorists. Best wait, and hope they take them out first," she advised. Belle realised the sense of her mother's advice, and kept under cover and watched as one of the fallen terrorists began to move, crawling across the ground to a position of better cover. She had seen him stagger and fall, and realised he must be wearing a protective vest under his suit.

The shots had come in from a distance, and had gone for body instead of the more difficult but surer head-shot. Khalid was lying there all bloody, either dead or wounded, but the three men were all still mobile. The tour-group was thinning out, as the attacking force, presumably SAS, where sheperding them away back down the access road, leaving a more defined field of fire.

*   *   *

Maddox ordered his driver to pull over just after turning up the access road, and as he and Gabriel got out, the two police cars began securing the junction, much to the consternation of the Solomon team in the minibus, who were now hamstrung. They couldn't move against the Italian Police. Forlornly, one of them radioed the news back to Falcone. There was nothing they could do. Laura and Belle were now on their own.

The screaming panicked tourists could be heard before Maddox and Gabriel saw them, and then the first of them crested over the rise, and a small tidal wave approached. Gunshots could be heard in the distance, as Gabriel and Maddox fought their way through the escaping tourists. Maddox had switched to a throat mike as he'd left the car, and he activated it as they approached the site. "Nick?" There was no answer. "Best take it easy. We don't want to walk into anything. We stay back and keep to the high ground till we know what's going on. Okay?"

"Okay," Gabriel agreed.

*   *   *

Nick Turnbull was too busy to answer Maddox's radio-call. He had finally spotted Torquemada moving diagonally across the site, using the ruins as cover, and he was working his way towards him. Gunshots were going off around him, as the rest of his men were trading shots with Achmed and Mustafa, and he must have shown himself, because one of them whizzed close by, before he ducked down. That action caused Torquemada to spot him, and he too began firing in Turnbull's direction.

Legs, arms, head. Anything would do except the torso, which the vests covered. But Torquemada knew that, and kept well down. A head-shot was the most difficult. He needed to get closer. Needed to get Torquemada to make a mistake. "Masoud, you fucker! There's no way out!" he shouted, letting Torquemada know just who was after him.

The taller man hissed as he crouched down behind a weathered piece of stone. Turnbull! Was there no escaping the man? Turnbull meant British/Europol forces, a small number by the gunfire. Where were the Italian Security Forces? If Turnbull was here, their escape route was blown. How now would he get away? He had seen Fatima fall. Of all of them, she had been unable to wear a vest because of her clothing. Two bullets had ripped her chest apart. Achmed and Mustafa were still mobile and firing back at their attackers. If they could keep drawing their fire, and if he could get rid of Turnbull, he might still be able to get away on foot, at least until he could finally contact Abdullah at the University and arrange for another way out of Italy.

He was breathing hard, still hyperventilating from shock and in pain from the bruising his own chest had taken from the impact of the two bullets, presumably from Turnbull's gun. He hated that little man. "Come on then, Turnbull! You and me, one last time! I'll fuck you just like I fucked that little sister of yours!" he taunted, tearing open old wounds.

Turnbull couldn't help but rise to the bait, and lunged forward, as Torquemada let loose with a salvo from the machine pistol he carried, almost taking Turnbull's head off.

Nick hadn't been totally honest in his recollections of his past association with the man. Masoud and his gang were flash, and always rolling in stolen money, and a succession of girls were always in tow, keen to latch onto that lifestyle.

His own sister Sally had been one of them, who wouldn't listen to either her brother or her parents. When she'd gotten knocked-up, the bastard had dropped her like a stone. Kicked-out by his parents, she had ended up having an abortion, and Nick had later found out she had ended up on the game to finance a drug habit that Masoud had gotten her started on. She had finally died of an overdose three years ago. He had a lot of reasons to hate Masoud!

"What was her name again? I can't remember. But she was a good fuck, all the same!" he taunted. "She earned me a lot of money when I put her on the game!" Turnbull moved fast, sliding over a fallen column, firing as he did so, and splinters of stone gashed Torquemada's cheek from the near-miss as he closed down the distance between the two of them. Another volley from the machine-pistol cut the air inches from Turnbull's arm.

Keep firing and missing, you cunt, Turnbull was hoping. Machine pistols were deadly, but they ran out of ammo pretty damn quickly if you weren't too careful.

*　　*　　*

Back on the main site, Achmed and Mustafa were outgunned, three to two, and the three SAS were maneouvring around them. As Palmer and Coverdale kept them pinned down, Dixon slid in around behind them. He got within twenty yards, before centreing the barrel on the back of Achmed's head, and then loosing off one deadly round, which dropped him like a stone.

The shock of seeing his friend killed so suddenly right next to him, made Mustafa jump up and panic, and he started to make a run for it, making himself an easy target for three guns, and he went down under a small fusillade of bullets, as they aimed at his unprotected legs. Coverdale went over as he lay there, bleeding and gasping from numerous wounds, and finished him off with a bullet to the head, with grim finality.

Palmer went over to check that Khalid was in fact dead, and he gave a thumbs-up to his two colleagues. That just left the big man and Nick out there, swapping bullets. "Let's try and outflank him. Don't get in Nick's line of fire," Palmer warned.

*　　*　　*

"It's all gone quiet down there, Masoud," Turnbull taunted back. "That means you're all that's left, and my men will be moving around now, angling for a shot on that ugly head of yours. No way out, no way back, no surrender. We can end this now, man to man, and you might have a chance to get away if you kill me before my men get here. You keep playing a waiting game and we'll box you in and finish you off." Torquemada could see figures moving out from the site lower down on the slopes, and vanishing off amongst the ruins and small trees. Turnbull was right. Not much chance if he waited any longer.

"Man to man? No guns?" Torquemada cried out.

"You know I'll keep my word, so let's see you chuck out your gun, sharpish," Turnbull suggested. Torquemada took little time to make his mind up. Time was of the essence. He held up the gun, where Turnbull would see it, and dropped it the other side of a fallen column. Turnbull stood up as he saw this, and made a show out of tossing his own gun down.

Torquemada stood up, and pulled a switch-blade from his pocket, activating the long shiny blade which hung down low. Turnbull pulled out his commando knife, and moved forward. This needed to be quick and dirty. Torquemada was bigger and had a longer reach. "You think you can take me, Turnbull?" Torquemada asked as the two men faced each other across a short clearing. Turnbull didn't speak, just moved in closer, cautiously, knife held down and low at his side, Torquemada held his own blade out in front of him, beckoning Turnbull forward.

Turnbull kept on coming, and when he was clear of any possible shelter, Torquemada dropped his knife and his hand whipped round under his coattails to pull a second automatic from the waistband of his trousers. Turnbull had nowhere to go, and less than a second to react.

The knife whizzed through the air, end over end, as Torquemada's gunhand came up, and the deadly point bit home in the shoulder of his left arm. He cried out, the gun going off once, missing, as Turnbull flung himself at the man, forcing the gun down, and twisting. Bigger and stronger, Torquemada dragged Turnbull down onto the ground with him, the two of them kicking and gouging at each other, as Turnbull tried to make him release his grip on the gun.

Struggling together, the two of them rolled around, till Turnbull's head caught and pressed against the knife still embedded in his shoulder, and the fresh burst of pain caused the terrorist to finally drop his gun, which Turnbull grabbed eagerly as he rolled free to one side. He levelled it on Torquemada, teeth bared, and finger tightening on the trigger. Torquemada froze. Turnbull had him dead to rights. Torquemada stood there, holding his injured arm and waited for the inevitable.

"Kill me and get it over with, then," he demanded, trying to stand tall as he looked into the face of his sworn enemy. "When I die, another will take my place. The Infidel will never win against the true believer," he promised.

"Whoever takes your place, we'll deal with him just the same. If I had my way, I'd nuke the fucking lot of you! Steal your oil, and generally fuck your countries up like you've done mine for the last thirty years!" Turnbull raised the gun, sighting it between Torquemada's eyes. "You Muslims aren't the only ones who can bear a grudge!"

"You will never win, Turnbull." Torquemada sank to one knee, favouring his wounded arm and trying to staunch the flow of blood, though he expected to die. "We are legion! Muslims have spread all across the western world, and we owe allegiance to no country, neither our birthplace, nor the countries that offer us refuge. All we have is our religion, and that is all we are loyal to. We are Brothers of the Faith, and no one can stand against us!" he rambled, the fervour back in his eyes as he spoke.

"You and your bloody Faith!" Turnbull scoffed. "Where did it come from, Masoud? Back home you were a typical scumbag, but that was just you. There was no religion behind it. You were into drugs, sex, and avarice. Somewhere along the line, you got brainwashed? Don't you think that if it was all true about assuring your place and rewards in Paradise for killing us infidels, blowing yourselves up as suicide-bombers, that your mullahs would be at the front of the queue to die? No, cos they're not that fucking stupid. Everywhere you look, its Muslim extremists here, Muslim insurgents there. Might only be a minority, but as long as the majority of Muslims keep quiet, that minority is all that's seen, all that's heard, and we're fucking sick of it! Your Jihad could be here a lot sooner than you think, Masoud," Turnbull admitted. "We can't tell the good guys from the bad guys any more, and your close-knit communities protect the guilty from facing what they see as persecution, when we see it as Justice."

"And we'll win, Turnbull. You can't stop the tide," he grinned, flashing his white teeth once more in a defiant snarl. Turnbull levelled the gun once more. "We'll drown you all eventually," he promised.

"This is the only way to deal with your kind. The only language a terrorist understands, and I speak it fluently!" Turnbull's finger tightened just a hair on the trigger, and the gun went off with grim finality, the back of Torquemada's head exploding in a red shower, and the tall man fell limply to the rocky ground. "We might not be allowed to win this war. But it won't be for the lack of trying!" Controlling himself, Turnbull fingered the throat-mike. "Secure the site. Torquemada has been eliminated. Repeat, Torquemada has been eliminated." Slowly, he went over to check the body, just to make sure, but half of the man's skull was missing, so no mistake. He tugged the commando knife free, and wiped the blade on Torquemada's coat before sheathing it once more. "Piece of shit!" Turnbull spat on the man's corpse.

The main mission was now completed. All the terrorists were now dead. Just the tidy-up still to do, and that involved the man called Gabriel!

* * *

Laura and Belle showed themselves once the other terrorists were killed by the three SAS men. They played it cool, for as far as they knew, the SAS didn't know that their plans were now known regarding Gabriel. "Where is he?" Belle whispered to her mother, still not seeing her father anywhere.

"Up there," Laura nudged her daughter, spotting Gabriel and another man approaching over the rise in the narrow road. The two women started walking briskly to join them, before Gabriel got closer to the SAS as they rounded up the terrorists' bodies. Belle wanted to run, but Laura grabbed her arm. "Don't alarm them too early," she warned, quickening her own pace. Gabriel and the other man were now stood looking down into the ruins and talking together. She guessed correctly that the other man was Maddox. Laura and Belle ran to meet the approaching Gabriel and Maddox, as Turnbull and the other special forces people checked the corpses of the dead terrorists. They needed to warn Gabriel of the doublecross planned for him. Gabriel smiled and waved at their approach, and Maddox guessed who they were, never having met them before, but unknowing of their intent.

Gabriel saw and recognised the two women as they approached, and waved, starting to walk down to greet them. Maddox identified the two women too, and inwardly groaned, not wanting further complications. "What are you two doing here?" he asked, smiling, as Maddox walked alongside him. The two women stayed silent as they walked towards the two men, and then Laura pulled the gun from her handbag, and held it to Maddox's head.

"Gabriel, it's all a trap. The British Government wants you dead along with Torquemada," Laura cried out in warning, as they approached. Gabriel turned to Maddox.

"Jim? What's this all about?" he asked. Maddox look a bit embarrassed, and he raised his hands.

"Calm down, and I'll explain," Maddox began to placate Gabriel, but seeing the raised hands, Belle took matters into her own, and her knife came out of its thigh-sheath as she lunged for his throat. Maddox saw it coming a second too late to react, for he wasn't as fit as he used to be. Fortunately, Gabriel was, and an outstretched arm deflected Belle's, preventing the fatal blow. Flustered, Maddox automatically went for his gun inside his coat, and as Gabriel wrestled with Belle, Laura dropped Maddox with a savate kick to his mid-section, following up with a blow to the back of his neck as he dropped to his knees.

A cry of alarm came from the Italian Special Forces coming up the road, who had witnessed the attack on Maddox, and it had also been noticed by Turnbull and his three men. "Will you two hellcats behave? We're in the shit now, alright," he cursed. "We can't go back up the road, and we certainly can't go down there," he said. "Quickly, stay close to me, and let's take cover in the ruins. It'll be dark soon, and we stand more chance of getting away without being seen as long as we're quiet." He took Maddox's gun, and the three of them headed at a tangent from the two armed forces. Vastly outnumbered, Gabriel knew they would need a lot of luck to escape. He risked a glimpse behind him and saw Maddox getting back to his feet, and strangely, waving to the Italians to keep their distance. Then he understood. This was to be personal. Regimental housekeeping. He could understand Whitehall's take on the situation. They didn't like bad apples coming back to haunt them. "Looks like the odds have changed a little in our favour," he nodded to the situation on the road, and the two women assessed it for themselves.

"Three against four? Should be easy to take them out or get past them," Belle commented. Gabriel sneered, watching Turnbull giving orders to his men. They split up into two teams of two men, now moving swiftly and silently to flank Gabriel and the two women.

"I don't think so. This is about to get very nasty. Turnbull and his men may not look like much, but they're SAS, and believe me when I tell you from personal experience, they don't come any better, or any nastier. Stay low and follow my lead," he ordered, moving off behind the crumbling stone edifices. The women discarded their handbags once they'd removed their own hand-guns. There was nothing important in them, and they would need to travel light.

Down in the ruins, the four SAS men were now on the move. Gabriel had only seconds to think of a strategy. The road was held by the Italian Security Forces. Cross-country they might have a chance in the dark of evening which was fast approaching, as long as they refrained from calling in air-support, and that meant involving the Italians. The sun was already out of sight on the horizon, and shadows were lengthening.

"We need to move quickly. We have to break free of pursuit and escape on foot. Head away from the road, and double back some time tonight and make for the coast. We have to get past Turnbull and his friends," he pointed out.

"They don't look so tough," argued Laura.

"Looks can be deceiving. They're the best there is. Don't underestimate them. The SAS don't pick their men on looks, just on what they can achieve. If we survive the next five minutes, we can discuss this again," says Gabriel, pushing the two women forward into the ruins. Looking back, he watched them deploy with a cold professional detachment, flitting like shadows as they started into the lower ruins.

*　　*　　*

Maddox struggled to his feet, cursing, now directing operations by secure frequency com-link to the ear-pieces of all four of the hit-team, and Turnbull teamed up with one of the other men, Palmer. Dixon and Coverdale paired up also.

*　　*　　*

They came forward fast, too bloody fast, one covering the other, playing overtake and catch-up. They'd obviously worked together before, and the odds on surviving the next five minutes weren't looking good at all. Time was the only thing Gabriel had going for him. The longer he could keep this firefight going, the more chance there was of the security forces getting involved, and that was driving the camouflaged figures towards him. They wanted no witnesses to what was about to go down. The SAS were acting on their own, and they weren't behaving with their normal professional cautiousness. If they'd had their standard gear, there wouldn't be much chance, but restricted to handguns only by the Italians, there remained a slim chance they could pull this off.

Belle stuck her head up from behind the stone plinth, rattling off a couple of quick shots. The fire was returned less than a second later, and she cursed as stone fragments cut her cheek as the bullets narrowly missed their target. Gabriel rattled off two quick shots as one cam-clad figure showed himself momentarily. He saw the figure stagger back, and then regain his footing before seeking cover. Body-armour, and the small caliber weapon he had wasn't powerful enough to penetrate it. He needed to get in up close and very personal.

"I need bait. You girls are it. Move out and keep low. Show yourselves for one shot at a time, then get your head back down before it's shot off. These men can be ghosts when they want to be, but right now they need a quick kill. That's all we have in our favour," he explained. "Circle round, and when you head back, don't show yourselves at all if you can help it." Belle and Laura set off, scuttling on all fours, as Gabriel reviewed his options. Those brightly coloured dressed weren't exactly good camouflage.

He had to take the fight to the SAS troopers before they realised what he was upto. One man against one pair. It was going to be fast and brutal. He needed to take the backmarker, just after his partner overtook him. Then it would be a matter of seconds only to make the kill, and turn his attentions to the second man.

Keeping low, he hurried back the way he had come, towards his attackers, staying out of sight of the approaching men whose whispered words he could barely pick out. They kept their conversation to a minimum, but they were getting closer.

Shucking off his shoes, he shoved them into his jacket pockets, and he began to climb the weathered column at the rear, where he remained out of sight. His hands and feet got a good purchase on the notched and weathered stone, and he soon reached the top of the column some twenty feet above the ground. Silently scrabbling over the top, he peered down over the other side, and risked a quick look down at the two figures approaching. One of them skirted the base of the column, covered by the other, as they progressed along the path they had seen Gabriel take with the women. They kept close, never more than five yards apart. Timing was going to be everything.

*   *   *

The shadows were lengthening now, as Maddox viewed the scene through binoculars, and he watched the dark silhouette climbing the weathered stone column. He gave a grim smile, and changing his view slightly, he saw Dixon and Coverdale approaching on a course that would take them just below that same column. He adjusted his throat mike, and whispered softly into it, alerting Turnbull.

*   *   *

Dropping silently down from his purchase on top of the weathered column, he took the rearmost man easily from behind. Coverdale had less than half a second to react, and taken completely by surprise, failed to do so. One hand over his mouth clamped tight, and the knife went in under his chin. Gabriel ripped the blade sideways. Dixon whirled at the sound of the gasp, and the hot blood gargling out of his partner's throat, and pumped two quick silenced bullets into the figure in front of him.

Gabriel shoved Coverdale's jerking body forward, onto Dixon, as he cried out, and followed up quickly before he had chance to get the body off him. One sharp hiss was all he had time for as Gabriel plunged his knife in between his ribs, the sharp blade easily penetrating the vest. He turned, listening, trying to locate the others.

*   *   *

The other pairing, Palmer and Turnbull, came upon the women from behind. Changing strategy, Palmer moved ahead, making a lot of noise, whilst Turnbull moved like a ghost. Preoccupied with the noise Palmer was making, Turnbull got the drop on them quite easily. Laura and Belle froze at the sound of a gun being cocked. "Don't be stupid. Drop your weapons, and stand up slowly. Our orders don't include you, so play your cards right girls, and you'll get out of this alive," he warned. At a signal from him, they dropped their guns on the ground.

"Now, slow and easy, step away from them." Laura and Belle turned slowly, looking at each other, as they turned.

Turnbull wasn't close enough to take without him getting at least one shot off. Palmer quickly joined the small group. "Let's have a little fun. He'll come out quicker once he hears the women screaming," leered Palmer, unsheathing his knife.

"Palmer," Turnbull attracted his attention, and he slowly turned to see Turnbull pointing his own gun at him. "This one's for Julie!" Turnbull put one bullet straight through Palmer's head, killing him instantly. The two women started for their guns, panicked momentarily, till Turnbull turned his gun back towards them warningly. "Easy. I'm a friend. Just stay cool. You remember me from Wales, don't you?"

"What about Gabriel?" asked Laura, worriedly.

Turnbull smiled wryly. "He's supposed to be the Top Knob, according to Maddox. Two to one odds should be no problem. I could take those two wozzacks, myself." The two women stared deliberately over Turnbull's shoulder as he held the gun on them. "Can't fool me with that old one, luv." Then he gasped as the barrel of a gun pressed against the back of his neck. No one had ever crept up behind him that silently before. "Jeezus . . . . Easy Guv'nor. It's not what it looks like," Turnbull quickly explained.

Gabriel's shirt was covered in blood, fortunately not his own. Turnbull turned around, and Gabriel recognised the younger man, who nods in professional appreciation. "I saw you kill him. That's the only reason you're still alive, Turnbull. What the hell is Maddox upto?"

"Best ask him yourself, guvnor."

Chapter Twenty Seven

"We don't always follow orders, as you know, Gabe," Maddox explained. "In the Regiment we do what we feel is right, and not always what Whitehall says is right. We police our own, and the three men killed today deserved killing, for reasons I shan't go into. I admit, I used you to help do it, and I apologise for that. I had a little personal agenda to take care of, and when Whitehall ordered me to make sure you were killed along with the rest of the terrorists, I hand-picked the team to do it. Under the circumstances, it seemed the most expedient way. Your affiliation with the Regiment, and your present activities were not deemed suitable by Whitehall, while this War Against Terror is going on. I did you a favour by helping you out against these terrorists, and you've done me a bit of favour with a bit of internal housekeeping. You also get the benefit of a funeral, as far as the rest of the world is concerned. Turnbull here is one of my best. Probably better than you, but his head's big enough already, without any more undue praise. I couldn't have done all this without his help." Turnbull stood there, smiling smugly, and eyeing Gabriel up and down. He winked, and Gabriel found it hard to repress a smile. Cocky bastard. "Hereford will believe our story about a successful conclusion to this mission only if you keep your head down. We'll say you were killed with the rest of them. We'll take care of the bodies. So do us all a favour and stay dead this time. Next time the people Hereford send after you might play the game by a different set of rules. Now get the hell out of here before the police show up. Going to be awkward enough as it is."

Turnbull shook Gabriel's hand as Maddox left to deal with the Italian security forces. "Don't let Jimbo kid you on. He's always told me you're the best thing since sliced bread. You've been my measuring-stick, so to speak. It's been nice to finally work together," he admitted. "The three of them raped a young girl back in Hereford. Left her in a coma. She's still in it. One of them made the mistake of boasting about it and letting me overhear the conversation. Whitehall is right. We do police our own. Her name was Julie Maddox, Jim's daughter." He paused to let the revelation sink in. "She was like a sister to me." He managed a grim smile. "Me and Jim were going to do the job ourselves, but the way Whitehall reacted to all this played right into our hands. Much easier to let them think terrorists did it, than have them investigating a triple murder at home. Sorry we couldn't fill you in on the details earlier, but it also gives you a head's up on the authorities, as long as you keep a low profile."

*   *   *

A few days later, Maddox collected Rebekah from the hospital when the medical authorities deemed fit to discharge her. He was strangely quiet, thinking of what Alexi had told him when he had talked to the Mossad chief to tell him Rebekah was safe, and that the mission was effectively a success. The boy had been his son. Rebekah had gone back to her childless marriage in the states pregnant with his child, and raised him with a stranger for a father. Possibly harsh thoughts, but he couldn't escape them. He didn't know all the reasons, or even if she admitted the real father of the child to her husband. The three of them eventually moved to Israel, and her husband and his son were killed by a suicide bomber whilst shopping in the supermarket. A life he had never known, and now would never know. His own daughter Julie tragically comatised by her attack and rape at the hands of those three scumbags, and now this. More heartache to deal with. Still, Rebekah was here now. What to do? What to say to her? Perhaps now was not the time, but some day he would discuss these feelings with her.

"Those deep silences don't become you, Jim Maddox." Rebekah smiled, reaching a hand to stroke his cheek, and Jim took it, kissing the back of her hand, smiling finally.

"You know me. Always the thinker. That's why they gave me this bloody desk-job," he joked. Reaching down he took her overnight bag, and the two of them walked out into the bright sunshine. "Come on, let's get you out of here. A couple of days of R&R, and you'll be as right as rain."

"Where are we going?"

"I know a little fishing port on the southern coast. Nice and quiet, lots of sun and sand, and crystal blue waters."

"Sounds like heaven," she smiled, accepting his arm and clinging to him as they walked out to his car. "Is Gabe going to be there?" she asked. Maddox shook his head.

"No, but I have a number where you can call him later. Gabe needs to keep a low-profile just now. The rest of the world thinks him dead, and it's better if it stays that way." He was glad Turnbull had offered to field all the reports and phonecalls back to Whitehall and Hereford. He had flown back to the UK earlier that morning.

*　　*　　*

Julie Maddox looked unchanged in her lonely bed, as the nurse let Nick into the room. He had called here before reporting to the Lines. Poor kid looked so beautiful as she lay there, as if dreaming sweet dreams. As he usually did, he drew up a chair by the bedside, and began talking to her as he took her hand. He often spent hours here, just talking to her in these one-sided conversations, rambling on about all sorts of things, and so he began telling her of what he and her father had just been up to in Italy, at least as much as he knew about it all, and bits he had guessed. "We got the bastards, Julie. All three of them. Call it revenge if you will, and I know you wouldn't want that, but me and your Dad aren't as charitable as you, love," he chuckled. He continued to talk, lost track of time as he normally did when he was in here, and then, just as he tried to let go of her hand, he found life in her fingers, found them reluctant to uncurl from his grasp. He gasped for a second, and then used his free hand to pull open the door. "Nurse? Nurse!" he shouted. "Someone get down here!"

*　　*　　*

Donatello Grimaldi played host to a reunion dinner, prepared with the help of his lovely Marianne. Gabriel, Laura, Belle and Lesya were all sat around the dinner table, enjoying the dessert prepared by his chef, and discussing their next moves.

"So are you going back to Kazakhstan, Lesya?" Donatello asked her. Light twinkled on her glasses as she turned towards him to reply.

"Yes, at least for a while. I have unfinished business there," she confirmed.

"Surely, now you are rich, you don't need to worry about your job any more?" Belle asked, moving her thigh so that it pressed against Lesya's own. Her eyes implored her to stay, and Lesya noticed her body language too. "Why not stay here a while with me, and I'll show you more of Italy?" Belle suggested.

"True, it was very nice of your Mr Maddox to let us keep the Al Qaeda money, and I don't really know what I will do with my newfound wealth. It hasn't really sunk in as yet. You really had no need to give me a share," she insisted, though was inwardly delighted with her unexpected windfall. There was so much she could do with the money. "But I know I must look after my family first and foremost. We honour our families above all else in Kazakhstan. It's just the way we are," she explained. "I do like my job, though. Money doesn't really come into it there."

"Giving the money away was the least Jim could do under the circumstances," Gabriel chuckled. "Too much paperwork if he kept it, and in way of apology for manipulating me and the situation. I already have more than I need, and so does Donatello here, so splitting it between you four girls seemed the fairest solution."

"I'm not complaining," smiled Laura.

"Me, neither," chuckled Belle, whose knee was pressing against Lesya's own once more, as their eyes met.

"Perhaps now Donatello will stop complaining about the credit card accounts I run up when I'm out shopping," joked Marianne, ruffling her fingers through Donatello's hair.

"You also deserved some recompense for the situation you found yourself in with Kovacs, Lesya, and he did send those men to kill you," Gabriel pointed out to her. "I'm sure you'll use the money wisely, and if you need help with investments, then talk to me or Donatello here, and if we can't help you, we'll put you in touch with other people that can," he offered.

"Thank you all, so much, for the kindness you've shown me," Lesya said, sincerely.

"Do say you'll return to Italy when your family business is taken care of. We could have so much fun together," Belle smiled persuasively, the pressure of her knee increasing slightly, and Belle noticed that Lesya was not pulling away from the contact. The eyes sparkled behind the glass lenses, and her mouth widened into a lovely smile.

"I'd like that, in a month or two, when I've settled a few things," she replied. "Italy has so much going for it, the opera, the fashion, the beautiful language, and of course, it's people," she complimented Donatello graciously, who bowed his head and laughed as Marianne made to hit him for his conceit.

"Well, I'll be here in Rome for a few months at least, and I'll make sure to give you my address and phone number before your plane leaves," Belle promised.

"Gabriel and I have to get back to Buenos Aires," said Laura.

"Yes, I have some work going on in one of my research centres which needs some input from myself," Gabriel admitted.

"I have made arrangements to get you out of Italy, through Sardinia, and then Malta once more. A slight change of appearance and new papers, and the authorities will be none the wiser, so long as Maddox keeps his promise and lets them think you're dead," Donatello grinned across the table to Gabriel.

"Playing dead is something I'm used to, by now, Donatello," Gabriel smiled. "It gets easier each time."

"Why don't you come visit us in South America, sometime, Lesya?" Laura suggested. "Marianne was telling me you have witches in your family," she chuckled, but Lesya didn't see the humour in the comment at first. "We have something similar in ours, too," Laura explained. "I'm supposed to be 'gifted' as well, though I wouldn't say so," she said modestly. "We have a friend called Juliana, who'd be delighted to meet you," she explained.

"I don't know. Maybe when I have finished my family affairs, and explored Italy a little more. I have an invitation to visit England too, and I also have some unfinished business there. We will see where the life will lead us." Lesya smiled that enigmatic smile. There was a lot hidden behind those beautiful dark eyes. But that's a tale for another time.

Past And Future Sins

The two women joked and chattered away merrily as they walked through the sukh. Both women were dressed lightly for the hot sun. Laura wore a thin loose white dress, while Belle dressed in slacks and a loose blouse. They had only arrived in Cairo a few days ago, and were still acclimatising, before seeing the Valley of the Kings, the Pyramids etcetera, in typical tourist fashion. In the meantime, a bit of retail therapy never goes amiss, and they spent some time touring the back-alleys and shops in search of bargains.

The old Arab shopkeepers were either very polite or very pushy, sometimes inviting them in for coffee and haggling, others just kept tugging very bad manneredly on their arms, to try and get them into their shops. It was hard to say no and get them to accept the refusal. The old curiousity shoppe caught their eye with the strange exotics display in the window, and the two women soon found themselves in an Aladdin's Cave inside, pouring over old tomes and strange objets d'art. Some of the books were covered with what looked like skin or flaking leather.

It was Belle that found the feather, larger than normal, and she assumed it was from some Eagle or other bird of prey. It had been made into a quill-pen, and was advertised on a little card as a genuine 'Angel-Feather' and the two women both laughed. "I bet Gabriel would just love it. I have to buy it for him," insisted Laura. "I'll see if the hotel will send it off by special courier for me."

*   *   *

The special delivery arrived later that week, and was delivered to Gabriel by his manservant Manuel, who left his master to open it in private. The card dropped out first, and it said simply 'Thought you'd enjoy this, Love, Laura.' Then Gabriel upended the package a bit further. It was so light, he wondered if there could be anything in it at all, and then out dropped the quill-pen, and the unmistakeable feather. He gasped, taken aback. The last time he had seen a feather like this had been in a laboratory complex in Madrid. It could be a fake or it could be genuine. The only way to tell would be to have it analysed, and the research facility in Cordoba would be able to do that quickly enough. They could also carbon-date it to tell how recently it had been grown. But unless Gabriel was wrong, this feather came from one of his kinsmen, another angel.